Louisa Devey

Life of Rosina, Lady Lytton

Louisa Devey

Life of Rosina, Lady Lytton

ISBN/EAN: 9783337123895

Printed in Europe, USA, Canada, Australia, Japan

Cover: Foto ©Raphael Reischuk / pixelio.de

More available books at **www.hansebooks.com**

LIFE

OF

ROSINA, LADY LYTTON,

WITH

NUMEROUS EXTRACTS FROM HER MS. AUTOBIOGRAPHY AND OTHER ORIGINAL DOCUMENTS,

PUBLISHED IN VINDICATION OF HER MEMORY.

BY

LOUISA DEVEY,

Literary Executrix to the Dowager Lady Lytton.

"LA VERITA E FIGLIA DEL TEMPO."

LONDON:

SWAN SONNENSCHEIN, LOWREY & CO.,

PATERNOSTER SQUARE.

—

1887.

PREFACE.

———◆———

In presenting to the public these somewhat fragmentary and imperfect Reminiscences, it is necessary that I should enter upon a brief explanation of the reasons for my decision to publish a volume which purists may consider a scandal, and Gallios a superfluity. In 1884 I was responsible for the publication of some three hundred letters of the late Lord Lytton to his wife, which I hoped would both aid in enabling the world to form a more accurate judgment of the private character of his lordship than had hitherto been obtainable, and also in clearing the reputation of his unhappy wife, whom I have the best possible reasons for asserting to have been a greatly maligned and misunderstood woman.

But Lord Lytton's son was of a very different opinion, and he obtained an injunction against me restraining their publication. He acted within his rights; and, having been adjudged at fault by a court of law, it does not beseem me to impugn the justice of its decision, although I must ever bitterly regret such a result. But I cannot help pointing out the remarkable inconsistency of the present Earl in the course he thought fit to adopt. For reasons, and doubtless very excellent reasons, of his own, he had always taken his father's part in the deplorable quarrels between his parents. He accordingly published a biography of Lord Lytton, in which he had every opportunity of laying his own case before the public. In this biography he claims to have given "from the only authentic record" all the circumstances relating to his parents' marriage, and states that his father's "own letters will now enable all candid persons to judge for themselves whether the writer of them could have been capable of the brutality, the cruelty, the meanness and selfishness attributed to him." But while I do not question the authenticity of the letters which the Earl quotes, I am at least entitled to claim equal value for those which I possess, written by his father's own hand; and it is only fair to the "candid persons" appealed to for judgment to allow them to inspect the whole of Lord Lytton's correspondence, and not merely a carefully selected portion. Was it not natural, therefore, that I should accept the challenge, made, as I supposed, in all good faith, and endeavour to publish the whole correspondence? For had I kept silence I might have been accused of casting a slur upon the memory of Lady Lytton, by shrinking, in order to screen her character, from daring to bring forth the whole truth; and thus I might justly have been called a moral coward and a false friend.

Moreover, it is necessary to bear in mind, as a criterion of the chances the present Earl enjoyed of forming a true estimate of his mother's character, the fact that, except during four months in 1858, he never saw her from 1838 down to the day of her death. The biographer also printed several letters written by his mother, which I, as that lady's executrix, had a perfect right to restrain him from publishing. I did not do so because I hoped to be allowed with impunity to publish Lord Lytton's own letters, merely by way of showing that there are two sides to every question, and also by way of vindicating his wife's memory. If these letters were a condemnation of Lord Lytton's behaviour, the censure, if any, proceeded out of his own mouth, and not out of mine.

But the Earl, being determined that one view, and one view only, of his father's character should be presented to the world, set in motion the machinery of the law to stifle my humble protest, and still threatens me with its terrors. He claims, therefore, for his father an exemption from criticism which few public men have either attained or desired. Even Bulwer himself was no advocate of the *nil de mortuis nisi bonum* system of compiling biographies; the inner life of Byron has been mercilessly dissected, the foibles of Carlyle have been unsparingly exposed, the love-letters of Keats have been recently sold by auction ; but of Edward Bulwer, novelist, poet, dramatist, and statesman, we are forbidden to know anything beyond what a dutiful son chooses with true filial discretion to impart to us. But I can plead another and a stronger motive for my so-called indiscretion. During the last years of the Dowager Lady Lytton's life I was her constant, I may almost say her sole, companion, and one of her very few remaining friends. It was her dearest hope that one day some attempt would be made to clear her reputation from the harsh judgment that had been pronounced upon it ; and I have in conversation frequently noticed her extreme anxiety that these letters and other papers which she had so long and so carefully preserved should be published after her decease.

She made me her executrix, and left to me the whole of her papers, with the strict charge that on no pretext, "however plausible and apparently truthful," should they be permitted to pass into the hands of the Lytton family. I should therefore have been guilty of a treachery towards my dead friend of which I hope I am incapable, had I not made an effort to vindicate her memory from the slanders which have blackened it so long. This effort having failed, there still remained to me the alternative of constructing out of the other materials at my disposal a short record of the life of this much-wronged woman ; and this course I have thought fit to adopt, being compelled to brave the anger of the living out of respect and love for the memory of the dead, as well as regard for the cause of justice and truth.

This being the case, I can emphatically deny that I am actuated by a wish to pander to morbid curiosity, or to gain notoriety. The task before me I regard as a sacred trust, which I am bound to fulfil to the best of my poor ability.

In compiling this biography it is inevitable that in many important points I should differ very materially from the version given by the present Earl of the relations between his parents both before and after marriage. This, as I have already indicated, arises partly from the son's ignorance of his mother's character, and partly from his having thrown in his lot with his father, and having formed his judgment solely from the latter's point of view. Thus, if Lord Lytton had known, as I know, that Miss Wheeler refused Mr. Bulwer no less than three times before she finally yielded to his solicitations, on the assurance of Mrs. Lytton's consent to the union, he could hardly have been responsible for such a statement as the following : "[Mr. Bulwer] would probably have been weaned from encouraging hopes and wishes associated with Miss Wheeler, had he

received ,from her a distinct assurance that she
was resolved not to marry him without his
mother's consent.   No such announcement came
in aid of his struggle."   Neither, if he had been
fully acquainted with the manner in which his
father ill-treated, neglected, and deceived his wife,
would he have passed upon him so indiscriminate
an eulogy as that "his errors were the errors of
a good man, and his virtues those of a great
one."

But this is not the place wherein to comment
upon Lord Lytton's well-meaning endeavours to
canonise his father. The discrepancies between the
two versions will, I trust, be made sufficiently clear
hereafter. My readers will doubtless be enabled
to form their own opinions; and, I venture to
say, will do so with a much better chance of
arriving at the truth than would be attainable
from a study of the Life alone.   Even if, like
Professor Goldwin Smith, they come to the
melancholy conclusion that the late Lord Lytton
was a "literary hypocrite," that is not a consideration which can deter me from the performance of a plain duty, for I submit that the
vindication of an injured woman's memory is
sufficiently imperative to justify the unmasking
of the faults of a deceased novelist, great man
though he may have been.

I have endeavoured to state the case of the late

Lady Lytton as fairly and impartially as lies in my
power, but I must claim the indulgence of my
readers if my knowledge of the persecutions she
endured has occasionally carried me across the
boundary which separates judicial statement from
special pleading. This much, at all events, I will
frankly admit: that Lady Lytton, being a warm-
hearted, impulsive woman, with strong passions
and a generous, sensitive nature, was driven by
outrage and insult into a course of action which
none can hesitate to condemn. But what I
wish to show is that she was not the aggressor,
but for many years the patient victim of
undeserved oppression, before at length her woes
found vent in bitter and passionate vehemence.
At thirty-four she was left to battle with the
world alone; her children were taken from her;
her existence was rendered miserable by the
calumnies of society, and the callous indifference
of those whose duty it was to protect her; and
at the very zenith of her husband's fame, she,
who should have graced his triumph, was immured by his orders in a private madhouse.

While he was rejoicing in the fulness of earthly
prosperity and success, rich, courted, overwhelmed
with honours, and sated with adulation, she, once
a noted beauty and wit, who had nobly for nine
long and weary years borne the burden and heat
of the day, slaved for him and for her children,

endured the trials and hardships of the life of a struggling author, unmurmuring, faithful and content, rewarded only by insult and violence, was condemned to live the life of a hated and despised outlaw, to eat her heart out in poverty, solitude, and neglect. Few women, assuredly, would have emerged from such an ordeal as pure and uncontaminated as Lady Lytton.

Can we, then, wonder that even her fortitude broke down under so grievous an accumulation of wrongs, or that she wrote in her despair, "Had an angel op'd the book of Providence and let me read my fate, my heart had broke when I beheld the sum of ills which one by one I have endured"?

LOUISA DEVEY.

MONTRÉSOR, UPPER NORWOOD.

CONTENTS.

LIFE OF LADY LYTTON.

CHAPTER I.

AUTOBIOGRAPHICAL.

"I'll speak of them as they are,
Nothing extenuate nor set down aught in malice."

"THE first mistake I made was being born at all,
though, like most of the serious errors that may be
laid at my door through life, I had no choice and
little part in the matter. But nevertheless it was
a double mistake, for I certainly did not want to
come into the world, neither did it appear that
I was wanted in it, at least so far as my father was
concerned, who, having already four ciphers in the
shape of daughters, was very anxious for a figure
in the shape of a son.*

"And I've heard my mother say that when, at
ten o'clock of a dreary, drizzling November morning, on the 2nd of that month, 1802, I was born
at Ballywire, my father's place near Limerick,†

---

* A son was afterwards born, but died in childhood; and two
daughters died in infancy, only Henrietta and Rosina surviving.

† Which, as he himself said, not having a son, he sold to his
uncle, the Hon. John Massy. It is now (1869) in the possession
of my cousin, Mr. Bolton Massy.

the whole household being aware that he had commanded a son, were afraid to announce to him the mistake. Mrs. Gifford, the nurse, positively refusing to do so, my aunt Bessie, my mother's maiden sister, undertook to be *chargé d'affaires* on the occasion, and announced the disagreeable tidings. She did so; and, the family archives set forth, met with so discourteous a reception that she hastily quitted the breakfast-room, muttering, 'Well, we can't strangle the poor little thing; since it has pleased God to send it, it must live.'

" Kindly meant, this, on the part of my poor aunt; but had I had a voice for anything but screaming at that time, and had I been consulted on the subject, I should have decidedly made the same reply that the French judge did to the thief, who said in extenuation of his misdeeds, 'Dame, Monsieur, il faut vivre,'—'Je ne vois pas la nécessité.' Indeed, it would have been far kinder of my poor aunt, had she, in the many caresses she bestowed upon me, given me one mortal squeeze, and so have prevented my living, to add another incontrovertible illustration to that most profound of axioms, that 'wrong never comes right,'—for truly

'My weary way to heaven has been one stormy day!'

"My father, Francis Massy Wheeler, was the eldest or rather the only son of Hugh Trevor Wheeler, of Ballywire, County Limerick, by his wife Charlotte, daughter of Hugh, second Lord Massy of Hermitage, in the same county. My mother was the youngest daughter of Archdeacon Doyle by his wife Anna Dunbar. Next to that most ill-fated thing a great heiress, my mother was that peril-begirt target, a great beauty and a portionless one. I don't think she much valued her beauty ; those who *really* possess

'Il dono fatale di belezza'

seldom do ; but what she was justly proud of was that Henry Grattan had been her godfather."

As regards her personal appearance, Mrs. Wheeler was, according to her daughter, "very tall, with one of those skins and complexions which look like snow with a few rose-leaves dropped upon it. Her face was a perfect oval, like an egg ; the forehead high, straight, and white, surmounted by very silky, rippling, dark chestnut hair. The eyes of a deep blue-grey, almond-shaped, with dark eyelashes and low straight eyebrows. The nose aquiline, but of extremely fine and delicate chiselling, as was the short curled upper lip of certainly, without exception in art or nature, the most beautiful mouth and teeth I ever saw—the former being a perfect Cupid's bow, the latter small, dazzling, and even as a row of Oriental pearls, beautifully arched in her head, and set in gums that resembled the finest and deepest shade of pink coral. This mouth had the most enchanting smile I ever beheld, literally realising Moore's simile of being

'Like any fair lake that the breeze is upon,
When it breaks into dimples and laughs in the sun.'

" My mother's figure (though on a larger scale than I admire) was as faultless as her face ; add to which her hands and arms were models both as to form and colour, and her feet and ankles equally good ;

as my father laboured under several serious disadvantages. First, he had been for the first sixteen
years of his life an only son and a spoilt child, and
for the last three an orphan and his own master.
Then he was heir to an estate which, like all Irish
estates, was three times greater nominally than it
was in reality. All these combined circumstances
made my grandmother ponder, and then tremble
in her high-heeled shoes. So she bethought her
that, as honours well and hardly earned were now
flowing in upon her dead husband's brother, Sir
John Doyle, she would write to him, and surely he
would at least advise her. The Egyptian war, to
which poor Sir Ralph Abercromby had fallen a
sacrifice, had just ended, but his dear friend and
protégé, my dear grand-uncle, had returned to reap
the laurels which his own and so much more noble
blood had irrigated. And so he received the thanks
of both Houses of Parliament and the freedoms of
the cities of London and Dublin, was moreover
created a baronet, and received the Grand Cross of
the Bath, and was at that time Secretary-at-War.
This from first to last kind uncle wrote back word
on no account to let 'the child' be sacrificed by
sealing her fate, till she had seen something of the
world and of other men, and could from comparison
form some fixed standard of her own feelings and
tastes ; and in order that she might do so, he would
the following spring take his two beautiful nieces
to live with him in London, and give them all the
advantages and opportunities of mixing in 'the best
society,' as our _haute volée_ is erroneously called.
But whether this truly kind proposition my grand-

mother stuck upon one of her sharpest arrows, barbed
with innuendoes and animadversions of her daughter's
penniless and dependent state, further steeped in the
gall of that extorted gratitude that elects to do away
with all choice, and fired it off incontinently from
her cross-bow, or whether the '*che sara, sara*' is always
to be exemplified by the Aryan simile of the Hito-
padesh, which asserts that a chariot moves upon two
wheels, and a life moves also upon free will and fate,
I know not. But certain it is that my mother forthwith raised the standard of rebellion, and announced
her determination of accepting my father's offer
instanter, vehemently disclaiming all wish to live
upon the charity of any of her relations. And thus
the 'free will' wheel giving the false impetus to
the vehicle of our lives, as is so often the case, and
having thereby pushed the wheel of fate out of its
proper groove, left it to bear all the brunt and blame
of the capsize.

"My mother, it is true, urged that it was acting
ungratefully by their good uncle, but she was soon
talked down by her sister. It is needless, perhaps,
after this to state that this ill-assorted marriage was
none of the happiest, and the quarrels of the sisters
drove my father out of the house, and more than
ever into the trammels of his designing uncle and
guardian, who moulded him to his purposes by an
unlimited supply of ready money, claret, and fox-
hunting, in order to obtain some of his property, in
which he eventually but too well succeeded. Often
was I the innocent cause of strife between the sisters,
through my childish restlessness or importunities,
when my mother would be stretched on one sofa,

deep in the perusal of some French or German philosophical work that had reached her translated *viâ* London (and who was unfortunately deeply imbued with the pernicious fallacies of the French revolution, which had then more or less seared their trace through Europe, and who was besides strongly tainted by the corresponding poison of Mrs. Wolstonecraft's book), and my aunt Bessie, reclining on another couch, was dropping a silent tear over the delicate distresses of some Minerva Press heroine. I, who, having in vain, by means of paper and pins, and the back of my spelling-book for a drawing board, tried to lithograph one of the large geranium leaves that stood boldly out on the light yellow-grounded chintz of the drawing-room curtains, and as vainly tried to seduce the ever good and obedient Henrietta from her book or work into making a noise, would then proceed, slate in hand, and kneeling down before one of the high, hard, gilt and painted cane-bottomed arm-chairs, would make a daring attempt to copy some of the wreaths of very scarlatina roses and cholera-morbus-looking forget-me-nots that meandered along the back of it. But being no genius, I only succeeded in making a most atrocious squeaking of the pencil against the slate, which would so irritate my poor mother's philosophical nerves that I generally received so strong a rebuke that it sent me screaming in such a manner as must have given a convincing proof, had any such been wanting, that the lungs of the Doyles (always so celebrated) had not degenerated. Then would my aunt Bessie, deserting her heroine, fly to the rescue, exclaiming, 'You ought to be ashamed of yourself, Anna, with your philosophy and your nonsense, to treat the poor darling child so. Come here, Rosie, my darling, and Aunt Bessie will give her a peach, and we'll go to the hothouse for it.' But at these offers of pacification I only screamed the louder, and rushed unappeasably out of the room, as I had seen Aunt Bessie herself do under similar aggravating offers of atonement on the part of my mother or father; and if in my flight I chanced to fall in with the latter, he'd catch me up in his arms, and muttering something, would say, ' What's the matter, Rosie my darling? What have they been teasing papa's fairy about?' And when, as soon as I could speak, from the big stag-like tears rolling like a cataract into my mouth, I had sobbed out an explanation of the affray, he would judiciously tell me not to mind them, but run back and just put my head in at the drawing-room door and say, ' Ah! I don't care, for papa is going to take me out to ride before him on Dare-Devil, and he says I shall sit up all night if I like, and have as much cake as I can eat.'

"Such was the auspicious commencement of my education. I remember little of my father, except that he was old-looking for so very young a man, for he was not then more than nine-and-twenty. I was too young to remark, or rather to wonder, why his hand trembled so violently of a morning,— for I *did* remark it, or I should not now recollect it so vividly; but all I felt then was that for the few brief moments I ever saw him daily that hand was laid kindly on my head, and therefore I thought I belonged to it, and it to me, and so I loved it.

For my mother evinced a decided preference for
my sister Henrietta, and I soon became that most
miserable of created beings, the neglected sister of
a favourite and favoured child.   Not that I envied
Henrietta for being loved, indulged, and privileged
on all occasions; for it was impossible not to love
one so gentle, so gifted, and so good.   I thought
it was a matter of course that every one must do so.
Still I did long for a little of my mother's love.

" Ballywire—for so was the home of my fathers
called at the time I allude to—was nothing more
than a long, straggling pile of white or rather grey
buildings, standing upon an eminence on that wildest
and most romantic of all coasts, the western coast
of Ireland.   It had been a castle once upon a time,
but all that remained of its architectural honours to
entitle it to the appellation was one solitary turret,
in which was situated our nursery; and as it overlooked the sea, poor Henrietta and I did not fail
to be threatened with mermaids and sirens, ever
on the watch to take us away if we were naughty —
or as Nelly, our Irish nurse, more tersely expressed
it, 'if we'd be bould.'   The entrance-hall at Ballywire was still paved with grey marble, but broken
and indented; around its walls were hung the colossal
horns of the Irish elk, and upon a huge granite slab,
which looked more like a Druidical table than an
altar, lay a stringless Irish harp, purporting, by a
parchment legend attached to it, to have belonged
to the last of the bards, the celebrated Carolan ;
while above this table was a large but frameless
picture, portraying the scene at Lord Mayo's in
which Carolan triumphed over the musical skill of

the Italian Geminiani. On the right-hand side of the entrance was a large barrack of a room, still dignified with the high-sounding appellation of the banqueting hall, while on the left was the dining-room, with its coarse scarlet moreen curtains trimmed with black velvet, and black velvet plague-spots bursting out about the draperies, according to the prevailing epidemic among dining-room curtains at the period (1812), when the war was raging, not only between France and England, but against everything like good taste, both in dress and furniture. Down the centre of the room rolled a long dark mahogany horseshoe table, which stretched forth its dinginess like an arm of the Black Sea,— for French polish was unknown in those days, and the green baize, bees'-wax and cork frictions bestowed every morning by the butler and his colleagues were neutralised by the stains of claret and punch shed upon it every night. Round this table were a set of *ci-devant* red morocco chairs, but which now looked like a detachment of the 24th Foot (for such was their number) marching into country quarters after a protracted campaign on active service, so tattered and deplorable was their condition, and so dimmed their once scarlet glory. At the end of the room, in an alcove supported by attenuated pillars (for this room had been modernised according to the most approved bad taste of the times) stood a long narrow isthmus of a mahogany sideboard, connecting the peninsula of two more red morocco chairs; and at either end of this piece of furniture were two colossal tea-urns, doubtless intended by the upholsterer as ornaments, but if so, shamefully frustrating his intentions. The legs of this mahogany nightmare were so thin and fragile as to look quite incapable of supporting so unwieldy a superstructure ; for, like all the furniture legs of that period, whether of tables, chairs, or pianofortes, they seemed to have been taken at a valuation from the Spiders' Company retiring from business on their own account. Over the mantelpiece, which was of a plain, ugly, and much-veined piece of white marble, too high for modern fashion and not high enough for that of the olden time, was a picture of my father going to cover on his favourite hunter, Dare-Devil, with Angus Troil, the huntsman, a *boy* of sixty-three, and all the pack round him, on the lawn before Ballywire, in the very kitchen of which, unfortunately for me, the claret still flowed as of old, though at that time, in most Irish houses, it had given place to water, or at least to strong waters."

CHAPTER II.

CHILDHOOD AT GUERNSEY.

For various reasons, which the previous sketch of Mr. and Mrs. Wheeler's domestic life may possibly explain, Mrs. Wheeler seems to have taken the resolution, in August 1812, of leaving her fox-hunting, claret-drinking, but apparently amiable husband, and of taking refuge with her uncle, Sir John Doyle, who was then Governor of Guernsey. Accordingly, "one dark and stormy night, when the wind was sending forth those mysterious wailings which are alternately like the low hollow moan of suppressed suffering and the loud frantic shriek of insanity, and when the rain was pattering against the casement panes, which the hurricane was shaking in their leaden, lozenge-shaped frames," Mrs. Wheeler, accompanied by her sister, the above-mentioned "Aunt Bessie," and her two children Henrietta and Rosina, and escorted by her brother John, embarked in Sir John Doyle's yacht, *Ocean Pearl*, on a voyage to Guernsey. The passage was exceedingly stormy, the yacht struck, and the party were compelled to make for Milford Haven in an open boat.

The *Ocean Pearl*, however, though considerably damaged, was eventually towed into Milford harbour by a friendly Government sloop; and after three weeks spent in repairing dilapidations, she was again ready for sea, and this time succeeded in landing her freight safe and sound at Guernsey.

In the times of Sir John Doyle the office of Governor of Guernsey possessed a dignity and importance of which after his retirement it was deprived. Moreover, this worthy and distinguished baronet himself did not count among his many virtues the merit of economy, for he left the island at least £20,000 in debt, in consequence of his careless liberality.

Without this explanation, Lady Lytton's account of the splendours of Government House and of the lavish generosity of her grand-uncle may appear somewhat hyperbolical.

On arriving at the island they were received with considerable state by Sir John Doyle and his staff, while the regimental band greeted them with the somewhat inappropriate air of "Lord Moira's Welcome to Scotland." They then proceeded to Sir John's official residence, escorted by a small cavalcade of the staff.

Sir John himself is described by Lady Lytton with an eminently characteristic enthusiasm. He seems from first to last to have commanded her unbounded admiration and love, and she always speaks of him as endowed with all the virtues of Sir Galahad and Colonel Newcome. He was, we read, "the dearest, kindest, and most unselfish of created beings, the only one whom I have ever known who was really

'In wit a man, in simplicity a child.

But there are natures (few and rare, it is true) so loftily noble, so unsulliedly pure, so broadly generous, and so incorruptibly conscientious, that to praise seems almost to profane—their own deeds being alone worthy to constitute their panegyric and embalm their names to the latest posterity ; and such was my grand-uncle Doyle. He possessed that rare talent of making himself quite as agreeable to children as he was to the wisest and most learned, by the solidity and breadth of his mind, the playful brilliancy of his wit, and the perfect encyclopædia of biography and anecdote with which his own extensive intercourse with men and things, aided by his quick tact and observation, had stored his most retentive memory. To listen to his conversation was like living over again in an easy-chair the most agreeable portion of the lives of the most agreeable people, with all the angles rounded, and the dross, which will alloy even the most brilliant lives, sifted from them ; for he had skimmed the cream of the greater portion of his distinguished contemporaries, and had even seen the setting sun of Burke, Goldsmith, and Johnson, whose glorious rays had not rested upon him in vain.

> ‘ For e'en as the tenderness that hour instils
> When summer's day declines along the hills,
> So feels the fulness of the heart and eyes
> When all of genius that can perish dies.’

And this tenderness and fulness of heart seemed to have penetrated into and hallowed his whole nature, truly making to the pure all things pure ; for though he had been private secretary to George IV. when Prince of Wales, and had with Sheridan often 'set the table in a roar,' yet had he come out of this contaminating ordeal unaffected, save by the perfect manners of the one and the exquisite wit of the other."

Lady Lytton was evidently an ardent hero-worshipper, and it would have been fortunate for her had her adoration never been bestowed upon less worthy objects than Sir John Doyle. But to resume the narrative.

At Government House they were received by an awe-inspiring array of "powdered footmen in their white liveries, blue facings, and silver shoulder-knots, blue plush continuations, and immaculate white silk stockings as unwrinkled as eternal youth. These gentry did not produce the slightest effect upon Henrietta or myself, and I doubt even if the size of the house and the splendour of its appoint-ments did ; but accustomed as we had been to the 'most admired disorder' of the drawing-room at Ballywire, the *pêle-mêle* confusion of our own nursery, and the rack-rent topsy-turvy of the whole house, the intense neatness and order that now surrounded us, the large, not to say elegantly furnished rooms that were allotted to us, the two silent and respectful English maids that waited upon us, only addressing us in an under-voice, their difficultly suppressed smiles when Nelly addressed them as 'ma'am,' and finally Mrs. Stillingfleet, the housekeeper, curtseying herself into the room in all the propriety of black silk and the purity of white muslin to know 'if the young ladies wanted anything,' were too much for our weak nerves. We felt a sort of grandeur of desolation steal over us, and simultaneously bursting into tears, we hid our faces against Nelly's arm, and almost for the first time thinking of our father during the excitement of the journey, we sobbed out an inquiry of 'when *he* was to come?'"

After a meal of *consommé à la Condé*, *épigramme d'agneau*, and roast chicken, served upon silver plate, the two children walked about the grounds, "which were both beautifully laid out and beautifully situated, commanding here and there through vistas of luxuriant foliage *échappés* of the dark blue sea beyond. There was also a charming summer-house, fitted up after the model of a Pompeian house, to which one ascended by a circular exterior flight of some eighty marble steps, the balustrade of which was green bronze acanthus leaves, intersected with gilt Roman battle-axes. The peristyle of this *Bel Retiro*, or rather *Bellos Guardos*, as it was called, commanded a most extensive and magnificent view of the sea. Its furniture was only classical in form, for nothing could exceed the luxurious comfort of the cushions and squabs of its couches, and small Persian carpets counteracted the chilling effects of its mosaic floor, containing the *obligato* 'black dog' and *Cave canem* in the centre. Outside each window, instead of *jalousies* or Venetian blinds was gilded lattice-work, which could be put back at pleasure. The subject of the fresco on the walls was the interior of a Libyan temple, with the priests and priestesses in the act of celebrating the rites of Neptune, while devotees were bringing cornucopias of pearl, coral, and gold to lay upon the altar. The curtains of this room were of Tyrian purple silk (but of the *real* Tyrian purple, which is a deep orange-red), and they

were trimmed with a key border of royal purple.
From the centre of the room was suspended a large
bronze Roman galley lamp, and when lit a flame
issued from each oar, while in the corners of the
room stood bronze tripod lamps, about five feet
high. There was no fireplace, but in lieu of it a
most beautiful antique brazier."

This description is perhaps sufficient to give some
idea of the glories of Government House; and as
"all sorts of reviews, sham-fights"—very sham they
must have appeared after the real ones they were
accustomed to at home—"races, and regattas were
got up in honour of my mother and aunt," while
Sir John entertained a series of more or less distinguished and agreeable personages, it is not perhaps
surprising that Mrs. Wheeler and her sister evinced
no disposition to return to the dreary dissipation of
Ballywire. Mr. Francis Wheeler seems to have
accepted this situation philosophically enough. He
declined to make his wife any allowance, remarking
that as she was living in such splendour she could
not want anything from him; and does not seem to
have made any serious efforts to induce her to
return. A correspondence, however, was regularly
kept up between Guernsey and Ballywire, the task
of writing to her father being usually deputed to
Rosina, who was his favourite daughter.

Accordingly, for the next four years Mrs. Wheeler
and her daughters remained at Guernsey, and Rosina
and Henrietta were educated by a French governess
and a variety of masters and preceptors.

Some of Sir John Doyle's guests were personages
of no small importance, and it may not be amiss

to transcribe here a few sketches of their various characteristics and peculiarities as they presented themselves to Miss Wheeler. The following relates to the Duc de Bouillon :—

" I have alluded to a very large folio edition of the ' History of the French Revolution,' bound in Russia, with splendid plates, which the Duc de Bouillon had made my uncle a present of, upon his having taken it into his head to fall in love with my mother. I may as well mention that circumstance here, lest I should forget it ; though I never can forget his kindness, or all the pretty *bijouterie* and delicious fruit and flowers he used to send to Henrietta and me, during the long siege of twelve years that he laid to my mother, accompanied with madrigals and epigrams at her, authenticated with his well-known signature, which looked for all the world like

PICCADILLY.

But considering, poor, dear old man, that he was nearly as wide as Piccadilly, no wonder that his name should look like it ; for at that time he was, if anything, larger than his cousin, Louis Dix-huit, though more like in face to the pictures of Louis XVI.

" We were much annoyed, when we arrived at the respectable ages of twelve and fourteen, to find that our mamma had refused the offer he had so dotingly made her—for he was then seventy-two. We insisted strongly that if she did not love him we did ; but somehow or other neither she nor he seemed to consider that sufficient, even though his son, poor Philip d'Auvergne, who was afterwards drowned, was also on our side. But when we arrived at years of discretion—that is, when Charles X. was king, and we found ourselves going to balls in Paris, and properly dressed—we were still more amazed that we had a mother who could have claimed a *tabouret à la cour* as Duchesse de Bouillon (though the poor Duke himself at that time was no more). We thought, in those robes of white tulle and white roses, that it would have been so pleasant to have called the King our cousin, even by marriage!"

To Guernsey also came the Duke of Brunswick shortly before the battle of Waterloo. He brought with him the German legion *en route* for Spain, and these soldiers seem to have made a lasting impression on Miss Wheeler.

"The word legion conjured up to my timorous imagination nothing short of a diabolical phalanx; and it was not till the dear good Duke had been domiciled with us a week, and had won every heart in the house, old and young, by his frank kindness and unaffected amiability, especially to us children, that my fears began to fade, though to the long beards and still longer pipes of the legion it took much more time to get used. But at last even the smell of tobacco was forgiven, for the sake of the exquisite harmonies with which they filled the air in the stillness of the night, as they sang in parts along the beach, with that perfect unity of time and tune of which Germans alone are masters. Even Henrietta, so good, so orthodox in all things, used to get out of bed and open the window to listen to them; and of a moonlight night these concerts

were infinitely more delightful than any I have
heard since, and such is the omnipotence of music—
at least of such music—that it completely banished
my *idées Napoléoniennes;* it was not because they
were got out of it, but my head was franchised from
absurdity altogether. This said German legion wore
black velvet caps, in shape something like a chimney-
pot, about a quarter of an ell long, at the other end
of which was sewn a flat round, about the size of a
dinner-plate, lined either with card-board or some
other substantial material, and embroidered outside
in circles of narrow gold braid, and this round hung
over, not ungracefully, on the right side.

Now, it was not to be supposed that in the
war, when everything was military, and ladies
were *à la lettre* always in battle array, bearing
about in their heterogeneous costumes either some
reminiscence of a victory or some tribute to the
hero of it, a whole family could let such an
opportunity escape of making themselves ridiculous.
Accordingly, two days after the arrival of the
German Legion saw us, one and all, inducted into
black velvet Brunswick caps, in compliment to the
Duke. I'm not sure that even Nelly had not
received orders to convert the immortal brown
beaver into a Brunswick *Oëls;* but I am very certain that she did not obey, not only because I heard
her soliloquising one morning about that time—'A
pity I don't endade go convarting meself into one
of thim outlandish sogers at wanchet; they'll be
expicting me to grow a beard next, I suppose!
Thim that sows may reape, but it won't be me,'
—but because also for many years after the brown

beaver, in its original form, or rather want of form, continued to 'brave the battle and the breeze!'"

The following may help to prove that the noble art of "making up" had in the time of the war risen to a pitch of perfection which it has hardly exceeded even at the present day. "At eleven o'clock that same night I was awakened with a gentle pinching of the cheek by my aunt. Was I dreaming, or was I awake? but there she stood, not frowning and angry, as I had last seen her, but radiant with smiles and beauty, and glittering with jewels. She was followed by a lady with peculiarly bright black eyes, dark hair divided down the centre, and flowing in ringlets upon a neck as white as the ceiling itself, and cheeks like 'the rose that's newly sprung in June'; her hands and arms, which were equally white, and models in shape, were covered with bracelets and rings. She wore a Brussels lace dress over pink satin, and very short petticoats—I suppose to display a beautifully small and well-turned foot and ankle. I afterwards learned that this flowing hair was a wig, this exquisite complexion paint, and the lady sixty-four; for it was the Margravine of Anspach. In the background of this tableau stood Mademoiselle de Guilleragues, Nelly, and the two English nursery-maids, looking very much as the seven burgesses of Calais may be supposed to have looked when going out to be hanged for the good of their country, before Queen Philippa begged them off."

My lady readers may also be amused by reading Lady Lytton's account of the dress and fashion of the beginning of the century.

"At length the happy moment came when we were to be dressed to go downstairs ; and I doubt if any bride of the present day, armed with all the seductive witcheries of Mesdames Minette and Palmyre, capped by Baudron, could be half so well convinced of the irreproachable perfection of their toilette as we, or at least as I was, upon being put into a large blue jelly-bag, made of an abomination called, in the war, Salisbury flannel, and (excepting its ugliness) only famous for two things—namely, palpable shrinking, both under the influence of fire and water ; and unmercifully scrubbing and scratching the arms and necks of the unfortunate young delinquents condemned to solitary confinement within the remorseless precincts of its woollen pillory.

"Nelly having made this addition to our wardrobe upon her own responsibility, had been determined to do the thing handsomely ; consequently, above each tuck was run a piece of tolerably wide blue and yellow braid, not unlike that which used to adorn old-fashioned liveries, only that this was silk instead of worsted : however, the three huge tucks of these lovely frocks need not have given themselves such airs, and stuck themselves out so, for all that ; for in those days (as far as the tucks of children's frocks were concerned, at least) there was no knowing how soon pride would have a fall ; for it no sooner pleased Heaven in the natural course of things that we should grow a couple of inches, than down went a tuck. I was not then aware that 'Nature' had the good taste 'to abhor a vacuum,' but I know that I did ; for nothing could be more abominable than the appearance of these deserted railroads skirting our garments, which never owned a swifter locomotive than a lukewarm iron, of which Nelly was the solitary stoker.   But on the present occasion the tucks had not all the finery to themselves, for on the front of the bodice the same braid (only narrower) was to be seen in an ingenious sort of puzzle, displayed in a pattern something like that of a lazy-tongs and the stripes on a backgammon board.

" Henrietta, from her more mature age and quiet deportment, was permitted the pomp and vanity of wearing her hair parted down the centre, and though docked close behind *à la* raw recruit, yet at either side of the forehead luxuriating into tufts of stiff flat curls, one laid over the other, as round as a set of wedding rings in their as yet harmless state— before they have left the jeweller's shop. Whilst I, on account of my more perturbed, that is, tom-boyish habits, was made to look still more brazen by having my hair brushed up into a sort of cataleptic rigidity, like nothing in the world but a scrubbing-brush which had received some sudden and terrible alarm from which its nervous system had never recovered. A pair of bright yellow kid shoes, a world too wide, completed my charming costume."

Thus fearsomely arrayed, Henrietta and Rosina were brought down to meet their uncle's guests at dessert. They were ushered into " the little brown dining-room, as it was called, though in reality it was a fine oval room of thirty feet by twenty-five, with the ceiling and panels painted in compartments by Capriani, and the carving round these panels, and also of the looking-glass over the sideboard, which was in a deep recess, was white picked out with brown, very like a chocolate drop, which, with the delicacy of the paintings, gave this room the air of a large *bonbonnière*, and from this brown-and-white carving and its brown velvet curtains it had derived the name of the brown room.

"This apartment opened into a drawing-room hung with yellow damask, and looking upon a beautiful terrace, to which one descended from one of the windows by a flight of steps. It was furnished with Louis Quinze *cabriole* chairs and *causeuses*, and choice *marqueterie* cabinets and *bureaux*, inlaid with old Sèvres, the part which let down for writing being covered with purple velvet, and the small drawer daintily lined with white satin. Most of these were presents from the Duc de Bouillon, and in one of them were some very costly old turquoise jewelled Sèvres dessert plates and coffee cups, containing portraits of the beauties of the courts of Louis Quatorze and Louis Quinze—that is to say, six of one, and half a dozen of the other; and of these, as they appeared on the china, the old De Maintenon and the young Du Barry were unquestionably the handsomest. There were also several crab-shaped gold snuff-boxes, with portraits let into them of Mademoiselle de Blois, the Duc de Maine, the Comte de Toulouse, and others of Louis Quatorze's children."

Here they found Sir John Doyle, his secretary Mr. Waltham, and the Duc de Bouillon, seated round the dinner table, the old Duc "being attired in a purple velvet coat and a white satin waistcoat, embroidered in rich wreaths at the pockets, with splendid lace ruffles and *jabot*, and being, moreover, redolent of *maréchale*—a perfume then unknown on this side of the Channel."

In the following extract, too, the costume then affected by English ladies is contrasted with the attire of Rosina Wheeler's French governess, as she first appeared before her pupil's astonished gaze.

" I must describe her, for there are no such ladies to be seen now, I promise you, nor were there even in the war, unless you went to Paris for them, which was not easily done then. Her appearance struck us as the more extraordinary, not to say ridiculous, from the fact of English absurdity of dress being at that time the very antipodes of French absurdity. The English *females* (dear fatal name, rest *never* " unrevealed " !) then really did dress with poke bonnets, like bathing machines, with green veil, union-jacks floating above them, very long waists, very short and very narrow petticoats, tea-coloured jean-boots, with rather thick soles, the said boots being laced up the centre ; a broad hem, unhidden by flounce or furbelow, was all the ornament ever tacked to their skirts ; a long tight plain spencer completed in those days the Anglo-Saxon female costume, exactly like that of the young ladies who went (I believe with the Prince of Wales) down to a public-house at Wapping to besiege that remorseless *crève-cœur* of an actor, as described in that extraordinary histrionic and historical nightmare of M. Frédéric le Maistre's, entitled, " Kean, Drame en cinq actes," except that the spencers aforesaid were not made of green baize, as represented on the boards of the Porte St. Martin.

" It will be perceived by this that the English style of dress in 1812 was the flat and horizontal, whereas the French style, on the contrary, was the perpendicular and the *bombé*, of which the lady now leaning on my uncle's arm was a florid and first-rate specimen ; for, though an *émigrée*, she had friends who kept her *au courant* to the Parisian fashions. She, therefore, on the present occasion burst upon our dazzled vision in all the facets of the following splendour. Instead of a bathing machine, she wore on her head a chimney-pot of white Leghorn ; for, without any exaggeration, the crown of her bonnet was half a yard high and quite perpendicular, only slightly bowed out at the back and curving forwards in front. This chimney-pot also did duty as a flower-pot, as at the very summit of it appeared a profusion of such exquisite roses, carnations, mignonette, and pansies as at that time were never seen in the British Isles, except growing in real *parterres*. The leaf, that is the front, of this stupendous superstructure, was shallow, being about the depth and shape of half a milk-pan. On each side underneath appeared little tufts of very short black ringlets, all kept in their place by a band of narrow black velvet round the head. She was thin and angular ; but instead of going the lengths the English ladies did, her waist, if waist that could be called which waist was none, went literally under her arms, the back at each side gracefully branching off like the sticks of a fan. She wore a black velvet spencer, with a fall of black blonde round

the waist, and slashed or what were then called top
sleeves.

"Her dress was composed of white cambric muslin,
but flounced up to the knees, each flounce being
deeply embroidered in a wheel-pattern (her own
work), and an insertion of the same embroidery
heading each *volant*. In her right hand she carried
a black velvet reticule with a steel clasp and chain,
and across the same arm hung a yellow or rather
a deep aventurine-coloured cashmere shawl, with a
palm-border to it ; but altogether the most miraculous part of her appearance to our uninitiated
warlike eyes was the exquisite make and fit of her
gloves and shoes."

CHAPTER III.

In addition to the various accomplishments which she acquired at the hands of this French governess and her masters, Rosina Wheeler managed at Guernsey to develop to a high pitch of perfection an unlucky talent for mimicry, which she, I believe, inherited from her father.

"I'm sorry to have to confess it," she writes, "but I was born a mimic, and for my further misfortune was endowed, as most mimics are, with a terribly keen sense of the ridiculous, and once knowing a person's peculiarities, I could not only imitate their face, voice, and gestures, but could extemporise whole scenes of adventures for them, and furnish dialogues of what they *would* have said had they been placed in such circumstances. But I beg that no one will run away with the common but very erroneous idea that ill-nature is the groundwork of all mimicry,—for it is not, and it was often those whom I loved the most that I imitated the best, provided they had any salient points to imitate; but parrots and ventriloquists might just as well be accused of being ill-natured and venomous as mimics, for mimicry merely arises from a peculiar organisation, moral and physical. Indeed, no one

can sing or speak oratorically well, or be a good
linguist, without possessing an imitative power, which
is the germ of mimicry."

She mimicked her governess and her Italian master
with such success that they both enjoyed so im-
mensely the caricature of their own peculiarities as
to applaud instead of punishing. She imitated the
poor Duc de Bouillon, and every one of marked
individuality whom she met at Government House;
and her mother and aunt used to encourage her in
her dangerous gift, for the purpose of ridiculing any
lady or gentleman who might at the time have incurred their displeasure. In fact, her talents in this
direction were turned to such account that she was
frequently asked to rehearse her performances before
her grand-uncle and his guests, and gradually became
possessed of quite a miniature property-wardrobe
of articles of dress which assisted her in the realism
of her impersonations. It is hardly necessary to
add that this unfortunate facility by no means assisted
to smooth her future passage through the world,
for through it she innocently made many enemies,
and it was frequently made use of to her discredit
by unscrupulous maligners of her character.

Sir John Doyle—good easy man—seems to have
been most unmercifully bullied by his handsome and
wilful nieces; and during the latter days of his stay
in Guernsey, besides being hampered by pecuniary
difficulties, he appears to have lived in no small fear
of domestic unpleasantness.

" About this time," writes Lady Lytton, " I became
acquainted with the only fault that the closest intimacy ever enabled me to discover in my uncle;

and though it is a fault common to most men—ay, to the wisest, the best, and even to the most physically brave—it is nevertheless one that produces the most baneful effects, the most fatal results to their own happiness, and to that of all with whom they are connected : I mean, want of moral courage. The fact is, my mother and aunt's society had already taken effect upon him, and he had begun to adopt the fatal code of 'anything for a quiet life !' A modern uncle, no doubt, would have asserted his authority, reminded them of the obligations they were under to him, and requested them to leave the house if they made it disagreeable to him ; and in this instance a modern uncle would have done right ; but he, from the very fact of its being his house, and of their being under obligations to him, transposed the order of things, and with a refinement of delicacy that made him at once the greatest victim and the most lovable of human beings, forbore, yielded, and obeyed on all occasions, as if *he* had been in the penniless and dependent position, for fear any of us should be reminded that we were. Peace, gentle spirit ! I forgive thee every childish tear thy one fault caused me to shed in remembrance of thy bright angel nature, of which no copy now remains !"

Sir John, moreover, seems to have acted the good Samaritan to such a horde of rapacious relatives that it is by no means surprising that by the time he left the island his affairs were in an exceedingly embarrassed condition. His great-niece, ever ready to put the best possible construction on her hero's weaknesses, explains matters thus :—

" All this preyed upon and worried my poor uncle,

—the more so that, notwithstanding his own fine private fortune, the munificent emoluments of his salary (for in those days all official appointments, whether embassies, governments, or missions, were splendidly remunerated), and notwithstanding the extreme cheapness of everything at Guernsey, from French wines and French silks down to French gloves and ribands, and all sorts of provisions and house rent, then so ruinously dear in England, yet, from the most unpardonable neglect, and the sort of perpetual saturnalia that was allowed unchecked to go on, he about this time found himself some twenty thousand pounds in debt. This was hard, to say the least of it, that he who had made a home for so many should see his own begin to crumble about him ; his household gods mutilated, if not quite destroyed, one after the other, in the shape of privations and retrenchments which are ever the hard coin in which extravagance exacts payment from generosity and principle. In short, he grew ill—ill with that weariness of soul for which there is no cure, save in the hands of Him who inflicts it."

In 1816 Sir John relinquished his office, and returned to London, accompanied by Mrs. Wheeler, Miss Doyle, Henrietta and Rosina, in the yacht *Ocean Pearl.*

" The whole population of Guernsey had turned out, and thronged the beach and the pier. My uncle was not to return there, as the appointment was to be given to an officer of inferior rank, and the salary to be considerably reduced ; but had the people of Guernsey been following his funeral, their silence could not have been more profound and mournful, or their tears have flowed more copiously. There is nothing in seeing women, children, and beggars cry, for tears are at once their vocation and their heritage here below; but when stern-visaged, strong-hearted men weep, the course of nature seems overruled, that feeling may be avenged, and one is awed before the miracle, as the Moabites and Amorites were before the sun and moon when they stood still in the valley of Ajalon. My uncle seemed equally affected—perhaps more painfully so—for it is a great charge for one heart to have to respond to thousands; but if ever heart were broad enough, deep enough, and true enough for the task, his was. He cordially returned the pressure of the hands within his reach, but uttered not a word. Oh! well and wisely, I ween, are things meted out; for how would half the world ever express their small ideas and smaller feelings but for great words? and how would great and intense feeling ever be expressed but for silence?"

They ultimately arrived in London, and put up at a "gloomy hotel" in Jermyn Street, of which Lady Lytton's recollections are not particularly pleasant, as "for the most part my mother and aunt, being unable to take us out unless one of them and one of us remained at home (the carriage being a chariot), our miserable time was spent in migrations, like perturbed spirits, from the large gloomy drawing-room to the still more gloomy bedroom leading out of it, and looking upon high walls and dingy leads, where the few faint sunbeams from a London sky had no chance of penetrating, with the fearful odds against them of fog, soot, and smoke."

To this dismal hotel came Grattan to visit Sir John Doyle, and to be drilled by him in the art of comporting himself with grace at a forthcoming *levée* of the Prince Regent.

" At this time Grattan was much bent, for it was only four years before his death. He generally walked with his hands behind his back, and his eyes bent on the ground as if intensely preoccupied by some engrossing thought—as, indeed, he always was—for when, during the course of a long, glorious, and consistent career, a man has had a whole people in his heart and a whole country in his head, as Grattan had, he has most indubitably sufficient matter for preoccupation. . . . But to continue : what with his white hair and his fragile appearance, the illustrious apostle of Catholic Emancipation gave gave to me the idea of a silver ash ; but there was a genuine expression of benevolence in his eyes, and a delicacy in the chiselling of the nose, which seemed to bear testimony to the former beauty of the face. It is perhaps needless to say that the inflections of his voice were peculiarly melodious ; for who can be really an orator without that organ being attuned to the most correct harmony ? "

The lesson was a failure, for Sir John found it impossible to make an elegant courtier out of the sturdy patriot, though, for all the history tells us, he may have gone through the ordeal itself with greater success than the rehearsal. From Jermyn Street Sir John moved into a small house in Lower Berkeley Street, and his grand-nieces were sent to a fashionable school in Kensington. Rosina bitterly details the misery which she endured at this establishment, accentuated by the fact that within a year her sister Henrietta was taken away to Dublin by Mrs. Wheeler; but it is unnecessary for the purposes of this narrative to dwell upon these girlish troubles. Suffice it to say that she presumably received the ordinary so-called finishing education, and in due time left school, and went to live with Sir John Doyle in Somerset Street.

During the next few years I have but scanty details of Miss Wheeler's life. She appears to have visited Ireland when about eighteen, and to have stayed with her uncle, the Rev. Charles Doyle. She then, for the first time since leaving Lizzard Connell, met her father, who came up from his own place for the purpose. Little or nothing resulted from the interview, for they never lived together again. Mr. Wheeler died in Ireland about 1820, and was buried with considerable pomp and ceremony, being a very prominent Freemason. I may here remind my readers that Rosina was his sole heiress, for her only brother died when a child, and her sister Henrietta died in Paris in May 1826. From this sister, to whom Lady Lytton was devotedly attached, and whose death was to her not merely a crushing blow, but a most irreparable loss, I have only one letter, which it may not be out of place to transcribe here:

"RUE DE GRENELLE, ST. GERMAIN No. 13, PARIS,
"*December 24th*, 1825.

"MY DEAREST ROSINA,—

"I was very glad to have received a letter from you at last, as I had indeed expected to have heard of you long before this; but as your silence has been accounted for in so satisfactory a manner, I have nothing more to say, save a hope of reformation

for the future. And although you must not expect a
correspondent that is very amusing, or that can give
you much news, or even invent any, a line now and
then can certainly do no harm. Mr. *Bentem's* * visit to
Paris, and my having had the honour of dining with him,
is no news to you ; but I must tell you that he is a
charming, gay old man, and made conquest of every one in
the hotel where he lodged. From his amiable manners,
he was very much run after here, and his arrival announced in the papers in the most flattering manner ;
but the funniest of all is, that in his hotel he passed
with some for a great sportsman, and with others for one
of the great poets of the age ; at all events they knew he
was a great man of some kind or other, but of what kind
they could not determine. We went with him one morning
to stay with him whilst he was sitting to a young statu-
ary of great genius for his bust. His two young secre-
taries were with us ; and as the conversation happened
to fall on Don Tomsono, etc., etc., it is needless to say
that the *atelier* resounded with shouts of laughter, in
which even the young artist joined most manfully. After
we had alternately related of him all the anecdotes that had
fallen under each other's knowledge, one of them exclaimed,
' Oh, but, Richard, you have not told Miss Wheeler of the
" *Harlequinades!* " ' I could hardly believe my senses.
But here is the story : Whilst he was stopping at *Bentem's*
he was one day with these young men in the library, just
equipped for going out—viz., the old plaid flannel petticoat
about his neck in guise of cloak, and that *séduisant* hat,
put on in the true Tompson cock, when they began talking
of the agility of Harlequin, when Tompson immediately said,
' I do declare to God that in less than three weeks I could do
the same.' ' Well, Mr. Tompson, but you should give us a
specimen of your talent.' Whereupon *mio caro uglissimo*
gathered his ' auld cloak aboot him,' and hat and all
capered, kicked, and frisked and flung about for some time
à la harlequin, whilst his enlightened and discerning audi-

* Jeremy Bentham.

ence were in strong convulsions on the floor. When he was
introduced to the young Comte de Miranda, who was complaining that a very hot climate incapacitated him from
great application to study, Tomsono advanced towards him
with a *pas de Zephyr*, and levelling his tins at him, told him
that this must be caused by a defect in his own intellect.
The young man at first stared, but had tact enough to
see how matters stood. However, all those political econo-
mists have their peculiarities, and many among them are
amiable men.

"I am afraid I must conclude for the present, with best
love to yourself, in which mamma joins, who is very happy.
Love to darling Bessy, General Doyle, and

"Believe me, dearest Rosina,

"Yours most affectionately,

"HENRIETTA."

This Don Tomsono admired Mrs. Wheeler ; and
her daughters told her if she dared to have anything
to say to him they would never let her have any
peace. Lady Lytton was a wonderful mimic, but
she told me she was a long time before she could
take Tomsono off. But one night she caught the
idea ; and their mother heard so much laughter in
their room that she called out, "What are you
making so much noise about?" "Oh," said Rosina,
"I have got him at last." She had found an old
scratch wig, and imitated him to perfection. Her
Miss Dulcibella B. was glorious. The only drawback was she could not speak, her mouth was
screwed down so tightly. Her changes were instan-
taneous.

I also know that Lady Lytton was in Paris
when Charles X. was king ; but beyond the foregoing there is practically nothing to narrate until
December 1825, the date of her first meeting with

her future husband, at which time she was still living in Somerset Street with Sir John Doyle, while her mother and sister were in Paris. Here I again call upon Lady Lytton to resume her narrative, premising that from the following I have omitted nothing of the smallest relevancy or importance. There are many bitter expressions which I might have excised, many asperities which I might have smoothed over; but I have deemed it best to let the whole stand, hoping that my readers will not forget that at the time it was written the iron had entered into the poor lady's soul, and she was smarting from the pangs of cruel outrage and neglect.

CHAPTER IV.

FIRST MEETING OF ROSINA WHEELER WITH EDWARD
LYTTON BULWER AND HIS MOTHER, AT MISS
BENGER'S, 1825 — "L. E. L." — PARTY AT MRS.
LYTTON'S.

AND now was about to dawn the most fatal era of
my life, when my *engoûment* for literary celebrities
led me to plunge headlong into the Bohemianism
of their perhaps more *émaillé* than magic circle.
Fed, as I had been, upon the rather "strong meat"
of my dear grand-uncle's traditions and personal
reminiscences of the magnates of politics and literature of his time—for "there *were* giants in those
days"—I had rather too much of a *cultus* for
the genus author, and at that time not sufficient
discrimination to perceive how the pure gold of
the olden time had been superseded by modern
pinchbeck for the million; and not very well gilt
pinchbeck either. It is true that the few live
authors I had met at my mother's—dear old Jeremy
Bentham, and the "Tom Toms," as my sister and
I irreverently called Moore and Campbell—by no
means filled the highest niches in my ideal Pan-
theon; yet still women are said to love fame, and
this is more especially the undiscriminating sin of
young women; and by the time they are old enough
to know better the mischief is done, and it is too

late to profit by the copy-book admonition " Evil
communications corrupt good manners." It was
peculiarly unfortunate for me that my mother, and
that wisest, kindest, truest friend I ever had—
my dear sister, were then in Paris. My grand-
uncle only accompanied me to my favourite aver-
sions—dinner parties, and to occasional squeezes at
great houses, and to the receptions at the Admiralty;
for the Duke of Clarence, afterwards William IV.,
was then Lord High Admiral.

My aunt never went anywhere, and only snapped
out what was very true—namely, that it was very
wrong to allow me to go out alone, and to let me have
the carriage when I pleased ; but she did nothing
either to obviate or remedy this. As she was con-
stitutionally objective and chronically implacable, her
animadversions had little weight, more especially
as she ever flavoured them with the family craze of
arraigning ugliness as a sin! for on one occasion, when
I had gone with Lady C—— P——, afterwards Lady
B——, to the Freemasons' Tavern, to hear my uncle
speechify as D.G.M., she for a whole week, *apropos
de bottes*, twitted and taunted me on every occasion
with " How you *could*, for the sake of going out, be
seen with so ugly a woman in public I cannot conceive!—I'd have stayed at home for ever rather
than have made such an exhibition." But it is very
certain that had my mother been in England I should
not have been allowed to take such " a header " into
the Slough of " Literary Society " as my evil star
led me to do at that time. The way of it was this.
" L. E. L." had just dawned upon the world by those
" Cameos from the Antique " of hers in the *Literary*

Gazette; and among the miscellaneous pieces at the end of one of her poems—"The Troubadour," I think—was a very charming little poem about a gallant achievement of my dear grand-uncle which she had heard from some old Chelsea pensioner, who had been an eye-witness to it. This was quite enough for me : I set off in hot haste to call on her, and ask if I might bring the hero of her poem, and present him to her. She was then living with her grandmother in Sloane Street. I was surprised, and somewhat scandalised, when I first saw her; for though only 2 p.m., she had her neck and arms bare, a very short, but elaborately flounced white muslin dress, and a flower in her hair,—but I thought, of course, that authoresses, like "charming women," might dress themselves just as they pleased. In later years her dress was thoroughly tamed to the conventional standard, but her manners were never entirely broken in. It was at her house I first beheld all the most curious specimens of the literary *menagerie ;* but I also met one of the most amiable and worthy, if precise, old ladies I ever knew in my life—Mrs. Roberts, the widow of Dr. Roberts, head master of St. Paul's School. If one could imagine Sir Charles Grandison having quitted his turbulent sex and exchanged into the Dowager Reserved Corps, placid and still, exquisitely polite, in the richest and softest of black *satin turque,* heavy with rich Chantilly lace, and surmounted by a snowy white blonde cap, that was a hybrid between that of a Quakeress and one of Greuze's *fanchettes*, he would exactly have presented the outward appearnace of Mrs. Roberts. There was also a prim pleasantry about the dear old lady, that always reminded one of "the cup that cheers but not inebriates." She was even a more enthusiastic admirer of "L. E. L." than I was, and indeed overflowing with kindness and consideration for all young people. Nothing could be more exquisite than the little dinners she used to give us at her house in Mansfield Street, but their goodness was all so solid, so decorous, so stately—to the noiseless, well-bred servants, that one felt if all one ate and drank (more especially the port) and saw was not in a bishop's palace, it ought to have been. The only thing not exquisitely in keeping with what Mr. Disraeli might call "the sustained" dignity rather than "splendour" of her existence was her carriage, or rather coach : *shabby* it could not be called—its paint and varnish and broadcloth lining were all too new and *point devise* for that—but there was about it too much of "the devil's darling sin, the pride that apes humility," for it was the exact model of a hackney coach, as hackney coaches then existed, only a hackney coach *endimanchée;* and the slow but very sure pace the sleek black horses went at, continued successfully the resemblance. But at these literary *Folkmotes* of "L. E. L.'s" it is impossible to describe, among so many strange and questionable-looking people, what an *ægis* one felt Mrs. Roberts to be ; for, unlike Lady A——, who, when asked to chaperone some English lady of cloudy character to the Tuileries, in Louis Philippe's time, said, "No, I have character enough for *one*, but not for *two*," Mrs. Roberts had such a plethora of character and respectability that she had enough to spare for all

Babylon. At one of these literary *menageries* it was that I first met Miss Spence, authoress of many immortal works, now widely forgotten: she was very stout, very short—in fact, very like a Sancho Panza in petticoats, before he became Governor of Barrataria and was condemned to such short commons. Her sleeves, like her skirts, were short, and in imitation of Madame de Staël she always twirled a sprig of something (quality if she could get it) in her fingers. Her nose was very thick, and wide at the wings, like a county hospital; her lips also thick; *mais en revanche* there was great economy about her eyes, which were very small, and so light that with false pride they seemed not to like people to know they had pupils. But her face had anticipated the recent discoveries in America by more than half a century, for it always looked as if it had just "struck oil." Like all the authoresses of that day, she culminated in a turban, or at least a caricature of one in gauze and wire, as unlike the real Moabite or Sibylline structure as the trade mark on the bottles of Bass's pale ale is like the Pyramids of Egypt. Poor Miss Spence's chief idiosyncracy was like Mr. Collins' in "Pride and Prejudice," always talking of "her humble abode." She never harpooned any one for her parties without the peroration "if they would condescend to honour her humble abode." And if Mr. Collins had his Lady Catherine de Burgh always ready, as a social battering-ram, wherewith to pulverise his inferior acquaintance into awe and admiration, in like manner did Miss Spence bring up her great gun Lady Caroline Lamb. This

was the manner in which she applied the match:
"If you will so far honour my humble abode as to
come next Tuesday, you will meet some *litry* (she
never said literary) celebrities; and, 'though last,
not least,' dear Lady Caroline Lamb, whom I honour
more for her *litry* abilities than for her rank,—though
when *she* condescends to honour it with her presence, others—of less litry and social pretensions,
need not be afraid to honour my humble abode."

Among all these "turban'd Turks," who did not
exactly scorn the world, there was one for whom I
had a sincere regard and esteem: this was Miss
Benger, the author of "Elizabeth, Queen of Bo-
hemia," and other historical works. She was that
little coveted but inestimable and rare excellence
which may emphatically be called *a good creature*,
for she *was* good in every relationship of life; and
trying and perilous were many of those relationships to her, but she came bravely, nobly, and
straitly through them all. Alas that so much
excellence should have been the unwitting cause of
so much evil! She had made it a point that I
should go to one of her parties; it was, as well as
I remember, the beginning of December, 1825. I
had been reading out to my uncle, or rather, had
just finished, a book that all the world was wild
about—"Vivian Grey." It was then just out; and
no one knew who had written it. There was a spice
of the prophetic in my uncle's critique as I closed
the book,—"Whoever has written that is a devilish
clever and somewhat unscrupulous fellow; he'll
leave his mark on the world's brazen wall, and would
be quite equal, I should say, to any and every

emergency, from a falling comet to an earthquake."
I was not only quite hoarse from reading aloud
so long, but had a dreadful cold beside. When the
carriage was announced, my uncle said, " My child,
you must be mad to think of going out to-night with
such a cold : you'll catch your death." " Oh no : my
furs—or rather yours, for I'll take one of your
Turkish pelisses—will defy both fog and frost ; and
poor dear Miss Benger would never forgive me if I did
not go, as I promised to take some people home for
her." And so I went. As usual, dear Miss Benger
was all kindness : in honour of my cold, she placed
me on a sofa near the fire, and propped me up with
cushions ; but presently my attention was arrested
by a long, intensely flat figure, with its back to me,
who was talking to some one on the opposite sofa.
Like the horse mentioned in the long-after-published
" Orpheus C. Kerr Papers,"—" as viewed from behind this figure was decidedly Gothic." But the
head-gear was *the* most extraordinary *tour de force*
I ever saw, even for what Miss Spence would call a
" litry " party, where I had seen many impenetrable
toilet enigmas ; for this one looked like a conglo-
meration of Turkish bath towels that had been
suddenly seized by the insane ambition of emulating
the serpents on the Laocoon, and were writhing
round and round the head of the lady in question.
Miss Benger, perceiving my inquiring glances, said,
sotto voce, almost bursting herself, " Don't laugh, if
you can help it : that is Mrs. Edward Blaquière ; she
has the reputation of being the ugliest woman that
ever was invented, not excepting Potiphar's wife.
She is the wife of Edward Blaquière, who was with

Lord Byron in Greece, and who has disappeared so
mysteriously; people say he is not dead, but only
pretending to be so, to keep out of the way of his
wife; and when you see her face you'll easily believe
the story." " But what on earth has she on her head ?
I have been trying for the last ten minutes to make
it out; I am used to turbans run to seed; but no
poppy-head in Brobdignag ever presented such an
outrageous appearance." Poor Miss Benger now
fairly exploded behind her fan, as she whispered to
me, " No, it has legitimately nothing to do with
heads of any kind; it is, *tout bonnement*, a pair of
Prince Mavrocordato's inexpressibles, which she
brought away, as one of her Greek trophies, and
has utilised as you see." " In fact," said I, "it is
not only a variation of the old charade about the
ostrich feather, but a *charade en action*—

<blockquote>
' In Africa's realm delighted to range,
   On the tail of my owner I fled;
  But in England experienced a wonderful change—
    I, instead of a tail, deck a head !' "
</blockquote>

" Exactly," laughed Miss Benger; and roused
by the laugh, the owner of the princely garment
turned suddenly round. Without for a moment
impeaching his courage, oh how I envied Mr. B.
his power of flight! The face now before me was
—white as the cotton turban that surmounted it,
and pitted with the small-pox like a cribbage board;
and very long, but to be sure it was as broad as it
was long, and as flat as a sheet of paper; while the
nose, though long, was so flattened into the face
that it gave one the idea of a giant having sat down

upon it by mistake.   Little attenuated jet black
ringlets, like corkscrews in an atrophy, dangled
down on each side, as far as the very high cheek-
bones, which they did not pass, apparently afraid
of so mountainous a journey.   Her figure kept the
unities perfectly, being as flat and as gaunt as her
face ;—this was cased in what I can only describe
as a sort of white satin armour, made perfectly tight,
without a vestige of trimming or fulness ; and being
lined with buckram, to insure greater rigidity, it
rattled like amateur thunder at every movement
she made.   But oh! the voice,—it was an antipodical voice, at once shrill and gruff, and so jerky
and spasmodic, with a metallic twang in it, that it
gave one the idea of a pair of tongs clanged across
the bars of a gridiron, in default of any more
harmonious instrument.

For one mortal half-hour the tongs and gridiron
twanged on, in the same strain—I in vain trying
to elicit some details about Lord Byron, beyond his
anchorite resistance of Mrs. B.'s attractions—when
fortunately "L. E. L." (Miss Landon) arrived ;
but was some time before she made her way over
to me, for she had to shake every one by both
hands *chemin faisant ;* for never was there any
one, even among the *literati*, who had such an
exaggerated and enthusiastic way of expressing
what she did not feel.   On the present occasion
she looked remarkably well : she had a sweetly
pretty blush-rose complexion, her forehead, eyebrows, eyes and eyelashes, were beautiful, the
mouth not bad ; the defaulter was the nose, if such
it could be called—being one of the most homœo-

pathic, ignoble little snubs that ever attempted to do duty for that important *juste milieu* of facial population. Her hands, feet, ankles were also very pretty; and her figure so light and *petite* that its flatness and angularity were almost unobserved.

While poor Miss Landon was still hurling down her avalanches of flattery upon my devoted head—which was really cruel, considering what a heavy weight it had already to bear, in the shape of a bad cold—there was a slight commotion, and a sudden cessation of voices, at the other end of the room; and Miss Benger said to me, *sotto voce*, "Oh! here is that odd, rich old woman, Mrs. Bulwer Lytton, and her son, her favourite son,—he is very clever, they say: his was the Prize Poem this year at Cambridge,—I must introduce you to them." "Oh no, pray don't, on any account!" I said, as Miss Benger hurried away to greet the new arrivals. As she did so, stopping at the door to shake hands with them, I had time to take an inventory of both; and both were new and curious in their way. The old lady wore a rather crushed had-been-white blonde cap, with still more oppressed artificial flowers trampled over it; her hair, which was not grey, but dark-brown, was so completely and chaotically frizzed over her forehead and eyes that it was impossible to see the latter *in extenso*, —only in occasional glints, as one does those of a Skye terrier from the same style of *coiffure*. Her very prominent aquiline nose was so large that it would have been an exaggerated feature for a man. Her mouth and teeth were both large, and the latter very long and prominent. She wore

a morning dress high up to her throat, of that
sort of dull-red slate-colour which, even in the
bloom of its youth, always looks dingy and faded,
so it might have been quite new; round her throat
was what used to be called "a frill," of thread lace,
upon which the blonde of the cap, though it had
long passed its grand climacteric, seemed scornfully
to look down. Round her neck, under the ruff, and
condescendingly reposing upon the dingy silk, was a
diamond necklace; and under the diamond necklace,
and in proper subjection to it, was a cameo necklace,
each cameo (small oval ones on dark shells) linked
together with small Venetian chains, as they used
to be worn at the beginning of this century; under
the cameo necklace came a thick but very dingy
gold chain; while in the centre of her chest—
though it had no apparent *raison d'être*, as it had
nothing to fasten—was a very large round topaz
brooch, surrounded by pearls, as if acting as a
full stop to all the above essays of jewellery. She
wore on each wrist a similar variety of bracelets,
which appeared like the lineal descendants and
heirs apparent of the necklaces. Her gloves were
of white kid, but unwontedly stiff and hard. In
her right hand she carried a pocket-handkerchief,
folded; and in the folds of the unfolded kerchief
was a very small white satin fan, labouring under
a confluent eruption of gold and silver spangles.
From the lady's left side dangled a sabretash-
shaped green velvet reticule, with a steel chain
and clasp—a little larger than an *aumonière* of
the twelfth century or a purse of Henry VIII.'s
time, when fashion exacted that the said purses

should be worn outside, which afforded such a
harvest to the light-fingered gentry that it gave
rise to their title of "cut-purses." It is proverbial
que les extrêmes se touchent; and the adage was
certainly not belied in the present instance, for
if this lady was the incarnation of the dowdy and
the out-of-fashion, her son, upon whom she leant
—and who had a grotesque expression, between
a suppressed strut and a primitive-Christian-
martyr-like amount of self-abnegation, as if wishing
practically to illustrate to the living mosaic of
science, philosophy, literature, and art, then and
there assembled, that

> " To bear, is to conquer one's fate ! "—

was altogether as antipodical an impersonation of
modes and fashions and *chics* considerably in
advance of their age.   He had just returned from
Paris, and was resplendent with French polish, so
far as boots went.   His cobweb cambric shirt-front
was a triumph of lace and embroidery, a combina-
tion never seen in this country till six or seven
years later, except on babies' frocks.   Studs, too,
except in racing stables, were then *non est;* but
a perfect galaxy glittered along the milky way
down the centre of this fairy-like *lingerie.*   His
hair, which was really golden, glitteringly golden,
and abundant, he wore literally in long ringlets, that
almost reached his shoulders.   The likeness to his
mother was striking ; only, reversing the usual order
of things, his features were, though very *prononcé,*
softened duplicates of hers ; he also was unmistak-
ably gentlemanlike-looking ; indeed, according to

his then surroundings, too patrician-looking. What
I mean is, that the fitness of things externally,
as well as mentally and psychologically, is always
marred by want of harmony ; and it has often
struck me that it amounts to a species of inverse
vulgarity to be more thoroughbred-looking than
any one else in a room, just as it decidedly *is*
vulgar to be the only one over-dressed person.
Now, looking round at the dim, thick-booted,
unkempt Herr Muddlewitses and Mufflechops by
which science was represented,—the philosophy,
which seemed, in "the interests of suffering
humanity," to be trying personal experiments of
strangulation *via* wisps of camomile-tea-coloured
mull muslin round their throats,—the literary
gentlemen, in gold nose-pinchers, who had converted thereby their noses into a supererogatory
parenthesis, and the literary ladies, who were
darting about like galvanised rag-bags, a man
who, as men *then* dressed, would have created
a smile and riveted a stare even at Devonshire
House or Almack's, certainly *did* explode upon
that literary *Folkmote* like a sort of sartorial
shrapnel ! Poor D'Orsay's linen gauntlets had not
yet burst upon the London world ; but, like the
little source of a mighty river, Mr. Lytton Bulwer
had three inches of cambric encircling his coat
cuffs, and fastened with jewelled sleeve-links. And
although it then wanted full five years till every
man in society, like a defaulting schoolboy, was
caned, he also dangled from his ungloved and
glittering right hand a somewhat gorgeously
jewelled headed ebony cane ; and the dangling

was of the scientific kind, that had been evidently "learnt, marked, and inwardly digested." Miss Landon and I, thus taken unawares, both laughed at the strange *tableau* of contrast at the door, as I exclaimed,—

"Sir Plume, of amber snuff-box justly vain,
And the nice conduct of a clouded cane."

The quotation was as involuntary as the laugh. Oh, Nemesis! I little dreamt with what a ruinous usury of tears you would make me pay that laugh through all my after life!

While Mrs. Bulwer Lytton and her son were still at the other end of the room, I heard Miss Spence's little nibbling *sotto voce* over my shoulder, beginning with her usual overture of "Oh, my dear" (or as she pronounced it, *meddear*), "don't let Miss Benger introduce you to that dreadful old Mrs. Bulwer Lytton, for I see her son has never taken his eyes off you, and she has behaved in the *meanest* manner to me. I sent her my last novel, which *La Belle Assemblée* and several other *litry* organs say is my best, and quite equal to Anthony Frederick Holstein's 'Star of Fashion,' or even 'A Winter in London,' which killed the Duchess of Devonshire and so delighted everybody. Well, meddear, would you believe it? though my book was only sixteen shillings, that dreadful old woman, when I sent it to her with 'The author's compliments' written on the fly leaf, which is always a compliment from litry people, sent me a sovereign for it by her housekeeper, and the woman actually *asked* and waited for the change, which of course she had her orders to do! So different from dear Lady Caroline,

who said in one of her sweet notes, in which she
enclosed me £10, that though she had not time to
do so then, she looked forward with great pleasure
to reading it, and asked me if I had sent a copy
to Isaac D'Israeli,—which I did not, *meddear*, as I
thought he was quite too learned and abstruse to
read novels." Miss Landon's laughing eyes and
keen sense of the ridiculous could not resist the
jest, and so taking up Lady Caroline's gauntlet about
Isaac D'Israeli, which might have lain for ever
perdu and unsuspected upon Miss Spence's *litry*
arena, said, "On the contrary, of course he reads
everything, as pabulum for his 'Curiosities of
Literature.'" Ignoring the interruption, the un-
suspecting Spence perorated her plaint with, "But
to return to dear Lady Caroline. She, of course,
is used to litry celebrities, and knows what is due
to them." "Exactly," interrupted I, "and therefore
knows how difficult it is to take change out of
them."

While Miss Landon and I were still laughing
over poor Miss Spence's latest contribution to the
"Calamities of Authors," Miss Benger made her
way back to us, and, bending down, said to me,
"You *must* let me introduce you to Mrs. Bulwer
Lytton : she has asked me so particularly twice to
do so, as she has a party to-morrow evening and
wants to ask you."

"Oh no, pray, on no account. I would so much
rather not ; and indeed my cold is so bad I ought
to stay in bed."

"Nay, to please me, I am sure you *will*, like a
dear, kind, unselfish soul, as I know you are ; for

if you do not take me you know I shall certainly
not go to the expense of a carriage."

"Of course not," said I. "You shall have the
carriage with pleasure, but don't ask me to take you."

"Yes! yes! yes! I know you *will* come *this once*,
to please me ; and I will never again ask you to
do anything you don't like," persisted Miss Benger.
" Besides," added she, "do you know, you have made
a desperate conquest of the young man ; and he is
so clever, and though a younger son, I daresay he
will be a good *parti*, as I believe his other brothers
are provided for, and he, they say, is the old lady's
favourite."

"Very likely," I said ; "but *partis*, as you may
have perceived, are nothing to me. I have up to
the present time—and I am just verging on the
superannuation of three-and-twenty—escaped all
partis. My uncle says if I go on I shall be an
old maid. I tell him yes, my vocation is to be a
sensible woman, which is the proper name for the
vulgar *sobriquet* of old maid."

"Oh! there they are both looking at us. You
really must let me introduce you to them, for as they
know I have asked you to do so, and that I am now
speaking to you on the subject, you *cannot* refuse
without being markedly rude, which I know you
never wish to be."

" But I really feel so ill and so stupid, and there
don't appear to be much inspiration in them ; and
what on earth can I talk to them about ?"

" Why, taste, Shakspeare, and the musical glasses,
and all the rest of it ; and you who are so fond of
poetry will be quite at home, as the young man's

was the prize poem at Cambridge this year, and is really very good, I hear."

"Of course all prize poems are : what was the subject ?"

" I forget ; but you must ask him, and that will be a very good opening."

" That is only for the Alma ; but what on earth shall I do with the mater, who looks truly formidable, unless I ask her if she has been sitting for the family picture as Mrs. Primrose, after that worthy matron had enjoined the limner to stud her with as many jewels as he could stick in for nothing ? "

" *Méchante !*" said Miss Benger, as she went back to her other guests ; "how do you know but that you are ridiculing your mother-in-law ?"

" I hope not," I replied ; "for without having the presumption to aspire to originality, one hates to be a mere echo."

As one should always confront the inevitable with calm and self-possession, even if one cannot do so with dignity, which albeit depends far more upon one's *entourage* than on one's volition, seeing Miss Benger now retracing her slow but sure way, with the mother and son in her wake, I had nothing for it but to resign myself to my fate, wondering parenthetically why Miss Spence, who was a free agent, and standing at the back of the sofa, did not move away from the approaching vicinity that she so much despised ; for as "silence is golden " and "speech silvern," she might be tempted verbally to jingle the four never-to-be-forgotten shillings in the ears of their too faithful custodian ; but she did nothing of the kind. She stood to her guns heroically, merely bending down and whispering to me, as Miss Benger approached with her convoy, "*Meddear*, remember." "Not twelve, but four," said I.

My having to stand up to undergo the ordeal of presentation completely hid Miss Spence longitudinally, though not in width; and when Mrs. Bulwer Lytton had told me that she was "at home" on the following evening, and should be "vastly" (or, as she always pronounced it, *vaustly*) happy if I would do her the honour of coming with Miss Benger— adding, as soon as I had conditionally accepted her invitation, if my cold was not worse, "Pray, my dear madam, be seated; though I'm sure you look so *vaustly* well no one could suppose you were labouring under any sort of indisposition,"—as of course I would not sit down while she remained standing, I moved on one side. The surprise was almost as great as when the screen fell and discovered Lady Teazle to Sir Peter, for there stood Miss Spence, her head, with its green gauze architectural fabric nodding *à discretion*, or rather *sans discretion*, like a Japanese joss, accompanying the same by a series of genuflections, while in her most nibbling pianissimo mouse-in-a-cheese voice she addressed Mrs. Bulwer Lytton with "*Meddear* madam, this is the first opportunity I have had of thanking you for your kind patronage of my last work, which I doubly value, knowing you have so much litry talent in your own family."

The lady thus addressed waved her right hand, as if, though perfectly aware she *had* done a noble deed, she yet was too additionally generous to wish to be reminded of it ; and so proceeded to efface this favour by conferring another, by telling Miss Spence she was at home on the following evening, and should be happy to see her. At which Miss Spence made a sudden Jack-in-the-box-like sort of spring, as if her head and very large bust were *en route* for the ceiling, and said, or rather exclaimed, with emphatic ecstacies, " Oh! *meddear* Madam, I shall be most proud and happy; though your parties, with all their hothouse luxuries, quite spoil me for my own, as in my humble abode, at my *litry réunions*, I can only pretend to purvey food for the mind."

Miss Spence having at length attended to her punctuation, and come to a full stop, the lady thus apostrophised only having had to " purvey " for persons who had a mind to pine-apples, and therefore not seeing clearly what pine-apples had to do with the mind, took refuge in the golden rule of silence, and with another wave of her right hand executed a sort of pantomime *congé* to her *litry* interlocutor, who, falling back out of the ranks, eclipsed herself behind the outworks—that is, the beard, spectacles, and rampant ears of a fat German professor.

Mrs. Bulwer Lytton had passed on in search of other " Curiosities of Literature," and left her son standing before me, evidently bent upon taking high degrees as a conversationalist, and carrying my wonder, and of course admiration, by storm. His first essay, however, was a *coup manqué*, owing to the fulsomeness of his compliments, which were quite in keeping with the foppery of his dress. They had such a nauseating effect upon me that I resolved I would not pay him in kind, and so never even mentioned his prize poem to him, with which Miss Benger had primed me. Finding me flattery proof, he glided into something like rational conversation, and toned down his fiatical manner so that I began to think that, despite his *soufflé* surface, there was something in him, but not enough to make me wish to meet him again so as to ascertain the fact ; and it was a relief to me when a telegraphic look from his mother summoned him to her side at the other end of the room. Whereupon Miss Benger came back to me, and asked if I did not think him very clever ? " Well—yes, perhaps so ; only he is too decidedly of your opinion on that point." I then pleaded my cold, which really was very bad, and entreated her not to ask me to go with her to Mrs. Bulwer Lytton's on the following evening, but the more I resisted, the more she urged her request ; and as even *then* I knew, what I know so much better now, that poverty is always more open-handed than wealth, and consequently, when one lends a carriage to those who have none, if one does not go in it oneself the person to whom it is lent is sure to give one's servants as much as the hire of a carriage would have cost them, this reflection suddenly occurring to me it was which made me say, with a sigh of resignation, " Well, if I'm alive, I'll call for you at half-past ten to-morrow evening."

Very soon after this the carriage, which I had ordered early, was announced. No sooner had I reached the drawing-room door than Mr. Lytton Bulwer darted across the room to offer me his arm to take me downstairs, and packed me up as carefully as if I really had been something of value.

"What splendid sable!" he exclaimed, as he inducted me into the Persian-green Turkish pelisse.

"Yes, is it not? As it is only borrowed finery, I may extol it. It is one of two that the Grand Vizier gave my uncle; and, scandalous to say, they have both been left tossing about for years hanging up in the servants' hall till I took possession of this one."

The night was rainy. I begged of him not to come out, but he *would* put me into the carriage, and regardless of the little cataracts that were falling from the servant's umbrella, still stood, hoping that I would honour his mother on the following evening.

A little note from Miss Benger the next day, just before dinner, nailing me to my appointment, left me no loophole of escape; so at half-past ten I called for her. She began by scolding me for never having mentioned Mr. Lytton Bulwer's prize poem to him. "Well, really," said I, "if you will drag people out of their beds who are only fit for pillows and hot possets, you cannot expect them to attend to *les bien-séances*, or even *les convenances*. I must only try and remember about the prize poem to-night. But how comes it that the mother is Mrs. Bulwer Lytton and the son is Mr. Lytton Bulwer?—for one really gets puzzled between the two. It is so hard to call people names when you don't know what names to call them." "Well, dear, Mrs. Bulwer Lytton was a Miss Lytton when she married General Bulwer; and two or three years after General Bulwer's death, her father, Mr. Lytton of Knebworth, died and left her his sole heiress. She then re-took the name of Lytton; and before that, as she was an heiress, all the children—viz., her three sons—were christened Lytton Bulwer."

Arrived at Mrs. Bulwer Lytton's house, in Upper Seymour Street, though I had not yet seen the pine-apples, Miss Spence was recalled to me by the "powdered footmen," who were so gigantic in that small house that they gave one the idea of being a *charade en action* of *multum in parvo*. The hostess was dressed as on the previous evening, only with two diamond necklaces instead of one. Not so her son. His costume was greatly subdued, and consequently he seemed much more gentlemanlike. From not being so exaggerated to look at, he appeared much more worthy of being listened to. His manner, too, had markedly improved: it was more subdued— subdued almost to diffidence, at least to an admirable imitation of it; and although from the moment I sat down, after speaking to his mother, there was an evident appropriation of me on his part, yet there was nothing offensively *prononcé* in the manner of it, for with the exception of rather too large a dose of his mother's gratitude for my coming, all the rest seemed as if merely a sort of drab punctilio of hospitality to welcome a guest who had never crossed their threshold before. Not to be too much in his debt, I then asked him the subject of his prize poem. He said it was "Sculpture." "A very far-sighted selection," I said; "for by this means you have insured your niche in the Temple of Fame being doubly filled by your works." He made me a very low bow, and of *course* assured me that such praise

was fame.   Soon after this he asked me to go down
and take some refreshment, as the heat of the room
was overpowering.   I did so ; but leaving all the
pine-apples for Miss Spence, only drank a glass of
water.   My companion was not, as he was on the
previous evening, *trying* to shine, and therefore was
much more interesting, and really agreeable.   I cannot,
of course, record half that was said on that evening,
and only wish I could forget it all.   Finding we
were the only two persons in the as yet uninvaded
refreshment-room, having drunk the water and
admired the flowers, I expressed a wish to return
upstairs.

"Oh! for Heaven's sake don't," said my companion; "it does seem such sacrilege to see you
among those old fossils.   Having found the spring
in the desert, and this oasis, don't let us be so ungrateful as to leave it so soon."   He then launched
out into satirical *silhouettes* of the human mosaic
above stairs ;—but although I could not help
laughing, neither could I be so ill bred as to join in
ridiculing his mother's guests, however ridiculous
they might be ; so when he placed Miss Spence
upon the easel, I said, "Now, really I cannot
allow this, as I take Miss Spence and her 'humble
abode' under my 'humble' protection, and always
do a little Jack the Giant killing in her behalf;
as I really think her an exceedingly kind-hearted,
well-meaning person—and inoffensive, when she
lays aside the 'litry,' that is, doffs the 'foolscap
uniform turned up with ink,' and returns to the
Mufti of muffins and marmalade."   He made me
a low bow, and with one of his set smiles, said,

"Had any one told me, a week ago, that I should ever envy Miss Spence to the extent of wishing myself like her, I should have brought an action for libel against him or her."

In the midst of all this *persiflage*, we heard Mrs. Bulwer Lytton's not very dulcet voice, chanticleering out, "Eddard! Eddard!" (as she always called her son Edward), "you really must not hide the star of the evening down here,"—and advancing towards me with her usual paddle-like wave of the right hand, she added, "So *vaustly* kind of you to come, my dear madam! that I cannot have you wasted down here," and then laid on her compliments so thickly and so coarsely, that I was considerably abashed ; and being really "unaccustomed to public speaking," and, like Mark Twain, "quite unprepared for the occasion," but unfortunately *not* having, like him, my speech all ready and elaborately written out, in my pocket, to prove my want of preparation, I muttered out something about having had great pleasure (humph!) in coming, and regret at being unable to stay long, at which she expressed herself "*vaustly* sorry," and then we were marched up-stairs. There was something so overpoweringly ludicrous in the mingled expressions of ill-suppressed rage and compulsory obedience and resignation in her son's face, that Hogarth's "March to Finchley" came into my mind, and if my life had depended upon it, I could not have helped laughing ; but, thanks to my cold, under guise of a cough, and holding my handkerchief before my mouth, this unlucky laugh was successfully

smuggled as far as the drawing-room door, from
whence we met Miss Spence emerging, towing
a little man in bristles and spectacles after her,
and just preparing to waddle down to the pine-
apples. " Oh! *Meddear*," said she, seizing my
hand, " had I known you were below, I should
have gone down sooner and joined you,—quite
as much on *your* account, Mr. Lytton Bulwer, I
assure you," she added, with a patronising little
triple bob major of nods. " For Bruce did not more
anxiously explore for the source of the Nile than
I do for *litry* talent in the young; and I have
heard so much of your prize poem, that I long
to talk to you about it: I forget, at this moment,
what the subject of it was?" " On PATIENCE!"
replied the ungrateful subject of this delicate
flattery; in a voice so loud, sharp, and curt,
that it bounded like one solitary, but potent clap
of thunder. " Nonsense, Eddard!" interposed his
mother; "he's so *vaust*ly playful! that's his *bodin-
narge* (*badinage*). Now *do* go down with Miss
Spence, Eddard, and talk to her about your prize
poem." Miss Spence, as if moved by a spring,
suddenly let go of the arm appertaining to the
bristles and spectacles, and made a dart forward, as
if to enforce Mrs. Bulwer Lytton's commands; but
that lady's son quite as quickly darted out of
danger, to the opposite extreme angle of the
doorway, and placing his hand upon his right
hip, darted a look at his mother, as he drew
himself up to his full height, which said, as
plainly as any words could have done, " Madam!
you forget that there *are* limits even to parental

authority, and consequently to filial obedience!"
Poor Miss Spence, whose moral cuticle, fortunately
for her, was of a rhinoceros texture, placed this
very unmistakable reluctance all to the score of
extreme modesty; so philosophically re-clutching
the only arm within her reach, said, with a little
patronising wag of her head over her shoulder,
as she pursued the *un*-even tenor of her way
downstairs, "Ah! well, true *litry* talent is
always modest; but that will not prevent my
speaking to you another time about your prize
poem, Mr. Lytton Bulwer."

We had no sooner reached the drawing-room
than, having found me a chair, he flung himself
into another beside me; and leaning back, as if
quite exhausted, asked me to lend him my fan.
After violently fanning himself for about a minute,
he said, "Oh! I should not so much mind if
there were only more Desdemonas in the world."

"What!" I replied, "that there might be more
women murdered by their lords and masters?"

"No; but because Desdemona loved the Moor,
for *the dangers he had passed.*"

"But," laughed I, "*you* could not possibly
advance such a claim, as it appears to me that
you ran away most unheroically from the danger,
and let *it* pass *you* very quietly on its way downstairs."

"Humph! it's all very well to credit Shakspeare
with having 'exhausted worlds, and then imagined
new.' But, if so, he ought to have imagined a
real appalling, overwhelming danger for Othello,
and have wedged him in the narrow landing of

a London staircase, with Paradise on the one hand and Miss Spence within clutch of him on the other!—*then* indeed he *might* have had some ' hairbreadth 'scapes ' worth telling of, instead of such ordinary vulgar squibs as battles and sieges ! '

"Well, but you see Shakspeare, with all his genius, and its deft handmaid imagination, had not *your* advantage of experience ! therefore, could *you* not immortalise this new phase of the terrible yourself ? "

" Hardly, seeing that there is no measure yet invented by which one can portray the im-measurable !"

" Oh ! then," said I, laughing, as Mrs. Bulwer Lytton was again advancing towards us out of the next room, where there were two card tables, "you must only fall back upon the Spenserian stanza, as the most appropriate."

" My dear," said Mrs. Bulwer Lytton, advancing towards her son, with a pack of cards in her hand, " I'm *vaustly* sorry to interrupt your agreeable *tête-à-tête* with so much beauty and fascination, and what *La Belle Assemblée* would designate as so much grace and fashion ! but Lady Winterton is waiting for a fourth to make up her whist party ; and you *must* come, *Eddard !* "

" Eddard " rose, and with his eyes cast up to the ceiling, that ubiquitously pirated edition of Heaven *qui est toujours à la porte de tout le monde*, and groaned out, " Lady Winterton be speedily—in the Elysian Fields ! " and so saying he stalked into the other room, and took his place at the board of green cloth, opposite to Lady Winterton, looking *literally*, as well as figuratively, *tiré à quatre épingles.*

Fortunately for me, soon after a servant entered by the front door of the drawing-room, and did not run the blockade of the card-room, and so found his way up to me without interception, to announce that the carriage had been waiting for an hour. So I rose, found Miss Benger, and beat, as I thought, a satisfactory retreat; but in this I reckoned without my *host,* for scarcely were we seated before Mr. Lytton Bulwer appeared at the door of the carriage, with a protest of " Surely you are not going yet ? it's scarcely half-past ten ; and there is going to be some music." "Pardon me, " said; I " it is a quarter to twelve.''

CHAPTER V.

IT is impossible for me to give any detailed record of the progress of Mr. Bulwer's courtship, for the very sufficient reason that the only adequate account of its varying phases is contained in his letters to Miss Wheeler, which I am forbidden to publish. Mr. Bulwer proposed marriage to his future wife some time in April 1826. His suit was accepted, though she writes: " I told him that both he and his mother would hate me when they found I could not minister to his unsatiable ambition. Alas that I should have been such a true prophet!"

And here I must say a few words upon a curious theory propounded by Earl Lytton in his life of his father. The biographer would have us believe not only that at an early age Mr. Edward Bulwer met with an enchanting, if somewhat mythical, child, who "died from love to him, and whose beautiful and steadfast nature appeared to promise all which he had missed in life, and for which he never ceased to yearn," not only that he flirted with this young lady by the waters of the Brent, and subsequently left her to pine, but that in consequence of this calf-love—Mr. Bulwer was then seventeen—his whole nature became warped and blighted, his capability of loving purely and devotedly destroyed, and his

heart changed into an aching void, which disposed
him "to seize with impatient avidity any apparent
promise of happiness from the exercise of his affec-
tions on a lower range."

Now, whatever may have been Bulwer's faults,
there is no sort of doubt that, at all events before
he married her, he loved Miss Wheeler with all
the passionate affection of which his nature was
capable.   He wrote to her hundreds of letters;
he persisted in setting at nought his mother's objections to the union; and although Miss Wheeler
broke off the engagement on no less than three
distinct occasions, it was each time renewed in deference to his own pressing solicitations.   But his son
would have us believe that it was Rosina's plain and
unmistakable duty to repel the advances of this
frenzied adorer with copy-book precepts, and cast
aside his ardent devotion with unrelenting scorn, to
steel her heart, which was no longer in her own
keeping, against his eloquent pleading, and to wreck
the happiness of her life in obedience to the wholly
unreasonable prejudices of that worthy but worldly-
minded old lady Mrs. Lytton!   Surely common
justice and charity will take a more merciful view of
Miss Wheeler's dilemma.   Edward Bulwer professed
that he loved her to distraction; and I have no
reason to doubt that at this period his professions
were sincere.   She loved him devotedly in return.
His mother was a notoriously selfish and eccentric
old dowager, who had an infinitely greater regard
for her son's success in the world than for his personal happiness or his domestic peace.   Is it therefore surprising that Bulwer's persistency should at

length have overcome Miss Wheeler's scruples, and
that, in the confident hope of a speedy reconciliation
with his mother, she should have consented to link
her lot with his?

The actual date for this unhappy union was
several times fixed and postponed, for Bulwer
spared no effort to obtain his mother's consent.
He argued high and low, with quotations from
Paley and the Schoolmen, in order to prove a fact
beyond the necessity of demonstration, viz., that
there are limits even to filial obedience, and that
a son is not bound to wreck his own and his
betrothed's happiness for life in deference to the
whim of an ambitious mother.*   It is of course
true that Mrs. Lytton had a large fortune in
her own right, and that her son was practically
dependent upon her, but how far this circumstance
influenced him in the course he adopted may
be left to the judgment of my readers.   December
1826 was the first date mentioned for the wedding.   It was put off, however, to the following summer, and did not actually take place until
August.   One reason for this delay appears to
have been that Mrs. Lytton had become possessed
of a theory that Miss Wheeler was much older than
she professed to be, and special messengers were
despatched to Ireland to obtain documentary evidence of the date of Rosina's birth.   This evidence
was of course forthcoming, but Mrs. Lytton did not
vouchsafe her consent, and the day was finally fixed
for the 29th of August.   Mr. Bulwer had meanwhile

* See Edward Bulwer's letters to his mother, "Life of Lord
Lytton," vol. ii., pp. 137, 140, 143, 145, etc.

taken Woodcot House, Oxfordshire, as a residence, a scrambling old-fashioned house buried in the depths of the country and desperately dull, and to this abode he took his wife immediately after their marriage. One or two points, however, remain to be mentioned before that event is referred to. First as regards the respective incomes of the couple. Bulwer himself, as his biographer informs us, had a capital of £6,000, out of which he settled £1,000 on his wife to bar dower. The reasonable suggestion of Sir John Doyle that more adequate provision should be made for her he treated with much virtuous indignation, and, with characteristic generosity, she not only persuaded her uncle to waive his request, but even lent her future husband £500, a sum which, I may here remark, he forgot to repay. I must also add that Mr. Bulwer subsequently induced his brother William, then the sole surviving trustee of the settlement, to hand over to him this £1,000. As regards the fortune of Miss Wheeler herself, the accounts I have are somewhat conflicting. It must be remembered that she was her father's sole heiress, for her only brother died in childhood, and her sister also died in Paris in 1826. There is of course every reason to suppose that Mr. Francis Wheeler dissipated by far the larger part of his patrimony before his death, but Lord Lytton's estimate of his mother's private income at £80 a year is distinctly an understatement.* In a letter from Dr. Roberts, Lady Lytton's trustee, written in 1873, he says that her income was "considerably more than £700 per

---

* I might suggest that Lord Lytton could easily verify his statement by publishing his mother's marriage settlement.—L. D.

annum," but this is not in accordance with other authorities, nor with Lady Lytton's own statement, for I always understood that £300 was nearer the real amount. This must have been chiefly derived from her Irish property, the remnant of which was sold before their separation for £2,774 17s., after having given Mr. Bulwer his qualification for his first seat in Parliament.

And now a few words about the personal characteristics of the bride. Rosina Wheeler may be described as an excellent type of most of the virtues and many of the amiable weaknesses peculiar to her nationality. She was, that is to say, warm-hearted, sensitive, and generous to a fault, of an intensely passionate and highly strung organisation, proud, no doubt, possibly too apt to feel keenly neglect or coldness, but ever ready to forgive even the most unpardonable offences. That she was jealous of her husband I do not pretend to deny; it was impossible for such a woman to love devotedly without resenting the infidelity of the man whom she adored; but that her jealousy was only too well founded will frequently appear in this narrative, and is indeed a fact that the most servile admirers of her husband have scarcely attempted to conceal. Mrs. Wheeler was certainly somewhat of a freethinker, but her daughter was one of the most fervently and truly religious women whom it has ever been my fortune to meet, and in this respect also afforded a striking contrast to the avowed agnosticism of Mr. Bulwer. As regards age, there were almost exactly six months between the pair, Rosina having been born Nov. 2nd, 1802, and Edward Bulwer May 25th, 1803,

and I may add that this trifling disparity was made
use of in subsequent years to such excellent purpose
by Mr. Bulwer, that he succeeded in inducing numbers of his friends to believe that he had thrown
himself away in boyhood upon a woman almost old
enough to be his mother.   Miss Wheeler was by
general consent a noted beauty, and might have
married a dozen times.   Even during her ill-fated
engagement she was besieged by offers.   A brief
account of her appearance may not be inappropriate
here.   She was tall, with an exquisite complexion,
dark hair, and bright grey, or, as she called them,
green eyes, sparkling and changing colour with
every emotion.   Her nose was finely chiselled, her
eyebrows delicately pencilled, her forehead broad
and high, her mouth small, her teeth perfect, and
her chin somewhat square and determined.   She
had a remarkably fine figure, bust, and arms, and
small feet.   As regards other attributes, I may
add that she was an excellent housekeeper and
accomplished needlewoman.   Literary talents of a
high order she undoubtedly possessed, not only in
the judgment of her friends, but of her husband.
Her reading was extensive, and her memory almost
to the last day of her life retentive to a very un-
common degree.   I have before dwelt upon her gift
of mimicry, and she also possessed a keen sense of
humour and a ready wit.   She spoke French and
Italian perfectly, and was familiar with Spanish and
Latin.   About the character of Mr. Edward Bulwer
it is not so easy for me to speak with a reasonable
hope of giving an impartial judgment, and I will
therefore leave it to the decision of my readers.

On Thursday, the 29th August, 1827, at St. James's Church, Piccadilly, Edward George Earle Lytton Bulwer, Esq., was married to Rosina Anne Doyle Wheeler, by the Hon. and Rev. William Bentinck. After the breakfast, Mr. and Mrs. Bulwer set off for Woodcot, near Nettlebed, Oxfordshire. Rosina Anne Doyle Wheeler was the only surviving child of the late Francis Massy Wheeler, Esq., of Ballywire, Lizzard Connell, Limerick, Ireland.

Of Mr. Edward Bulwer's early married life at Woodcot I have, unfortunately, no very full details, but one can scarcely imagine it to have been of a very enlivening character. Bulwer's avowed object in selecting a house buried in the depths of the country was to lead a life of absolute seclusion, and to devote himself to almost unremitting literary toil. With an income of £500 or so a year the couple lived much beyond that rate, and the money had to be found, and I do not deny that it was found, somehow or another. But for a young and beautiful woman to be shut up in a gloomy mansion without society, friends, or amusements, in company with a husband whose toils prevented him from seeing her for more than an hour or so during the entire day, was surely a very severe trial of affection. Nor was this all that she had to endure. Bulwer's love was of a type more sensual than imaginative, and after a very brief honeymoon he found it imperatively necessary for his prospects to indulge in prolonged visits to London. I do not mean to assert that these periodical absences were entirely without justification.   Literary men must interview their publishers, must to a certain degree mix in the world of letters, and keep themselves well in view of the public, if they do not wish to incur the risk of falling into oblivion.   But Mr. Bulwer's absences from home were so frequent and so prolonged that I can scarcely believe them to have been always prompted by considerations of necessity or of affection at this early period of his married life.

In the spring of 1828 Mrs. Bulwer was expecting her confinement, an event which took place on June 27th, and here I am compelled to narrate a truly deplorable incident which was told me by Lady Lytton herself as a striking instance of her husband's cruel and violent temper.   This episode occurred about the end of May 1828, nearly a month before the birth of her daughter.   She was in the constant habit of assisting her husband as much as possible in his literary labours, and on that occasion had been helping him by getting down books for reference from the library shelves.   Worn out and exhausted one evening, she had lain down on the sofa, when her lord and master ordered her to hand him down another volume, and for that purpose to mount a step-ladder.

" Really, Edward," she said, " I cannot do more, I am so tired."

In a sudden fit of fury, he sprang to his feet and kicked her in the side with such savage violence that she fainted from the pain.   In after-years, when Mr. Bulwer committed a still more brutal outrage upon his victim, a friend* of hers remarked,

* Dr. Lushington, when she told him that Mr. Bulwer had bitten her cheek.

"That man has been ill-treating you for years past," and upon Mrs. Bulwer inquiring his reasons for such a theory, he answered, "Because I do not believe that any one could suddenly develop into such a cruel tyrant." That his suspicions were only too well founded is proved by many flagrant instances of Bulwer's violence and cruelty.

A month later on, June 27th, 1828, a daughter, Emily Elizabeth, was born. In her confinement Mrs. Bulwer suffered very severely, and there is but little reason to doubt that her agonies were in great measure, if not entirely, caused by the above-mentioned exploit of her amiable spouse. Of the unhappy life and squalid death of their unfortunate daughter it will be necessary to speak hereafter; but I must, in justice to Lady Lytton, say a few words with reference to a singular misconception of her son's that the care and society of children was distasteful to her. During Mrs. Bulwer's life at Woodcot, and for some years after, she continually assisted her husband in his literary toils. At a subsequent date a friend asked Mrs. Bulwer what she had been reading lately; and her answer was, "I have been studying the Newgate Calendar to help Edward with 'Paul Clifford.'" Such being the case, Mr. Bulwer, that is to say, not only requiring his wife's undivided attention, but even looking with jealousy upon the affection she lavished on his child, he determined that the infant must at once be sent out to nurse, lest it should interfere with his domestic arrangements. In his elegant phraseology he declined to allow his wife's time "to be taken up by any damned child," and the little girl was accordingly handed over to the care of a neighbouring farmer's wife. The consequence of this enforced separation was that about the middle of July Mrs. Bulwer's eyesight became affected by constant weeping; and in the following September the doctors, being unable to afford her permanent relief, ordered her to Weymouth, whither, accordingly, she went with her husband on September 19th. For the next three months they stayed together at Weymouth, but in December Mr. Bulwer's presence in town was again indispensable, and there he remained for upwards of a month. Mrs. Bulwer left Weymouth about the 20th of January, and was obliged to perform her cold and dismal three days' journey back to Woodcot alone, her husband not deeming it necessary to accompany or meet her. He had, in act, conceived a violent hatred for that rural retreat, and up to the time when he finally quitted it, about six months later, his visits there were very few and far between. Thus for a great part of February and March he was absent in London, and in April they removed for a time to Tunbridge Wells. But the air of Kent did not suit Mr. Bulwer much better than that of Oxfordshire, for during May he remained in London, looking for houses and engaged in literary and other business, in spite of his wife's repeated complaints of the dulness of Tunbridge and frequent entreaties to be allowed to see more of him. As regards houses, he finally decided to buy 36, Hertford Street, Mayfair, for £2,570, and this house continued to be Mr. and Mrs. Bulwer's London residence for several years.

CHAPTER VI.

I MUST here again apologise to my readers for the scanty nature of the materials I possess for framing a connected narrative of the next few years of Lady Lytton's married life. A very brief recital of her chief movements may be given; and then I will return to the testimony of the injured wife as told in her own language, and to the evidence of other witnesses to her husband's proceedings. Mr. and Mrs. Bulwer removed to Hertford Street in the autumn of 1829. A son, Edward Robert, was born November 8th, 1831. They left England in the autumn of 1833, and arrived at Naples on the 17th of November that same year. Her life in Naples Lady Lytton frequently mentioned as having been one of the happiest periods of her existence, but any gratification she derived from her sojourn there must have been grievously marred by her husband's brutality and violence, as will hereafter appear. I have a short fragmentary journal, or rather diary, written by her at Naples; but it contains nothing but the briefest possible notes of her movements, and is not worth reproducing *in extenso*. It is chiefly a record of social functions, dinners, dances, and so forth, and seems to have served also

as a memorandum of the number of lessons Lady
Lytton took from her Italian master and the number
of carriages she hired.   There are no entries for a
few days prior to January 14th, 1834.   However, at
that date I find an entry: " Dined at Lord Hertford's ; taken by Lady Cullum," which is somewhat
important as tending to corroborate the following
deposition, sworn to by Mrs. Rosetta Benson, whose
maiden name was Byrne, for several years maid to
Lady Lytton.

DEPOSITION OF MRS. ROSETTA BENSON (WHOSE
MAIDEN NAME WAS BYRNE), MAID TO LADY LYTTON.

" I, ROSETTA BENSON, Widow, whose maiden name was
Byrne, and who lived for some years as Lady's-Maid with
The Right Honourable Lady Lytton—then Mrs. Edward
Lytton Bulwer, when her Ladyship married—from 1827 to
1845, being prevented by the present state of my health
from going to London to give my evidence in the Divorce
Court—should it be necessary—Do hereby depose on Oath
—before The Revd John Batt Bingham, Magistrate, Herts,
that during the whole of that period I never knew any
Gentleman treat a wife, more especially such a good and
irreproachable wife, so hardly and so badly as the present
Lord Lytton, then Mr. Edward Lytton Bulwer, did her
Ladyship, not only as to cruel neglect and infidelity, but
also as to acts of brutal personal violence, amongst others
on one occasion, when travelling in Italy in 1833.   One
night at the Lake of Bolsano he so dashed the things
about, and at her Ladyship, that even Luigi the courier
vowed he would not continue the journey with him.   Again
at Naples, after having in one of his brutal rages kicked
and bang'd her Ladyship against the stone floor at the
Hôtel Vittoria till she was black and blue, and had to keep
her bed.   A few days after—because people began to talk
of this at Naples, he made her, poor lady, get up and dress
herself to go to a great dinner at Lord Hertford's.

"After we got back to London, his temper continued awful towards her Ladyship; for having asked him for money to pay the House Bills left unpaid when they went abroad : so one day, in July 1834, at dinner at their House, 36 Hertford Street, May Fair, London, he seized a Carving knife, and rushed at his wife, when she cried out, ' For God's sake, Edward, take care what you are about !' when he dropped the knife, and springing on her like a Tiger, made his teeth meet in her left cheek, until her screams brought the men Servants back into the Dining room, and he has ever since hunted her thro' the world, with Spies and bad Women, and does not allow her enough to live upon, for a Lady in her station.

"As every one knows of his cruelty in Kidnapping her Ladyship, and shutting her up in a Madhouse on 22nd June 1858—from which the poor Lady was released, thro' the public outcry it caused—at the end of three weeks :— I have nothing further to add—but that a better, more devoted wife no man, rich or poor, ever had ; she was far too good a Wife for Lord Lytton.

" ROSETTA BENSON.

" *Witness*, JOSEPH HUGGARD, 11, Ann's Terrace, Fulham.
    "MARY ANN RUSSELL,   ,,   ,,   ,,

"The above is the declaration of Mrs. Rosetta Benson, before me, The Revd JOHN BATT BINGHAM, Magistrate of Hertfordshire.

"J. B. Bingham, J.P., October 4th, 1867."

Endorsed by Lady Lytton :—

" Byrne wrote the foregoing deposition at her own house where she died, in George Street, Hemel Hempstead, Hertfordshire."

It is characteristic of Lady Lytton that, although herself suffering from straitened means, she had for several years previously allowed the poor maid, who was dying from a lingering disease, £20 a year, besides frequent gifts suitable to her condition.

Lady Lytton's own account of this and other episodes is given in an unpublished manuscript entitled "Nemesis." As I shall frequently have to quote from this work, I must premise that it is written in the form of letters, addressed by "the shade of Lord Byron" to "the rising and risen male generation of Great Britain," and contains a very full account of the various trials and persecutions which Lady Lytton endured.

"Suppose, then," says the *umbra*, "instead of leaving my wife, as I did, her child and all her property, I had tortured her as a good drudge and general *souffre douleur* for eight or nine years, kicking her within an inch of her life about a month before her first child was born, which she, poor soft-hearted, conscientious fool, might endure for the sake of that unborn child, and in the hope of reclaiming me, all which silly forbearance on the part of a wife, you are aware, is what our charming laws in their rigid virtue call 'condonation'! and preclude her getting any further redress. Well, if, after this pretty little prelude, the moment her first child was born, I had it turned out of my house, saying I would not have *my* wife's time or attention taken up with any d——d child! and after this amiable and praiseworthy proceeding, I let her cry herself blind, but never would yield to her entreaties of letting the poor little martyr be brought back, till I found the world was beginning to talk about me! and then, with a prudential view to my own interest and that scrupulous deference which must always be paid to *public opinion* in 'moral England,' I allowed my child to be smuggled into my house, on the express proviso that it was not to entail upon me an additional servant, and that I was never to find my wife one moment absent from her post of attendance upon me; and that thereupon my wife, having a silly habit of always serving people when she could, implored me to let her ask a homeless but very vulgar old maid, whom she had once known, to come and stay with her, as she was such

a good soul, so pious, and so fond of children—in short,
she devoted her whole time between Bibles and babies, and
would look after ours, and so save a head nurse; but in
order that she might not fancy or feel herself a dependant,
my silly wife insisted úpon her always dining with us, and
heaped her with dresses, kindnesses, and presents of every
description to try and make her presentable (which, by-the-
bye, is the way in which that most venomous of all reptiles,
the domestic viper, is generally brought up by hand, till it
turns upon you, and inflicts a deadly wound for your
pains). Suppose, further, that I varied my cuffs and kicks,
and—*Tremontanos*, of demoniac passion and other little
incidents, which women cannot tell even to their lawyers;
and which very young women, however disgusted they
may be at them, are still not aware that they have *legally
a right to do so*—but supposing I varied all these charming scenes, in our domestic drama, by occasionally telling
my victim that she had been perfection to me as a wife,
and that I could not even think of her without tears
in my eyes, etc., etc., etc.; at the same time telling others
that I did not give her much credit for her Griselda of
a temper, as I thought it was constitutional. Made bold
by the security of knowing that she would not even hint to
her own mother my conduct—such was the sort of sacred
seal that she had set upon her endurance—I now begin to
bring my mistresses into the house, and insist upon her
being civil to them as long as they were *women in society;*
and if any of these ladies' relations presumed to interfere
about my conduct, then my plan was to get my wife
abroad, first taking a *solemn oath* to her that everything
was at an end between me and Mrs. ——, whereas, as soon
as the packet was in the middle of the Channel, who should
she see but the lady in question, and I lying (in every sense
of the word) at her feet? when upon landing, as I took
care my wife never should have a shilling in her possession,
and therefore knew she could not return, I told her in
a bullying tone, seasoned plentifully with oaths, not to
make a fool of herself, that she *must* give Mrs. —— a place
in her carriage to save her character! More condonation

this, for I was astutely calculating every move as I wove each fresh mesh of the toils for my victim ; and after a wretched journey of kicks, cuffs, and every insult to her, we returned home " (?), " I *naturally* irritated at having spent more money in *vertu* than I could afford, which, from great economy in virtue, I thought I had a right to do. My wife, however, goes on as usual, inviting a set of fellows of the critical press, reviewers in fact (a sort of animal whom she both despised and disliked), to the house, on account of my being an author, and even entreating me often, for prudential motives, to lend them money, which, by-the-bye, where literary gentlemen are concerned, means *give*, for they never offend one by returning it, except in paper currency, so that, after all, this sort of thing does not exactly come under the head of generosity, but is merely a value-received sort of transaction.   Still further suppose (for no railway is so rapid as the progress of evil) my next calculation is that it will not do to leave my victim the slightest shadow of independence, for then I should not get her so completely into my power. So I affect to be in pecuniary difficulties, though at that time I had a mother living, who, having tutored and encouraged me in every vice, readily supplied all my extravagance, my wife's little property having given me a qualification for the first borough for which I sat ; but my real object being to get my victim completely into my toils, the money must be got out of *her*, for men may do very bad things from impulse or necessity, but they cannot be considered geniuses, or master minds, in wickedness unless every villainy is premeditated, and made a matter of profound and cold-blooded calculation.   Well, of course, with such a silly wife, that little point would be very soon achieved."

With reference to this trip to Italy, mentioned above, Lady Lytton writes elsewhere :—

"He had been intriguing with a Mrs. R——, and her husband's relatives were so scandalised at the way they *affiché*'d themselves that they insisted upon the scandal ceasing. For a few days he became most suspiciously kind and cajoling to me, and then I was ordered, at six hours' notice, to get ready to go to Italy. Suspecting the *dessous des cartes*, I told him so, whereupon he knelt down and took the most solemn oaths that everything was at an end between him and Mrs. R——. But the next day we had not been an hour out in the Channel, when this woman appeared reclining on a bench on the deck, and he sitting at her feet fanning her, while her husband sat by smoking his cigar. Before leaving England, I could not get a farthing from him to pay the house bills, which amounted to £540, and as in Italy he spent as many thousands on pictures and statues, he came back in such an impecunious state as to be like a raving madman, as my poor cheek for months could testify."

Mr. and Mrs. Bulwer returned to England early in the year 1834, and lived together at 36, Hertford Street, until July of the same year, when the gross personal outrage to which reference has already been made led to the first mention of a separation between husband and wife. After this exploit Mr. Bulwer retired to the Castle Hotel, Richmond. Lady Lytton writes :—

"The 'provocation' I gave this man was this: upon his asking me with whom I was going to the christening of Mr. Fonblanque's child that night, and I replying, 'With Lady Stepney,' he then repeated as fast as he could, a dozen times running, 'My mother calls her that ugly old woman.' He then called out, 'Do you hear me, Madam?' 'Of course I hear you.' 'Then why the —— in —— don't you answer me?' 'I did not think it required an answer.' 'D—— your soul, Madam!' he exclaimed, seizing a carving knife (for we were at dinner, and he had told the servants to leave the room till he rang), and rushing at me, cried, 'I'll have you to know that when-ever *I* do you the honour of addressing you, it requires an answer!' I said, 'For God's sake, take care what you are about, Edward!' He then dropped the knife and, springing on me, made his great teeth meet in my cheek, and the blood spurted over me. The agony was so great, that my screams brought the servants back, and presently Cresson, the cook, seized him by the collar; but he broke from him, and seizing one of the footmen's hats in the hall, rushed down Piccadilly.

"After his sanguinary exploit, he had taken himself off to Richmond. I, like a fool, went down to forgive him, not indeed for *his* sake—for I cordially despised him—but for that of my then baby children. Of course I found that he had no earthly thought of selling everything up and going abroad; he had been boating about the Thames, amusing himself, and was in treaty for the purchase of Lady Dysart's villa."

Lady Lytton writes further in " Nemesis " :—

"I knew very well that I should bring the fool to my side, after her usual fashion of ridiculous and overwrought generosity, reversing the relative positions and taking all the blame upon herself. She did come, forgave all, brought me back, never reproached me except with her tied-up face, which was tied up for some weeks, and was what the French would have called a *reproche sanglante*. But though she never hinted at such a thing, I felt she must despise me for the mock generosity of having pretended to leave her everything, and the lie about having arranged all with the lawyer, when in reality I had not the slightest idea of doing anything of the sort, and had been boating about the Thames, amusing myself, and in treaty for the purchase of a villa."

"Like a fool," elsewhere writes Lady Lytton, "even this I hushed up and condoned for my then baby children's sake, to be, in less than two years after, turned with them out of our home to make way for one of his legion of mistresses, and implacably hunted through the world ever since."

Mr. Bulwer rewarded his wife's generosity and forbearance by sending her off to Gloucester with the children, from which place she writes in November 1834 : " I have now been here four months—alone." During her stay at Gloucester Mrs. Bulwer wrote the following two letters, copies of which have been preserved. They will further explain the painful circumstances already alluded to, and the reader must judge for himself of their weight in contradiction of the very different statements to which they are opposed.

COPY OF A LETTER IN MRS. BULWER'S HANDWRITING, FROM GLOUCESTER.

[The wife's appeal.]

"*About the end of November* 1834.

" To say that your letter of this morning has wounded, galled, lacerated me to the quick, is to say nothing ; but as I can only look upon it as the will of God that I should be so treated, persecuted, and afflicted, I shall endeavour to humble myself to ' His will,' and bear it as I ought, not, indeed, without at first, I fear, great repining, but eventually, I hope, submitting patiently.

" If what you have been told about Mrs. S—— and Mrs. W—— be true, I am certainly a very unfortunate person, and might claim pity, even from my husband ; but having met them both in very respectable, though second-rate houses, I could not even have formed a suspicion of their impropriety; but I am peculiarly unhappy in my female acquaintance, for since I have returned to England, I have often been asked ' how I could possibly have travelled to Paris with such a woman as Mrs. R. S—— ?'

" In answer to your questions about my having acquainted Lady S—— or Mrs. W. L—— with our separation, I solemnly *assure* you, or if you prefer it *swear* to you, that I *never have ;* the only two letters I have written to Lady S—— since I have been here were written in a gay strain,

about herself, her books, and her acquaintance ; the only
one I have written to Mrs. W. L—— was in answer to one
of hers, meant to be very kind, telling me she had heard I
was unhappy, and that was the reason she wrote—in reply
I said that I had indeed been very unhappy at my poor
dear uncle's death; the rest of the letter was all about my
domestic enjoyment with my children and praises of Miss
Greene, which was a *quietus*, for I have never heard from
her since ; nor am I likely to do so, for, previous to my
leaving town, I thought she had behaved very unkindly to
me, though you did tell me, coming home from L⁴ Hertford's
last ball, ' that you thought I had behaved d—d ungratefully to her,' which I was not only hurt, but surprised at,
considering you had so often expressed a dislike to my
associating with her.   For the rest, not even to your
mother (as you seem to dislike her knowing anything quite
as much as any one else) have I hinted at our separation in
my letters, and so tenacious have I been of appearances on
that subject, that I got your pamphlet the moment it was
published, that people might think you had sent it to me,
and lent it to all the influential people here; and all the
political news I heard I said was from you.   When I
thought there would be a dissolution, I wrote to you from
my heart, wishing to serve you ; but you never condescended to answer my letter, which I concluded arose from
the usual reasons of your being busy and not requiring the
services I offered.   As to reports, they are nasty things ;
they will get about, if there is only a shadow for
their foundation.   The night you bit my cheek, Lady
S—— called in an hour afterwards, to take us to Mr.
F——'s.   I was out—God knows what she may have
heard—perhaps the truth !   Edward Bulwer, it might have
been worse—you had your hand upon the carving knife—
you brandished it at me—and if, instead of lacerating my
cheek, you had cut my throat, and in your turn forfeited
your life to the laws of your country, you could hardly
call *that* a calumny, or accuse *me* of having ' grossly
injured you.'

"Now, if you forget all this, I candidly tell you I have

kept all your letters, in which you will scarcely have *calumniated yourself*—Edward! Edward! put your hand upon your heart, look at home, be above the meanness of infallibility, and acknowledge to *yourself* (I ask you not to do it to *me*) that for the last year and a half, ever since that business about Mr. Mildmay, you have not acted kindly, justly, humanely, by me. *Do this*, and to-morrow I will go back to you, and devote my life to making *yours* happy, and refuting, or rather annihilating, every report that may have arisen about us. If you would but judge yourself with a *just* judgment, you would feel that you did owe me (even by your own showing) some reparation. I only know that, had life depended on it, I could not have studied every thought, wish, and even caprice of yours more than I did ; and my reward has been personal ill-usage, unkind words, neglect, shattered health, and a broken heart, upon which, for your respectability's sake, I have always put a smiling appearance. I have now been four months at Gloucester *by myself*, and I will venture to say that, *through me* and *my friend*, your *private* character stands as high here as your *public* one does everywhere.

"As for me, it has been my fate through life to suffer from the conduct of *others*, not from my own ; but there is this consolation, that even in this world we cannot eventually *firmly stand* or *wholly fall* but by *our own conduct alone ;* others may, and do for a time, gild or tarnish it, but the reality depends upon ourselves solely. And now about appealing to F. D——. Surely, surely, you do not for a moment suppose my reluctance to do so arose merely from the fear of troubling him, or with the slightest reference *to myself!* In doing so, I thought of *you*, and *you only*. I am ready and willing to do so *immediately*, if it is still your wish. You have asked me to give you an acquittal. The fullest, the most unquestionable, and above all the most beneficial to you would be my returning to live with, to love you (if you will let me), and to serve you in any and every way I can—this I am willing to do; but a written acquittal I could not give you, without branding all we have *both* written with falsehood, which must invalidate anything I could say, not only in our own eyes, but those of the world.

"I have only to add that not even to Mamma, who has written several times to know how long I meant to remain at Gloucester, have I said a word of our separation.

"God bless, guide, and forgive you as entirely as I do !

"R. L. B.

"I am very glad to hear by a letter I have just got from Mamma that you are looking better and stronger than she ever saw."

(True copy.)

COPY OF A LETTER FROM MRS. BULWER TO HER HUS-BAND, IN HER OWN HANDWRITING.

[Left her no earthly hope.—Her seven years' forbearance.]

"GLOUCESTER, *December* 14*th*, 1834.

"When you last demanded an acquittal of calumnies that had been set afloat about you, you did not *specify what* those calumnies were; therefore how could I refute them ? Now that you have told me the infamous reports about Mrs. S—— and her husband, of course I can deny them in the solemnest manner, and by telling the *exact* truth, most fully clear you from so base, so groundless, so black a slander. My acquaintance with Mrs. S—— originated in her having found my reticule, with my card-case in it, in a shop, and bringing it to me. A short time after I met her at a party at Mrs. D——'s. She got introduced to me. I thanked her for my bag ; the next day she called ; I saw she was dreadfully vulgar, but did not think *that* a sufficient reason for hurting her feelings, and after many pressing invitations went out to drive with her. You expressed a *great dislike* to my knowing her (as, to do you justice, you did to my knowing *every* one with whom I am acquainted), on the score of her vulgarity, which was of course *the only thing* you then knew against her, any more than myself. You afterwards went with me to a ball at her house, and there ended the acquaintance.

"I also here *most fully* acquit you of being dishonourable and ungentlemanlike, as ill-treating a wife is, I believe,

considered neither. As for my keeping your letters, I have
been guilty of equal treachery to myself, as I keep copies
of all my own that I write to you, for fear I should at any
time misstate to you anything I may have formerly said,
and I keep yours as, from having so many things to think
of, you are apt to forget, and consequently to deny, things
and promises you have made to me; there are many instances of this short memory ; you recollect the Emperor
Claudius after he had ordered his wife to be murdered !
Having quite forgotten the trifling circumstance, he next
day sent an angry message to know the meaning of her
disrespect to him in not appearing at dinner. So, upon the
whole, it was lucky the headsman had the imperial warrant
to produce ; and as I stand in the double capacity of wife
and executor of your commands, it is doubly necessary for
me to retain the proofs of my vindication.

"It was finding that a seven years' pursuance of this
forbearance, this softness, this silence, had failed, that
induced me as a forlorn hope to appeal to your justice,
your heart, your compassion ; in so doing, I appealed to
what does not exist. No wonder, then, that nothing
has been the result. Who for seven years has lavished
on you the care, the consideration, the early and late
attention to your wants, wishes, fame, and well-being,
in great things and in small, that I have? And who in
return has received from you ill-treatment, ingratitude,
injuries, and contempt? Unfortunately there are reciprocal duties in all our relationships of life, and however
individuals concerned may dispense with the share due to
them, the world in its judgment of facts will not do so :
it would certainly be much more agreeable, and give us
more room for gratitude, if every servant in our house
would do the work of two, without either food or wages,
and bear a great deal of ill-treatment besides ; but it would
be hardly reasonable to expect that they should.

"You have now left me no earthly hope of redress but
from the laws of the land. Fatherless, brotherless, almost
relationless, your conduct has not perhaps been the most
generous and high-minded in the world ; but let that pass.

It is true I have few influential earthly friends ; but with God and justice on my side, there is still hope, and may be redress, *even for me*."

After Mrs. Bulwer's departure from Gloucester, which took place about the spring of 1835, her husband took for her and the children Berrymead Priory, Acton, which I find described in " Nemesis " as follows :—

" I took chambers in the Albany, and furnished them sumptuously for myself, and took a villa for my wife which had not been inhabited for years, and therefore looked like the very abomination of desolation, the grass growing up to the hall door. Thither I packed her off, and her two children, not allowing her any carriage horses, which was the first retrenchment I made, not simply as a retrenchment, but as a means of keeping my wife safely imprisoned, without the power of getting out ; on arriving at this damp, dreary, desolate place, she found she had not even a bed to lie on ; but the housekeeper told her, with great indignation, that a very sumptuous one of crimson damask, lined with white silk, had been put up the day before, but the upholsterer had returned in a great hurry, saying he had made a mistake, as that bed was for *me* at my chambers. So again my victim had nothing for it but to kneel to her God upon the rock of resolution and en- durance, and implore Him to send her courage to the end ! There were not wanting plenty of kind friends to tell her the disgraceful way in which I was going on. By this time she had got to despise me for the innumerable lies I had told her, my horrible ostentation, coupled with the most despicable meanness, to say nothing of the petty tyranny I exercised over her, like a permanent cat-o'-nine-tails. Thus, love having died a natural, or rather an unnatural death, it had nothing more to suffer. So poor Rosina devoted herself to teaching her children, and making her prison habitable and cheerful, for on the two occasions I had honoured her by going down there, I had vowed I could not remain in such a desolate place, whereupon she set to work and had the library most beautifully and comfortably arranged, and the whole house *en suite*, which considerably annoyed me, as I wanted some excuse, however shadowy, for absenting myself. One evening, some months after she had been there, I returned (after a two months' absence with my new mistress, whom I had taken over to Paris for her *accouchement*). It was late, about nine, when I arrived for dinner, and brought a *roué* friend with me, that I might not be exposed to the disagreeable risk of a *tête-à-tête* with my wife; for to be alone with those we have deeply injured is always painful to what my Genoa acquaintance Lady Blessington would call 'the highly sensitive refinement of genius!' When I went in my wife was teaching our son, a child of five years old, his letters. I merely frowned at the mother and child, bit my lip sharply, and said, 'What! is not that d—d child in bed yet?' and then, motioning to my friend, we took ourselves off to the dining-room, where I told my wife she need not follow, for at a glance I perceived that she was guilty of that highest of all high treasons against marital tyranny—tears!"

While at Berrymead Mrs. Bulwer wrote the following journal of her monotonous existence.

CHAPTER VII.

LIFE AT BERRYMEAD PRIORY.

"BERRYMEAD PRIORY, ACTON,
"*December* 13*th*, 1855.

" I HAVE always remarked that every one in solitary confinement, from Baron Trenck down to Fieschi, has taken
refuge in a journal, I suppose on the same principle that
madmen talk to themselves : they have no one else to talk
to ; at all events, it is an innocent substitute for society,
with this advantage, that one inflicts one's egotism on no
one but one's self, the *only* human being to whom it would
not be obnoxious. So much for the fitness of things. We
have had journals from purgatory, *vide* Fanny Kemble's,
begun on board an American steamboat ; but I know of
none from the other place, unless the 'Divina Commedia'
can be considered as such. Young D'Israeli has given us
'Ixion in Heaven,' with infinite *Ju*cundity, but these are
all wide fields to journalise upon, except the Baron's and
Fieschi's, with whose may rank the ingenious Frenchman's
most ingenious little book 'Le Voyage autour de ma Chambre.'
Now the circumnavigation of one's own room may suit the
patient perseverance of a Cook, but I doubt it being palat-
able to the enterprising genius of a Columbus, and in life's
masquerade we would rather play the part of the latter.
But necessity has no law, except that of chamber council
in the present instance ; and the only way in solitude to
have 'thoughts that breathe' is to read them aloud as soon
as one has written them, and as for 'words that burn,'
they are easily secured by committing one's journal to the
flames as soon as it is finished. Poor M——! how I miss
her ; the house seems like a body without a soul, now
that she is gone, and I am literally 'alone'! I would fret
more about her chances and changes but that I am convinced God is as much with and for her as she is with

and for Him. Poor little Emily too, poor child! She is happy with her little friend and companion. This is as it should be; we ought to get a little happiness on account in childhood; it prevents fate being too much in arrears to us. What a life has mine been! A sunless childhood; a flowerless youth; and certainly a fruitless womanhood, the few good qualities I possess utterly wasted or rather despised. I hate looking back on the last eight years of my life; I so thoroughly despise myself for having wasted so much affection, zeal, and devotion on so *worthless* an object. I forgot that nothing ever takes root in a stone but weeds; those of pride and selfishness are rooted there with a vengeance, and yet the eternal complaining of want of *sympathy!* Sympathy must be *given* before it can be received, just as *respect* must be paid before it can be expected in return. Above all, sympathy, like electric fluid, must find a corresponding vein before it can be communicated, and therefore self-love annihilates all sympathy, because self-love is indivisible. It would amuse me if I were not sick at heart to hear ——, who cannot remain two days at home, and who, the moment he for a short interval dismounts from the whirlwind of his ambition, instantly busies himself in providing some *new* and *solitary* enjoyment, which would be marred for him if another shared it, complain, like a poor domestic, home-rid man, of having his household gods shivered about him, and his hearth devastated, because he has the misfortune to be tied to one who does not think it an all-sufficient honour to share his *name*, in perfect and uninterrupted loneliness, or to see him at distant intervals, when, like a sea-captain, he puts in occasionally to his home harbour, and makes his house like a tavern, with a few boon companions, eating, drinking, smoking, then blustering about the bills, and off again, till convenience or necessity once more drives him homeward.

"I could not help smiling the other day at dinner, when Mr. R—— told us of Mr. N—— having said that were he to marry again, he would not marry a 'show wife,' at ——'s remarking that it showed what a sensible

man N—— was ; not so sensible as himself after all, for
N—— does not *prevent* his wife from opening her lips
or writing books, and, moreover, he does not shut her
up in the country without horses, which would be the
most effectual way of preventing her 'outglaring' him
in personal appearance, as she is so handsome, and he
so much the reverse. The epithets —— is so fond of
applying to women always anger and disgust me. When
Mr. H—— was pitying the usage Mrs. F—— had
received from her husband, —— added, in his usual well-
bred way, 'Oh! that is the story of the d—d woman's
friends.' The sort of mother a man has had may, generally speaking, be pretty correctly known by the estimate
he entertains of her sex. There are two kinds of mothers
who invariably engender in their sons a respect for woman.
One is the woman of superior intellect, properly evinced
in the education of her children, and concealed in the
presence of her husband. The other is one who without
many intellectual advantages possesses that sort of moral
pre-eminence and right-mindedness which, proved by every
act of her life, induce her sons to believe, and rightly too, that
a good woman is the best counsellor and friend that a man
can have. On the other hand, if a man can only think
of his mother's understanding with contempt, and her
caprice with disgust, he is wondrously apt to confound
all the rest of the sex with her, while the very vices her
own imbecility has so carefully nurtured, the vanity she
has manured with flattery, and the selfishness she has
grafted with jealousy, all conspire to choke even the faint
impulses of tenderness towards herself that nature might
have implanted in him ; and, with characteristic wisdom,
she is the first to deplore and wonder at the result of her
own work, the worst part of which is that *she*, the cause of
all the mischief, only suffers from it in a minor degree, for it
is reserved to some wretched wife to become its victim.
My boy is but four years old; he came this morning
praising himself for having kept some grapes and given
them to his nurse. I told him he had better not have been
guilty of this piece of generosity if he thought so much

of it as to boast about it. He had been reprobated hitherto
for being a selfish child, and sharing with no one, so he
stared at me, and did not seem to know what I meant.
No matter; I hope he will fully understand it and act upon
it by the time he is twenty. I'm sure the secret of forming really estimable, lovable characters is not to praise
children for doing right, but to make them very much
ashamed of doing *wrong*, for we have daily experience
that many persons are extremely tenacious of their *characters* who are not at all particular as to their *conduct.*

"I dread going to bed, for there this gnawing pain and
low fever consume me. I cannot sleep, and therefore
cannot dream, which makes loneliness doubly lonely,
for dreams are a sort of phantasmagoria of life : they are
kind things, for even if horrid, we wake, and are so thankful it was *but* a dream, taking it all as a jest on the part
of Somnus, a *mauvaise plaisanterie* certainly, but then he
is but a benighted half-witted creature; whereas if they
are happy ones, they are to us sleeping what letters are
to us waking, and bring tidings of those we love from
the happy, sunny past into that miserable, barren little
segment of life— *The Present !*

" *Monday, December* 14*th.*—A letter from dear M—— and
the money. I'm sorry it is too late, for I am silly enough
to be disappointed at ——'s disappointment ; but of course
he got what he wanted, or he would not have set off.

"What's this? an illegible scrawl from that little
H. B——. More about the cloak ! which has not, however,
made its appearance, and of course never will, for to
promise is his mode of giving ; not that it is any loss to
me, for I am sure Hercules was not more uncomfortable in
his poisoned shirt, than I should be in wearing anything
that came from him.

"What a blessing it is to me that Mrs. —— is not in
town, and thinking it necessary to make me one of her
periodical, ceremonious, truly professional mean-nothing,
do-nothing visits, flattering up the children, and making
fools of them for a whole week after, though they have the
sense to ask if she was not laughing at them ! Her senti-

ments give me a perfect idea of the third echo at Killar-
ney, which is but the *echoed echo of an echo.* She is, God
bless her, the most unmitigated goose I ever met ; I wonder
how I can keep my countenance, for the style and turn of
our *conversation* always forcibly remind me of the words
of poor H——'s song of the jackdaws.

(AIR, *Le Petit Tambour.*)

" ' Said an old jackdaw
To a young jackdaw,
As they was a-walking together,
Says the old jackdaw
To the young jackdaw,
" I think it's wery fine weather." ' '

" Poor little Ted told me a piece of sentiment *de sa part*
to-day, which, if worked by a skilful lover into a sonnet
to his mistress, would not in tenderness and delicacy be
exceeded by anything Boccacio ever felt towards his
Fiametta, or Petrarch ever invented about Laura. He
said he went every morning to feed the birds at his sister's
window. I asked him why he did not feed them at his
own nursery window? ' Oh!' said he, ' because I wish
dem to tink dat Emily still feeds dem, for she has fed dem
so long, dat dey must love her de best, and dey might not
eat de crumbs if dey thought she was gone !' For four
years old, *ça ne va pas mal.* I can think of nothing better
than this, and so will leave off.

" *Tuesday,* 15*th.*—No letters. I have sent off the
books and basket to ——, and such a regal-looking,
profuse bunch of dear sweet Neapolitan violets as
an English December seldom produces. So *she*, I hope,
will at least have half an hour's pleasure in unpack-
ing the basket, eating the fruit, and kissing the violets
—at least, I suppose she will kiss them—as I always
do ; and they are such double darlings to come in
this black, atrocious, Newgate-looking weather. *À propos*
of darlings, there is the queen of them all, that dear
dog Fay ; no wonder I doat upon her as I do : the little
creature, with her big, loving, diamond eyes, seems to think

it incumbent on her to make up to me for the rest of the
world, for she not only sings her Mazurka with double the
alacrity she used to do, but sits up, or rather walks about,
on her hind paws all the time, so emulating Taglioni, as
well as Grisi, which she never did before; and when I cry,
the little silver silken paws are instantly round my neck,
and the little velvet head under my chin, and then the
little low sympathetic moan, and every canine consolation
she can think of.   Then the game of teetotum with
T——, and the way she knocks it down with her paw (as
if to enter into the spirit of the game) when we say, 'Which
number will Faizey have?'   And yet some fools wonder I
should love that dog; ay, that do I, and the more that
she is a dog of character, and has 'a lick' for those she
loves, and 'a snap' for those she hates.   I have been
casting up my bills—no friends—and am not so badly off,
after all, for I have *one* certain, dear M——, who has been
tried and proved so often, as to be quite suspicion-proof.
Then I think dear —— really loves me, though I have sometimes thought she was too happy and too well off, as far as
this world goes, to be capable of paying the tax of genuine
friendship, great self-sacrifice on all occasions, but her last
letters have been *very* kind, very *genuine*, and very consola-
tory; and to have time to *think* even of poor me, in that
paradis des femmes, much more to write me such long
affectionate letters, is certainly friendship put to one of
its tests.   Her faults she has borrowed from others, which
must be their excuse; but her youngness of feeling and
singleness of disposition are her own, and they must have
been of the nature of the asbestos to have gone unscathed
through the fiery ordeal of prosperity and pleasure; but
like many others, she will never get the credit she deserves,
for she *acts* better than she *talks*, a great mistake in the
present era, when cant and quackery are the 'open Sesame'
to character and reputation.   Poor —— too!   I once
thought her very staunch to me, and returned her supposed
affection with all sincerity, as is my wont.   *Mais qui sait?*
As a burnt child dreads the fire, so do I dread, or rather,
doubt, all the 'irritable tribe;' then the insufferable *volto*

sciolto, gli pensieri of them all, which is, and ever has been, their distinguishing badge, to say nothing of their flattery to one's face and their treachery to one's back: they are perfect beehives—all honey if you take their works, all stings if you come in too close contact with themselves. One can't have a greater type of an author's insincerity, carried to a pitch of sublimity, than Voltaire's saying to Swift that reading his (the Dean's) works made him ashamed of his own ! *He* could not think this, nor indeed could any one else. One only wonders, that the insincerity of his *nature* could have been so much more powerful, than the vanity of his *art;* but the mystery is solved when one remembers, that he said this at the conclusion of that letter which he had begun by requesting Swift's exertions in getting up an Irish subscription for the Henriade !

"*Wednesday,* 16th.—A letter from ——. Not a word about the violets, and too many about the books and the theatricals, but *real* generosity never does ensure gratitude. I would rather have had a tooth out, than part with a violet at this time of the year, much less such a bunch ! and therefore of course I am not thanked for them ; whereas the Spanish melon, which was a complete B——r gift, given merely because I did not want it, or know what to do with it, was received like an heir-apparent. I am called away to Thomas Millar, the English Burns and Nottingham basket-maker. Well, I have seen him ; in person he is like a hazel-nut ; said the *pooblic* had indeed appreciated his works (for a moment I was in the *basket,* and did not know whether he meant literary or wicker), but soon discovered it was the *former,* as he had the authorly egotism strongly upon him, and seemed to labour under what Pope and Swift so bitterly complained of in Gay, and which the latter designated as 'a painful intenseness about his own affairs.' He deprecated the illiberality of the reviews raking up his and Burns' sphere of life, and therefore only praising them comparatively. I said, that of course genius, to attain the highest rank, neither required to pass through college nor the Herald's Office, but that were I

he, I could easily pardon any missiles directed at me
that were at the same time aimed at Burns, as, though it
might, with true critical spleen, be killing two birds with
one stone, yet it showed they were considered 'birds of
a feather,' and *that*, in my opinion, was honour enough
for any man. He said he had had 'a very sweet' (that
was his phrase) letter from Moore, and had seen all the
live authors worth seeing, from my Sposo downwards;
but that it had not at all turned his brain! (No, to be
sure, for he had only *seen* them!) Next to his own
poems he spoke more *con amore* about Newstead Abbey,
Lord Byron and his Mary (Mrs. Musters), than anything
else; he said her beauty was perfectly angelic and
unearthly, and that her husband was a perfect brute.
Cela va sans dire if *she* was an angel. He talked
fanatically about woods and flowers and violets; yet he
never even noticed mine, that were breathing out their
purple souls from their golden baskets round the room.
Oh, those violets! I'm sure I shall fight a duel about
them yet! He said when he had written for many hours
together, he could neither eat nor sleep, and could not
account for the throbbing pulses and burning pains in
his head. I told him that I could, for that the body was
a sort of wife to the mind, and would not allow it to go
gadding, amusing itself and others, and reaping fame
and profit, to the eternal injury of *her* health from want
of exercise and starvation, without twitting and worrying
him when he at length thought fit to remember her
existence, 'whereat,' like Queen Elizabeth, while pocket-
ing the Countess of Suffolk's over-rich comfit cake, he
'waxed exceedingly merry.' He would not eat anything,
but said he would take some 'purple' (*vulgo* red) wine.
When I gave it to him he said, 'Thank you kindly, Lady;
my *respects* to you, and my respects to you, pretty little
master.' On which, like a little cub of four years old
as he is, T—— burst out laughing. Millar then wrote a
very pretty sonnet in my album, for which I thanked
him much; and I bought five baskets which he had
brought with him. He then took leave, yet still he

lingered, and when he at length reached the door returned (very gratuitously, as I thought) to tell me the only vice he had was smoking! and that he could not conceive why most authors were so much addicted to it. I said I supposed it was to ensure themselves plenty of puffs, whereat he laughed afresh, thinking, doubtless, that this execrable pun came from his namesake's emporium. Poor man! he wished much for Tennyson's poems, which he said he was not able to buy, so I have sent them to him, and since dinner have read some of his, parts of which are really beautiful, and there is one line Shakespeare might have put into Puck's mouth, *i.e.*,

'The bee went round to tell the flowers 'twas May.'

I lent him my Florentine basket that kind, agreeable Mr. Landor gave me at Fiezole, filled with those delicious figs, gathered from his beautiful gardens, in the sunniest nook of the Val d'Arno. The very shape of the basket breathes of Boccacio. Millar was enchanted with it, and hoped to make a fortune by imitating it. T—— said a very good lesson to-day, and read a story about a lion who did not eat a dog; the story ended by saying, 'And ever after the lion and the dog lived on very friendly terms together.' I asked him if he knew what 'living on *friendly* terms' meant; he considered for a moment, and then said, 'Yes; I'm sure Faizey and Juno will never live on friendly terms *todeder*, for Faizey snaps at Juno to this day.'

"17th December.—In too great pain to write, and nothing to write about.

"18th.—A letter from dear M——, which I have answered. A note from Mr. R——, with his book, the note beginning, 'My dear Mrs.,' and saying that he cannot bring himself to address me with form! so it appears, for this is free enough, God knows. The wonderful cloak has at length arrived, and is worthy of the donor; in a place like London he must have found it difficult to get so shabby a one, but it is the idiosyncracy of genius to overcome great difficulties; it is a mile too short. However, I may console myself on the old Joe Miller reflection, that it will be long enough before I get another! I am now going to read Mr. R——'s book.

" 19*th*.—I am too ill to write, or do anything but lie down and die—if I could, but that would be too happy a release for me.

"20*th*.—I have read Mr. R——'s book; it is extremely well written, but quite too horrible; there is, however, one masterstroke of knowledge of human nature in it: in describing that most odious character the parricide's father, he says, ' He neither possessed any positive virtue, nor positive vice; and I know of but two words that will accurately describe him—he was eminently *selfish* and *insensible.*' In these two sentences all his atrocities are fully accounted for, the first being the Alpha and Omega of all *vice*, and the latter a barrier which no virtue ever passes; but still I think (as I told him) the moral of such powerful materials would have been more subtle, and infinitely more useful, had he made both father and son equal monsters, equal destroyers of their own and others' happiness, and still kept them within the *pale* of the *law*, for then it would have been sufficiently *vraisemblable* to have borne a comparison with the dire hourly and daily realities of life, *all* rising out of the same sources, parental neglect, selfishness, egotism, and vanity, let loose like so many vicious, unbridled brutes, enacting the part of wild horses to that *doomed Mazeppa* their possessor's fate! One thing this book convinces me of, *i.e.*, that the writer is a perfect Æneas of a son, though, no doubt, more than half that discriminating monster, the world, will vote him a parricide, and his book an autobiography, actions being of no import whatever, thanks to the omnipotence of the press; therefore, in order to attain the reputation of great morality, people have only to write books filled with the following claptraps, ' benevolence,' ' philanthropy,' 'virtue,' 'civil and religious liberty.' The greatness of nations has always been achieved by the people! and the greatest happiness of the greatest number, which, being interpreted, means a *total* and most immoral disregard of the happiness and well-being of any and every *individual*. In short, to succeed in this enlightened age, when the march of intellect has billeted even every subaltern mind on that Marquis de Carrabas of our social system public opinion, to *seem* is *everything;* to *be* is *nothing;* therefore let all that would propitiate this autocrat follow the example of Glaucus (the son of Hippolochus) and forthwith exchange the golden arms of reality for Diomedes' brazen ones of assumption. Poor Mr. ——! complaining of the acrimony of editors and sub-editors, he little knows that those who contrive to mollify them generally play the Quintus Curtius to their own fame—they save it, but they engulf themselves.

"Poor little T—— said a very good lesson to-day. He really is an uncommonly quick, clever child, and if I can but root out the *selfishness, egotism,* and *vanity,* that is already *dreadfully deep-rooted,* in so young a child (for they actually *seem part* of his blood, bone, and muscle), I may make a fine creature of him; if not, I would rather he had been a born idiot, for mere intellect, however highly cultivated, without an equally cultivated disposition, is but like a brilliant beacon, placed on the summit of a barren and isolated rock, which, by revealing the perilous and miserable void beneath, only warns and repels by that very light which, differently situated, could not fail to vivify and attract. Oh! when will those who have the training of embryo men and women remember and educate upon this golden maxim : '*que l'on est plus sociable et d'un meilleur commerce par le cœur, que par l'esprit*'?

"21st.—What another dreadful night I have had! No sleep, and in torture the whole time. My nature must be a happy mixture of asbestos, cast iron, and feline unkillability, for no fever will consume me, no illness break me, and, worst of all, no grief will kill me.

"Had a note to-night from Count d'Orsay offering me his box at the Adelphi on Thursday ; very good-natured of him to think of me. Answered it in bad French and worse humour, at not being able to avail myself of the offer, for as my lord and master takes such infinite pains to assure me that I am older than any of the ladies of thirty-eight and forty now extant, I don't see why I should not have some of the benefits of my antiquity, and issue forth like the Prayer-books (*cum privilegio*); for the sort of life I am *compelled* to lead, I might as well have the misfortune to be a beauty of fifteen. So had I been well enough, I should certainly have accepted the box, as I am sure Mrs. L. S—— or Mrs. W—— would have been delighted to have gone with me.

"This evening read Swift's character of Mrs. Johnson (Stella), and never was much more disgusted in my life ; I have, in common with other sages, always prayed Heaven to defend me from my *friends*, but by this it would appear, one ought to extend the petition to one's lovers.

"*Tuesday morning, December 22nd*, 1835.—Another dreadful night—no sleep, and pain than which, I'm sure, the rack cannot be worse. A letter of 'tender inquiries from the poor D——'s ; they really are what J. C. B—— said wives were, *i.e.*, clean, cheap, and thankful : clean, for they write on the nicest of all possible paper ; cheap, for I never have to give them above two dinners a year ; and thankful, since for those they are grateful. What's this ? another letter, and comes to one shilling and fourpence ; it is too costly, with its large seal and all. Ha! ha! ha! an invitation from H. B—— to go to B—— ; a promise of an opera-box and a seat at church! with an apology for coupling them. 'No offence, sir,' for, as I have told him in my answer, I merely look upon it as one of those little confusions that he and his brother Radicals are eternally making between the *vox populi* and the *vox Dei*. He goes on to say, ' M—— may' (well-bred this) ' accompany me as a chaperon *if* she likes.' I am sure both the invitations are given in perfect sincerity, from the conviction that they will not be accepted ; however, I ought to be grateful, as it is by far the best attempt he has yet made at kindness and sincerity, to say nothing of the laugh it has given me to *envisager* dear M—— and myself, first, *en route* for the Island of Calypso! next our arrival! Then my conjectures as to whether his Penseroso Majesty of —— would recognise in the portly (for I won't call

myself by any more disadvantageous name) matron of past
twenty-eight the girl of nineteen that he used to call 'the
dark-haired sylph.' *No*, most assuredly, for there is a *fat-
ality* attends me in all things *now*.   And then what fun we
would have in writing to dear M. A—— and Blurt, who, I
daresay, would tell us, out of *envy*, that we were two women
'she had not the slightest respect for'!   It seems quite omi-
nous that I should have been reading 'The *Impossible*
Enchantment' and 'The Palace of Ideas' just before I got
this epistle.   Could I have achieved this exploit, it would
have been delicious, even in my mind's eye, to have seen
my lord and master's face when he returned, and found that
'Est il possible!' *herself* was gone off.   The plot thickens ;
a brace of pheasants and a hare from head-quarters.   Went
out for the first time these ten days ; described to the
gardener about making the flowerpots into baskets, and
dug the first circle of the Northern Star myself ; kissed and
talked to poor darling Fiddlestick, who licked my hand,
rubbed his innocent head against me, bleated, and, in short,
appeared more delighted to see me, than any other relation
I have in the world.   Came home ; had a greater bevy
than ever of robins in the room, and that fat red-hooded
cardinal of a fellow, that always eats the most, and flies
upon the bed and even upon Faizey's head of a morning,
jumped upon my shoulder.   The Misses W—— called ;
I like the eldest very much, there is something so kind-
hearted about her ; they asked me to spend the day to-
morrow : I am not well enough ; they bespoke me for New
Year's Day! have promised if I am able.   Kept T—— up
till half-past seven ; he is growing lovingly fond of me.

"Read Mr. Willis's 'Pencillings by the Way,' and very racy
and pleasant they are ; all about Austria is cordial and spicy,
like mulled Burgundy in December, and then all about the
Ægean is perfectly delicious, like iced lemonade at the Café
della Fiore at Venice.   Poor man! how well one can enter
into his feelings on beholding Ionia for the first time, his
head full of Homer, and his heart full of Byron.   Then
landing, ard the first sounds that salute his ears to be from
a Mrs. Flack, an English greengrocer : 'Sir, it is *wery 'ot;*

von't you 'ave a glass of water?' Alas! alas! is there not always a *very* hot or *very* cold upon the realisations of our brightest imaginings? Yet still had he to go farther and fare worse, 'Oh ye Athenians,' to find the Byron-loved, the Moore-sung, the matchless Teresa Makri, in short the immortal 'Maid of Athens,' turned into Mrs. Black, the better half of a respectable Scotchman, with no earthly mitigation of her crime but the acquisition of a Scotch terrier who bit at the Yankee tourist's heels as he entered her sacrilegious abode!

"Played on the guitar for an hour, and sang many songs I had heard or dreamt. A blaze sprang up in the fire, and fell full upon the picture of Napoli di Posolippo. I flung down the guitar. Again was I returning from the dear balmy, happy, sunset drive on the Strada Nova; again did I feel the soft breeze on my cheek from across the bay, freighted with a warm kiss from Vesuvius; again did I cast my eye along the Ciaja, and as I saw Lord H——'s palazzo, where the ball was to be held at night, call to poor stupid, often scolded, but still more often regretted Francesco Firmate alla casa di Jacopo Tonere Riviera di Ciaja, to order another wreath, with more myrtle and fewer roses. Ah! Naples, dear Naples, you are the *only* place in which I ever *felt* young (for I did not do so as a child), and what was the result? did I commit more follies? No. '*Mais qui vit sans folie n'est pas si sage qu'il pense.*'

"*23rd.*—A letter from dear M———poor M——!—and a letter from Mr. B——, overflowing with morbid sensibility for himself and repudiating me! Be it so. How foolish it is of me to let these reptiles irritate me as they do, nor would I but that with their abominable assumption of know-ledge and superiority, they have the power of crushing and injuring me every moment. Our Saviour even seems to have had the same contempt for their species in His time, for at the beginning of the Christian era, Plato and Epicurus found amongst the Pharisees and Sadducees their chief followers, and *against them* are all Christ's animadversions directed. St. Paul, too, than whom no man 'was better versed in Grecian literature, philosophy, and science, such

as it then was, had an equal contempt for those pseudo-
sages, who affected to assert that 'Virtue' was the chief
good, without being able to decide *what virtue was*, or
fix it into an immutable standard, as it varied, according
to the passions or perceptions of its votaries, from health
to riches, and from riches to honour, and St. Paul especially
warns Timothy to ' avoid profane and vain babblings, and
oppositions of science falsely so called;' and, again, he
cautions the Colossians to 'beware lest any man spoil them
through philosophy and vain deceit.' Like St. Paul, I know
them *too* well, so am in no danger, further than my temper
is concerned, unless indeed Paraciades (the fisherman in
Lucian), who knew so well how to bait his hooks for this
infinitely small fry, were to come and angle for me, as
he did for the philosophers, with gold and figs; then indeed
I might be caught, for I have as great a craving for the
former as any reforming patriot now extant, and am as fond
of the latter as any *beccafica* in all Italy. How often
I make a resolution (only to break it) that these B——s
shall not anger me. There is nothing so horrible as hatred,
except being hated, which is perhaps worse, inasmuch as
there is something very infectious in one's own unpopu-
larity, that puts one out of conceit with one's self, and this
is one reason why women are always pleased at, and
grateful for, being loved, even if they cannot love in return;
it makes them of consequence in their own eyes, just
as some persons value a cat's eye—the ugliest thing in
the world—merely because they know there are those who
would give twenty guineas for it. It is different with men.
Love with them at best is very apocryphal, lust being
generally the feeling they dignify with that name, and
nine times in ten their vanity leads them to fancy themselves beloved where they are not even thought of; and
when they really have a woman's happiness in their power
they seem to consider that the same privilege is attached
to it that a child attaches to a new toy, *i.e.*, that of
destroying it at discretion. How fond I am of biography!
it is like living other people's lives at second-hand, or rather
skimming the cream of theirs to enrich the milk and water

of one's own. I have lately been struggling, and hoping, and dining, and triumphing, and desponding, deceiving, and maddening with Swift. I have been to the printer's with him with the last number of the *Examiner*, and called on 'poor Patty Rolt' by the way; who had but £18 a year to live on, and seen her eyes sparkle at the 'guinea, which patched up twenty things;' I have returned to the Thatched House, dined with the Lord Treasurer, Mr. Secretary St. John, Dr. Arbuthnot, and the Duke of Ormond, laughed at the suppressed lampoon on the Duchess of Somerset, drunk some of the 'flask of the grand Duke's wine,' sent for my Lord Keeper, waited in vain for his return from the House, and so crossed over to sup with Lady Masham on 'boiled oysters and scraps of private news about the Queen, who hath been confined for the last few days with the gout in her hand.' Then I have walked home (in spite of the Mohawks), stood by while 'Patrick' was being sirrahed and cudgelled for his hundred and fifty-fourth achievement in inebriety; that over, I've held the candle while the Dean wrote lies to Stella of loving her better than his life, while he was daily telling Miss Vanhomeigh the same thing, and summing up the evidence in 'the little language' till the candle has gone out. As for my idol Pope, I am afraid Lady M. W. Montagu was right, that he was *un peu avare*, and a terrible legacy-hunter; nevertheless, 'I love him hugely,' and really cried that night that *we* were overturned in my Lord Bolingbroke's 'coach and six,' and that he got immersed 'in the Thames up to the knots of his periwig,' and cut his hand so terribly. Well! at least he was a paragon of a son, that nobody can deny, and the solicitude with which he attended to his mother makes one forgive the frugality of the dinners at Twickenham, and even the two-pronged forks which drove Swift into the abomination of eating with his knife, and thereby got him into such disgrace with the Duchess of Queensbury; but 'out of evil cometh good,' for this forced him into spending £30 on three-pronged forks. Then how well I can fancy the still more scanty suppers, with nothing

plentiful but the fruit, which Swift could not, and Arbuthnot *would* not touch, the early withdrawal of the host,
the 'little half-pint of wine,' and his everlasting parting
address of 'Gentlemen, I leave you to your wine,' and
the Doctor's good-humoured gibe of 'Yes, but you don't
leave *your* wine to us.' Then I think I see the conclave
examining the broken pen-knife with which Guiscard
stabbed Lord Oxford, and their feverish anxiety for his
recovery. As for Lord Bolingbroke, I never did, and
never can, admire him, and for the 'all-accomplished'
I would read 'all-pretending St. John:' he was a happy
mixture of fop, stoic, statesman, and philosopher; there
was an eternal straining after effect and nothing *real* about
him, not even his scepticism, and his meanness in depreciating the indisputable learning of Bayle, that he, with all
the pedantry of a Scaliger, might the more safely crib from
him, disgusts and provokes one; his letters in exile
are so overlaid with laboured classical quotations, that they
quite destroy the circinatous tone he wishes to affect; however, I respect him for having *once* spoken the truth, which
was when he said, 'If I must despise riches, let it be
with Seneca's purse, for then I shall have the advantage
of wealth and philosophy both.' When Sir Walter Scott
praises him for his active zeal in obtaining for Swift the
£1,000 from the Queen, during the three days of his ad-
ministration, which his friend Lord Oxford had failed to
get for him in so much longer a period, he does not seem
to perceive that Lord Bolingbroke was spurred on much
more by his implacable hatred of Lord Oxford into a wish
of outdoing him, than by pure friendship to Swift; in
short, though Lord Chatham, when a young man, was
surprised, on going to see Lord Bolingbroke (then an old
one) at Battersea, to find him, as he describes, 'pedantic,
fretful, and angry with his wife,' I am not the least
surprised to hear it, for there was no longer a motive for
display, which had been the governing principle of his
life. One of the most unfeeling things I know anywhere is a passage in a letter of his to Swift, about a month
after Stella's death, in which he says, 'My wife' (his

second wife, the Marquise de la Vilette, Madame de Maintenon's niece) 'writes to you herself, and sends you some
fans just arrived from Liliput, which you will dispose of
to the present Stella, whoever she be.' Now, considering
that Swift, notwithstanding the way in which he had
behaved to her, really loved her, and was in a state
of distraction at her death, this was perfect brutality
on the part of my Lord Bolingbroke; but some persons
are apt to make great mistakes when they take it for
granted that others are as unfeeling as themselves.
This fan sprightliness is just such a piece of pleasantry
as H. B—— would be guilty of, his only ideas of wit being
profanity or want of feeling.

" *January 4th*, 1836.—Poor Mamma came in all the frost
and snow to see me—very kind of her; gave me a nice
warm shawl, ermine muff, and boa.

"*6th.*—A letter from poor dear Elizabeth. She still
continues ill. What a martyr she is! But like me, if she
were dying, I believe she would contrive to laugh at Tommy
the Great. His letters from Algiers are indeed as dismal
as *lettres de cachet*. However, Parnassus has two ascents,
one sacred to Apollo, the other to Bacchus, and though
he may have failed in reaching the summit of the former,
he has soared most triumphantly to the pinnacle of the
latter.

> "' So though he's not Valerius Flacchus,
> He might pass any day for Bacchus.'

" *January 7th.*—Too ill to write.

" *February 20th.*—My jailer returned with his amiable
epicurean debauchee friend, Mr. F. V——, after a *five weeks'*
absence; and ill as I have been, too, he could not be here
one day alone.

" *March 1st.*—From crying, coughing, and violent agitation, I have burst a small blood vessel. Oh, my God! my
God! when will You take me?"

The journal abruptly breaks off here.

CHAPTER VIII.

FINAL QUARREL AND SEPARATION (1836).

THE end of Mrs. Bulwer's earthly existence was fortunately, or perhaps unfortunately, still far distant, but the separation from her husband was approaching more rapidly than even she herself could have anticipated. Very soon after the conclusion of the journal at Acton an event occurred which led to a final rupture between the ill-assorted pair. Of this episode I have several accounts; but I prefer to give Lady Lytton's own version, as written in " Nemesis," adding a few explanatory remarks for the guidance of my readers. Bulwer had promised to dine one night with his wife at Berrymead Priory. She waited until nine o'clock, when a groom arrived in haste with a note saying that he was very ill, and quite unable to leave his chambers. Mrs. Bulwer, fully believing the truth of this statement, at once started for London in considerable alarm, taking with her medicines and other comforts for her ailing spouse.

"When she arrived at my chambers in the Albany," writes Lady Lytton in " Nemesis," " it was eleven o'clock at night. I had purposely sent my man out of the way, so my fool of a wife rang and rang, till, thinking, notwithstanding my *soi-disant* illness, I must be out, and the servants in bed, she was just about to go away, when I, on

my side, supposing these loud rings might herald some
note or invitation that I should not like to lose, went to
open the door *en chemise*, with my dressing-gown hastily
thrown over my shoulders.   Upon opening the door, I was
for a moment so taken aback at seeing my victim that I
actually staggered, while rage and indignation made her
stand firm as a rock, as she beheld through the drawing-
room door our cosy salver with tea for two on it, and Miss
Laura Deacon making a precipitate retreat into the bedroom, but unfortunately dropping, after a Parthian fashion,
in her flight, all her arrows, *vulgo* her bonnet, shawl, etc.,
on the sofa. 'Good God !' exclaimed I, 'what on earth
brought you here?'

"'Your note, sir, with its *circumstantial details* of your
pretended illness, which, of course, like yourself, was an
incarnate lie!' she rejoined, with bitter contempt ; and, so
saying, rushed back to her carriage."

Bulwer's rage and mortification at being detected
in this precious intrigue knew no bounds. He had
evidently made up his mind to get rid at all hazards
of a woman whom he had long since ceased to
love, and whose presence reminded him so inconveniently of the vows he had broken, the outrages
and insults of which he had been guilty, and the long
series of deceits and infidelities he had practised.
Consequently he announced to her that he had
finally determined to separate from her at once
and for ever. Under these circumstances, there
was but one course open to his victim. Her
womanly pride forbade her to cringe for forgiveness to a man who had so cruelly scorned, insulted,
and wronged her ; and she was forced to accept the
inevitable, and to agree to whatever terms her lord
and master might think fit to dictate. Knowing
it was useless to appeal for mercy, she wrote the

following pathetic and dignified letter, which I may recommend to the attention of my readers as containing a cogent refutation of the charges of pride, violence, obstinacy, and extravagance, so often and so unjustly ascribed to the character of this much-wronged woman.

FROM MRS. BULWER TO EDWARD LYTTON BULWER.

[Her forgiveness.—His banker's account.]

Undated, but probably written in April 1836.

"I thank you for your letter, and am sorry that poor Mary's zeal and kind feelings for me should have offended you; but be not angry that I have *one* friend on earth: it is not long that I shall want even that one. For the rest, I do not wish to have blame imputed to any one— that is solely due to me.

"Upon the first intimation of your casting me off, I *did* say I would not take less than £600 a year, for that I could not support and educate my children upon a smaller sum. I felt bitterly, too, at the time, as I had seen your banker's account, by which it appeared I had had £180 in eight months, and in six you had spent 2,000 some hundred and odd pounds, and that without appearing to have paid any heavy debts. But these and every other feeling of resentment have, thank God, now subsided, and I solemnly assure you, so far from *now* wishing to tax your luxury of getting rid of me at so dear a rate as the sacrifice of half your tangible income, I would not, were my poor little *unhappy children out of the question*, under any persuasion take more than £200 a year from you; as it is, I beg explicitly to state that *no* illness, no want, no privation, shall *ever* induce me to accept *one farthing* from you beyond the stipulated £500: *if* I live, I can make more.

"And now, do not, I implore you, attribute to vindictive or unforgiving feelings *my unalterable* determination of never again 'cursing your existence with my presence.' Upon reflection, you must feel convinced that, without any feeling

of resentment, no woman of common delicacy, no woman
of the most latent and dormant pride could, when once
publicly expelled from her husband's house, ever UNDER
ANY CIRCUMSTANCES think of returning to it, especially
when that husband had spoken of her to a third person
in the terms you have of me, for which, however, I most
freely and sincerely forgive you.

"I do not contemplate the possibility of being able to
leave this before Midsummer, as, housekeeping being
out of the question, it will not be so easy to find the sort
of thing I want. I hope you have let this place for a great
deal more than you gave for it, as the house, which had
not a door or window that would shut, is now in good
repair, and the garden, that was knee-deep in weeds when
I came here, and destitute of even a potato, is now in
perfect order and thoroughly stocked with everything.

"And now, once for all, may God bless you and prosper
you! May those new ties, which make it indispensable
for you to part with me, be to you all that I have failed to
be! May your friends be as zealous in promoting your
interests and your comforts as I *tried* to be, and may they
have none of the irritability of temper and easily wounded
feelings which in me destroyed and cancelled all my best
intentions—in short, may you henceforth be as happy as
I have made you the reverse—is the sincere hope and will
be the constant prayer of her who was your wife.

"ROSINA LYTTON BULWER.

"*Berrymead Priory, Acton.*"

At this period, unhappily, Mrs. Bulwer was to
all intents and purposes friendless. Near relatives
she had none, and of her many acquaintances, no
one seems to have had the power or the inclination
to save her from being bound by the fetters of a
most iniquitous and one-sided deed of separation.
This precious document I append hereto, and its terms
will doubtless reflect an additional lustre upon Mr.
Bulwer's reputation for generosity and unselfishness.

8

COPY OF DEED OF SEPARATION BETWEEN E. G. E. L.
BULWER AND ROSINA ANNE BULWER.

"19 *April*, 1836.

"This Indenture, of four parts, made the nineteenth day
of April, One thousand eight hundred and thirty-six,
Between Edward George Earle Lytton Bulwer, of Acton,
in the County of Middlesex, Esquire, of the first part,
Rosina Anne Bulwer his Wife, of the same place, of the
second part, Eliza Barbara Bulwer Lytton, of Knebworth
Park, in the County of Hertford, Widow, and the Mother
of the said Edward George Earle Lytton, of the third
part, and Sir Francis Hastings Doyle, of Wimpole Street,
in the said County of Middlesex, Baronet, and The Reverend
Sir Thomas Gery Cullum, of Hardwick House, in the
County of Suffolk, Baronet, of the fourth part. Whereas
unhappy differences have arisen and still subsist between
the said Edward George Earle Lytton Bulwer and Rosina
Anne his Wife, by reason whereof they have agreed to live
separate and apart from each other for the future—And
whereas the said Edward George Earle Lytton Bulwer
hath proposed to allow unto or in trust for the said Rosina
Anne Bulwer during the said Separation the yearly sum
of £400 as a provision for her maintenance and support, and
a further yearly sum of £50 for each of the two children of
the Marriage so long as he, the said E. G. E. L. Bulwer,
shall consent that each such child shall remain with the
said Rosina Anne Bulwer, to enable the said R. A. Bulwer
to clothe and maintain them. And for the better and more
effectually securing the due and punctual payment of the
aforesaid annual sum of £400 and the two several sums of
£50 for each of the said children so long as the same may
continue to be payable, the said E. G. E. L. B. Lytton
has consented to enter into the covenant hereinafter contained for that purpose. Now this Indenture witnesseth
that in pursuance and performance of the said Agreement on the part of the said E. G. E. L. Bulwer, he,
the said E. G. E. L. Bulwer, Doth covenant, promise,
and agree with and to the said Sir F. H. Doyle and Sir

T. G. Cullum, their executors and administrators, by these presents in manner following, that is to say, that notwithstanding the Marriage between him, the said E. G. E. L. Bulwer, and R. A. Bulwer his wife, it shall and may be lawful to and for the said R. A. Bulwer from time to time and at all times hereafter to live separate and apart from him, the said E. G. E. L. Bulwer, in such sort and manner as if she, the said R. A. Bulwer, were sole and unmarried. And that he, the said E. G. E. L. Bulwer, shall not nor will compel the said R. A. Bulwer to live with him, the said E. G. E. L. Bulwer, by any Ecclesiastical censures or proceedings or otherwise howsoever. And that she, the said R. A. Bulwer, shall be absolutely and to all intents and purposes whatsoever freed and discharged from the power, command, will, restraint, authority, and government of him the said E. G. E. L. Bulwer. And that it shall and may be lawful to and for the said R. A. Bulwer from henceforth to have, take, and enjoy to her own separate and absolute use, with full power and disposition by Delivery, Deed, or Will, or any writing of a testamentary purport, notwithstanding, her coverture, All such furniture, wearing apparel, jewels, articles, and things whatsoever in the nature of furniture, wearing apparel, and jewels, as now are or which at any time or times hereafter shall be hers or reputed to be hers. And the said E. G. E. L. Bulwer doth further covenant, promise, and agree with and to the said Sir F. H. Doyle and Sir Thomas G. Cullum, their executors, administrators, and assigns, that he, the said E. G. E. L. Bulwer, will well and truly pay or cause to be paid unto the said Sir F. H. Doyle and Sir T. G. Cullum, or the survivors or survivor of them, or the executors, administrators, or assigns of such survivor, or unto some one of them, during the said Separation the yearly sum of £400 of lawful money of the United Kingdom by even and equal quarterly payments on the 10th day of July, the 10th day of October, the 10th day of January, and the 10th day of April, in every year. And shall and will make the first payment on the 10th day of July now next ensuing, the day of the date of these presents, without deduction or abatement on any account whatsoever, Upon trust that they do and shall thereout, in the first place, indemnify the said E. G. E. L. Bulwer, his executors and administrators, of, from, and against all or any debts, charges, or expenses which shall or may at any time or times during the said Separation be incurred by the said R. A. Bulwer, or which he, the said E. G. E. L. Bulwer, shall or may be liable for or on account or in respect of the said Rosina Anne Bulwer, And subject thereto do and shall, so long only as the said R. A. Bulwer shall live separate from him, the said E. G. E. L. Bulwer, and shall not use or take any ways or means to compel him to live with her by any Ecclesiastical censures or proceedings or otherwise howsoever, or molest, interrupt, or disturb him in anywise howsoever, pay the same sum of £400 or such parts thereof as shall not be applicable for or towards indemnifying the said E. G. E. L. Bulwer in manner hereinbefore mentioned by quarterly payments, to be made on the quarterly days hereinbefore mentioned to such person or persons only and for such intents and purposes only as the said R. A. Bulwer shall, notwithstanding her coverture, from time to time by any writing or writings signed by her with her own hand, but not so as to dispose of or affect the same by any sale, mortgage, or charge, or otherwise in the way of anticipation, direct or appoint, And in default of such direction or appointment, into the proper hands of the said R. A. Bulwer for her sole and absolute use exclusively of the said E. G. E. L. Bulwer. And the said E. G. E. L. Bulwer doth further covenant, promise, and agree with and to the said Sir F. H. Doyle and Sir T. G. Cullum, their executors, administrators, and assigns, that he the said E. G. E. L. Bulwer will, in addition to the aforesaid yearly sum of £400, well and truly pay or cause to be paid unto the said Sir F. H. Doyle and Sir T. G. Cullum, or the survivors or survivor of them, or the executors, administrators, or assigns of such survivor or unto some one of them the yearly sum of £100 of lawful money of the United Kingdom so long as he, the said E. G. E. L. Bulwer, shall consent and agree that both the said children shall remain with the said R. A. Bulwer, and the yearly sum of £50 of like lawful money of the United Kingdom when one of the said children shall have ceased to reside with the said R. A. Bulwer, and so long only as he, the said E. G. E. L. Bulwer, shall consent and agree that the other of such children shall remain with the said Rosina A. Bulwer, The aforesaid sums of £100 or £50, as the case may be, to be paid by even and equal quarterly payments at the days and times hereinbefore mentioned respecting the aforesaid sum of £400, Upon trust that they do and shall pay the aforesaid sum of £100 or £50, as the case may be, by such and the like quarterly payments as are hereinbefore stated respecting the aforesaid annual sum of £400 to the said Rosina Anne Bulwer to enable her to clothe and maintain the aforesaid two children, or one of them, as the case may be, during such time as the said E. G. E. L. Bulwer may consent and agree that both or one of the said children shall remain with her, the said R. A. Bulwer. And in pursuance and performance of the aforesaid Agreement, the said Eliza Barbara Bulwer Lytton doth hereby covenant, promise, and agree with and to the said Sir F. H. Doyle and Sir T. G. Cullum, their executors, administrators, and assigns, that when and so often as any or either of the said payments hereinbefore covenanted to be made by the said E. G. E. L. Bulwer shall be in arrear and unpaid for the space of thirty days next after each of the days of payment hereinbefore particularly named, and after demand thereof, she, the said Eliza Barbara Bulwer Lytton, will well and truly pay or cause to be paid unto the said Sir F. H. Doyle and Sir T. G. Cullum, or the survivors or survivor of them, or the executors or administrators or assigns of such survivor, or unto some one of them, during the aforesaid Separation, and so long only as the debts of the said R. A. Bulwer shall be fully paid by her and shall not exceed the sum of £400 per annum, such sum or sums of money which may be then due and owing by the said E. G. E. L. Bulwer, and to be applied and disposed of according to the true intent and meaning of these presents.

"In Witness whereof," etc.

As will appear from the foregoing, Lady Lytton's
trustees were Sir Francis Hastings Doyle and the
Rev. Sir Thomas Gery Cullum, and for the benefit
of those who are averse to the technicalities of legal
language, I may recapitulate the leading provisions
of a document which bound my unhappy friend for
the term of her natural life, and embittered her remaining years by the tortures inseparable from a condition of abject dependence and grinding poverty.
Four hundred pounds a year, payable during his life,
is the magnificent sum which Mr. Edward Bulwer
thinks sufficient to allow the woman who had been for
nine years his faithful and devoted wife, who had
endured for the sake of her children his infidelity,
violence, and neglect, and whom he had turned out of
his house because she had been the unwilling witness
of one of his numerous intrigues. Fifty pounds a year
is granted to her for each of the two children so long
only as it shall suit his wishes that they shall remain
in her custody ; and out of this sum she is expected
to feed, lodge, clothe, and educate them. She is of
course rigidly prohibited from anticipating, mort-
gaging, or otherwise charging her allowance, and
Mr. Bulwer is careful to protect himself from all
liability for any debts which she may afterwards
incur.   Such were the terms which Mrs. Bulwer
was forced to accept from a husband whose income
was certainly not less than £3,000 or £4,000 a year,*

---

* On page 155, Vol. II., of the Life, Lord Lytton writes : " At
that time " (*i.e.*, in the third year of their marriage) " she and my
father were living in London at the rate of not less than £3,000
a year."   At the date of the separation Mr. Bulwer's income must
have been considerably in excess of this estimate.

and who, in addition, had expectations of the most
definite character of succeeding to the large fortune
and estates of his mother. I may add that the
income tax was subsequently deducted from this
miserable pittance, in spite of the clause which pro-
vides against "deduction or abatement."

In 1857 Lady Lytton writes upon this subject as
follows :

"Surely Lady Cullum cannot forget—or, at all events,
if she does, she will remember it on her deathbed—the
perfect agony with which I for two hours paced her drawing-room at the Green Park Hotel, Piccadilly, saying that
I would not sign that infamously one-sided deed, and how
she followed me with ' You know, dear, Sir Thomas would
not let you do anything against your interests,' until, like
a fool, I was at length cajoled and exhausted into doing
so, and being then young, and cowed by bodily and chronic
fear of that monster, I also dreaded the threat that my
children would be taken away from me if I did not sign
the deed, for it is through my children he has always
tortured me."

It is certainly difficult to imagine how Sir Francis
Doyle could have been induced to agree to the
terms offered by Mr. Bulwer; but his character, as
described by Lady Lytton in "Nemesis," may afford
some explanation of his strange indifference to her
interests :

"He was an elderly gentleman, who, being one of those
thoroughly honourable, high-minded men of the old school,
perfectly incapable of shuffle, quibble, or trick himself, but
withal of an Anglo-Saxon coldness of heart, was doubly
ripe for my cold-blooded scheme, having, moreover, just
recovered from a severe paralytic stroke, and therefore
being totally divested of even his ordinary very homœopa-
thic quantum of shrewdness." '

The interview between Mr. Bulwer and Sir Francis is thus described in "Nemesis:"

"I commenced by placing my handkerchief before my eyes, to hide the tears I ought to have, but could not shed; and said in a tremulous artistically modulated voice: 'My dear sir, I come to you this morning on a painful mission. I need not, I hope, assure you that no one can estimate Rosina's many good and noble qualities more than I do, for nobody can be half so well aware of them as I am; but unfortunately her temper of late—— '

"'Her temper!' interrupted Sir ——, with unfeigned surprise! 'Why, I have always understood you to say, that you thought her temper perfection, but that you did not give her as much credit for it as others might, as you considered it constitutional.'

"'Ah—well—yes—exactly so—but—a—somehow or other of late—she has given way to the most extraordinary fits of jealousy—and—— '

"'Jealousy!' again interrupted Sir ——, 'for which by all accounts she has ample cause; for all the world are talking of your fresh *liaison* with some Miss Deacon, a *ci-devant* governess, and recently the mistress of a Colonel Q——, living at Raven Cottage, Fulham.'

"At this nothing daunted, I seized a large Bible,—for we were in the library,—and solemnly swore upon it that such a report was perfectly unfounded! After which pretty little perjury, I assumed a more bullying, determined, and aggrieved tone, saying, 'But you must be aware, my dear sir, that no man would or could submit to being *watched and followed about* by his wife.'

"'Decidedly not,' replied the orthodox and ever-proper Sir ——.

"'Therefore,' I resumed, 'I have come to the irrevocable resolution of separating from Rosina; but it is more to frighten her than anything else.'

"Sir —— here made a stiff *Amen* sort of bow, supposing that by not offering the slightest resistance to this summary and, at all events, perfectly novel arrangement, he

upheld his relative's dignity. Which perceiving with all
the quickness in which *he*, good easy man, was so totally
deficient, I pulled a paper from my pocket, which, according to my usual mode of proceeding, I had prepared, all in
readiness, and with one of my most hollow parchment smiles,
blandly requested he would sign.

" 'What may this be ?' he inquired.

" ' It is,' I replied, ' that I merely wish you to sign this,
certifying that I have behaved honourably to my wife in
pecuniary matters, as far as my present means will allow.'

" ' And, pray, what allowance *do* you intend making
her ? '

" Rather nervous at naming so paltry a sum after the
rate at which he knew I had been living, lest, obliging as
he had hitherto been in letting me do whatever I pleased
with his cousin, even he should be staggered by such
grovelling meanness, I stammered out, 'Four hundred
pounds a year.'

" ' Four hundred a year !' exclaimed Sir ——, in alto.
'No ; really that *is* too little, considering that you have
been living at the rate of four or five thousand, and she has
been accustomed to every luxury. No, no ; with two
children, I don't see how she can do upon that.'

" ' I feel,' said I, in my most honeyed and plausible tone,
'that it is indeed very little ; but although I make a great
deal of money by writing, that is uncertain, and I have as
yet no tangible property ; and the very fact of my having
lived at the rate I have done makes it now imperative on
me to retrench.'

" ' Well, but,' resumed Sir ——, who began to have a
vague sort of uncomfortable feeling that he had no right to
aid and abet in so completely wrecking three innocent and
defenceless victims, 'you should at least put in a clause
that in the event of your coming into landed property, you
will *then* adequately increase your wife's allowance.'

" ' Oh,' said I, assuming a solemn and tender air of
filial delicacy—though I used occasionally to boast in my
own domestic circle of the manly and amiable exploit of
having '*felled my mother to the earth* '—' Oh, my dear Sir

——,' said I, *avec un air pénetré*, ' much as I should desire
to do so, were I to insert such a clause as *that*, it would not
only be anticipating my mother's death, but assuming that
she must leave me her property, at which she might very
justly be both hurt and offended.'

" This bait of a seeming propriety and delicacy of feeling
of course took with the proper Sir ——.

" ' Oh, my dear Sir ——, you may implicitly rely *upon
my honour* to do everything I ought in money matters the
moment I have the power to do so.'

" With this he actually signed the infamous document I
had prepared. He signed it; and for a moment I felt
almost more paralysed than he was. But when I had
secured it I quitted the house, feeling light and buoyant, as
if I had borrowed Mercury's winged heels.

" I ordered her to leave my house, much as I should
have done my housekeeper or any other servant, merely
adding that nothing would induce me to live with her
any longer; but to my astonishment, instead of the violent
and upbraiding letter I had expected, she wrote me one
calmly cold and temperate, saying that as for separation,
we could not be more separated than we were, but as she
thought it rather too hard, after having borne so much and
so long as she had, with my own statement that she had
been to me '*perfection as a wife*,' *she* should now be turned
adrift, because, foolishly believing in the falsehood of my
illness, she had caught me with my mistress, and that for
her children's sake she would not deprive them of a roof
over their heads, therefore she, being blameless, would *not*
be turned ignominiously out of her home.

" This of course, as attempting to thwart my plans, put
me in a fury, and I resorted to an expedient which, I
hoped, would be a quietus. But no; the silly fool again
wrote to me, and this time it was in an agony, the paper
all blotted with her tears.

" She said : ' If you have no human feeling for, no mercy
upon, *me*, have *some* on your poor helpless children, if I
am in your power. I doubt whether *even* the immoral
clique among whom you live would approve of such very

cowardly and unmanly conduct as that of crushing and
outraging a poor defenceless victim merely because she
was in your power! Remember, too, that when I had it
in my power to crush and expose *you*, *I* shielded and forgave you.'

"My only reply to this latter truth (which as a *truth* I of
course considered an insult) was : 'More fool you not to
have crushed me *when* you had the opportunity, for you
may rely upon it, I will never give you another.'

"After this I believe she hated and despised me so
cordially that she began actually to pant to quit a house
where she had suffered so much ; and things progressed
swimmingly."

On the 14th of June, 1836, Mrs. Bulwer, with her
children, quitted Berrymead, her husband's home,
for ever.

CHAPTER IX.

MRS. BULWER'S POSITION—SHE GOES TO IRELAND, 1836.
—HER CHILDREN TAKEN AWAY, 1838—LIFE AT
BATH.

GREAT as were the troubles of Mrs. Bulwer's married
life, and bitter the sufferings she underwent while
living under her husband's roof, they became almost
insignificant as compared with the squalid misery,
the unremitting persecution, and the mental and
bodily torture she endured after the date of her
separation. For nearly forty-six years was this
unhappy lady condemned to protract her weary
and joyless existence, and during this dismal period
she experienced such a series of unmerited misfortunes, insults, outrages, and disasters, that none
can marvel that her amiable disposition became
soured, her views of life and of human nature
embittered, or that occasionally her agony found
a vent in extravagances which she herself in calmer
moments and under happier circumstances would
have been the first to condemn and repudiate. But
though I do not attempt to defend the tone of some
of her writings, or the virulence of certain of her
utterances, I am confident that when my readers
are made acquainted with the gross provocation
she received, they will pity rather than condemn

a woman whose virtues were all her own, and whose faults were created by the persecutions of others. But to resume. When Mrs. Bulwer left Berry-mead she went over to Ireland to live with Miss Greene, the woman who was once, according to his own views, Mr. Bulwer's bitter enemy, but who afterwards became his subservient and devoted tool.

"Things having proceeded thus far," writes Lady Lytton in "Nemesis," "my wife, poor wretch, was sadly put to it where to find a shelter on the beggarly pittance she now had *pour tout potage*, and hearing the sister kingdom was very cheap, and still wishing to serve the pious Bible-and-baby lady whom she had, much against my will, harboured for seven years, told her to write and ask her sister, a widow, who was living rent free in a large house, what she would take her and her two poor little children for, the one being nearly seven, the other four, without even a maid, stating at the same time how crippled she was in means. The modest reply was 'three hundred and fifty pounds a year,' which my wife, knowing nothing about that sort of living, acceded to, though this sum was not to include coals! I may here state that though I of course made a great favour of letting my wife have the children, whom I detested, and whom, even if I had not done so, no man likes being bored with at that age, I generously allowed her an additional £100 a year, so that after the £350 paid to the pious Bible-and-baby lady's sister, she would have the munificent sum of £150 a year to educate and clothe herself and her children ; for this I knew to be the real way of keeping her out of society, the true and only crusher.

"At this crisis, the lawyers told her she should make out a list of what plate she wanted. She said if such was her *right*, let them exact it ; but if it were a favour, she would perish before she would accept a glass of water from me. They said it was doubly her right. She then, feeling it was absurd to take plates or dishes, or even salvers, when she could not afford plate powder to clean them, only put down what the lawyer laughed at as a too modest list— viz., twelve spoons and forks of each sort ; but when it was submitted to me I drew a line through it, saying *half* a dozen were quite enough for her and her brats. But this story getting wind and telling considerably against me, I cleverly ordered a silver gilt breakfast service at what is now Hunt and Roskell's, but was then Storr and Mortimer's, and gave out that it was a parting gift to my wife, as if *she* would have accepted it, though I really intended it as a present to Mrs. Beaumont, and it afterwards figured both at my Pompeian house and at my *déjeûners* at Raven Cottage. My wife foolishly refused to accept the six spoons and forks ; nor did she take a single thing out of my house with the exception of *one*, which I shall mention presently. It is customary in cases of separation to pay the first quarter of a wife's alimony, as the lawyers call it, in advance, but such laxity of pocket was foreign from my habits ; therefore I did not pay hers till three months after it was due, and as there were no railways or cheap travelling in those days, and all I had doled out for her long journey, with four persons, was £40, she found herself so hard run that she actually took the unpardonable liberty of selling an old travelling chariot, for which she only got £10 ; but this gave me an opportunity of inveighing amain against her sordid and grasping disposition. Poor wretch ! had these two (in my estimation) prudent virtues figured among her catalogue of qualities, she never would have given me the power of crushing out her heart, and trampling upon it, as I have done.

"So my wife, having arrived at the ' miserable goal of her journey,' proceeded to do her best to become reconciled to her sadly changed circumstances. The neighbouring people called upon her, and she returned their visits ; but she felt too wretched, broken-hearted, and it may be too ashamed of her *locale* to accept their invitations until Miss Greene told her that, as a matter of principle, she was acting extremely wrong in retiring from the world, for with such an unscrupulous, unfeeling villain to deal with, and also for the sake of her children, she ought to appear as much in society as possible. She at length yielded, and, from long habit and a foolish sensitiveness and over-delicacy of fearing to hurt other people's feelings, in the case of relatives or very intimate friends with whom she could take such a liberty, she used privately to beg of them to include Miss Greene in their invitations, though, being herself now only on sufferance in society and no longer a personage with a fine house to ask them to in return, she could not venture upon anything of the kind with mere acquaintances ; and, indeed, the friends and relations very soon grew restive under such an infliction, and used to appeal against it with an imploring 'My dear Rosina, it is very hard we cannot have the pleasure of seeing you and your children without always being hampered with your *verd antique.*'

"As time went on Miss Greene began to show the cloven hoof. First she (Mrs. Bulwer) was taxed with having made a perfect lodging-house-keeper of Mrs. B——, Miss Greene's widowed sister, because fine people and fine carriages not only called on Mrs. Bulwer, but added insult to injury by leaving cards or invitations, as the case might be, for her and none for Mrs. B—— or Miss Greene. Then other and more portentous signs of the times manifested themselves; for instance, Mrs. Bulwer felt naturally annoyed when her children began to call that antidote, or rather bane, Miss Greene 'Aunt,' and when she would return to Mrs. B——'s after a visit of a fortnight to some country house, she would be greeted on her return by the poor little unconscious accomplices of the conspiracy with 'Oh, Mamma, look here! wasn't it so kind of Auntie to give me this doll!' or 'this pony!' or what-ever the thing might be, which Mrs. Bulwer had either sent or given Miss Greene the money expressly to buy for them. In the course of two miserable years (1836-38) this under-mining system increased to such a degree, and the children were getting too big to be any longer subjected to such vulgar associations with impunity, and were, moreover

with alarming rapidity acquiring the peculiar accent and
dialect of the country, that my wife determined to change
her quarters. So having met two ladies who spoke highly
of the cheapness and abundance of good masters in a
certain magnificent provincial city in England (Bath), also
of the goodness of the houses and the excellence of the
market, and added that if they would club their three
incomes together, how much better they could live; and,
moreover, the eldest would take all trouble of housekeeping
off her hands; these ladies being the orphan daughters
of a field officer, and both their parents having held a high,
respectable, and respected position in society, my wife
thought she was perfectly safe in *monté*-ing a menage with
them, and truly thought it would be a reciprocal advantage to all; for though she greatly disliked settling down
in an English provincial town, yet, as beggars cannot be
choosers, she resolved to make a virtue of necessity.
Above all, she hailed the plan as giving her a fair and
legitimate opening for *congédié*-ing Miss Greene, which
she did by telling her that for the sake of masters she was
about removing to England, and that as the children's
education would now begin to be onerous, she could no
longer afford to retain Miss Greene as a fixture, but would
be happy occasionally to receive her as a guest. Whereupon the antique vestal not only showed the whole of
her cloven foot to an enormous extent, but lashed out her
tail into the bargain for drawing up the whole length of
her fifty-six winters. She replied, that 'she hoped she
knew her duty too well to refuse to give up the children
unless *both* parents *agreed* to take them from her.' Here
was a thunderbolt of insolence and ingratitude with a
vengeance, as the wretched mother was not till then
aware that *her* children were in Miss Greene's custody.
Nor were they, but the pious spinster knew very well that
in being guilty of this unfeeling and unparalleled outrage
to the woman who had sheltered and befriended her for
years, she was playing a sure card. So that very night
she wrote to me, saying it grieved her to the heart to
observe that 'my wife was now what she never used to be,

,

wholly given up to the world, and therefore neglected
her children, for which reason *she* could not bear the idea
of entrusting them to her alone, as she was going with two
strangers, whose acquaintance she had only recently made,
to live in England, but that if I would give her a house,
however small, and only £50 a year, *she* would take them.'
This was hitting the right nail on the head, appealing at
one blow to my two ruling passions, vindictiveness and
avarice; in short, my patron the devil had thus unex-
pectedly thrust upon me an infernal stretch of power, in
which even *I*, devoid of every human feeling, of honour,
probity, or nature, as I was, would never have dared to
take the initiative and grasp! I instantly, and by return
of post, closed with her only too tempting offer; ordering
my wife at the same time to be officially informed that till
I knew *where* she meant to live I could not think of leaving
my children with her; for whenever I had occasion to
torture her, it's astonishing how punctilious my sense
of *paternal duty* became. Of course I was instantly
besieged by letters of appeal against such unheard-of
tyranny and cruelty; but as Faust had always Mephistopheles at his elbow to incline more and more the downward
plane for him, so that sublimest of rascals, my attorney, ever
ready to take any sudden journey in the way of spying,
or any other dirty work, was always at mine, instigating
all my schemes of villainy; for without such unscrupulous
assistance it is not every man, with all the desire in the
world, who is aware to what lengths of infamy the law
allows him to go. So it was formally proposed to my
victim that if she would sign a bond pledging herself never
to dine out or drink tea, or even turn the corner of the
street in which she lived, I might consent to allow her
children to remain with her a little longer. She, poor
fool, was actually going eagerly to do this; but her lawyer,
seeing through the black quibble, and resenting so insane
a piece of tyranny, would not allow her to do so; and
Loaden and I, fearing that the impertinent world might
begin to talk of these cruel and repeated outrages upon
a blameless wife by so notorious and unscrupulous a

profligate as myself, we concocted another impossible facility, that is, he wrote to say that with *my usual kind consideration for her feelings*—for he was the greatest adept I ever saw at thickly and smoothly spreading out the grossest possible insult, and then sprinkling it with the cantharides of ironical civility and compassion—I would allow her to see her children once a month for half an hour, with Miss Greene in the room, but never alone. This was, of course, indignantly rejected, and the poor young victims were torn from the only parent who had a human feeling for them, to be starved morally and physically with Miss Greene, with whom, however, they would have the *one* thing that I thought needful instilled into them, viz., to have their father puffed into a demi-god, and that *his* commandments were to be obeyed even before those of God ; while their too deeply injured mother's name was never to be mentioned to them, as if it had been a crime more heinous than any forbidden in the Decalogue, which, in truth, was a work of fiendish supererogation, as the mere monstrous, unnatural, and unpardonable fact of bringing up children away from a mother whose moral conduct has given no warrant for such an outrage is quite enough to erase all natural affection from their hearts, for it is impossible to love those whom we never see, and the fondest memories of whom, all things possible and almost impossible are done to obliterate and to desecrate. Meanwhile the new triumvirate, Loaden, Miss Greene, and myself, gave out that the children were placed with her by the consent of *both* their parents. Such a very likely story that *any* mother would consent to have her children taken from her and consigned to the custody of a base and ungrateful traitress."

Mrs. Bulwer's children were accordingly taken from her and handed over to the mercies of Miss Greene in 1838. The son was at this time about six years old ; and, except for about four months subsequent to his mother leaving the lunatic

asylum in 1858, when he induced her to go
abroad, all personal intercourse between them may
be said to have terminated from this date. The
daughter, aged about ten, was permitted the like
restricted communication with her mother that
was provided by her father's "kind consideration."
She died in 1848, under circumstances that will
be best described hereafter in the words of an
eye-witness.

The bereaved and desolate mother quitted Ireland
in February 1838, and took up her residence at
Bath with the two ladies I have mentioned above.
With the fatal ill-fortune which seemed constantly to
pursue her, she speedily found that her choice of
companions had been anything but judicious. The
family consisted of three persons: Miss Katherine,
the elder sister,

" ' A feather-bed sample of obese plainness,' Miss Bella,
the younger, ' a skewer-like specimen of ugliness,' and an
uncouth *bon vivant* of a brother. Miss Katherine was an
excellent *menagère*, always providing the things that everybody liked, and as each morning Mrs. Bulwer used to give
her money for the daily expenditure, of which she would
render a satisfactory account, with the change all *en règle*,
she very naturally was rejoicing in the luxurious idea of
paying ready money for everything and not owing a
shilling. Her fat friend, moreover, was kind and *préve-
nante*, and always supplied her with the earliest violets,
the most premature lilies of the valley, and the most
precocious peaches. However, when the first quarter's
rent came to be paid, which was, according to their
covenant, to be paid by three general contributions, some
delay had happened to the Miss B——s' dividends; and
they were obliged, though ' very reluctantly,' to trouble
Mrs. Bulwer to settle the whole amount. Of this she
thought nothing; but when the next quarter came round,

and even a third, and the same hitch again occurred, she began to feel not quite so comfortable, as the house was a larger one than she should have liked alone to be liable for. But she consoled herself with thinking that, at all events, all the other household expenses, for food, etc., were duly and regularly paid.

"Shortly after this, there was a fearful quarrel between the brother and sisters; and Mrs. Bulwer, who had seen enough of the trio to be convinced that they certainly did not add to her respectability, said, that as such constant disputes were very distressing and unpleasant to her, and as there was always some difficulty about paying the rent, she thought it would be much better that they should separate. Miss Bella said, she and her brother had thoughts of going abroad, but that nothing would induce them to live with their eldest sister. This quarrel occurred at night after a ball, when the brother was more than half-seas over, which, from his being a sailor, some persons might have considered merely professional, more especially as he looked yard-arms and cats-of-nine-tails at the unfortunate Katherine, and hiccupped out the most dreadful innuendoes about her, which she was by no means backward in recriminating, in much more explicit terms.

"When, in a few days after, Miss Bella and her brother, to Mrs. Bulwer's great satisfaction, took their departure, she had to undergo a dreadful scene with Miss Katherine, who on her knees, with a perfect cataract of tears, implored her not to turn her out of the house, as she had no earthly place to go to, whereupon my wife, who was always a fool at the appearance of distress, whether real or assumed, reluctantly consented to her remaining three months longer, but said she positively then *must* seek some other place, as she was going to remove into a smaller house, which she did immediately, but had not been there three weeks before Miss Katherine came one day, in an agony of tears, to know if she could, to save her from ruin, lend her for two months £100? Now she knew that an old lady, the widow of a relation of mine, who had come down to see my wife, had made her a present of that sum, otherwise it would

have been in vain to ask for it; and the story Miss
Katherine concocted was, that an undertaker was about
to arrest *her* for the expenses of her father and mother's
funerals, who had died within three months of each other.
'Well, but surely,' said my wife, 'they would have come
upon the executors for those, or, at all events, upon your
brother and sister also, and not you *alone ?*' 'Oh!' replied
the Greek, not Grecian daughter, 'one of the executors is
since dead, the other is abroad; no one knows where
Collingwood and Bella are; and so they have come upon
me, I being here, and the only tangible one.' 'Well, but,'
said my wife, still hesitating, 'how *can* you repay me in
two months? and if you do not, it will put me to terrible
inconvenience.' She then had recourse to another falsehood, asserting that there were £134 that she *must* receive
in less than seven weeks. At this, and another Niagara of
tears, my silly wife wrote her a cheque for the money;
but albeit, unused to the sort of Rothschild grandeur of
having a whole spare hundred pounds at her banker's,
she made a mistake, and first wrote a cheque, dating it at
two months' distance, for the quarterly £100 due to her
by me; but Miss Katherine immediately perceived the
mistake, and called her attention to it, whereupon she
crumpled it up and flung it very foolishly into the fireplace,
instead of tearing it, and then wrote another draft for the
available £100, merely saying, 'Pay to Miss Katherine
B—— or bearer the sum of one hundred pounds—
£100.' The two months soon came round, and brought
January; and as the old lady who had given her the £100
had passed the Christmas with my wife, and a gentleman,
a widower, whose wife had been exceedingly kind to Mrs.
Bulwer when she was at Mrs. B——'s, it was very lucky
that she was not quite alone to meet the pitiless storm that
was about to burst upon her devoted head; for although
—— January had come, it had *not* brought the £134 which
Miss B—— was so *positively* to have received, and so all
Mrs. Bulwer could do was to urge her strongly to try and
get it immediately, as Christmas bills are always heavy,
and to write for her own quarterly £100. But what was her

horror and consternation when her own *two* cancelled
cheques were returned to her, with a civil letter, saying
that *both* had been presented and cashed, the allowance
one only within the last two days! Had my wife been the
culprit, she could not have turned more deadly pale. The
letter fell from her hand; the room seemed to swim; she
tottered to the bell, and desired Miss B—— might be sent
to her; when she came, and my wife, unable to utter a word,
merely held out the two cancelled cheques to her, the
wretched creature fell upon her knees, confessed all, shriek-
ing out rather than speaking: 'Oh! save me! save me!'
'I don't know that it is in my power to do so,' said the
latter; and the back drawing-room, where this terrible scene
was going on, being only separated from the other by
folding doors, the old lady and the gentleman, who were
both sitting there after breakfast, came rushing in on hearing her screams; and when she herself had told them what
she had done, they were furious against her, and insisted
that the law should take its course. 'No, not if I can help
it,' said Mrs. Bulwer, and then added sternly, turning
to the still kneeling woman, 'But out of this house you
must go *instantly*, and never under any pretext enter it
again.'

"After this she hurried up to her own room and wrote a
letter to the London banker, who happened to be a personal
friend of hers, saying how sorry she was for the *mistake*
which had occurred, and begging him to tell his cashier
that it was an oversight of hers, that the money was
all right! and she would explain to him (the banker) the
whole affair when she saw him in town. On going down
to dinner, she inquired whether Miss B—— was gone? the
servant said no, that she was not in a state to go. 'Then,'
said my wife, 'you had better send for a doctor.'

"'Doctor, indeed!' echoed the old lady and the gentleman
in the same breath; 'we have sent for two policemen, for
brandy seems to be her only complaint, which now fully
accounts for the palsied tremulousness of her hands;' and
of course the servants, who, according to their usual habit,
'never warn one till the deed is done,' had now plenty

to tell my wife of her horrible and long-standing habits
of intoxication.

"But this was only the beginning of the drama; no
sooner had the police removed her from the house to
that of a relation of hers in the town, than the plot began
to thicken, and the very next day bills from all quarters
came showering in—from butchers, bakers, poulterers,
fishmongers, fruiterers, etc., etc., not one of whom she
had paid for the last twelve months. The only fortunate
individuals who had been paid were the upholsterers,
who had ministered to the comforts of 'the ministry;'
and to them, it would appear, had been devoted the
amounts of the fancy bills of which my wife had been
in the habit of receiving the change. At this discovery
she was naturally very angry with the tradespeople for
having given Miss B—— such long credit, without ever
apprising or applying to her for their bills, as they
must have supposed that *she* would not go on so long
without paying them. Their reply was that they *knew*
she gave Miss B—— ready money for everything; and
that therefore they did not think she was ever legally
bound to pay them; and that as long as Miss B——
continued in my wife's house, they had not the heart to
worry her about their bills, feeling sure (Miss B——'s
parents having lived so long in the town, and having been
in every way so honourable and so highly respected)
that Miss B—— herself would make it all right in
time. I might now indeed well call my wife 'poor
wretch,' for she groaned, and covered her face with her
hands, as she said, 'I don't know whether I am bound
in *law* or not to pay you; but I am in honour, and if
you will only give me *time*, I will do so to the uttermost
farthing.' To which they not only acceded, but many
of them even offered to lend her money, on no security
but her simple word, so much did they feel for the
cruel position in which she was placed; and besides those
poor tradespeople, there were other good, aye actively
good Samaritans in that town, who were never weary of
doing real kindnesses for her, and, what is far more

wonderful, amid such a black whirlpool of treachery and ingratitude as this world is, have remained good, and true, and actively kind to her ever since.

"Meanwhile the old lady, wound up by so many screw propellers, actually (though she came of the same stock—or *stocks?*—as that other old lady who, when she fell among thieves, exclaimed in an agony, 'Oh! good Mr. Highwayman! for heaven's sake take my life, but spare my money'), seeing the terrible urgency of the case, lent my wife £400 for six months; and in order to repay her, Mrs. Bulwer was driven to commit scribbledom, a crime which, as the sequel will show, I registered a vow never to forget or forgive.

"Meanwhile it must not be supposed that Loaden and I slept at our posts, though ordinary mortals might think that from such an influx of misfortunes coming on a poor injured creature whom I had turned out of her home because, not content with being for nine years one of the most tyrannical and profligate husbands in London, I, at the end of that time, thought fit to rid myself even of the nominal shackles of marriage—it might be thought, I say, that having thrown her on a cruel world out of the lap of luxury to struggle with all the temptations and, far worse, all the tramplings and tyrannies of poverty, while my vice was revelling in gilded rooms, I should feel some touch of conscience, some twinge of remorse, for having flung her into such a fearful arena. But the very reverse was the case. So the moment I heard of her misfortunes, which, thanks to the subtly organised system of espionnage I have kept up towards her ever since I turned her out of her home, I did as soon as they occurred, I instantly sent Loaden down to Bath, thinking that as Miss B—— had got her into debt all over the place, the people would be only too glad to say or do anything against her. But, unfortunately, we reckoned without our host; for not only did every one speak well of her, but when, as a *pis aller*, he then tried to asperse her character by going to the house where she had lodged, and, after taking the most minute topographical survey of the rooms, asking the woman of the house, with a sneering smile, 'if *the gentle-man* who had been here on a visit at Christmas had not slept in the room next my wife's, although the door of communication was *apparently* nailed up?' 'Oh dear, no,' said the woman; 'Mrs. F——r, the old lady, slept there; and the gentleman slept upstairs.' But when Loaden hinted to her that it would be much more to her interest to transpose the geography of the bedrooms, the honest creature indignantly turned him out of the house; but nothing daunted, as he found it hopeless to attempt to get up any conspiracy against her *there*, he actually, to insult and outrage her,—and considering how stringently I had tied her up, so as that she could not run me in debt a shilling, it *was the* very grossest outrage,—put an advertisement in all the county papers, warning the tradespeople not to trust her, as if she had been the runaway wife of a grocer or a cheesemonger; and on his return to London, to amuse his fellow-passengers in the mail, he brought her name on the *tapis* by inquiring if they had heard the late terrible swindling case at *Bath?* and then talked of her terrible habits of intoxication, and how much her charming and gifted husband was to be pitied. An impromptu stroke of genius this on the part of Loaden, which I so much admired, that a year after, when I sent him on an embassy of special espionnage abroad, I ordered him again to have recourse to it, and have ever since pursued the same plan with immense success; for in this way I can get every and any lie disseminated and keep myself cautiously out of the scrape, and at the same time give double force to the calumnies, because when those who are made the innocent propagators of them add, 'Oh! I heard it in a steamboat or on a railway,' why the sequence must be, that it is a matter so notorious, as to be the public talk."

CHAPTER X.

SIR EDWARD BULWER—he had been made a baronet in 1838—had now succeeded, as we have seen, in driving his unfortunate wife to a condition bordering upon desperation. Her children had been torn from her and entrusted to the care of a woman whom, rightly or wrongly, she despised and detested; her character had been mercilessly defamed by his agents; her almost penniless condition had been brutally thrown in her face by advertisements in the public press; insult, indeed, had been heaped upon injury to such an extent that it was idle for him to expect consideration from one to whom he had denied not only mercy and forbearance, but common humanity. Owing to the circumstances I have already detailed, Lady Lytton's meagre allowance was wholly inadequate to discharge the debts she had incurred by her own generosity and ignorance of the darker side of human nature, and in her distress the unfortunate lady endeavoured to turn her talents to account by writing for a livelihood, a resolve which entailed upon her a persecution of tenfold bitterness.

Lady Lytton possessed abilities of a very high order, as she had already proved by various fugitive writings; and, under favourable circumstances, there is little reason to doubt that she would have achieved respectable, if not brilliant, success. She had passed very much of her time among literary personages, and, instigated perhaps by their example, had produced work which had excited warm admiration of the most competent critics ; even her husband had condescended to praise her talents, and had certainly made use of them considerably to his own advantage. I may here insert a few early letters of the noted Miss Landon, who seems to have had a very high opinion of Miss Wheeler and her attractions, both mental and physical.

FROM MISS LANDON TO MISS R. WHEELER.

"About 1825.

" Many thanks, my dearest Rosina, for your kind letter. Glad I am to hear from Miss Spence that this epistle will not find you in Somerset Street ; ay, glad, for sick am I of the utter cold worldliness, whose prudence is but the decent password of selfishness, which would say such affectionate, such disinterested friendship can be without its reward. I shall enclose this to Miss Spence, as I have just now such constant opportunity of sending backwards and forwards, leading just now a very pretty, pleasant, and peaceable life. You must pardon my want of *les frais de conversation*—'news.' I have eaten, drunk, and talked quite as much, and peradventure a little more than ever St. Denis did after his head was cut off. The only heavy misfortune befell me at Harrowgate, where I got wet through, and my bonnet spoilt, and verily my rural tastes are not even yet sufficiently developed to prefer the cottage shape, which has succeeded, generally speaking.

' Je suis bel esprit,
Et n'ai de sentiment que pour mes ecrits.'

But *this* I did feel very deeply ; add to this, I caught cold

in one eye, which was for a week poulticed and eclipsed by
a black handkerchief tied over half my face, and not at all
resembling

> ' Such mask as shades
> The face of young Arabian maids,
> A mask that leaves but one eye free
> To do its best in witchery.'

I had a very pleasant day the day I went to Leeds, a town
where the spirit of steam has erected its shrine. On our
first approach I began to anticipate another drenching, ' so
darkly gloomed the thunder-cloud upon the distant hill ; '
but I spouted Scott and anathematized Coles in vain—it all
ended in smoke. I do not know whether the Leeds people
are a very godly race, but of this I am sure, they are out
of sight of heaven. I think it would be a question well
worthy the notice of their philosophical society whether
there *is* a sky above the place or not. The only thing
resembling an adventure was that I nearly murdered an
old woman by almost breaking her neck down the steps
of a cellar which seems placed in all the streets at Leeds
to endanger the lives of her Majesty's subjects ; but
old women never *do* die, so we mutually escaped with
a fright and a shake. I was very much amused with the
exhibition ; there were some good pictures, and the
common quantity of portraits, doing their *possible* to look
fine and foolish : one in particular haunted me—'a lady,'
who must have either been Lady Mayoress of Leeds, or
else have kept its principal inn, one who must have been
the death of the unfortunate man who drew her, one of
those red and yellow dames whose clothes and complexion
are all of a cast. I had *un petit accès de fièvre* contem-
plating her crimson gown and more crimson cheek.   I
think artists might with great justice make the same complaint with the author of ' Rouge et Noir,' and say of their
sitters, as he does of his countrywomen landing at Calais,
' florid and flushed, sea-sick and sea-green.' The ugliest
come on purpose to disgrace us. We have passed divers
rural days, dining in woods, etc., to my taste more
picturesque than pleasant ; while a chair and a table are to

hand, I shall infinitely prefer them, in their rosewood and mahogany shapes, to making a chair of a stump, a table of my knees, and, *par conséquence*, a tablecloth of my frock. Much as I like my relations, I prefer taking my dinner with any than my *ants;* and, I am afraid, in spite of the poetry of the place, prefer water from a pump to water from the prettiest spring that ever showed the mud at the bottom of its clear depths. And now for a parting charge. Take care of yourself. Remember the old proverb, backing itself with all the authority of Ecclesiastes, 'Love thine own soul; comfort thine own heart; for sorrow hath killed many, and there is no profit therein.' I am sure for myself, were I asked which of all my actions I repented most, I should say, 'My good ones.' Experience, as far as mine goes, has read me a lesson of so much disgust, that I really do sometimes lament I have no means of becoming desperately wicked, in order to ensure every advantage of life. But I must say good-bye, dearest Rosina.

"Your very affectionate

"LETITIA ELIZABETH LANDON.

"P.S.—Write to me, my own love, and that soon. *Encore adieu, belle des belles.*"

MISS LANDON TO MISS R. WHEELER.

"13th October, 1825,

"I have regular classifications for all my acquaintance; but truly, *ma charmante et belle Rose*, I know not under what denomination to class you. I cannot class you among pretty young ladies whose qualifications are scorns, silliness, and simpers, who go the length of news and nonsense; neither can I content myself by only niching you among the beauties, who deem to look is to live; neither can I class you among the blues (for all you do quote Latin), all books, barbarisms, and bores. You must go therefore unclassed. But this is a preamble for my objection to a character I understand Miss Benger has pointed out for yours, Lady Delacour. I admit the beauty, grace, wit, *esprit de billet;* but these are only sparkling ornaments.

You have such in common ; it was no mental Sir Thomas
Lawrence that drew such portrait of you : at least, to me it
is unsatisfactory. I am dazzled by Lady Delacour, but I
could not love her ; for there is an unattractiveness about
her, nothing of that tenderness and gentleness which is the
poetry of woman. I have even thought Lady Delacour
resembled one of those roses formed of precious stones we
read of in fairy lore, but where in such a flower is the
fragrance, the freshness of my charming Rose ? I have Mrs.
Roberts on my side to testify to the likeness of your
portrait. I shall take the pet and pout if you thus depre-
ciate my pictorial talents.

"This letter has lain at this point for nearly two days.
I have had one of my most violent headaches, but am
sufficiently recovered now to fairly write your patience out
of pocket. Shall I not meet you at Miss Spence's next
Wednesday week ? I hope and trust so, so pray go. I
rely upon it, and you could not have the heart to dis-
appoint me. But perhaps I may see you before. I have
written to solicit the honour of the aforesaid lady's company
on the Wednesday previous to her own show. I have
taken it into my head I could form a very decent menagerie,
but really I have not time to hunt up what would make
a regular shilling-a-head exhibition, so I do not rate next
Wednesday above a twopenny sight, but if you would come, I
should forthwith raise the value to sixpence ; but, badinage
apart, I do want to see you. I want you to come that
evening to urge another request—that of spending a whole
day with me *tête-à-tête*. Am I not greedy ? So you must
come next Wednesday. As to your epigram, I am
delighted with it, and could not resist showing it and the
caricature to Mr. Jerdan, who says he will submit to your
'braining him with a Latin quotation' if you will not
assassinate him with an epigram, and at the same time
asserts he thinks it too bad and too exorbitant of you to
be both the beauty and the wit.

"I am happy to tell you, you are nearly dead. When I
next see you, I will show you the portrait of your lover ;
but I won't send it you, as it may be an inducement to

come. I have heard from my brother, and tidings of the picture. It was put with his things by mistake, and taken into the country, instead of being sent to you. I saw Mrs. Roberts the day before yesterday; if you were not yourself, I should quite hate you as my rival there.

"God bless you, my dearest Rosina.

"Your truly attached

"LETITIA ELIZABETH LANDON.

"Wednesday.

"Miss R. Wheeler,

"Sir John Doyle, Bart.,

"Somerset Street, Portman Square."

MISS LANDON TO MISS R. WHEELER.

"*October,* 1825.

"Many thanks, *ma belle Rose,* for your most entertaining of epistles. If it were for vanity alone, you should write to me : a letter is *un vrai trésor de campagne ;* and, believe me, affection has no point of distance so enhancing as absence— not but that I have a very proper appreciation of your presence. Dearest Rosina, why do you end your letter with ' as impossible as that I should ever be happy ' ? it makes me more melancholy than suits my style of face ; how well I remember the first time I *saw* you (I do not count our introduction anything), gay, brilliant, like the personification of your diamond cross, taking a mortal shape for mortal eyes. I went home envying you, not the envy that would have robbed you of either curls, colour, or cross, but that pleasant kind of desiring *admirativeness* which wishes nature had cast you in such a mould. I had such a wish to see you again, and now I will not be disappointed. Happy you must be. To quote an old and elegant proverb, ' good luck knocks once at everybody's door ;' if it has yet to knock at yours, *tant mieux.* You do not enjoy pleasure unless you appreciate it, and it is only by previous want we can appreciate possession. In spite of the miseries of human life—and their name is Legion—I do also most firmly believe every pain has its twin pleasure ; your best part of life is to come. I have but small taste for the reminiscences of childhood, standing in the corner with a certain paper pyramid, boxes on the ear, bread-and-water, stocks and dumb-bells, grammar with all its auxiliary horrors, geography with its twin brother history, two monsters at a birth, and that climax the multiplication table. Out upon lamenting the childish hours of *a, b, c,* and 1, 2, 3! No, *carissima,* I will tell you what you must do : marry, by all means; and marry well. *Dieu de l'amour* forbid I should desire you to change Miss into Mrs. on the strength of a set of diamonds, a Brussels lace dress, and a coach and four, but I must say in calculating matrimonial *agrémens* the most important are those which will outlive the honeymoon. I have no faith in the happiness of love matches: marriage should be a treaty in which every concession is duly weighed, every article carefully examined ; and how can this be done when every object is seen through the magnifying, diminishing, or rose-coloured glasses of love's observatory ? Marry, *ma charmante Rose,* and your London season will be the wonder of the *Morning Post,* and in the country your husband will be returned member for the county on the strength of his wife's popularity. You must not expect much detail from me. Since I last wrote I have been quite a round of dinner-parties, very pleasant to myself, but very indescribable ; it will not be very entertaining to hear how very fine the pines were at one place, and how very good the ice was at another, and that at one the table was so covered with gold plate, that I began to look somewhat anxiously for a dish that had something in it, with the old epigram running in my head,

> ' Your pride, but not your victuals, spare,—
> I came to eat and not to stare.'

I can assure you my canvassing powers are held in no small estimation by my young cousins, for I have actually, by dint of quips and quirks and wreathed smiles, persuaded an old gentleman near to give a ball at his house. I have really been very happy since I have been down here, I have met with so much kindness, and glad as I shall be to see 'the friends I left behind,' I shall be very truly sorry to say good-bye to Aberford. I calculate on returning in about a fortnight. I am most truly sorry I cannot ascribe any Irish conquest *à mes beaux yeux*, for I have neither seen nor heard of Mr. O'Driscol ; it is really very unfortunate that my conquests are something like the passage to the South Pole or Wordsworth's cuckoo, ' talked of, but never seen.' Pray write again ; it is a charity, a pleasure, and a favour to me. I have not written a line of poetry since here I arrived, so your unfortunate lover lies with only one curl and an eye finished ; I fear he must wait for London polishing. I am glad you liked my portraits.

> " ' Farewell : be pleasures, like the air you breathe,
>   Constant around you ; would I had a gift,
>   A fairy gift of happiness and hope,
>   And I would share it with you.'

> "Your most affectionately attached
>   " LETITIA ELIZABETH LANDON.

"There is nothing in future so wonderful but I will be-lieve it. Thomson married ! who has made such a dying speech and confession of a forlorn hope. Well,

> ' Loving goes by haps ;
>   Some Cupids kill with arrows, some with traps.'

But what, in the name of matches, did he kill with ? You must remember me most affectionately to dear Mrs. Roberts. Hope you'll excuse the wafer."

The following Ode may be read not only with interest, but admiration. It was written by Lady Lytton in 1833, at the Hotel Vittoria, Naples, and appeared in " Fraser's Magazine," April, 1838.

" ANACREONTIC."

1.

> " Bring me the purple wine !
>   The bright Falernian bring ;
>   And myrtle fetters twine
>   To chain the boy-god's wing !

If he unruly proves,
　　Invokes his mother's doves,
Or scorns our soft control,
　　Plunge, plunge him in the bowl!

II.

" I'll drink the rosy draught;
　　Venus shall smile to see,
Soon as the god I've quaffed,
　　The urchin's pranks in me,
And wish she had sooner smiled
　　Ere I had stolen her child.

III.

" Lesbia no more shall fling
　　Her scornful glance at me;
Arm'd with the tyrant's wing,
　　'Tis my turn to be free!
I'll barb his keenest dart,
　　And when I've pierced her heart
I'll leave her to her fate,
　　Sighing, ' *It is too late !* '

IV.

" Thais, whose every look
　　Was stolen from Love of yore,
Shall give back all she took,
　　And vow to steal no more.
Thus charms, the most Divine,
　　By right of love are mine!

V.

" And cold Ianthe, too,
　　Blanch'd in Diana's beam,
Whose pale cheek never grew
　　Bright with the heart's warm stream,
Shall woo Endymion now,
　　With kisses on my brow,
And leave the chaste, cold moon
　　To bask in Love's warm noon!

VI.

" But for the Nubian maid,
Who gave me love of old,
I'll seek the almond shade,
And pay her back tenfold,
Till mighty Jove above
Shall envy us our love !

VII.

"Sweet Love—young Mirth—bright Wine !
Take, take them all away !
Yet no—I feel Love's mine :
He in my heart must stay ;
Breathe a Lydian measure,
Steep my soul in pleasure :
Soft Sleep her balm now brings ;
Down, Love! keep still thy wings !"

Lady Lytton told me that Walter Savage Landor *
said to her he would rather have written these lines
than all the works he had composed.

Lady Lytton accordingly wrote her first novel,
" Cheveley," and began to treat for its publication.
Naturally enough, her husband soon heard the news ;
and did all in his power to prevent its issue by
endeavouring to intimidate the authoress.

Sir Edward's threats were, of course, treated with
the contempt they merited, for, as Lady Lytton
continues :—

"She was at that time writhing in every fibre of her
heart under the first effects of the vile conspiracy about
her children, whose distant periodical letters were beginning
to assume the measured curtness and coldness derived
from passing through the joint infernal machine of Miss
Greene's dictation and their father's supervisal, so that on
hearing of his menaces the only effect they had upon her
was to nerve her arm, with the strength of a Judith, into

* See Appendix, III.

drawing the strong sword of defiance and flinging away the scabbard; and the *only* reply she vouchsafed to it was to write to Mr. Bull, her publisher, telling him to hurry the publication of her book. But in reply, he wrote in great consternation, saying that Sir Edward had come into his shop the preceding day, and said that *he* did not care what Lady Bulwer published, but that *her* relations would not hear of her publishing anything, and that her cousin, Sir F. Doyle, positively insisted that the book in question should *not* be published, and therefore Mr. Bull must discontinue the printing of it! Now, though Mr. Bull, with his long experience of publishing business, did not exactly see what earthly right relations, and more especially such very distant and neutral ones as cousins, had to interfere in the suppression of a work, and that, moreover, only a work of fiction, still he was a nervous, tremulous, unquiet little man, with none of the brass for which publishers in general are so distinguished, and a great deal of the honesty by which they are, alas! so rarely distinguished. So, not knowing very well how to act, he wrote to Lady Bulwer, requesting to know what she would wish him to do. But before she answered him, she wrote the following letter to the tepid relative who had, with such gentlemanlike and imperturbable composure, made her and her poor ill-fated children over so completely to the tender mercies of her unscrupulous husband.

"'Sir,—

"'Is it possible that, not content with having wrecked me and my poor children eternally—as far as this world is concerned—by a total and unprecedented disregard of our commonest interests, you have now presumed to take upon you, without the slightest natural, or even conventional, authority so to do, to interdict the publication of the novel I have sold to Mr. Bull, written for the purpose of discharging debts which I never incurred, and which, owing to your most extraordinary passiveness in making me over so completely into the power of the most unprincipled man that ever existed, I may look upon as only the beginning of a long series of humiliating and irreparable misfortunes? Awaiting your immediate and explicit reply to the above inquiry,

"'I remain, Sir, your obedient servant,

'ROSINA BULWER.'

To which, by return of post, she received the following laconic but conclusive answer:—

"'MY DEAR ROSINA (for I will not address you in the same tone in which you have done me), I beg most explicitly to state that not only have I never interfered in any way to stop the publication of your book, which, in the first place, as you truly say, I should have *no right to do*, but, in the next place, I could *not* have done so, inasmuch as that your own letter just received was the very first intimation I had of your intention to publish.

'I am yours sincerely,

'F. H. DOYLE.'

"This letter Lady Bulwer thought it better to take to Mr. Bull; so a young friend very kindly, at a moment's notice, having obtained her mother's permission so to do, accompanied Lady Bulwer to London, her older and married sister having, with equal kindness, lent her the money for the journey. As I before said, there were no railroads then, so, to save time, they travelled all night, and surprised Mr. Bull by an early visit the next morning, when she placed her cousin's letter in his hands; no sooner had the little man read it than he threw up his hands and eyes, exclaiming, 'Well! well! It passes my comprehension how any man calling himself a gentleman could come into my shop and tell me as many falsehoods as Sir E. Bulwer did the other day, the chief of which this letter so completely refutes. And now,' continued he, 'if your Ladyship can only remain three days in town, I shall have the proofs of the third volume ready, in which I want you to insert something.'

"Poor Lady Bulwer coloured up to her temples as she felt her attenuated purse, and said that ' she was very sorry, but that she should be obliged to return immediately. But the publisher, with great delicacy and kindness, guessing pretty well the real necessity of her immediate return' said—

"' Really, my dear madam, you look much too tired to recommence your journey so soon; and as I let apartments, —my rooms are by no means bad upstairs,—and as they are now vacant, if you would do me the honour of occupying them, not as a tenant, but as a guest, for a few days, it would make me very happy, and I should be much flattered. Kindness from such quarters is generally genuine, and whenever and wherever and from whomsoever it is so, the best present return that can be made for it is to accept it ; and, as a good heart is always well-bred, Lady Bulwer did accept the worthy publisher's hospitality, and in less than half an hour his equally kind wife had, in their very nicely furnished upstairs rooms, prepared a most excellent breakfast for her and her friend.

"No sooner had Sir Edward's cowardly attempt to intimidate his wife become a subject of conversation than he solemnly denied it, and roundly asserted that it was an invention of hers. Nice accusations for a woman to forge against herself! But it is an old remark that there is no falsehood so absurd but what there will be some fools found to believe in. Next, out came the book, and from that time forth Sir Edward's own particular pressgang were indefatigable and unscrupulous in the personal nature of their attacks upon it and its authoress.

"However, *à tout malheur quelque chose est bon ;* and as Lady Bulwer's ill-fated novel had at least had the merit of eliciting some new psychological definitions in criticism, so it had also the still greater merit of causing to be given to the world a new literary curiosity, as it furnished Sir Edward with the opportunity of writing a charming little poem, in which he launched out into the following

truly poetical ecstacy upon his own excessive personal loveliness and genius as contrasted with his wife's extreme
antiquity :—

> " 'He' (*i.e.*, Sir Edward) 'was a gifted boy, with golden hair
>   And eyes of heaven's own blue ;
>   While her maturer charms but shone
>   With a faint lustre borrowed from his own.' "

But in spite of the organised opposition to its
success, "Cheveley" sold well enough . to induce
Mr. Bull to accept Lady Lytton's next novel, " The
Budget of the Bubble Family," in the following year ;
and that it enjoyed a considerable amount of popularity I have ample evidence to prove. The testimony of a few friends will be found in the following
letters, which I subjoin both as aiding my narrative
and as being not without interest from other reasons.

On April 28th, 1839, Alaric A. Watts writes :—

> "Ember Lodge, Thames Ditton,
> "*April 28th*, 1839.

" DEAR LADY BULWER,—

"It would be impossible for me to convey to you
in writing anything like a definite idea of the impression
which has been produced on the minds of myself and wife
by your last painfully affecting packet. The treatment you
have experienced surpasses in atrocity everything that I
have ever heard of or could have conceived possible, and
at once puts an end to all delicacy and forbearance towards
its author from either yourself or friends. Indeed, on my
return last evening from town, I found Mrs. Watts in a
paroxysm of indignation, and I can truly say that we have
spoken and thought of nothing else since ; nor could I
peruse your thrilling account of your persecutions and in-
dignities without a feeling of shame on behalf of the species
to which your oppressor belongs. When I assure you of

our deepest sympathy, I am satisfied you will give me full
credit for sincerity ; for the details you have been pleased
to communicate to us have made us more warmly interested
in your future welfare than I could have thought possible
on so slight an acquaintance.   Certainly, under all the circumstances, I should not, had I been privy to the intended
publication of 'Cheveley,' have advised its suppression.
I took the part of 'Cheveley' as a stranger, a mere looker-on,
should invariably take part when a woman is even reputed
to have been oppressed.   To enable me to form an idea of
the exact position in which you stand with Bull, you had
better send me a copy of the agreement you signed with
him.   As for injunction or prosecution, it was a mere bug-
bear ; but it is perfectly true that if your *MSS.* pass *directly*
from your own hands to those of your publisher, and the
copyright is not paid for at the time it is delivered, Sir
Edward can at any time possess himself of either the *book*
or the *money* to be paid for it.   I see a catchpenny adver-
tised to which you refer in your letter.   My belief is that
the object of the *annonce* is merely to harass you, and
that it will never make its appearance.   But do not, I
entreat, publish anything *yourself* without due advice and
consideration.   Do not write to or notice any of these
vermin *yourself*.

" We gather from the tone of your last note that you are
ill, and that you are labouring under great excitement of
mind.   We earnestly entreat you, for the sake of your
children, to keep yourself as quiet as possible, and not to
seek unnecessary occasions of fresh excitement.   Your
case is as strong as it can possibly be, and if you labour
under temporary calumny, ' bide your time,' and all will
be right.   My wife will write by an early opportunity.
She joins me in the wish that you could spend a week or
two of perfect repose in our cottage, which is pretty and
pleasantly situated ; and as I am only an hour and a half's
drive from town, you might settle all your matters with
Bull, arrange for another book with some one else, and
gain from change of air and scene renewed health and
spirits.   You and Mrs. Watts should drive out every day.

Certainly, should anything call me near Bath, I will not fail
to visit you for a day; and if you will make our cottage
your home when you come to town, Mrs. Watts will take
a trip to Bath some day for the pleasure of passing a day
or two in your society.

> "I remain, dear Lady Bulwer,
>> "Faithfully yours,
>>> "ALARIC A. WATTS."

In a subsequent letter from the same writer
occurs the remark: "The edition of 'Cheveley'
now selling is the *third.* Of this I have proofs."

The following was also written about the same
date :—

> "EMBER LODGE, *Monday.*

"MY DEAR LADY BULWER,—

"I have thought over your affairs until I hardly
know what course to recommend. One appears to me
imperative, and in the prosecution of that I will do all I
can. I mean a simple statement of your wrongs, supported
by such documentary evidence as can be obtained from
various sources. Above all, Byrne should testify to what
she knows, to the worst points, of course; and I think she
might safely say that there had been some parts of
B——'s conduct which a sense of decency made it impossible to detail. Mr. Hume should testify to what Miss
Greene told him of B——. If he denies its truth, it will at
least show with what kind of woman he has placed your
children. I sincerely hope Bentley may have accepted
your terms, but I fear not.

"I was so overwhelmed with my own avocations that I
found it impossible to call on you on Saturday, but I saw
Mr. Hyde, and suggested what I thought best with regard
to Bull. I shall make a point of being in time on Tuesday,
when I will go to Sir Francis Doyle; and if I cannot see
him, which I hardly hope to do, I may see his son. Meanwhile collect all the material together for your statement
that is likely to add to its force, and any written declara-

tions illustrative of the narrative will be most important, and I will do my best to meet your wishes.

"I remain, dear Lady Bulwer,

"Faithfully yours,

"ALARIC A. WATTS."

Charles Kean, who was a favourite *protegé* of Lady Lytton, writes :—

"DUBLIN, GRESHAM'S HOTEL. *April 9th*, 1839.

"A thousand thanks, my dear Lady Bulwer, for your kind letter ; but I really am very jealous that you should have sent the 'Man of Honour' to my mother so long before I am honoured by his company. The poor old lady is quite enchanted with *my chapter*. But, pray, what is the reason that it cannot be procured in Dublin ? for hundreds are on the tiptoe of expectation, and yet are unable to procure it. I hope and trust, my dear madam, that you will visit London in *June*, and see the farewell at the Haymarket, for one *may* be blown up on the way to America, or *Lynch law* be my lot when I reach it. Your friend Colonel D'A—— is in wretched spirits ; the loss of his child and the approaching trial of his friend and schoolfellow Lord S—— are preying upon his mind. He speaks of you most kindly! I have not yet seen the new Lord Lieutenant, but his staff have received orders to attend chapel prayers every morning at half-past nine. Report stated that the private box would not be retained at the theatre, so great were his religious scruples ; but this is not correct, as a contrary order has been received, as 'had been the custom with his predecessors.' We are very dull and stupid, as everybody of respectability is out of Dublin, and the Radicals that are here are full of O'Connell and Lord Fortescue. Once again let me hope you will be present at my *last moments* in London, or I shall be deeply pained ; and believe me, my dear Lady Bulwer,

"Ever yours sincerely,

"CHARLES KEAN."

"Cheveley ; or, The Man of Honour," Lady Bulwer's first novel.

"DUBLIN, *April* 16*th*, 1839.

"I cannot sufficiently express to you, my dear Lady Bulwer, how gratified I feel by so many indications of your regard, and how deeply sensible I am of the kind interest you have taken in my welfare. Your parcel has just arrived, and I only regret that I cannot borrow *your pen* on this occasion to enable me to describe the unfeigned pleasure your kindness has afforded me ; but conscious how incompetent I am at all times to express my feelings, let me pray you to pardon this poor acknowledgment, and believe that I thank you from my heart. I am rejoiced to think there is every probability of seeing you in London, as it would have given me pain indeed had I contemplated my departure from England without the hopes of personally bidding you farewell. My engagements concluded here last night, when the house was crowded to the roof ; but I remain in Dublin until my appearance in Liverpool requires me on the 27th. Our new and saint-like Lord Lieutenant, much against his inclination, I believe, visits the theatre in state to-morrow evening, and has commanded *The Lady of Lyons* as the performance, having heard, he says, that Claude Melnotte is my best character.

"His Excellency is not theatrical. The potentate of Covent Garden has announced his intended abdication. There will now be a meeting of the gang to petition his Majesty to resume the government, unless indeed he anticipates the House of Commons will bring in a Bill stating that the welfare of the country requires his Majesty should continue in office, with this amendment by Talfourd, that Charles Kean must play second to him.

"Pray present my compliments to Miss Boys, and say how grateful I am to her for the beautiful manner in which she has etched my initials. *The* handkerchief will make its first appearance on any stage next Saturday, when *Hamlet* is repeated for the last time. I am perfectly ashamed at sending this apology of a letter in reply to yours, but can only repeat that my heart thanks you ; and

though one of the *evil gender*, I *can* feel, and with sincerity
subscribe myself,

"Ever yours sincerely,

"CHARLES KEAN."

"MANCHESTER, *May 24th*, 1839.

"MY DEAR LADY BULWER,—

"I intrude this letter upon you for the sake of
urging speech to your kind intention of being in London
next month, as I am all anxiety to know that you will
be present on my *first* appearance at the Haymarket,
3rd June.

"Very much depends on the *first* night of a *London*
engagement, and I ardently hope you will not desert
me on such a trial. Although I passed the Rubicon
at Drury Lane, yet I feel my enemies are so strong and
so vindictive, that I know every engine will be set in motion
to endeavour to crush me on this occasion ; and therefore
I solicit the presence of one who has so powerfully and
generously aided my cause to encourage me against
Fusbos and his gang.

"I shall reach my home, after an absence of nine months,
on Sunday evening. And glad enough I shall be to quit
this horrid place.

"The Chartist excitement here is so great, that
the military are constantly parading the streets ; and
another regiment, together with some cavalry, have just
entered the town.

"To-morrow is the meeting, and the troops are ordered
to be under arms.

"*What think you of our gracious Queen?* What a
capital speech the great Duke made in the House of
Lords !

"Pray send me one line to 30, Old Bond Street, telling me you will be in London by 3rd June, and confer
a heartfelt obligation on

"Yours ever sincerely,

"CHARLES KEAN."

I have not been able to discover who was the writer of the following, which relates to the effect produced by "Cheveley" upon a certain lady of rank :—

"April, 1839.

"MY DEAREST ROSINA,—

"Do not be alarmed at hearing from me so soon again, but I *must* relate to you a laughable scene which has just been told to my father by the pretty mistress of a circulating library within a few doors of this. My father went to obtain 'Cheveley' for a friend who is staying with us. Upon receiving the work, he asked her if she had read it. She said she had done so in a hurried manner. My father gave her a *key* to the characters. When he came to Lady Stepastray, the poor woman started and said, 'Oh, sir, you have accounted for a curious scene which took place here last night, and for which I was quite at a loss to account. Lady S—— came in and asked me to recommend her a new book. I instantly named "Cheveley." Her Ladyship seemed in a moment overcome with violent passion, and stamping with her foot, exclaimed, "Oh, that horrid *bad* book, written by that horrid woman ! I would not allow it to be on my table. *Not* that I have ever *seen* the book." She then bounced out of the shop, exclaiming, "Oh, the horrid, disgusting, shameful book ! "' The *enlightened* librarian asked if it were possible any man could be so bad. Upon being assured it was not only a possibility, but a *reality*, she added, 'Well, sir, I never had a very good opinion of Sir Edward Bulwer since he cheated me out of nine shillings.' Deeply do I lament the annoyances which beset you ; but if the fate of women in general be but a *triste affaire*, what can you, the gifted, the beautiful, and the *persecuted*, expect? The women abuse your book—they don't know why ; the men because you know *them*. From such judges there is no appeal.

"Your sincerely affectionate friend,

"C. E. H."

EXTRACTS FROM FRIENDS' LETTERS.

"*February* 1st, 1839.

"MY DEAREST ROSINA,—

"Your new work, I see by the papers, is to appear the first of March. The power of that monster, *Law*, made by men to gratify their own selfish and vindictive passions, leaves a woman so entirely at the mercy of a husband, that I cannot help wishing that every page of your 'Man of Honour' may be revised by a lawyer before it passes to the public. However harmless the shafts of satire may fall on the shameless swell mob, by fraternal convention called *gentlemen* and men of honour, it is not expected, and therefore never pardoned, when a woman tears the *mask* from any individual amongst them. Therefore *caution!* caution! for none can tell what wounded self-love may do, aided by power and unchecked by conscientious feeling, to double, treble, the injury you have received. You have a right to exercise your talent and increase your income by writing books, and, fortunately, you bring great ability to your task ; but for every motive that *prudence* can suggest, make your just indignation less pointed towards the individual, and more towards the general delinquency of men, their laws and institutions, which sanction them in degrading generally, and ill-treating individually, every woman *equal in intellect* and superior in moral practice to themselves.

"There never was a period when the *public* and the intelligent also among women were more prepared to sympathise with a work of this kind. Mrs. Jameson and other women of the present day have nobly fought their battle in this way, and have been responded to by public sympathy, and there is none other worth writing for.

"Ever most affectionately yours,

"A. W."

CHAPTER XI.

LADY BULWER went to Paris in the autumn of
1839,* and then, she writes,

"began the organised system of *espionnage*, by anonymous letters and foul conspiracies, which have never for
one moment ceased, and which, though of course it is very
easy to deny, it is also, thank God, from clouds of
witnesses and carefully preserved documents, equally easy
to prove indisputably, could the victim of them ever be so
fortunate as even to obtain the tardy justice of a public
tribunal. But what earthly hope or chance has a penniless
martyr?"

The only drawback that Lady Bulwer found to
her *séjour* in Paris was that Sir Edward happened
to have a brother there at the time as secretary
of legation, "who was in every respect worthy of
him;" but as he was physically as well as morally
utterly insignificant, it was very easy to pass him
without having the annoyance of seeing him, which
she accordingly made up her mind to do. And

---

* In the Paris correspondence of the *Court Journal* for September
7th, 1839, I find the following:—

"Among the recent arrivals is, I understand, Lady Bulwer, who
intends to remain here twelve months, during which she will follow
up closely her literary avocations."

one day, when dining at Lord Aylmer's, Lady
Aylmer told her that she had invited all the Corps
Diplomatique to a ball she intended giving the
following week except Mr. Henry Bulwer, the
little secretary.

"Pray, my dear Lady Aylmer," said Lady Bulwer,
"do not leave him out on my account, as I shall
have so many more agreeable objects to look at
that I should not even see that he was in the room."

But Lady Aylmer persisted in not inviting him,
and the ball took place accordingly without being
graced with his presence.

About a week after it Lady Bulwer was again
dining at Lord Aylmer's, when, after dinner, one
of his pretty nieces took up the *Morning Post*,
and said, "Good heavens, Lady Bulwer, have you
seen this?" pointing to a paragraph and handing
her the paper, adding as she did so, "What an
abominable falsehood, when he was not even invited!"

"No!" said Lady Bulwer; "what is it?"

The following was the paragraph in question,
which appeared in the *Morning Post* of Friday,
October 18th, 1839 :—

"A curious scene occurred here the other evening at the
soirée of Lady Aylmer. Lady Bulwer, who is resident
here, and whose connubial wrongs are a motto of notoriety,
is occupied, it is said, with a novel which, like 'Cheveley,'
may strike home to many persons. Sir Edward Lytton
Bulwer's brother, Henry Bulwer, principally known by
a book on French statistics, the materials of which he
stole from the works of Moreau and Louis Goldsmid, is
chargé d'affaires here during Lord Granville's absence.

At Lady Aylmer's Mr. Henry Bulwer met Lady Bulwer and ventured to bow to her, the consequence of which was that her Ladyship, to his great discomfiture and the amusement of all present, pulled certain wry faces, the meaning of which could not be mistaken. The scene is described as having been most grotesque upon the precipitate retreat of England's envoy. I may add that Lord Granville's absence is deeply regretted by men of all shades of opinion. Personally his Lordship is highly respected; and, at all events, while *he* is here the dignity and character of our country are not compromised."

This ridiculous libel appeared also in the *Court Journal* of October 19th, 1839, in which paper the following highly imaginative account of the episode appeared :—

"A scene took place a few evenings since at Lady Aylmer's soirée which has afforded the Parisians much food for gossip and comment. Mr. Henry Bulwer, who represents Lord Granville during his Lordship's absence, was passing through one of the elegant saloons, when he encountered Lady Bulwer, who has been residing in Paris for some time, to whom he politely bowed. Her Ladyship, who, it is said, had gone to the soirée with the express intention of insulting her husband's brother, made a dead stop as he passed, and placing her arms akimbo, commenced a series of grimaces that have scarcely been equalled since the best days of Grimaldi, and con-tinued her vulgar gestures until Mr. Bulwer had passed beyond her sight. The affair has created a feeling of disgust in the minds of all persons here, and it is probable that her Ladyship will not have another opportunity of displaying her grotesque performance either at Lady Aylmer's or elsewhere."

The difference between the two versions arises of course from the fact that Mr. Henry Bulwer was, for certain reasons, a *persona gratissima* to the editor of the *Court Journal*, who lost no opportunity of singing the praises of his patron. Thus in the *Court Journal* of September 28th, 1839, I read :—

"Mr. Bulwer is said to be a great favourite, not only at the French Court, but also with the President of the Council. . . . . It is reported here that Lord Ponsonby is about to retire from Constantinople, and that he will be succeeded by Mr. Bulwer."

And again, on October 5th of the same year :—

"Mr. Bulwer, whose conciliatory manners have procured him many friends here in the Court circle——"

and so on.

Lady Bulwer, though at first disposed to treat the attacks of her enemies with silent contempt, was advised that she could not allow the matter to rest, and accordingly wrote the following letter, which appeared in the *Morning Post* of October 31st, 1839 :—

LADY LYTTON BULWER TO THE EDITOR
OF THE "MORNING POST."

"30, RUE DE RIVOLI, PARIS, *Oct.* 28*th*, 1839.

"SIR,—Disagreeable as it is to me to have my name dragged before the public, it is something more than disagreeable to have my life *lied* away. All other injuries as a woman I have been compelled to submit to; but, for my children's sake, I will not tamely submit to be grossly vilified and defamed in newspapers. In one of your journals of last week there was a paragraph from your Paris correspondent purporting to be a description of a scene that had taken place at Lady Aylmer's, wherein I was described as acting like a *poissarde* towards Mr. Henry Lytton Bulwer. Now I have no doubt you will be as much surprised as I was to see such a falsehood

in your very respectable journal when I tell you that
no such scene ever took place, inasmuch as Mr. Henry
Bulwer was not, nor ever has been, at Lady Aylmer's
since I have been at Paris, as her Ladyship, with great
delicacy of feeling, avoided asking him on my account,
though I can have no possible objection to meet any
member of the Bulwer family, *I* never having injured them,
however much they may have injured me. I know it is
their object, if possible, to hunt me from society; but
surely they might resort to more honourable and gentlemanlike stratagems than that of propagating gross
falsehoods of me through the medium of the public press.
When the above-alluded-to paragraph appeared in the
Morning Post I was advised by all my friends here to
take no notice of so palpable a misstatement, but having
this day received letters from England telling me that
it had been repeated more violently and with greater
exaggeration in the *Court Journal* of the 19th, I am compelled to call upon you to publish this contradiction of
so cruel a calumny in the columns of your next paper,
which, I am sure, is conducted on principles of too much
justice to wilfully contribute to the unmanly oppression
of a persecuted woman. Knowing as I do the contemptible source from which the *Court Journal* got its malicious
falsehoods, I cannot degrade myself by thinking it worth
while to contradict anything it may, in the plenitude
of its insanity, think fit to pander to the profligate and
amuse the public with. I have the honour to be, Sir,

"Your obedient servant,

"ROSINA LYTTON BULWER.

"P.S.—I think it further right to state that I have
never yet met Mr. Henry Bulwer in any society in Paris,
so could not ever have had an opportunity of acting as
described."

The Paris correspondent of the same journal
subsequently wrote an apology, which was published

in the *Morning Post* of November 11th, 1839. It ran
thus :—

"RE LADY LYTTON BULWER.—TO THE EDITOR OF
THE 'MORNING POST.'

"Having perused Lady Lytton Bulwer's letter in the
Morning Post of October 31st, justice to her Ladyship
requires me to state, upon strict inquiry, I find that
no such scene as that described in my correspondence
of October 18th has taken place at Lady Aylmer's.

"I deeply regret that, relying upon the affirmation o
persons who alleged that the story was told them by Mr
Henry Lytton Bulwer himself, I should have been the un
intentional means of giving pain to Lady Lytton Bulwer
and that a purely political paragraph should have
annoyed her Ladyship in the slightest manner, which
was far from the object of your Paris correspondent."

After this Lady Bulwer deemed it unnecessary
to take any further proceedings against the *Morning
Post*, but with regard to the *Court Journal* she was
otherwise advised. To resume from " Nemesis ":—

"Her solicitor, Mr. Hyde, wrote to her immediately
on the appearance of this infamous libel, and told her i
possible to try and be calm under such an outrage, as i
might turn out to be the most fortunate thing that had
ever happened to her, as he should instantly bring an
action for libel against the editor of the *Court Journal*
and that would afford an opportunity of showing in open
court of what the amiable brothers Bulwer were capable
in point of truth and honour."

Mr. Hyde's anticipations were unfortunately
over sanguine so far as a complete exposure o
the brothers was concerned. The trial duly came
off; but Sir Edward Bulwer, with unexampled
generosity, not only permitted his wife to bring

the action (being a married woman, she was unable to sue without his consent), but even added his own name as nominal plaintiff, thereby diverting attention from the part which he and Mr. Henry Bulwer had played in the matter, and leaving the editor of the *Court Journal* to bear all the blame and defray all the expenses. At this trial Mr. Hyde had retained Sir Frederick Pollock for Lady Bulwer. She writes regarding it :—

"The impudent and, even for English apathy, rather too improbable defence which the libellers set up was that Lady Bulwer had libelled herself to bring herself into public notice! Whereupon Sir Frederick Pollock, in the very able and eloquent speech which he made on the occasion, observed, 'Why, even in a court of justice it would appear that this poor lady cannot be secure from the base stratagems of her calumniators,' in reply to which the clumsy counsel for the amiable brothers asked, with an air of Brummagem candour, 'What motive could Sir Edward Bulwer or Mr. Henry Bulwer possibly have for libelling Lady Bulwer?' 'The motive,' rejoined Sir Frederick Pollock, 'is set forth plainly enough, indeed, rather too much so in the last line of the libel, namely that the conduct attributed to this much-outraged lady would exclude her from all society.'"

The result was that Lady Bulwer obtained a verdict for fifty pounds and costs, which very possibly, as she says, "only served to heap fuel on the fire of their black malice, for from that time the plot began to thicken."

I will insert here a letter written some time afterwards to the editor of *Galignani's Messenger* with reference to this trial by Mr. Henry Bulwer himself, and copied in the *Court Journal* of March 28th, 1840 :—

"RUE DE COURCELLES, *March 23rd*, 1840.

" SIR,—

"Having observed in your report of the proceedings in the Cour Correctionnelle of last Friday a passage from which it appeared that M. Berryer had said that Lady Bulwer had brought an action against me for libel and had gained her suit, I thought it necessary to apply to M. Berryer to request that if he had ever asserted or insinuated that I had anything to do with the action brought against the *Court Journal* by Lady Bulwer, he would retract so unjust and improper a misrepresentation.

"M. Berryer replied to me by saying that he did erroneously assert in the first instance that the action was brought against me, but that he had immediately corrected his mistake, and explained that it was brought against the newspaper, and that my name was only used by him in this explanation as having been mentioned, together with that of Lady Bulwer, in the article which gave rise to the cause. M. Berryer's reply being perfectly satisfactory (since the article prosecuted was some foolish fiction as to a meeting between Lady Bulwer and myself), and removing every impression on my mind as to an unjustifiable statement having been made and persisted in (a circumstance which I could never have submitted to), I deem it due to myself and M. Berryer, who seems to have been honourably anxious to correct an unintentional mistake, to request that by publishing this letter you will rectify the report which attracted my attention.

" I have the honour, etc.,

" HENRY LYTTON BULWER."

The editor of the *Court Journal* appends to this the following note :—

" With reference to the proceedings above alluded to,

we feel it necessary to repeat that the matter in question
which formed the subject of Lady Bulwer's action was
received from an anonymous correspondent, and that we
have never been in communication with Mr. H. L. Bulwer
or any member of his family.   The action brought by
Lady Bulwer was not against Mr. H. L. Bulwer, but
against the proprietors of the *Court Journal*, upon whom
the costs of the proceedings and the verdict fall exclusively.—ED. *C.J.*"

The best comment upon this editorial explanation is that of Lady Bulwer herself.

" This was," she writes, " as the lawyers say, proving too
much with a vengeance, for, as the other papers of the
day truly remarked, ' the law of libel is far too stringent
in England for any editor to run so ruinous a risk as to
publish so gross a one simply upon anonymous authority ;
and in the next place, if it were anonymous, how could
the editor take upon him to assert so positively that it
came neither from Sir Edward Bulwer nor from Mr.
Henry Bulwer ? '   Here again came the beautiful dis-
crepancy between public statements and private facts,
for in all the editor's carefully preserved letters to Lady
Bulwer he most bitterly and categorically complains of
the cruel and unscrupulous manner in which Sir Edward
Bulwer and his brother had first entrapped him into
publishing the libel, and then betrayed and left him in
the lurch to bear the brunt of the onerous proceedings
against him."

This guileless editor was, in fact, seduced by the
blandishments of Mr. Edwin James, who for many
years acted as a sort of jackal and man-of-all-work
to Sir Edward Bulwer, and on this occasion procured the insertion of the libel by guaranteeing
its literal truth on the authority of no less a
personage than Sir Edward himself.

But enough upon this subject.   One plot having
disastrously failed, it became necessary for Lady
Bulwer's enemies to devise another of a more
dangerous and unscrupulous sort ; and it will be
needful for me to deal with this at some length
in another chapter.

CHAPTER XII.

At this time Lady Bulwer was living at 30 bis, Rue de Rivoli ; and though she has unfortunately left no record of her social life in Paris, I may quote a few fragments from contemporary papers which prove that she mixed in the highest circles of Parisian society, was much admired, and considerably run after.   Thus I read in an issue of the *Court Journal* for December 28th, 1839 :—

" Lady Granville's first *soirée dansante* for the season was given at the British Embassy on the 20th.   There was a most numerous assemblage of English nobility and fashionables, including Lord and Lady Canterbury, Lord and Lady Clarendon, Lady Aldborough, Lady Lytton Bulwer, etc."

Again, January 11th, 1840 :—

" The ball given by the Russian Prince Tonfakin and the soirées of the Sardinian Ambassador, the Marquess de Brignolles, Countess d'Appouy, Lady Bulwer, and the Viscountess Canterbury are a theme of comment among the *élite* of this gayest and most brilliant of capitals."

One more extract, February 22nd, 1840 :—

" Lady Lytton Bulwer was also a component in the galaxy of female loveliness."

This state of things was, however, anything bu

agreeable to Sir Edward Bulwer; and in the latter
part of 1839 he began to set on foot inquiries as
to his wife's character and behaviour, from which
he evidently hoped to elicit something scandalous,
or at least unfavourable to her reputation, and
thereby deprive her of the position which her
beauty, talents, and misfortunes had won.

I subjoin extracts from a letter written at Bath
by a friend, and dated October 4th, 1839 :—

"DEAREST LADY BULWER,—

"I hope you will as soon as you possibly can
after you receive this set off for England, as there is a
vile conspiracy hatching against you, headed, no doubt,
by Sir E. L. B. I went to Clifton for a few hours
yesterday, but on my return found poor Mrs. Stockman,
full of indignation and zeal, awaiting my arrival to
tell me that in the morning, about eleven o'clock, a gentleman, medium height, hair dark and brushed up and
rather rough, in age about forty, white silk stockings,
pumps, and evening coat, called upon her, and began
asking numerous questions, the answers to which he
took down in writing. The principal questions were if
Mr. H—— had ever taken or paid for lodgings in her
house? if ever she had seen anything to make her
believe Mr. H—— was otherwise than on the footing
of a friend? if a person sleeping in the garret could hear
the door between the dressing-room and your room open
in the night? if she knew anything of the removal of
a chest of drawers, and a key being lost, and a plate
being put on the keyhole? if you had ever received money
from Mr. H——? where Anne and Harding were? and
a great many more questions, which Mrs. Stockman, had
she been tutored, could not have answered better; for the
man was much provoked by her asseverations, and said
musingly, 'Very strange; I must have been misinformed.'
He knew every circumstance of your life, even the most

minute particulars. He was two hours with Mrs. Stock-man, and it is impossible to tell you all he said, but you have been very closely watched by some one. He said Mott met you in Paris, and lodged opposite to you; that he remained in your rooms till twelve or one at night; that you were going to Naples because he was going; that some conversation that took place between Miss B—— and Mr. H—— relative to the dog one night when you were out could only have been told to you by Mr. H—— in your own room in the middle of the night, as Mr. H—— had retired when you came home, and was not up when you told Miss B—— that Mr. H—— had told you of it; that Mr. H——'s mother and sister had said that Mr. H—— had made you a present of his carriage, that you had had his arms taken out and your own inserted, that he had ruined himself for you, that you had broken his wife's heart. He asked all sorts of questions relative to Mr. H——'s illness, and if you were not up with him all night in your dressing-gown? that your former flirtations with a great personage had been the cause, together with your temper, of the separation between Sir E—— and yourself; that you had tried every means in your power to reconcile him to you. He asked if you did not live very extravagantly, and how you could support such extravagance if you did not receive money from Mr. H——? Mrs. Stockman said I had advanced you money before your book came out, and then that had helped you materially; she said that you were to pay her in October. . . . Mrs. Stockman gave the most appropriate answers. She said you were a most virtuous and high-minded lady, and neither she nor anybody else could say with truth that they had ever seen you behave otherwise; that Anne's and Harding's testimony was not to be taken, from their abandoned characters, neither Miss B——'s, for she went to bed drunk every night. He said, 'But if she did, she could be sober again at three in the morning, when she heard the door open between Mr. H——'s and your room.' Mrs. Stockman said, drunk or sober, she would defy anybody to hear that from the garret. . . . . Take care whom you come to England with, for you will be very closely watched. . . . . Mrs. S—— is now here ; she says the man was followed to some place where he was a long time in conversation with White, the charwoman ; he then went to Walcot Street to find out Rory O'Toole, because Rory knew where that horrid Anne lived. . . . . He had told Mrs. S—— he had been to Ireland and to France to gather particulars. . . . . When Mrs. Stockman said Sir E. L. B—— was living with Miss Deacon, the man's face flushed, and he looked savage."

The object of these inquiries is of course obvious enough.   Sir Edward Bulwer was desperately anxious to get rid of his injured wife altogether, and he spared no pains or expense in endeavouring to collect evidence against her character which would justify him in instituting proceedings for a divorce with fair hopes of success.   Failing utterly in this amiable design, he resorted to the gentlemanly and honourable expedient of employing agents in Paris not only to carry on the system of espionage, but to purloin her private papers and correspondence from her lodgings.   The history of this episode will be told in Lady Bulwer's own words :—

"A very brief time had elapsed after the action for libel, when the first night Lady Bulwer went to the Tuileries, which happened to be the then King's birthday, there were great illuminations, which, of course, all the servants turned out to see ; and on her return from Court, her maid said, while undressing her,—

"'If you please, my Lady, Phœbe wishes to speak to you.'

"Now, Phœbe being the cook, Lady Bulwer could not

imagine what she could want at that time of night, and asked if the morning would not do as well? but the maid said she had particularly requested to see her mistress that night.

"'Oh, very well,' said the latter; 'as soon as I have my dressing-gown on she may come up.'

"When she did so, after apologising for her intrusion at that hour, she said,—

"'But the fact is, I thought it better to lose no more time in telling your Ladyship that for the last fortnight every time I stirred out I have been followed by two men—Englishmen, one a great, fat, red-faced man, the other a lean, sallow, lame man, who have always been trying to enter into conversation with me, but I never would answer them; however, to-night, when your Ladyship went to the Tuileries, they stood beside the *porte cochère* to see you get into the carriage, and as soon as you had driven off, they offered me a *drageoir* of bonbons, and asked if I would not like to go and see the illuminations? I said I was going to do so by-and-bye with a friend. Still they stayed on, and at length asked me if I did not live with Lady Bulwer? I said, "Yes," at which they began asking me the most infamous questions, which put me in a terrible rage; but I thought it better to dissemble and answer like a simple fool, to let them think I was a simple fool that they could get anything out of, so that I might the better find out what they were at ——'

"'That was very well judged of you,' interrupted Lady Bulwer, 'but, pray, what were the questions they did ask you?'

"'Why, really, my Lady, I am almost ashamed to tell you, only I think you ought to know, and to let some lawyer know, as I am convinced there is some wicked plot going on against you.'

"'Nothing more likely; but what questions did they ask?'

"'First, if when gentlemen called you did not send the servants out of the way?'

"'"Oh, dear no," said I, keeping down my rage as well

as I could, " for, as there are but three of us, nothing makes
her Ladyship so angry as that any of us should stir
out; besides, the only gentlemen that do call are old
General H—— and his daughters, and that little Mr.
H—— and his wig, and Lord and Lady A——."

"'"Well, now, but, upon your honour, did none of you
ever return and find the drawing-room door locked?"

"'I could have spit in the fellow's face, but again I
mastered myself, and all I said was, "No! upon my
honour, or *upon my oath*, if you like that better."

"'"Come now, my good girl," said the fat brute, chuck-
ing me under the chin, " I see you are a sensible woman;
couldn't you, for three or four hundred pounds, swear
the very contrary?"

"'"No," said I, indignantly; "I could not perjure
myself even for three or four hundred pounds; so you had
better take yourselves off, and let me alone."

"'"I should like very much to come and drink tea
with you some night when your mistress is out," persisted
the fellow, nothing daunted, "for you are a very pretty
woman."

"'"*That's* a lie, on the *face of it*, at all events," said I,
" for I'm as ugly as the business you seem to be upon."

"'At this both of them set up a great laugh, and the
fat wretch said, " Well, you are no fool, at all events, and
I do wish you would let me come and drink tea with you
the first evening your mistress dines out; will you? *do* say
you will."

"'Now, my Lady, the thought struck me that it would
be a very good plan if we could get these wretches into
the house, and you have a lawyer here to confront them,
so I hesitated, that he might press me, which he did; and
then I said, "Well, perhaps, but I don't know what day
her Ladyship may dine out next; but good-night now,
for I must not stay talking any longer;" and with that
I ran upstairs, and shut the door in their face.'

"'You acted very well, Phœbe, and I am very much
obliged to you; and to-morrow I'll send for M.
Ledru, and consult with him as to the best plan of un-

masking this conspiracy before it goes any farther; and I am very grateful to you for putting me on my guard.'

"The next morning poor Lady Bulwer, who had indeed, as her amiable and honourable husband had reminded her, neither father, nor brother, nor any other earthly help to turn to, sent for M. Ledru, the *jurisconsulte;* and in the meanwhile, when she expressed her fears of the fresh and still more infamous conspiracy that was now got up against her, had to contend with the usual amount of apathetic English twaddle as to *what motive* Sir Edward Bulwer could possibly have for such conduct.

"When M. Charles Ledru came, his advice was that the next time Phœbe met the fat spy, and he asked her to let him come and drink tea with her, she should agree to it on the proviso that her mistress dined out, and return home on the pretence of finding out, but in reality to let Lady Bulwer know, who would then send for the *jurisconsulte*, who would arrange the farther programme. They had not long to wait, for two days after Phœbe returned home in haste, saying she had met the fat spy in the Marché St. Honoré, and she had come back to find that her mistress did not dine out, and therefore returned to tell him that she did, and that he might come at eight that evening; meanwhile Lady Bulwer wrote to M. Charles Ledru to tell him to come immediately. He did so, and arranged to be there with two *gens d'armes* in the evening, advising Lady Bulwer to have no light but the firelight in the drawing-room, and to leave the door ajar that led from it into the little boudoir where she used to write of a morning, and, moreover, to leave the key in her *secrétaire* and her letters temptingly about, as most probably the fat spy's great anxiety to get into the house was for the purpose of tampering with her papers, and unless they could catch him *en flagrant délit*, they could have no pretext for arresting him; for although coming to drink tea with the maids may be *fellowing*, it is *not* felony. Lady Bulwer accordingly unlocked the iron box in which they were generally kept, and took one or two packets of

Sir Edward Bulwer's letters, red-tape-tied and temptingly endorsed, giving the heads of their contents, and laid them carelessly on the slab of the *secrétaire.*

"Nor were the rest of the household idle. Phœbe donned her smartest cap, and made a barmecide preparation of a great display of tea-things and vacant muffin plates pompously covered, as if containing ample supplies, and according to the time immemorial high-life-below-stairs custom when the masters and mistresses are from home, laid them out in the dining-room instead of in the kitchen, while the *Pipelets* of the *concierge,* the ugly porter, his buxom wife, and *piquante* daughter, were all on the *qui vive* to usher in the fat filibusterer, M. Charles Ledru and the two *gens d'armes* also waiting breathlessly in the drawing-room to do honour to his arrival.

"True as never lover was to a trysting, as the clock struck eight, the old porter's sonorous *tambour majeur* voice was heard saying, 'Allez toujours; prennez le grand escalier; mi Ladi dine en ville,' an injunction which he lost no time in obeying, and still more with the eagerness of a lover than the cautiousness of a spy; clearing four steps at a bound, his hand was on the door-bell, which resounded to his touch, and Phœbe lost no time in replying to the summons.

"'Good-evening, my dear,' said the blood-red knight, *sotto voce.*

"'Oh! there's no occasion for whispering,' responded the nymph; 'her Ladyship is out, and you may speak as loud as you like;' and as there is nothing like example, it must be confessed she uttered the amiable permission in the shrillest and most shrewish tone possible.

"'I say, my dear,' said the stout gentleman, suddenly stopping as he strode across the ante-room; 'I want to see the little room off the *salle à manger* where Lady Bulwer writes of a morning.'

"'La!' cried Phœbe pertly; 'one would suppose that your trade must be drinking tea with all the maids that have lived in this apartment, you seem so well acquainted with the way the rooms lie.'

"'Perhaps,' grinned the fat philanderer, 'but you'll let me see it, won't you?' said he, placing his hand on the lock of the drawing-room door.

"'Yes, to be sure, but not there; this way, through the dining-room;' and the next minute, through the partially open door leading from the drawing-room into the little boudoir, by the lamp that Phœbe held, which threw its red glare on the spy's still redder face, Lady Bulwer, M. Ledru, and the two *gens d'armes* could see all that passed. The lawyer put his finger on his lip, and held his right hand out to keep the others back, as much as to say, 'Not yet;' but presently the spy turned the key in the *secrétaire*, let down the leaf, and seeing the temptingly endorsed packets, seized them with a long-drawn 'Ha!' of satisfaction, at which crisis the lawyer rushed in upon him, and collared him, exclaiming, 'So, wretch! this is the second time this month that I have caught you at your dirty work!' while Phœbe stood laughing, and pointing at the detected spy, as she gibingly said, 'I'm a *very pretty woman*, ain't *I?* at all events, I'm a very *true* one; and handsome is that handsome does. Ha! ha! ha! you'll come and drink tea with me again *soon*; now won't you? for three or four hundred pounds. Now couldn't you take another cup, without quite so much *green* in it? Ha! ha! ha!'

"'Silence, viper!' gasped the springed spy almost apoplectically; 'this is an infamous trap in which I have been caught.'

"'It is indeed a *most* infamous one,' said Lady Bulwer, now making her appearance, 'but one of your own setting and baiting; and now you have had a taste of its quality, I hope you like it: as for your accurate knowledge of the topography of my apartment, as it was his *friend* Lady S——'s, that of course you acquired from your *honourable* employer, Mr. Henry Bulwer.'

"'I am not bound to say who my employers are,' panted the now perspiring pilferer.

"'No, you needn't,' put in Phœbe, holding up a small hand glass before him; 'but don't you think that you look a nice young man for a small tea-party!'

"'Do take that woman away, or I shall do her a mischief.'

"'No, you won't, for there *is* two GENTS DE *armes* to take *you* away.'

"And hereupon the *gens d'armes* stepped forward, and the spy was taken in the snare which he thought he had so cleverly laid for others; there was, however, some informality in what we should call the warrant, so that the lawyer and the *gens d'armes* were obliged to release him for that night, when he lost no time in hurrying out of the house, even faster than he had come into it, and rejoined his coadjutor, the lank, lame man, who was hobbling up and down outside, anxiously waiting to know the result of 'the *beau* stratagem.'

"As soon as M. Ledru had relieved his mind by the energetic enunciation of a few 'Les lâches! les misérables! les infâmes!' he informed Lady Bulwer that the fat and lean spies were two English attorneys living in Paris, of the names of Lawson and Thackeray, whose chief business consisted in doing dirty work of the same kind as that in which they had so signally failed on the present occasion.

"But, as will soon be seen, all this was but the commencement of a long and dastardly conspiracy, often so paltry and comparatively motiveless as to excite incredulity rather than compassion; and to produce such an effect was of course one phase of the calculated plan upon which this honourable and gentlemanlike plot was organised. It must not be supposed that while there was so much dirty work doing, and still to be done, so great an adept at it as Mr. Loaden was idle; far from it. He was sent over to France to play his old game of bringing Lady Bulwer's name on the *tapis* in steamboats and other public conveyances, and thereupon disseminating every lie that his honourable client could possibly desire. Meanwhile poor Lady Bulwer was receiving the pleasing intelligence that Mrs. B—— had been figuring in divers Continental towns and English watering-places as Lady Bulwer, and, of course, leaving no very enviable or reputable *renommée* after her; but, like all that the amiable Sir Edward did, this was only another item of the deep-laid scheme to additionally outrage and insult his already too grossly injured wife and blacken her name by having her confounded with this infamous woman.

"Mr. Loaden's *modus operandi* was as follows. He went about ringing at every door where Lady Bulwer visited, and whenever he could gain admission commenced operations by saying, 'My dear madam, I understand you are intimate with Lady Bulwer; now, really, as you have daughters, I come to warn you she is not a person with whom you ought to allow them to associate.' He met, however, with much the same indignant reception and summary dismissal at every house where he called, and had nothing left but to go to M. Ledru and say that he had come, for Lady Bulwer's sake, to try and get him to persuade her to withdraw her action against Lawson and Thackeray, as it would be her ruin.

"'Not only she, but her friends,' said M. Ledru, 'are so convinced that a public tribunal is the only thing that can redress her grievous wrongs, and expose beyond the power of future lies the infamous conspiracy that has been going on against her, that even were she inclined to waive the punishment of Sir Edward's emissaries, no friend, much less any lawyer, would allow her to do so. Finding he could do nothing with any one, at least on his client's terms, which were always to grasp everything and give nothing, Loaden next wended his way to Lady Bulwer's house, and began interrogating the porter as to what hour he would be sure to find her at home."

Lady Lytton's account of this interview, when it came off, is as follows :—

"Everything was circumstantially reported to Lady Bulwer as it occurred by her faithful servants, and so she knew at once, from the description, that the mysterious visitor who would not leave his name was Loaden. Accordingly she convened between twenty and thirty ladies and gentlemen to witness his summary ejection on the following day, when he made his thief-like call.

"The next day came, and they were all waiting in breathless expectation for the little reptile's arrival.

"Two o'clock, and nearly half-past, when a little sneaking ring was heard at the ante-room door; and presently Fritz—the great, tall, impassible German—threw open the folding doors and announced 'Monsieur Loaden,' whereupon Lady Bulwer rose, drawing herself up to her full height, and pointing at arm's length to the wretched little attorney the whole time she was speaking, said, 'Fritz, you see that man? look at him well, that you may know him again, for you are not likely, with one exception, to see another such ill-looking fellow in all Paris. Now show him out; and never, under *any* pretext, allow him to darken my doors again.'

"The cowardly Loaden, cowering with rage and fear, and collecting the skirts of his coat, as if about to clear a puddle at a leap, said, casting a furtive glance around, 'Nobody's going to touch me, I hope, for that would be an assault.'

"And as the little reptile walked through the rooms Lady Bulwer stood mutely and rigidly, pointing at him to marshal him out, till the doors had closed upon him, when one loud 'Bravo!' burst from the assembled spectators. 'You did that beautifully! I was afraid at first you would excite yourself, or condescend to address a single syllable to the fellow, but nothing could be better.'

"These two months that were to linger on before this trial could take place were both weary and costly ones to Lady Bulwer, as, besides the four lawyers, she had to keep the servants of several families in Paris, who had been tampered with by the spies, as witnesses at her expense, as the families with whom they had lived had gone; so that at first and last this charming little conspiracy cost her several hundred pounds, the only means she had of paying which was by writing: and it was chiefly upon this account that Sir Edward and his equally honourable clique felt it incumbent on them to cut the ground from under her, by doing everything, as far as in them lay, to crush her books by the grossest, not even reviews of *them*, but personal abuse of her. As long as poor Mr. Bull lived, their malice was in a great measure defeated, as he always gave her large sums down, and behaved honourably to her in every respect; but no sooner was he dead, poor man, than she had the pleasure of finding that every single publisher of any note had had value received in some shape or other, through the powerful literary and political influence of the clique, to have nothing to say to her; so that she was driven into the exact strait that they wished, namely to publish with penniless adventurers, who first swamp a book by never advertising it, and then swindle the author in the most barefaced and unscrupulous manner.

"As when this action against Lawson and Thackeray was over Lady Bulwer was intending to go to Italy with a large party, she was looking out for a travelling servant; and one morning a slip of paper which had been left with the porter was sent up to her, upon which was written, 'If Lady Bulwer will call on Madame ——, No.——, Rue de ——, between two and three o'clock this afternoon, she will hear of a most excellent travelling servant, who can be highly recommended.' She laid the paper on the table, resolving to go if she had time, but was very busy that morning writing to her English lawyer, good Mr. Hyde; but, providentially for her, Sir H. W——, who, with his wife, lived next door to her, and who, from being a very good linguist, used obligingly to copy any letters or papers, which this charming conspiracy had given rise to, into different languages, as they happened to be required, called that morning to ask her to dine with them, as they had a box for that evening at the opera; and after she had accepted the invitation, he said as usual, 'Well, is there anything I can do for you to-day?'

"'Why, yes,' said she, handing him the slip of paper which had been sent up to her from the lodge; 'if you have time, I should be *very* much obliged to you if you would call at this address, and inquire about the character of this servant, as men can always better find out the character of men-servants.'

"'Good God!' said he, stamping his foot, as soon as he had glanced at the paper. 'Who on earth gave you this?'

"'I am sure I don't know,' said she. 'It was left with the porter this morning, and he sent it up about an hour ago.'

"On hearing this, Sir H. W——, without another word, seized his hat and rushed out of the room; nor did Lady Bulwer see him again till dinner-time, at his own house, when he came in, accompanied by M. Ledru, both of them exclaiming, 'The dastardly blackguards!' and then gave the following account of their morning's adventure.

"'As soon,' said Sir H——, 'as I left you, the carriage was fortunately at the door, and so I thought it best to take M. Ledru with me; for I must tell you the pretty escape you have had of falling into one of the most damnable snares that ever was laid, as the house you were so kindly directed to in search of a servant was nothing more or less than one of the most notorious houses of ill fame in all Paris. And when we drove up there, who should be walking up and down, eagerly looking out, no doubt, for *your* arrival, accompanied by H——, of the Embassy, but Henry Bulwer! Now H—— is a great ass; but, hang it! I acquit him of *knowingly* being an accomplice in so diabolical a plot. *He*, of course, was innocently decoyed into the stroll, no doubt to be an eye-witness of *your* abandoned infamy in going to such a place.'

With this sample of the unscrupulous devices of Lady Bulwer's enemies, I pass on to the trial of Sir E. L. Bulwer's agents, Lawson and Thackeray.

CHAPTER XIII.

THE action against these individuals is of the highest possible importance, affording as it does practically conclusive evidence, not only of the systematic persecution to which Lady Bulwer was subjected, but also of her amiable husband's complicity in the designs of the spies, informers, and slanderers who for years made her life a burden. I have accordingly deemed it advisable to report the case simply as it appeared in the contemporary newspapers, without giving Lady Bulwer's version or any comments of my own beyond what are absolutely necessary for explanation. The following extracts, therefore, will speak for themselves :—

"*Morning Post*," *March* 21st, 1840.

"PARIS CORRESPONDENCE.

"To-morrow Lady Bulwer's affair comes on in the Sixth Chamber of the Correctional Police. The case excites here the deepest interest both in English and French circles, and the court will certainly not hold the multitude which will throng to hear this curious lawsuit. The counsel engaged for Lady Bulwer are MM. Berryer, More, Chaix d'Est Ange, and Charles Ledru. The latter is also principal in the action for libel against Mr. Thackeray, Mr. Lawson's clerk. M. Delangle, *bâtonnier*, chief of the order of advocates, acts also for M. Charles Ledru, as the custom of the

profession is that when an advocate brings an action he
mnst be assisted by the chief of the order. The process
on the part of Lady Bulwer is against Mr. Lawson, an
attorney, and Mr. Thackeray, his clerk, for having conspired and attempted to carry off the private papers of
Lady Bulwer by fraudulently penetrating into her house ;
secondly, for subornation and bribery of witnesses ; and,
thirdly, the action is against Thackeray alone for defamation of Lady Bulwer by a letter which he published in the
Gazette des Tribuneaux, in answer to one from M. Charles
Ledru, detailing the circumstances of the former being
found in Lady Bulwer's house. M. Charles Ledru brings
an action against Mr. Thackeray for the same letter. I
understand that French laws are not very clear upon the
point of violation of domicile, or what we may term trespass ;
but the object of the prosecution appears to be more for
the purpose of affording Lady Bulwer's counsel an opportunity of making known to the world her persecution and
her persecutors. It is thus more an appeal to public
opinion than a recourse to criminal justice."

" *Morning Post*," *March* 28th.

" The two actions brought by Lady Bulwer and her
counsel, M. Charles Ledru, against Messrs. Lawson and
Thackeray for subornation of witnesses and bribery, came
on in the Tribunal of Correctional Police on Friday ;
but the causes were postponed till Friday next, on the
application of counsel for the defendants, to enable
M. Odilon Barrot to appear for Sir E. L. Bulwer."

Same Date.

" LADY LYTTON BULWER'S PROCESS IN PARIS.

" The action brought by Lady Lytton Bulwer against
Mr. Lawson, an attorney practising in this capital, and Mr.
J. G. Thackeray, his clerk, came on this morning in the
Sixth Chamber of the Tribunal Correctional, under the
presidency of M. Periondel. The case excited great
interest, and at an early hour this small court was crowded
with elegantly-dressed ladies. Mrs. Trollope was present,

and appeared to watch the proceedings with great anxiety.
Lord Howden, Colonel Webster, and numerous other
English gentlemen were also in the court. The French
auditory was also considerable, attracted probably by the
fact that the celebrated advocate M. Berryer was engaged.
Long before the case opened the court was filled in every
part. At eleven o'clock it was called on.

" The counsel for Lady Bulwer were MM. Berryer, Chaix
d'Est Ange, More, and Ledru ; and for the defendant,
M. Blanchet. Mr. Lawson and Mr. Thackeray stood below
the bar assigned to prisoners. The latter was a fine-looking
man, with an open expression of countenance. The former
was by no means prepossessing. To the usual questions
put by the President, Mr. Lawson said he was born in
Jamaica, and practising as an attorney in Paris. Mr.
Thackeray said he was born in Madras, and was clerk to
Mr. Lawson. The President said that as M. Ledru's action
was against the same defendants, the same judgment should
apply to the two causes. The President then said that he
had received a letter from M. Odilon Barrot, the counsel,
stating that he held a brief for Sir Edward Lytton Bulwer,
but that he could not plead that day, as he was waiting for
the instructions of his client.

" M. Berryer : I cannot reply to M. Odilon Barrot in his
absence. Our action is neither against Sir E. L. Bulwer
nor Mr. H. Bulwer, but against Lawson and Thackeray.
The facts of the case are these. Lady Bulwer has been
living in Paris for some time. Her husband is in England,
and a deed of separation exists between them. She has
been in Paris the object of inquiries and observations, and
every means of bribery have been resorted to with her
servants. Many persons have essayed to obtain from them
certain declarations contrary to the honour of this lady.
The sanctity of her domicile has even been violated to procure evidence against her ; and one of the accused, Mr.
Thackeray, has been arrested in her house, having introduced himself by attempting to corrupt her waiting-woman
in order to obtain false declarations against Lady Bulwer.
This attempt was particularly directed against her papers.

This fact is the principal object of the action : the fact of
a fraudulent entrance by Mr. Thackeray whilst Mr. Lawson
was waiting at the door of Lady Bulwer's house. This led
to an explanation in the newspapers on the part of Mr.
Thackeray, whose letter was found so insulting to and
defamatory of Lady Bulwer that she found it necessary to
bring this action ; and M. Charles Ledru has pursued the
same course for libel in the same letter. This is the nature
of the present cause.

" The President : The presence of Lady Bulwer may
perhaps not be indispensable, but it might be useful.

" M. Berryer : It is not the custom in England for ladies
to appear in court on such occasions ; but if it be necessary
that she should be here to give explanations, the wish of
the court, however unpleasant it must be to Lady Bulwer's
feelings, must be obeyed.

" M. Blanchet, counsel for the defendants, now came
into court. He said, ' M. Odilon Barrot is to appear for
Sir Edward Lytton Bulwer, who is now in London ; and
Messrs. Lawson and Thackeray are his agents here. Sir E.
Bulwer wishes to take cognisance of the affair to know if
it be expedient to authorise or to assist Lady Bulwer in
the dispute, or, on the other hand, to refuse her that
assistance that she has not thought proper to claim from
him. M. Odilon Barrot can appear this day week.'

" M. Berryer : The tribunal is accustomed to authorise
the wife to bring an action without the assistance of the
husband when she is interested to obtain the prompt reparation of a wrong caused by a fact designated as a crime
(*délit*). I must add that the deed of separation drawn up
between Lady Bulwer and her husband in conformity with
the English laws permits her to act for herself. This
cannot be denied, for it is but a few days since Lady
Bulwer brought an action in London against Mr. Henry
Bulwer, her brother-in-law, for libel, and obtained fifty
pounds damages.

" M. Blanchet (interrupting) : That is a mistake. Mr.
Henry Bulwer's name did not appear in the cause in
question.

" M. Berryer : Mr. Henry Bulwer was certainly not condemned ; nominally the action was against the editor of
the *Court Journal*, for an article the writer of which he
refused to give up. I contend that the wife of an alien
here is authorised to have recourse to a court of law for any
wrong she may receive, and she cannot be met with a nonsuit. However, I attach great interest to what Sir E. L.
Bulwer's intervention may lead to. I can therefore be the
first in asking, since the interference is now announced, that
the cause may be postponed till this day week.

" M. Ternaux (King's Advocate): In a week you will
be in the same position. It is a question to know if the
wife can sue isolated or alone.

" M. Blanchet : Mr. Lawson might take upon himself not
to insist upon the objection, but he is in a delicate position.
He represents here the interests of the husband. He has
acted by the precise orders of the husband. This is the
reason that he is obliged to wait till Sir E. L. Bulwer has
sent his instructions to M. Odilon Barrot, who will plead
for the husband.

" The trial was then postponed till Friday, March 27th, to
the evident disappointment of the numerous assemblage,
who retired from the court immediately. The turn which
this curious affair will take next Friday is, I need scarcely
add, the object of universal speculation. It was reported,
but I could not learn the fact positively, that Sir E. L.
Bulwer had arrived in Paris."

" *Morning Post," March* 30*th*, 1840.

LEADER.

" Lady Bulwer's action against Messrs. Lawson and
Thackeray came on before the Sixth Chamber of the
Tribunal Correctionnel de Police on Friday, in pursuance
of the adjournment to enable M. Odilon Barrot to appear for
Sir E. L. Bulwer. M. Barrot, in a long legal argument, contended that neither the English nor French laws authorised
Lady Bulwer to proceed in this case without the consent
of her husband, which he, from consideration for public
decency, thought proper to withhold. M. Berryer replied

in a most energetic and eloquent speech, quoting the deed of separation and an opinion of Lord Ellenborough in a similar cause to prove that it would be a monstrous oppression not to permit Lady Bulwer to proceed against these parties for their misconduct. The court, after deliberating a considerable time, decided that as the English laws required the consent of the husband in a civil suit, and as that consent had not been obtained by Lady Bulwer, she must be nonsuited. It appears from the report that this decision will only lead to further delay, as Lady Bulwer has still a remedy by the French laws to pursue her action against the defendants. M. Charles Ledru's action against Thackeray for libel was adjourned for a fortnight.

" We really think that Sir E. L. Bulwer's conduct is open to serious comment ; for how is it possible that he can take advantage of miserable quibbles to prevent his wife's case from seeing the light if there be not strong apprehensions on his part that the actions of his avowed agents in Paris have compromised himself as well as them ? It is not by concealment that the world will exonerate Sir E. L. Bulwer, for public sympathy must naturally incline to an unprotected lady who says that she has suffered grievous wrongs, and yet is prevented by her legal, if not natural, protector from obtaining redress from her oppressors on account of a technical objection."

" Morning Post," March 30th.

" LADY LYTTON BULWER'S PROCESS."

(Extracts from Report.)

" The process of Lady Bulwer against Mr. Lawson, an attorney practising in Paris, and Mr. Thackeray, his clerk, is for subornation and bribery of witnesses and for fraudulently penetrating into her domicile to purloin her papers, as also for libel on the part of Mr. Thackeray. The action of M. Charles Ledru against the clerk is also for a libel in the same letter published in the *Gazette des Tribuneaux.* It may be remembered that the case was adjourned last Friday to enable M. Odilon Barrot to receive instructions from Sir Edward Lytton Bulwer, who is now in Paris. This may be truly enrolled among the *causes célèbres*, for rarely has a case excited deeper and more general interest. Considerable curiosity was raised, inasmuch as, by order of the judges, Lady Bulwer was placed in the distressing situation of having to appear in court. Long before the proceedings commenced every corner of the court was occupied, and amidst the dense mass were most elegantly dressed ladies, the *élite* of English and French fashionable society. . . . The same counsel appeared as on the previous occasion. The appearance of M. Berryer was looked for with interest from his magnificent speech in the Chamber on Wednesday last, and his 'forensic' display was anticipated with equal curiosity. He has a very commanding figure, with a remarkably fine head, searching and expressive eyes, his action distinguished by its ease and grace, and his voice rich, round, and melodious. M. Odilon Barrot is a stern-looking man, with a conventicle tone of voice.

* * * * * *

" The case was a melancholy one, the exposure to the world of one of its severest miseries and heaviest inflictions. The proceedings were nevertheless unavoidable, for even a separated wife must not be suspected ; and if she has suffered wrong by a system of espionage, and the sanctity of her dwelling has been violated, she is bound to seek for protection and redress, however painful to her feelings, from the hands of justice. M. Blanchet opened the proceedings by stating that Messrs. Lawson and Thackeray had been obliged to call upon Sir E. L. Bulwer to become a party in the case. Mr. Lawson is the representative in France of Sir E. L. Bulwer in making certain inquiries as to Lady Bulwer, his wife. Mr. Lawson accepted the delicate mission, and in the course of its fulfilment the circumstances arose upon which this action is founded. Messrs. Lawson and Thackeray . . . did not think it right to afford Lady Bulwer an opportunity of pursuing the system of defaming her husband she had hitherto followed. . . . They were unwilling that Lady Bulwer, by accusing them of violation of domicile and other crimes, should proclaim facts which ought to remain private." After a protest from M. Berryer and some legal argument, the President called upon Lady Bulwer ; "and she" (to resume the report) "entered the court, accompanied by Mrs. Trollope. Her Ladyship's appearance created some sensation, and evident marks of sympathy were evinced for her excessive agitation. The French criticisms were that she was a *belle dame* and quite an *élégante.* Two chairs were placed beside the box of the King's Advocate for Lady Bulwer and Mrs. Trollope. To the customary questions as to name, residence, etc., of the President, she replied in French that her ordinary residence was 30 bis, Rue de Rivoli, and that she was of no profession. I am ashamed to say that French politeness is eschewed in legal forms, and she was asked that most delicate of all questions to put to a lady—her age. I think she said thirty-five. M. Odilon Barrot proceeded to explain Sir E. L. Bulwer's conduct. His only object was to avoid public scandal. M. Barrot then read the following letter which he had received from Sir Edward :—

"'I have to ask at your hands the support of your oratory and of your character in a distressing circumstance which concerns me. An action has been brought before the French tribunals against Mr. Lawson, my agent, by Lady Bulwer. I have informed myself of the facts which serve as a pretext to this process, and I feel persuaded that they have been got up with the sole purpose of provoking scandal and to prejudge the wrongs of which I have myself to complain at the hands of Lady Bulwer as a husband and a father. I must now put in my interdiction against my wife bringing such an action in a foreign tribunal.

"'In all countries the married woman, even if separated from her husband by legal means, cannot bring any action without his consent or that of the law. The English courts of justice will appear to you, as to me, more capable of appreciating and judging the discussions the publicity of which is provoked, and which interest the honour of a whole family, as well as the future welfare of my children.

"'I have the honour, etc.,

"'E. L. BULWER.'

"'Sir E. Bulwer,' continued M. Odilon Barrot, 'is now ready to repeat verbally his refusal. We have only to discuss a question of law, which is at the same time one of public decorum.' M. Barrot then argued that Lady Bulwer could not prosecute her action without her husband's consent unless she first appealed to the tribunal to set aside her husband's authority.

"M. Berryer, in an eloquent reply, commented strongly upon Sir Edward's conduct in protecting men who were admittedly his own agents against the consequences of an outrage on his wife. He contended that Lady Bulwer had a right to sue in her own name by the terms of the deed of separation, and concluded : 'If I were in England, I would say to the tribunal, "In the name of the Queen of the three kingdoms, I plead for a woman whose husband has refused to her his authority to demand justice;" and I would ask for that woman the reparation which the law was bound to grant her. This is the law of the case. What is its morality? It is said that we seek for scandal. Scandal, indeed! the scandal is in the protection which is given to the guilty.'

"Both counsel again addressed the court; and then M. Ternaux, substitute of the Procureur du Roi, summed up the case in a manner adverse to Lady Bulwer's claims. The Tribunal retired at ten minutes to one, and at a quarter past two delivered judgment to the effect that Lady Bulwer could not sustain the action in her own name, that she was therefore nonsuited, and that she must pay the costs of the proceedings."

"*April 4th*, 1840.—Sir E. L. Bulwer and his solicitor, Mr. Loaden, are still here. The latter has been attempting a compromise with Lady Bulwer, but Lady Bulwer ordered him out of her house this afternoon."

"*April 6th*, 1840.—Sir E. L. Bulwer's affair with Lady

Bulwer stands thus. His solicitor wrote to her Ladyship that she had better apply to the Court of Chancery in England for the redress of her wrongs in Paris; that is, apply to a court which has no jurisdiction over the offenders residing in Paris. The letter in question was couched in such offensive terms (and I can have no hesitation in saying so, since Mr. Loaden says in it that it is intended for publication), that Lady Bulwer, when he called on her, ordered him to leave her house. M. Ledru, her counsel, declines to listen to the compromise not expressly offered, but hinted at, by Mr. Loaden when he called on the former. The appeal of Lady Bulwer against the decision of the Police Correctionnel stands good at present, as also M. Ledru's action for libel against Thackeray, fixed for next Friday. The case attracts great attention here."

This last paragraph from the *Morning Post* produced the following curious epistle from Mr. Loaden himself, which was published in that journal on April 7th, 1840 :—

"SIR EDWARD AND LADY LYTTON BULWER.—TO THE EDITOR OF THE 'MORNING POST.'

"SIR,—

"In your paper of this day you have thought proper to insert the following misstatements connected with my name in the affair of Sir E. L. Bulwer with Lady Bulwer." (Here follows the passage in *Morning Post* of April 6— "His solicitor" to "former.") "I beg in reply to state that I never hinted as to any compromise whatever to M. Ledru : that he himself (in an interview with me upon a wholly different professional subject) "regretted that there should be any such differences between husband and wife, and that I expressly told him that I had no power whatever from Sir E. L. Bulwer to treat the matter ; and I even refused to mention to Sir Edward what M. Ledru had said on the subject, although requested by M. Ledru to do so. Secondly, that I told him that I wished to see Lady Bulwer on a matter between herself and myself,

Thirdly, it is false to state that in my letter to Lady
Bulwer I referred her to the Court of Chancery on the
subject of the present French lawsuit. I informed her
simply that in consequence of the inquiries instituted
by Sir Edward, he had felt it his duty to withdraw from
her Ladyship the liberty of access he had hitherto granted
her to her children, especially her daughter; and that,
by a recent Act of Parliament, she could apply to the
Court of Chancery for that access; and that then all
her general complaints against Sir Edward could be
heard; but with respect to the particular suit, I distinctly
referred her to the proper tribunal in France, with which
Sir Edward could not interfere, and by which, if her
accusations were really tenable, her suit would be tried
without cost to herself, in proof of which, and in reply
to the charge that my letter was couched in offensive
terms, I beg to enclose a copy of it, and request you
to insert it.

" I am, etc.,

"WILLIAM LOADEN.

" We decline to print the letter that Mr. Loaden has
enclosed.—Editor *Morning Post.*"

It need hardly be said that this epistle does not
greatly redound to the credit either of Mr. Loaden or
of his distinguished client. It had already been acknowledged in open court both by M. Blanchet and
M. Odilon Barrot that Lawson and Thackeray were
employed by Sir E. L. Bulwer to act as spies and
informers with regard to Lady Bulwer's movements
and actions, and now we have a categorical confession from Mr. Loaden as to the objects of these
inquiries. They were, it is abundantly clear, firstly,
to secure evidence which would enable the baronet
to sue for a divorce; secondly, to blast his wife's
reputation in society; and, thirdly, to justify him in
forbidding her access to her children.

Being unable, by fair means or foul, to obtain the proofs he desired, Sir E. L. Bulwer nevertheless proceeded to carry out part of his plan in utter defiance of every rule of justice and humanity.   For, to resume Lady Bulwer's narrative,—

"after the iniquitous suppression of this trial against his emissaries, Lawson and Thackeray, in Paris, Sir Edward's next move to torture his hapless victim was to put a total stop to even the simulacrum of a correspondence which had subsisted between her and her poor children ; and although it had never been anything beyond the six stereotyped lines of Miss Greene's dictation, commencing with the obligato 'Dear Mamma,' still the words, meaningless and measured as they were, had been traced by their little hands, and were therefore precious to Lady Bulwer's poor desecrated heart; but for that reason even this faint reflected ray of happiness was to be denied her."

The only important event which occurred to Lady Bulwer during the remainder of her stay in Paris was the having one day lost a very pretty little Blenheim dog in the Bois de Boulogne, which luckless event made her acquainted with that great man Vidocq, and it was only right that having, for a short time, got rid of the thieves, she should fall in with the great thief-taker.   Every morning he used to express his sympathy for her loss upon rose-coloured paper, and until the poor little dog was found he used to call twice a week, with his brown wig and his endless fund of amusing anecdotes.   The following letter may help to prove the great detective's energy in Lady Bulwer's cause :—

" Le 2 Janvier, 1840.

"MILADY,—

    "Ainsi que j'ai eu l'honneur de vous informer j'ai fait continuer les explorations les plus étendues pour découvrir votre chien et se mettre sur ses traces. Les diverses rues de Chaillot et toutes celles de Passy ont d'abord été l'objet particulier de l'investigation de mes hommes ; les boutiquiers, commissionaires, marchands, ambulands, revendants sur la voie publique, tous ont été questionné, mais infructueusement. J'ai donné l'ordre de pousser les investigations aussi loin que possible, et d'explorer également la commune de Neuilly, les diverses routes qui aboutent près au bois de Boulogne, et qui communiquent avec les chemins qui conduisent à Passy ; toutes ces démarches n'ont pu être couronnées d'aucun succès.

" Esperons mieux du résultat des affiches.

    " J'ai l'honneur d'être avec respect, Milady,

        " Votre très humble serviteur,

            " VIDOCQ.

" P.S.—Les affiches sont posées."

Lady Lytton's appeal to the Cour Royale was never prosecuted, owing, no doubt, to her lack of means ; and later in the year 1840 she quitted Paris for Italy.

I append here a few letters received about this date by Lady Lytton from Mr. and Mrs. Trollope :—

FROM MRS. TROLLOPE.

"3, WYNDHAM STREET, BRYANSTON SQUARE.

"I have no heart to write to you, dear friend, and yet I could not see my son sending off a letter without one word from me. Oh! how your kind warm heart would pity me could you witness the anxious misery I am enduring! My poor darling lies in a state that defies the views of his physicians as effectually as it puzzles my ignorance. It is asthma from which he chiefly suffers now ; but they say this can only be a symptom, and not the disease. He is frightfully reduced in size and strength ; sure am I that could you see him, you would not find even a distant resemblance to the being who, exactly three months ago, left us in all the pride of youth, health, and strength.   Day by day I lose hope, and so, I am quite sure, do his physicians; we have had three consultations, but nothing prescribed relieves him, nor has any light been thrown on the nature of his complaint. Let me hear what your proposed movements are.   Alas! the sad change from the gay hopes with which I left you!   Not all the engrossing anxiety that has been upon me from the hour of my arrival has prevented my thinking much of you.   During the days that Tom was giving every moment he could spare from me and his poor brother to seeing after Colburn and publishers, I was very unhappy about your MS., and repeatedly believed that all the dark prognostics for which I used to scold you were to prove true prophecy.   That you *were* right in a very great degree, I am quite convinced, but this without losing the slightest portion of my confidence in the professionally recognised value of any work from your hands.   But in this case there was a great propensity to let *fear* predominate over even a *certain* prospect of gain.   Under these circumstances (the existence of which cannot be doubted), I hope you will not hesitate about the present offer.   The same person who braves the danger now will not be likely to shrink before it in future, for it would increase; and the more you write, the more imperative will the call for your works become.   Do yourself but justice by giving yourself quiet unbroken leisure to write, and I will readily stake my judgment on a brilliant success—so brilliant as to defy all cabal to smother it.

" God bless you, dearest Lady Bulwer.   Do not forget to love me should our hoped-for meeting be delayed for long, very long.

" Ever affectionately yours,
" F. TROLLOPE.

" Pray remember me kindly to Mr. Hume."

FROM THE SAME.

" 3, WYNDHAM STREET, BRYANSTON SQUARE,
" <i>Friday, July 3rd</i>, 1840.</div>

" You are a thousand times kinder to me than I deserve, albeit I really do love you heartily, and would serve you

too, dear friend, if I knew how. What can I feel but
pride and pleasure at your offered dedication? I accept
it, dear Lady Bulwer, gratefully. But both here and in
your preface, let your old woman preach to you; and bear
it, dear, as sweetly as I have seen you do heretofore, when
most literally 'love conquered fear,' and enabled me
to lecture you upon prudence and forbearance as never
any one so circumstanced was lectured before. You
have great powers; and though I will not say they
have been unworthily used in being lent to the painful
purpose of exposing a little part of what you have so
wrongfully endured, I will say that no one who loves
and admires you as much as I do, and who knows
even no more than I do of the public, but would
deprecate the idea of your again dipping your brilliant
wing in the dirty troubled waters of personal affairs.
Walter Scott, with all his talent multiplied into itself, could
not have stood against the killing blight of such a mildew
as this would wrap round your name as a writer. I saw
the Herculean strength and vigour of Byron's literary
reputation almost strangled by his

'Born in the garret, in the kitchen bred,'

and well do I remember hearing one of the cleverest men in
Europe, and a greatly attached friend of Byron to boot, say,
'If he goes on wiping his eyes thus upon the public, it is over
with him; it is downright snivelling.' I stake my sagacity
on your success as a writer if you keep clear of this pitfall.
My poor Anthony is so very nearly in the same state as when
I last wrote that I have not a word to say that can
help to give you information of our future movements.
Had I the power to move, my will is as fixed as ever
towards Italy; and the journey thither with you would
be a *surcroit* of pleasure that I should value as it deserves.
But at this moment I *dare not* think of pleasure; I *dare not*
plan a future. I have seen the dear Pauncefotes with real
pleasure. I think very highly of them, and if I must give
you up myself, would rather yield you to them than
to anybody else. They have right principles, right feelings,

and right tempers. Poor dear Judith ! How I love you for
going to her. Trust me, your vocation is not to scold,
either in public or in private. Your nature is kind,
noble, generous, and warm-hearted. You have a great many
things to thank God for, That you have been *sorely
tried* is true; but you have that within you that *ought*
to enable you to rise unscathed from it all. Now do
not shake your head and say, 'Foolish old woman!' but
be good, and mind what I say to you, and I shall live
yet to see all the world admire you as much as I do,
and I shall be proud of my friend. Kiss Taff and tell
him I should know him amidst a thousand.

"God bless you, dear friend, and believe me,

"Ever affectionately yours,

"FRANCES TROLLOPE."

FROM MR. T. ADOLPHUS TROLLOPE.

"*Friday, July 3rd,* 1840.

"DEAR LADY BULWER,—

"I have this instant received your letter. Pray
do not talk so much of thanks for my little attempt to render
my very useless existence in any degree of service to some-
body. I do thank you, however, for the illuminated post-
boy you have sent me, for that is something 'out of the
common.'

"And now to business. I am vexed that you, and
Hume as well, seem entirely to misunderstand the nature
of the offer Mr. Bull makes respecting the second £400.
You and Hume, in his letter to me, both say that you wish
the second £400 to be paid in a bill given at the time of
publication. Of course you wish it; so do I; so would
any one. It is simply converting a contingency into a
certainty, a very different (I am sorry to say) sort of terms,
which of course I should have obtained for you if it had
been possible. The terms, which I thought I did right to
accept from Bull, more especially as they are accurately
the same as you had determined on accepting from Colburn,
are these : £400 to be paid on delivery of the MS. (mode

of payment not definitively arranged, but doubtless might be, as you say in your letter, by a bill at three months) for the right to print 1,250 copies ; then £200 to be paid contingently on going to press with 750 copies. These were the terms you determined on accepting from Colburn. Bull will give you the additional guarantee of a letter to his printer to account to you the number printed. Since writing the above I have been to Bull. He would not hear of altering the terms as you propose, saying, truly enough, that it made *all* the difference, and would be throwing an infinitely increased risk on him. He said, ' Is it to be considered all up, then ?'

" ' Not at all,' I answered ; ' I shall immediately send your answer to Lady Bulwer, and my impression is that she will accede to your terms.' Was I wrong in so doing? I dreaded having the negotiation with him broken off, as I know not to whom I could go next; and somehow or other news circulates through the trade so quickly that it is a very dangerous experiment to hawk a book about more than can possibly be helped from one to another. The freshness of a new novel's name and reputation is injured almost as easily as a peach's bloom.   Besides, I have NO hopes of obtaining a *certain* £800, or of course I should not have closed with Bull's terms.

" Respecting the illustrations, he appeared very unwilling, saying that the book would sell as well without, and that it would be an expense *de plus* for nothing. However, I insisted; and he has promised to have six plates by Cruikshank if possible, which, it seems, is very doubtful.

" As to the mode of paying the £400, I pressed, according to what you say in your letter, for a bill at three months, which he will give you on delivery of the MS. if you require it; but he begged hard that it might be divided into two bills, one at three, and the other at four months' date. I do not like to take Hyde to him to witness the agreement; it is unusual. It is needlessly offensive to a man with whom we had better keep on agreeable terms. It is also useless, seeing that I shall take care that the agreement is drawn up in the usual manner and properly signed; and all the lawyers in the world can do no more. Will you, when you send your MS. to Mr. Hyde, ask him to send me a line announcing its arrival?

"I have said a great deal to Bull respecting the printing, and he swears by his gods that it shall be carefully done. He grumbles about the *length* of ' Cheveley; ' and I much fear that the ' Bubbles ' is as *least* as long. It goes to my heart to give 'the public' a measure running over into their ungrateful bosoms. I scraped mine off close along the top of the bushel, and put by all that was over for another time.

"But you have no notion of economy. I hope you are already thinking in earnest of your next book. Do you remember my suggestion that upon some slight thread of a story you should string the adventures, sayings, and doings and seeings of a ludicrously composed English party making the grand tour ? Begin with them at Paris; and then take them over the ground which you purpose traversing this autumn, etc. I am sure the idea is a good one, 'though *I* says it, as shouldn't.' My brother is unquestionably *much* better. We must not, as his sententious Esculapius says, ' cry, " Whoop ! " before we are out of the wood ; ' but I am in great hope that he will now rapidly gain ground, and that our plans will resume their course. The Pauncefotes have no thoughts of leaving Paris till October, and will then, I fear, certainly proceed direct to Naples by Marseilles ; whereas if we are able to leave England in time to be at Venice in October, we shall take that route, in order to meet Chateaubriand and Madame Recamier there, which my mother much wishes to do. What do you intend doing during the summer and early autumn ? My mother has written to you and to Madame de Montalc, but she will send her letters by the occasion you speak of. This will go forthwith, as it is desirable to lose no time in concluding with Bull. Pray give my best regards and wishes to M. de Montalc, and to Hume, whose commission shall be attended to ; I am much obliged to him for his letter, to which this is an answer, as it was all about your book.   Many thanks for the interest you take in my scribblement ; it is going on swimmingly.   This pen never learnt to write when it was young ; and now in its hebetated old age, when all its faculties are blunted, it is disgusting.   Pray excuse *its* scrawl ; and believe me,

" Always sincerely yours,

" T. ADOLPHUS TROLLOPE."

FROM MRS. TROLLOPE AND T. ADOLPHUS TROLLOPE.

" *July 9th*, 1840.

"Knowing, dear friend, that when you say, 'Write by the post,' you mean it, I take up my pen as soon as possible, in the nature of things, after putting down your letter, and proceed to tell you, not all you desire to know, but all I know myself.   First, however, let me forestall a portion of the epistle at present reposing in Mrs. Pauncefote's travelling trunk, that is to say, let me thank you heartily and affectionately for the honour you propose to do me, and assure you that such a proof of your regard is very precious to me ; I accept it joyfully.   Now if I forestall still farther, and tell you that the rest of the said Pauncefote despatch is a sermon, perhaps you will burn it.   But don't, dear, for if you do, you will lose one proof of my affection.

"Anthony goes on decidedly improving, but so slowly as to make every morning's inquiry one of fear and trembling.   Still I DO hope and believe that we shall be able to leave England early in September ; and if so, we shall proceed *viâ* Paris direct to Venice by diligence and with diligence (absolute ablative case, if not ablative case absolute), from whence we shall proceed to Naples, seeing as much of the writable about places as we can *en route*.   At Naples, where we hope to arrive in November, we propose remaining till it is time to remove to Rome for the Holy Week.   After that I know nothing, but think it very likely we shall pass our time at Florence.

"Could we not meet at *Venice?* Ma'dame Recamier would not have *seemed* to like you had she not done so. Where she does like her sweet nature leads her to show it, but if she be a flatterer, her flattery is only for those she loves. She keeps people at arm's length more steadily, *courageously*, and effectually than any one I know. *Do* let us meet at Venice! I should like it in all ways. In the first place, the uncertainty of our movements will by that time be as much over as ever happens, I suppose, in human doings; and, secondly, our economical and therefore of *necessity* disagreeable going-ahead travelling must be over, or, at least, by far the worst part of it. And besides, if, on comparing notes together at Venice, we discover that we should do better by travelling to Naples in different ways, we can do so. But I have a great feeling that I should like to be at Venice with ——. There is eternal interest in the place. There is interest in Chateaubriand and his charming old friend —— and ——. In short, I hope we *shall* meet at Venice. Most surely you are wise not to remain at Paris through the dog-days; why should you? Your Rhenish route would give you a somewhat longer, but much more agreeable journey.

"My highly gifted and very interesting friend, Mrs. Fauche, is with her beautiful little girls at Heidelberg; and for a few weeks, if you liked to halt there, you would find her a delightful companion. If you would like such a halt, tell me so directly, and I will write to her, and she will receive you with all the kindness of her most kind heart; and when you get to her, my principal fear will be that I shall not be able to get you away again. But if you threaten any false-heartedness towards me, you shall have a heavy packet by the post once every day containing the words, '*Meet me at Venice.*' But here I must stop, for the Signor is away to Bull; and I must let this sheet convey the result to you. God bless dear warm-hearted Hume (I don't mean Joseph). I wish I had his strong steadfast will, moving in some direction in which it could be useful. But he is *wrong*,

wrong, wrong.   Give my kind regards to said Hume, and tell him he is a very lucky fellow for not knowing more about this vile publishing work, but he does know very little indeed."

ADDED BY T. A. TROLLOPE.

"Dear Lady Bulwer, I am vexed at your letter to my mother.   Do not think me impertinent for saying so; but allow me to point out one or two passages which appear to me delicately tinged with the slightest possible measure of unreasonableness, a womanly failing, and the only one which I attribute to women in a greater degree than to their 'owners:' £400 is *not* a 'beggarly' price for a novel, with another £400 contingent; James, a decidedly successful novelist, has only £500 for the copyright.   My mother, after her *very* successful book on America and a most flourishing review-in the *Quarterly*, had only £400 for her two first novels.   *You* say that 'you will be cheated as much as he can possibly cheat you.'   But I do think that Bull's opportunities of cheating you will be as small as they can be in any case.   You complain that 'to repay himself for the paltry sum he gives you is all that Bull cares for.' Unquestionably it is.   What on earth else should he care for?   Permit me to assure you that the views of all publishers are (lamentable as it is) absolutely and un-mixedly mercenary, and that all hopes of a race of publishers, who shall consult their author's interest instead of their own, must be deferred to those promised days when the lion shall lie down with the lamb, and other heterogeneous associations come to pass.   You agree to accept Bull's terms 'if he will give you a written promise that the illustrations shall be done by Cruikshank.'   But how is he to promise for another man?   He undertakes to do all he can with Cruikshank; he is as anxious to have him as you are.   But this is by no means easy. He wishes me also to go to Cruikshank; to see and testify that no endeavours are wanting on his part to induce him to undertake it, and also to assist in flattering him

into compliance with *your* wishes. This I shall do if
Bull does not ·succeed with him. I have this morning
been to Bull, and have caused the enclosed agreements
to be drawn up.   The one signed by Bull you must
keep, and return the other signed by yourself.   Will
you return it with the MS. to Mr. Hyde ? What must be
done with the bills paid by Bull should they be paid in to
any banker here? I took your note to Mrs. Willoughby's
this morning ; she had started for Paris. The people, however, *would* keep the note. Pray do not be very angry
with me for all that I have here written ; and believe me,

"Always faithfully yours,

"T. ADOLPHUS TROLLOPE."

CHAPTER XIV.

THE next two years, 1840—1842, were spent by Lady Bulwer at Florence ; and here she seems to have enjoyed comparative immunity from persecution. During these two years she was told that the spies were in full force ; but, as for fifteen months of that period she was suffering from a severe and lingering illness, the only proofs of their activity which she experienced were occasionally receiving open through the post (that is, with the seals no doubt purposely broken, that they might be read upon Mr. Loaden's plan for the diffusion of knowledge) letters of the most infamous description, varied in their signatures from " Frederick " to "Charles" or "Henry." It is certainly barely possible that these letters may have been *bonâ fide* travellers and really addressed to the deputy Lady Bulwer, the woman Beaumont.

Of course the diplomatic relations kept pace with those at Paris wherever she went for marked rudeness and neglect. As soon as Lady Bulwer felt well enough to re-encounter the abominations of an Italian journey she resolved to return to England, but unfortunately at Geneva she heard of the death of poor Mr. Bull, her ever-liberal publisher. This was a serious loss to her, as she had still heavy legal expenses to meet on account of the Paris conspiracy ; and the new publisher whom she entered into a negotiation with, like his order, ever eager to seize upon any pretext to mulct their natural prey an author, wrote her word that Mrs. M——, with her long-flowing ringlets, had been to threaten him unheard-of persecution on the part of her then friend Sir Edward Bulwer, and that if he published for her in the first place, he would take good care that any book of hers should be effectually crushed by the reviewers.

At Geneva Lady Bulwer spent four years. Of the early part of her sojourn there I have no record, but it may be presumed that she was almost continuously engaged in literary labour. From a mass of correspondence with all sorts of personages I extract the following letter from Georges Sand :—

FROM GEORGES SAND (PARIS), CE 6 DECEMBRE, 1842,
À MADAME ROSINA LYTTON BULWER À GENÈVE.

"Nous vous connoissons, Madame, sans nous être jamais rencontrées ; vous avez prêté votre génie à un époux indigne de vous, et vos œuvres collectives ont illuminé l'Angleterre et la France. J'ai versé, moi, mes rêves et mes douleurs dans des romans qui ont fait plus de bruit qu'ils ne méritent ; vous avez souffert : j'ai souffert aussi—notre route est la même. Ne vous étonnez donc pas si je viens vous tendre la main. Les écrits récents qui portent votre nom m'inspirent pour vous la plus vive sympathie. J'aime à voir votre étoile graviter seule dans l'orbite que le ciel lui a tracé ; le génie est solitaire, et contrairement à l'ordre établi, c'est vous qui êtes le soleil : l'autre n'a brillé que de votre reflêt ; vous devez mépriser l'honneur mâle comme je le méprise. Acceptez mon amitié ; lignons nous toutes deux contre un sèxe qui ne nous a donné que déceptions et tortures ; consolons nous réciproquement ; et prouvons au monde que la femme jetée par le malheur en dehors de sa sphère reprend le

sceptre de l'intelligence à ceux qui lui ont arraché vio-
lemment la baguette magique du cœur.

"J'attends un mot de vous, et je l'espère.

"GEORGES SAND."

It was at Geneva that Lady Bulwer received news
of the death of her mother-in-law, Mrs. Lytton,
which occurred in 1844.

"So," she writes, "Sir Edward Bulwer attained the
object of his lifelong exertions, namely the possession
of her unentailed property, Knebworth Park, for which
he took her maiden name of Lytton, and so became
Sir Edward Bulwer Lytton; but the only change this
accession of fortune produced to his victim was to
have her pittance more irregularly paid and to receive
an insolent notification from Loaden that it was Sir
Edward's desire that she should not assume the name
of Lytton, but restrict herself to that of Bulwer, while
the same post brought her a letter from good Mr. Hyde
directed to Lady Bulwer Lytton by royal assent! But
in this letter he told her that in order to sue her husband
for a proper maintenance, proportionate to his present
fortune, she must return to England, as she could not
do so outside the jurisdiction of the court. But at that
time she had not the funds for the purpose; and good
care was taken, as will be seen hereafter, to prevent any
facilities for her doing so; and another year rolled on
like a dark cloud, as every year was now to her. One
evening, as she was sitting at the window of the hotel
after a more than usually miserable day, looking alternately at the lake, with its clear blue waters, and the
muddy carriages and *fourgons* that drove up to the door,
an *avant-courier* dashed, with his splashed boots and
jingling bells, up to the door, and alighted in all the
haste of his order. After his friendly greeting with the
waiters at the door he drew a large pocket-book from his
side-pocket, and opening it, took from out a wilderness
of passports and tariffs a letter; and Lady Lytton thought,

as he handed it to one of the waiters, that she heard
her own name, coupled with the words 'Est-elle ici'?
Nor was she mistaken, for shortly afterwards the man
to whom the letter had been given brought it in. This
letter to all appearance might have passed for a bridal
announcement; the envelope was of that white, highly
glazed enamelled paper then in vogue, with a delicate
tracery of silver round it; above the seal the coronet
and supporters were also in embossed silver; and, like all
foreign epistles, this one was redolent of patchouli. Now,
there was nothing in all these accessories to excite alarm
any more than in the bold yet delicate and ladylike
writing; and yet a sharp pain shot through her heart, and
she was some seconds before she could summon courage
to break the seal. At length she did so, and read as
follows, the letter being from Madame de S——, wife of
the chargé d'affaires at Frankfort:—

"'FRANKFORT-ON-THE-MAINE, *Thursday, June,* 18—.

"'DEAREST LADY LYTTON,—

"'The ——s leave this to-morrow for Geneva,
which gives me an opportunity of sending you a packet
safely; and, although it is now two in the morning, I
cannot go to bed without telling you what I fear will
give you pain; and yet, knowing as I do how you yearn
after any intelligence of your poor darling children, and
judging by my own feelings, I think you would even rather
hear the sad tidings I have to tell than remain ignorant of
them. Strange to say, at N——d there is now living a
Madame de W——y, who had formerly been Sarah's and
my governess; and so far I can reassure you that she
is a most ladylike, accomplished person, though I do
not think she possesses what I, and I know *you*, regard as
far more essential, a grain of feeling. Now it appears Sir
Edward has placed your dear girl with her; and as I am
not on terms with Madame de W——y, who did not
behave well to Mamma, I heard of poor E——'s arrival
in a strange way from the landlady of an hotel here.
It seems she came with that horrid Miss Greene, whom,

unseen and unknown, I so cordially detest for her base
ingratitude and treachery to you, and the evening of her
arrival the woman of the hotel, going into the room
for something while Miss Greene had gone out, saw poor
dear E—— sitting on the sofa, with her feet tucked
under her, *à la Turc*, whereupon she said to her, "My
dear, put down your feet; that is not a pretty way for
a young lady to sit." "Oh!" said the poor child, "I
cannot put them down, for I have but two pairs of
stockings! one is not unpacked, and the other pair, that
I had on, is gone to be washed." I feel, dearest Lady
Lytton, as my own tears blot the paper, how cruel it is
to write this to you, and yet perhaps it would be more
cruel to withhold it; and what I further elicited from
the Frau —— may give you a gleam of comfort. I
know it did me, as it is the beginning of retributive
justice on that wretch Miss Greene. It appears that
Madame de W——y was so *effarouchée* at Miss Greene's
appearance and vulgarity to match, that she said she
could not possibly undertake Miss Lytton's education
unless such an appendage was got rid of. Miss Greene
then *improvisée*'d an alarming paroxysm of hysterics,
and wanted to intimidate poor E—— into writing to
her father to say that she should die if separated from
Miss Greene; but the dear child, apparently only too
enchanted at such an unhoped-for opportunity of getting
rid of her, steadily refused to put pen to paper for any
such purpose; so the battle ended in the total defeat
of Miss Greene, who was *congédiée* at last. I feel
that after writing you such painful details as these, any
attempts at consolation would be almost a mockery; but
you may rely upon it, dearest Lady Lytton, that I will
not lose sight of your darling child, and shall keep you
au courant to everything concerning her, as far as I can
possibly collect it. As I look at my own little calmly
sleeping treasure, I feel almost a monster to add another
wound to your poor lacerated heart; would to God that
I could pour comfort into it instead, but HE alone can
do so, who has given you such a varied experience of

(humanly speaking) apparently unmerited trials—unmerited, but not unnecessary. The furnace has been indeed fierce for you, but it has been to purify, and not to consume; where all is so solemnly sad and impenetrably mysterious, reason might well despair, but faith has a deeper sense than reason; and we greatly tried ones know that our choicest fountains are fed from the darkest clouds. And when the sun of worldly prosperity is setting, as set it *will,* in endless night on your cruel and unmanly oppressor, may you, dearest Lady Lytton, find, like the aged patriarch, "that at evening time it is light,"

"'Is the fervent prayer of

"'Your sincerely affectionate

"'S——t de S——e.'

"The next day Lady Lytton sold a bracelet and sent the £20 she got for it to her kind friend Madame de S——, entreating that she would at least buy the poor innocent little martyr some clothes; but after keeping this money eight months Madame de S—— returned it, saying that she had found it impossible either to convey it, or in any way to gain access to the poor child, and that the only additional information she had been able to reap about her was that Sir Edward, with his usual hypocrisy of always getting up some solemn sham to dupe the public with, had taken poor Emily to Baden-Baden with him for six weeks, in order to play the amiable father to that little Babel of gossip and gambling; and although the sum total he allowed Madame de W——y for her education, food, etc., was £100 a year, yet on his return from this excursion he had actually wanted to deduct these six weeks from that magnificent stipend!

"Two more miserable years crept slowly on; and Madame de S—— having left Frankfort, the unhappy mother could gain no more tidings of her ill-fated child."

Nor did better fortune attend her efforts to communicate with her son.

"To return to that delectable state of things from

which not only all reason, but all humanity, was banished, Lady Lytton heard, through the friend who had kindly promised to take her packet for her poor daughter to England,* that her son was now at a public school, and knowing very well that his father was not very likely either to consult or comply with his boyish tastes, and that before boys know or heed the value of time, a watch forms an epoch in their lives, as does a chain as long as its links are fragile and golden, she sent him a watch and chain, with a small enamel portrait of herself; and oh, the hot tears that fell upon the latter, as she thought how cold and tearlessly those mimic eyes would meet her boy's deep loving ones! Yes, they *were* always full of love, and *must* be still; and she knew, she *felt* all his young being would rush in wild tumults to their brink, and his heart leap into that deep flood of love and sorrow gushing from hers then.

"Poor soul! Such was her fervent faith, for there is no fanaticism like that of a mother's love; truly it hopeth all things, endureth all things. Her boy being younger than his poor sister, she had only written him a short letter of love and counsel, such as a boy could understand, might *feel*, and would remember; and as the weeks went by her heart stood still at every letter that was brought into the room, straining its every nerve to see the round schoolboy hand which she thought *must* come at last; but no, not even that; and then indeed, as hope died away, like Tennyson's Mariana,

> " ' Her tears fell with the dews at even ;
> Her tears fell ere the dews were dried ;
> She could not look on the sweet heaven
>   Either at noon or eventide :
> She only said, " My life is dreary,
>   He cometh not," she said ;
> She said, I am aweary, aweary,
>   I would that I were dead.'

---

* This lady was unable to find an opportunity of delivering the packet.—L. D.

"One day an English lady and her husband and their three blooming children were sitting with her; the lady, charming in every respect, was a model wife; and oh, rarer far, the gentleman *par excellence* was a model husband. They were preaching from the old text to her, to hope against hope, when a servant brought in a parcel and a letter; both were from England. Lady Lytton opened the letter first; it was only three lines, and they ran as follows:—

"'BEDFORD ROW, LONDON, *June* 1846.

"'MADAM,—

"'Master Lytton, having received a watch, chain, and miniature from you, begs to return them, and desires that for the future he may not receive any more parcels.

"'I am, Madam, your obedient servant,

"'WILLIAM LOADEN.'"

Such were the only episodes which varied the monotony of the unhappy lady's existence.

"Four miserable years had she lingered on at that wretched little Calvinistic town which Voltaire truly described as

"'Cette ville froide et fade, où tout est entamé,
    Où l'on calcule toujours, et ne sent jamais,'

though she, it must be confessed, had some noble-hearted friends there, but they were the exceptions that proved the rule, being a few of those bright golden links in that long chain of lead which men call life.

"It is an old remark what a quantity of killing women take, and poor Lady Lytton was a notable instance of this. There had now been a delay of several weeks in the payment of her miserable pittance; and as she was in the habit of settling her bills at the hotel quarterly, this of course caused her the greatest inconvenience and annoyance; and she wrote and wrote to her trustee without success. Poor Lady Lytton! As the long, tedious, blank days lingered one after another, she knew that she still existed, because she felt that she suffered; and each letter caused a fever flush, not indeed of hope, but of expectation, which was invariably doomed to a sudden death of disappointment. One morning, as she was eagerly trusting that her pittance would come at last, her letters were brought to her; no, they only announced another of the infinitesimal meannesses of Sir Edward and his clique.

"One letter said, amongst other things :—

"'Heath was with me the other day, and wanted, as I told you, permission to engrave that picture of you by Chalon for "The Book of Beauty;" but before your consent arrived he returned in great consternation, stating that Lady Blessington had gone to him in a great hurry to say he must not on any account think of such a thing, as Sir Edward would be furious, as having heard of Heath's intention, he had told her he would not have it appear on any account. Poor Heath was dreadfully annoyed at this, as he thought it one of Chalon's happiest *chef-d'œuvres.'*

"Another letter by the same post continued the theme more energetically :—

"'I should be in a towering rage at that infamous Gore House cabal having prevented your picture appearing in "The Book of Beauty" were I not convulsed with laughter at the sequel. I have just heard the history of Sir Edward's forbidding it, which was that he said to his dear friend Lady Blessington, "If Heath wants beauty, let him engrave *my* portrait." Now I don't think that this is one iota too good to be true, when we know that when Mr. N. P. Willis had committed the *gaucherie* of putting an elaborate description of you and your rooms into his first "Pencillings by the Way," the charming Lady Blessington was deputed to hint to him that it would be more agreeable if that were omitted in all future editions, and an account of Henry Bulwer substituted of whose perfections Lady Blessington forthwith furnished him with a fancy inventory. However, *cara mia*, it is a comfort to think that although *your* portrait does *not* appear, the world have lost nothing, for *en revanche* they are to have Mrs. Disraeli, at the blooming age of sixty,

in "The Book of Beauty;" but then, to be sure, she goes
to Gore House.'

"Had Sir Edward Bulwer Lytton's conspiracy against
his victim been merely confined to this sort of Gore House
manœuvres, it would only have afforded her a hearty
laugh when she could not afford a box at the play; but
his was a far deeper scheme, that of literally hunting
her to death, by subjecting her to every insult, every
privation, and every difficulty which malice could conceive.
The landlord of the hotel where Lady Lytton had now
been for three years and a half, finding that her parish
allowance did not come, made this a pretext for charging
her hotel prices, a sadly inflating process compared to the
moderate fixed sum at which she had hitherto been living.
At this rate she saw ruin staring her in the face, and that
was precisely the motive for which her pittance was retarded;
and from the landlord's subsequent shameful breach of faith
with her, she had no doubt he was in the plot."

In this dilemma Lady Lytton was prevented from
borrowing money of friends who were willing to
lend it because "no honest person would accept
money they saw no means of repaying;" and an
arrangement was finally come to with the landlord
by which he agreed to wait for his bill provided she
would leave her rooms at the hotel, and at the
same time solemnly promised that under no circumstances would he apply for payment to Sir
Edward. So she quitted the hotel and took up
her abode at a *pension* about three miles from
Geneva, "kept by a horrible old woman, with
dinners to match; however, the rooms were
excellent, the grounds beautiful, and the price only
two hundred francs a month for Lady Lytton and
her maid." But even to defray this modest charge
she was compelled to sell her watch.

"First, in a moment of bitterness, she thought of selling the watch her son had flung back to her. Yet no! Perhaps he had not done it. Alas, poor human hearts! what costly hopes and ponderous fears you are ever suspending on and trusting to the frail tenure of a 'perhaps'! So she left it there, and took her own watch. Oh the deep humiliation of those moments when necessity overcomes without annihilating pride!—instances when extremes meet, for nothing can look more like a thief going to steal what belongs to another than a poor lady or gentleman going to sell what belongs to themselves. She went to one of those quaint old shops in the Rue Basse; but although the watch was a Bréguet, she only got twenty-two pounds for it; and no doubt, from the confusion of her manner, the worthy Genevois concluded she had stolen it.

"She that very evening went to her new abode. As Sir Edward Lytton is such a patron of the arts, and has such a love for the beautiful, I wonder what he would think, as an addition to his collection at Knebworth, of a double picture in the style of Parmegano's picture of Adam and Eve, on two separate panels, divided by a golden bar: of himself in his baronial halls, surrounded by his parasites and all the magnificence of gold cups and chargers, with the parcel-gilt goblets which he so much affects, on the one side, and on the other his poor hunted wife prowling down back streets in the twilight to sell her watch to pay for her daily bread.

"At this *pension* Lady Lytton had stayed about six weeks, when two ladies drove out to see her, joy beaming in their countenances, to tell her that a most extraordinary thing had happened at the hotel, which they were sure was the harbinger of great good to her. The wondrous tale which they had to disclose to her was that an Englishman ('sans doute un grand seigneur!') had arrived at the —— Hotel, and had asked the landlord if Lady Lytton had not been staying there a long time, and if she did not owe him a large sum of money? to which K——, the landlord, replied in the affirmative. Whereupon this travelling St. Anthony answered, 'You are aware, M.

K——, that Sir Edward Lytton is now a very rich man, *et je me fais fort de vous faire payer.*'

"Upon hearing this poor Lady Lytton burst into tears, intuitively perceiving that there was some fresh conspiracy afloat on the part of her dastardly persecutor, and said to her friends, 'For heaven's sake, when you go back this evening, call at the hotel and tell K—— on *no* account to have any conversation with this man about me or my affairs, but to come and tell me his name, at least what name he goes by, and describe to me his appearance, for, depend upon it, no gentleman, or indeed any honest man, would ask the landlord of an hotel such questions about a person who is a stranger to him, at least not for any good purpose;' and her fears instantly pointed to Loaden, and with these fears she so infected these kind friends that they departed in haste to warn the landlord of the hotel not to be too communicative to this stranger, but go and speak to Lady Lytton as soon as he could. Accordingly the next day but one M. K—— arrived, followed by a tremendously tall man, who announced himself with a low bow in the following negative communication: 'Ahem! I am not a lawyer, madam.' A man not well versed in synonyms might have responded, 'Then who the d——l are you, sir?' But what Lady Lytton said was, 'Indeed! then, pray, may I inquire who you are, and, above all, by what authority you busy yourself about my affairs?'

"'Certainly, madam, by all means; my name is B——; I am connected with the *Galignani;* in fact, madam, I an *agent d'affaires*, and collect bad debts.'

"'Sir!' interrupted Lady Lytton, her eyes flashing as she glanced indignantly at the fat landlord, who stood foolishly looking into his empty hat, 'there is no bad debt that I am aware of between myself and M. K——. Owing to a long and most scandalous delay in the payment of my very paltry allowance, I was, it is true, on leaving his hotel six weeks ago, unable to settle his bill, when he consented to give me a full year to do so, whereupon I volunteered to give him six per cent. for his money;

consequently, till the stipulated year expires, and I *then* should fail in the fulfilment of my promise, I take it, there is no question of a bad debt between me and M. K——.'

"'Oh! no, no, clearly not, madam; I merely thought that, with Sir Edward's present fortune, it was a great shame that you should be left in such a position, and that he ought to be, and can be compelled, to pay your just debts.'

"Poor Lady Lytton then had the humiliating task of entering into an elaborate and minute detail of her pecuniary position to this debt-collector to convince him that applying to her honourable husband would not ensure quicker payment to M. K——, but would only plunge her into deeper ruin,—by giving her cowardly persecutor a feasible pretext for continuing to deprive her of the means of existence, at the conclusion of which explanation Mr. B—— affected to be so thoroughly convinced of the justice of her statement that he departed with his fat friend, both of them faithfully promising that no application should be made to Sir Edward for the bill, and that she should have the originally promised year to pay it. But every day poor Lady Lytton was growing more nervous and more wretched, for her pittance had not yet arrived. She had, out of the £22 got for the watch, paid £12 to the old woman of the *pension*, and would soon have another fortnight to pay her; and having paid £5 to her maid (her quarter's wages), where was it to come from, and what *was* she to do? Moreover, Geneva was in a very disturbed state. There was nothing but wars and rumours of wars, or at least their small change, revolutions; and at the very name the English, according to their wont, were all striking their tents.

"Truly misfortunes never come singly. It was only three weeks from Mr. B——'s invasion, and her beggarly pittance had not yet arrived. She took a letter hopelessly and abstractedly from the packet, and broke the seal. It was from her trustee, Sir Thomas Cullum, and ran as follows :—

"'Hardwick, *October*, 1846.

"'Dear Lady Lytton,—

"'I am sorry to inform you that Sir Edward, having been sued for an hotel bill on your account by M. Jules K——, of Geneva, your allowance must be further stopped till the same is paid.

"'I remain, dear Lady Lytton,
"'Yours truly,
"'Thomas G. Cullum.'

"This curt climax to all her pressing, harassing, goading miseries fell from her hands; and had it been a thunderbolt instead of a simple sheet of paper, it could scarcely have stunned her more."

Penniless, friendless, and desperate, Lady Lytton appealed to Sir Thomas himself not to leave her to perish of sheer want in a foreign country, reflecting that any advance he might make to her could be stopped in instalments out of her allowance, which passed through his hands as trustee.

"She concluded by describing the state of insurrection Geneva was in, and her not having one sou wherewith either to go or remain, and imploring him, by every sentiment of humanity and Christianity, not to leave her in so horrible a strait, and above all to let her have an answer by return of post, as that day week she was to be turned out of her present shelter. That day week, while the cannon were roaring from the ramparts of Geneva, the clash and clang of steel echoing through the town, the yells of the victors and the groans of the dying rolling like a muffled drum accompaniment to the shrill clarions of anarchy, and the gates of the town were just thrown open by the victorious rabble, while the rain was descending in Alpine torrents, as if endeavouring to wash away the blood that was flowing through the streets, old Madame G——, the ogress of the *pension*, rushed into her room, exclaiming, 'Dieu merci! Les Bouzingots ont gagné! V'là vos lettres; vite, en route! car le contingent sera ici à l'instant même!'"

Lady Lytton despatched her maid for a vehicle of some description or another,

"and hastily broke the seal of Sir Thomas's answer to her urgent appeal. Amid the dull echoes of carnage and the booming of artillery, now lessening into irregular and distant volleys, which came rolling heavily from the town, amid the rattling rain, there was something almost supernaturally placid and peaceful in the imperturbable tenor of Sir Thomas's epistle. Here it is:—

"'HARDWICK HOUSE, *October*, 1846.

"'DEAR LADY LYTTON,—

"'I am extremely sorry to hear of the uncomfortable position in which you are placed; but, in justice to myself, I cannot pursue any other course than that of stopping your allowance till M. K——'s demands on you are satisfied.

"'I am, dear Lady Lytton,
"'Yours truly,
"'THOMAS G. CULLUM.'"

CHAPTER XV.

"SIR THOMAS'S letter, coming in the midst of all this elemental and social strife, had, it must be confessed, fallen cold and crushing, like an avalanche, upon this poor wanderer's homeless, houseless heart. Where go? What do? How ever pay the hard old harpy of the *pension*, since of the current coin of the realm all she now possessed in the world was twenty-five francs three sous? In every painful crisis of life there is no climax, because no stumbling-block, so insurmountable as a financial one. Oh! how hard it is in such peril-fraught moments of impending wreck and ruin to see God in everything; to believe that all that befalls us, however mysteriously dark and crookedly hard, is still but the integral parts of a stupendous plan of wisdom, nay, more, of mercy and of love! Yet so it is; the arm of Omnipotence is never so strong to save as when its hand is heaviest upon us. And were we not thrust, hungry and unpitied, from the gilded halls and sumptuous banquets of the Dives of this world into life's cold, desolate, ever-lengthening highway, we should never meet with those good Samaritans who have compassion on us when the priests and the Levites pass by on the other side.

"Eugénie, at the end of half an hour, returned, with the son of the village *voiturier*, or rather *charrettier*, a lad of about thirteen, who said that his father had not a carriage of any sort, neither had any of the neighbours, but there was one Paul Chappuis who had a cart, which would do for the luggage, but it was out, and would not be in before two

(it was then half-past ten); and that, moreover, on account
of the great demand every sort of conveyance was in, he
asked sixteen francs to go with luggage as far as Geneva.

"This was a terrible inroad, certainly, into five-and-
twenty, more especially as poor Lady Lytton did not on
earth know where she was to find shelter for the night
when she got to the town, as after M. K——'s gratuitous
treachery to her (though perhaps it was anything but
gratuitous) she had rather a dread of hotels ; but the first
thing to be thought of was, how to get the £12 she had to
pay Madame G——, when she suddenly recollected a very
kind-hearted English or rather Irish woman who was
married to a Swiss colonel, who had served in the English
army, and gained many laurels and medals in the Penin-
sular war. As this lady had suffered much from many
vicissitudes in life herself, and was not overburdened with
money, she could feel for others, which, in this millennium
of mammon, mediocrity, and selfishness, none of those
whose fates are set in gold ever do ; so poor Lady Lytton
concluded what the Minerva Press would have called her
'mental soliloquy' with 'Yes, I know poor kind Mrs.
G——e will do it if she can.' Her next step was to ask the
carter's boy what his name was, and if he would take a note
to Colonel G——e's house in Geneva, and bring her back an
answer, for five francs ? To the first question he replied
that his name was Grégoire Bertholt, and to the second,
'Je veux ben.' This point settled, she wrote a note to
Mrs. G——e, telling her exactly what had happened, about
the scandalous stoppage of her allowance, and her penniless
condition, till she could get into Geneva to convert something into money.

"In the shortest space of time possible that Grégoire
could have gone over the three miles and back, he returned, drenched to the skin and out of breath ; and when
Lady Lytton perceived that he did not make any attempt at
unearthing a note either from his pockets or cap, her heart
sank down into an almost deathlike absence of pulsation.
But as soon as Grégoire could speak he panted out, 'La
demoiselle va venir.' And even while she was paying him

the wheels of a vehicle and the trab-trab of a horse's hoofs
were heard splashing through the mud; and the next
moment a *char-à-banc* drove up the avenue, and stopping
before the door, the eldest Miss G——e emerged from its
crab-like interior, and her magnificent Oriental dark eyes
looked doubly beautiful from the diamond drops of kindness in which they were floating. 'Poor dear Lady
Lytton!' said she; 'Mamma told me to give you this,'
placing a packet in Lady Lytton's hand; but evidently
afraid of being thanked, she hastily added, 'But I can't stay
a moment; for if I don't get back directly, they will be
frightened to death at home, thinking that I have fallen into
the hands of the *Bouzingots*, as you know, I suppose, that
all the English fled the day before yesterday?'

"And before Lady Lytton could say a word, or even
open the packet, she had sprung into the car, and driven off.
Upon opening it, Lady Lytton found that, instead of the
£12 she had asked for, it contained £24; but as the tears
streamed down her cheeks at this proof of poor Mrs
G——e's prompt and abounding kindness, she resolved, the
moment she reached Geneva, to return the other £12,
although when the sixteen francs were paid to the man for
taking the luggage, her capital would then be reduced to
five francs three sous; and Mrs. G——e, with all the delicate
and princely generosity which only the *poor* know how to
extract from their own necessities, when they afterwards
met, urged her in the strongest manner to keep the whole,
as she should not want it for at least a year to come.

"The old beldame of the *pension* insisted that all her
then inmates should, without a moment's delay, turn out,
and, as some were bound for France, others for Germany,
and others for Lausanne, every available post-horse for
three leagues round was in requisition, so that neither horse
nor conveyance beyond the before-mentioned cart was to
be had for love or money. In vain Lady Lytton implored
her hostess to let her remain one day more, or even a few
hours longer, till the storm should have, in some degree,
abated; she was inexorable, so they had nothing for it but
to leave the pitiless landlady for the only less pitiless storm

and wend their melancholy way through the mud and rain after the slow and heavily laden cart into Geneva.

"The gates of the town had not been many minutes reopened to comers and goers, but instead of the ordinary impassible, stolid-looking Swiss soldiers, pacing up and down as sentries, were drunken Bouzingots, with their blood and mud-smeared blouses, the only trophies of their ignoble victory. The lamp-posts had been torn up, the bridges burnt, with now a narrow plank thrown across as the only means of transit; and as the dead and dying were still lying about, the streets were running with blood. At this horrible spectacle poor Eugénie had another fit of hysterics, and no earthly power could induce her to venture through the town in its then state till she had ascertained the fate of her lover and brother, so her mistress had nothing for it but to wade through all these horrors alone, or at least with only her poor faithful dog, and leave the maid there with the luggage while she went in quest of some place of shelter. All the English having fled from Geneva at the report of the first revolutionary popgun, what to do or whither to go she knew not. In this cruel perplexity she suddenly recollected that there lived on the Place St. Antoine a Madame George, who was in the habit of letting houses to the English, and also of hiring out plate, linen, and furniture; so, with a faint heart, she began toiling up the steep hill that leads to the Place St. Antoine, the ascent of which was now rendered doubly arduous by the slippery, miry state of the roads.

"When she at length arrived at the Maison Duval, as Madame George's house was called, her heart literally seemed to sink into her shoes, for was she not, for the first time in her life, going to implore charity? And of whom? Of a Swiss! and her empty pockets appeared to be suddenly inflated, as it were, with a condensed hurricane, croaking out, 'Point d'argent, point de Suisse!'"

But Lady Lytton's misgivings were luckily falsified, and once more she found kindness and generosity in a quarter where she had the least right to expect them. No sooner had Mademoiselle George heard her piteous story than she insisted that Lady Lytton should at once take possession of a suite of rooms in the Maison Duval, on the terms that she should be called upon to pay for nothing whatever until it happened to suit her circumstances to do so. Unwilling as she was to trespass upon this generous woman's kindness, Lady Lytton's embarrassments left her no choice in the matter; and at the Maison Duval she accordingly took up her residence.

"That winter," to resume the narrative, "which Lady Lytton had dreaded, thinking it would be the most wretched of her wretched life, was, on the contrary, made, by the active and ceaseless kindness of genuine friends, one of the happiest she has to look back to."

Early, however, in 1847 Lady Lytton began to make arrangements for quitting Geneva, a course which she had only been prevented hitherto from adopting by the helplessness inseparable from poverty. A kind friend, Mrs. Sandby, offered to give her temporary shelter in her native country until such time as Sir Edward could be compelled to put his wife's affairs on a satisfactory footing and make her an allowance commensurate in some degree with her necessities; and having found this welcome asylum, it only remained for her to prepare for departure.

"But there was much still to be done before Lady Lytton could quit Geneva; there was still £500 owing for the legal expenses of the Paris conspiracy, and, inclusive of

Mademoiselle George's claim, about £200 in Geneva. Upon this Mr. Sandby kindly lent her £200 at five per cent., and Mrs. Sandby more kindly applied to a friend of hers, a Mr. Berrington (would that I were at liberty to inscribe the real name in golden letters), nor was the application in vain : he said he once travelled with an American who gave him a harrowing account of the dreadful usage poor Lady Lytton received from her amiable husband, and that ever since he had felt the greatest commiseration for her, and instantly wrote a cheque for £400. When Lady Lytton received it a thousand complex feelings of gratitude and humiliation, pain and pleasure, seemed rushing upon her, as it were to suffocate her. She wrote endeavouring to thank him, as far as words could do so, and acknowledged the debt at five per cent. interest. He returned this acknowledgment to her torn up, with such a charming letter, in which he said that, 'of course, were she ever in the proper pecuniary position that she ought to be, he would not offend her by refusing to take back that trifling sum ; but till then she must not even remember that he had ever sent it.' Alas, alas ! to this day that £400 remains unpaid.*

"But that spring of 1847 seemed to have produced a perfect harvest of good Samaritans, for this £600 being instantly appropriated to its predestined use, and Lady Lytton's munificent allowance being still in arrear, on account of the hotel bill, she was personally as destitute as' ever, when, not to leave the work half done, La Reine de Mont Blanc,† with her usual active kindness, procured from two admirable women, Les Sœurs Tirard, in the Carraterie, another £100, to be repaid in two years, and also a supply of clothes, of which Lady Lytton was sadly in want.

"But truly 'man never is, but always to be blessed,' for though it had been so long her most earnest wish to get out of Geneva, that little narrow-minded republic, which

* It was repaid in 1859.—L. D.

† This lady, the Comtesse d'Angeville, was so called because she was the first woman to make the ascent of that mountain.

was so withering and uncongenial to her in every way, yet, now that the hour of her emancipation drew nigh, she only thought of the kind faithful hearts she was leaving behind —hearts which had so generously, so delicately, and so unceasingly ministered to hers in all ways and sheltered her through that long rigorous winter 1846-47 and her still harder fate.   But it was not only the pain of parting that awaited·her : she had another struggle to encounter which she certainly had not anticipated.   The moment she received Mr. Berrington's most generous loan she flew to discharge the very least part of her debt to Mademoiselle George, but that excellent and decidedly unique woman resolutely put her hands behind her back and obstinately refused to receive one sou.   Long and obstinate was the contest on both sides ; but Lady Lytton was at length obliged to yield, as the only concession that Rothschild of good Samaritans, Mademoiselle George, would make was allowing her guest to refund the amount of all the little bills she had been secretly paying during the winter.

" That 11th of May, 1847, though one of the finest days that ever came out of the heavens, was yet a dark one in Lady Lytton's heart ; is it that coming events do indeed cast their shadows before ?   She then thought it was only the sorrow of parting from such very kind friends."

CHAPTER XVI.

So Lady Lytton started on her return journey in
company with "a very stupid Swiss maid," and after
experiencing a considerable amount of discomfort
duly arrived at the country house of Mr. and Mrs.
Sandby on the 29th of May, 1847.

"Never did a fairyographer (there is a nice and much-
wanted word!) imagine or describe anything more beautiful in its way than that cultivated happy-looking scenery.
Those green, green lanes, with all their leafy affluence, vocal
with innumerable birds, which burst into view on every side
as they approached the rectory, the air embalmed with a
perfect mosaic of perfumes, above all of which, however,
the queenly may predominated, the brilliant rays of the
morning sun playing bo-peep, as it were, with the spring air
through the timid quivering leaves, the soft yet penetrating
odour of the flowers, the song of the birds, the kiss of the
gentle genial air—all seemed so many affectionate greet-
ings in voiceless words, of which nature has so many,
and which the heart alone can hear, but to which the eyes
alone reply ; for extremes do indeed meet, and sorrow or
great joy have but one language—tears !

"It was a very pretty modern Gothic-Elizabethan, gable-
end pile of buildings, built to correspond with the old Hall.
As the carriage stopped before the gates the beatings of
Lady Lytton's heart became so tumultuous as to be painful in the extreme, and no sooner did Mrs. Sandby hear

the wheels than she and her little girl came to the door, and as the carriage turned round the sweep of the avenue Lady Lytton could not wait for it to arrive at the hall door, but jumped out, which, the carriage being a brougham, she was enabled to do without breaking her neck, and the next moment she found herself clasped in her friend's arms."

I pass on to a description of Lady Lytton's host.

"The Rev. Mr. Sandby was a jovial country gentleman-looking man, who might from his appearance with equal propriety have represented the younger son of a duke in an agricultural county, or that which he did represent, an independent clergyman of the Church of England, who had graduated at Christ Church. He laughed off Lady Lytton's thanks, and said, rubbing his hands merrily as he looked at her,—

"'Well, truth is stranger than fiction. I am very glad to see you at Flixton, and should like to see the enemy's face when they really know you have arrived, and your ' eagles begin to flutter among the Volsci.'

"In short, he was exceedingly kind and hospitable.

"A day or two after Lady Lytton's arrival at Flixton, Mr. Hartcup, Mr. Sandby's solicitor, came over ; and it was arranged that as he was going to town in the middle of June about a Chancery suit, Mr. Sandby should accompany him, and they should jointly make a personal application to Sir Edward Bulwer. But Mr. Hartcup, who had just returned from London, had already called upon Loaden, intimating to him that he had better advise his client, Sir Edward, to make some prompt and amicable arrangement about allowing his wife something at least approaching to a competency, as otherwise she was determined to proceed against him in the Ecclesiastical Court.

"But Mr. Hartcup's journey to London was repeatedly put off, so that she had that sharpest fang of the serpent sorrow, suspense, added to all the others. Shortly afterwards she received an invitation from a Mrs. Dennett, who had a villa on the Thames in one of the outskirts of London ; and having no desire to again see London, where she had suffered so much, and to see it more especially under the miserable and destitute circumstances she was then placed in, she accepted this invitation conditionally, leaving it very doubtful whether she should be able to go to London or not. But this contemplated visit was easier in theory than in practice, as where was the money to come from ? The July quarter of her parish allowance would have to be sent off to Geneva, and then she must make some arrangements to leave her present quarters.

"At length Mr. Sandby and his solicitor went to London ; and as Sir Edward, like all other great men, never was to be got at without an intermediary, in reply to Mr. Sandby's note requesting an interview, he was referred to Mr. Beavan. But alas for the frail tenure of all earthly powers ! for this negotiation with Mr. Sandby was almost the last little episode of dirty work Mr. Beavan was enabled to transact for his friend Sir Edward previous to his being compelled to leave his country for his country's good for some fraudulent proceedings.

" Now it may be here necessary to observe that it was a sort of *ruse en permanence* of Sir Edward and his whole clique always to begin as if they had every inclination to accede to the propositions made to them on Lady Lytton's behalf. Consequently, when Mr. Sandby had represented to Mr. Beavan that, with Sir Edward's present large increase of fortune, he thought the pittance allowed his wife scandalous, and therefore he hoped he would increase it to something like an adequate income without compelling her to sue him in the Ecclesiastical Court, Mr. Beavan leant forward and said,—

" ' Ah, yes, certainly ; with his present fortune, £400 a year is very little, too little, I should say, for Lady Lytton ; and I'll represent this to Sir Edward, and endeavour to get him to increase it, but, at the same time, I must warn you not to expect too much, for he's as near as the very devil ; but perhaps a personal interview might be

better, if you would meet him here to-morrow between one
and two.'

"So Mr. Sandby wrote to Lady Lytton by that day's post
detailing this interview with Beavan, and saying he had no
doubt he should get her £800, but he feared not more.
Meanwhile that great man Sir Edward Lytton, after
hearing Mr. Beavan's report of the enemy's forces, or rather
weakness, resolved to take the field in person. The following day, when Sir Edward entered Mr. Beavan's office,
it was with the air of a lawgiving conqueror; and, after
taking the initiative with a sort of permit-you-to-live bow
to Mr. Sandby and his solicitor, he began by announcing
that instead of making his wife an additional allowance it
was his wish to get a divorce; and if he brought an action
against her (not intimating with whom she was to be
accused, for that, of course, he had still to invent), he would
allow her to defend herself, but on the express proviso that
she did not recriminate upon him!

"Now, will it be believed that this superfluous outrage,
which, like most of Sir Edward Lytton's proceedings, would
have been too ridiculous had it not been too infamous, was
actually communicated to Lady Lytton, not as a mere
report of the interview with her brutal tyrant, but as a
proposition? It is utterly impossible for any language to
describe the bitter and burning feeling of indignant disgust
and contempt that seized poor Lady Lytton upon receiving
this unheard-of insult. As it was, she wrote back that any
action Sir Edward chose to bring against her for murder,
adultery, or any other crime he chose to invent, so long
as it was in open court, she would be glad to meet; but
as for recriminating, she certainly would not wait for that,
as Mr. Hartcup had her instructions instantly to proceed
against him in the Ecclesiastical Court for the recent affair
at M—— with Miss ——'s companion, Miss P——. Now
when it is remembered that this much-outraged woman
had been originally turned out of her house for having,
on the strength of one of his own lies, gone to his
bachelor chambers in the Albany, believing him to be ill,
and caught him with one of his mistresses, the woman

Deacon, and that then, even under such flagrant and
scandalous circumstances, she had not only no human
being to protect or right her, but merely a very distant
relation to reverse the positions, and put her completely in
the power of this unscrupulous and unparalleled villain,
and when it is further taken into consideration the manner
in which this wretch had ever since conspired against and
hunted her, the disgraceful Paris plot, followed up by the
recent one at Geneva, and, above all, the reports of the vile
treatment of her poor innocent child, which were rankling
in this outraged mother's heart, the violence of her indignation may be comprehensible."

Mr. Sandby's solicitor threatened a process against
Sir Edward in the Ecclesiastical Court on account of
his intrigue with this aforesaid companion ; but finding
that it was impossible to collect evidence of a sufficiently conclusive character to establish his unfaith-
fulness, they were compelled to abandon the suit.
Naturally enough, Lady Lytton did not accept her
husband's generous offer to obtain a divorce on condition that while he accused her of wrong-doing
with some imaginary lover, she, on her part, should
refrain from publishing any of his numerous infidelities
—a truly astounding proposal, which, were it not for
indisputable evidence, I should have had considerable difficulty in ascribing even to Sir Edward
Lytton.*

"In due time Mr. Hartcup's services were followed by a
long bill, amounting to £75, of which she ultimately paid

A year later this offer was renewed, namely, that "she should
connive at her own dishonour by allowing her husband to sue for
a divorce, with the same special clause that she should not recriminate upon him, and the additional stipulation that she was not to
breathe a word of this arrangement to any mortal, as if it was
known that there was anything like collusion, it would prevent the

£20, though upon getting the bill taxed by another solicitor, he said that the £20 Mr. Hartley had received was just £15 too much for what he had done or rather not done.

"It is scarcely possible to describe the *chevaux de frise* of conflicting tortures by which poor Lady Lytton felt herself hedged in on every side : despair at her total friendlessness and powerlessness, which placed her completely at the mercy of her cruel, unscrupulous enemy ; humiliation and disgust at not having a sou wherewith to leave her present quarters, for it was then only June, and the next quarter of her parish allowance—the first free since the payment of M. Jules K——'s bill—was not due till July, and even when she had it she was in perfect ignorance as to knowing how or where to live on such a sum in England. Clever Sir Edward Lytton ! How scientifically you calculated the perilous straits, the bitter insults, the degrading necessities with which you would compass your penniless victim ! She finally resolved, *coûte que coûte*, to accept Mrs. Dennett's invitation ; but where was the money

Bill passing the Lords, but that if she would consent to this, he would pay her debts and give her a sum of money to start upon."

With reference to this proposal, Lady Lytton wrote as follows to Mr. Hartcup :—

"*March 24th*, 1848.

"I beg most explicitly to disclaim ever having written one word to you in reference to yourself individually which you could with any shadow of foundation construe into unwarrantable irritation against you personally, as, notwithstanding the just cause I had for unbounded indignation and contempt at the proposition contained in your letter of January 5th, I did not, in my reply to it, even express my surprise that you, as *my* solicitor, should have done otherwise than indignantly decline to Mr. Beavan to be made the medium of such an insulting proposition, the more insulting and ridiculous from not having been made at the outset of the negotiation, if they dared to make it at all, than as a *pis-aller* at the end of nine months' frivolous and vexatious falsehood and equivocation.

"I have the honour, etc.,

"ROSINA BULWER LYTTON."

When the letter containing this insulting proposal arrived, Miss Planché was present (Mrs. Curteis Whelan).

to come from? The only available thing she had was
a silver-gilt *déjeûner,* consisting of a cup, saucer, cream-
ewer, sugar and slop-basin, which had been the grateful
offering of a poor working jeweller whom she had got out
of prison at Geneva for a political offence. She was,
indeed, sorry to part with the poor man's gift, but she
at length made up her mind to do so; but its being
foreign was made a pretext for depreciating its value, and
the mighty sum this beginning of a series of sacrifices
brought was £12 15s. Well, it would do to take her to
London and to keep her there for a few days; so, with
a solitary sigh for poor Taffy, her faithful dog, who had
been left in charge of good Mrs. Howard, once more, with
a heavy heart, she entered the modern Babylon."

Lady Lytton stayed two or three weeks with this
Mrs. Dennett (her real name was Mrs. Leicester
Stanhope, afterwards Countess of Harrington).
She then returned to Mrs. Sandby's, and left in
October, 1847, for apartments at East Ham. In
1848 she left East Ham, and went to reside with
the assistant chaplain at the Tower of London.

The following is Mrs. Whelan's account of her
first meeting with Lady Lytton in 1847, and of the
impressions she received of that lady and of her
misfortunes.

MRS. CURTEIS WHELAN'S NARRATIVE.

"*July,* 1847.

" In the summer of 1847, my father, Mr. J. R. Planché
with my sister and myself, were invited by the Hon.
Mrs. Leicester Stanhope, afterwards Countess of Harrington, to a garden party at Ashburnham House. On reaching
the lawn, where most of the company were assembled, my
attention was drawn to a lady of remarkable beauty, who
stood in a group with some others a short distance off.
On asking my father who it was, he said he did not know,

but he would inquire, and discovered very quickly that this beautiful woman was the wife of the novelist Bulwer Lytton, 'from whom,' my father said, 'she is separated, mind, if you are introduced to her.' The introduction followed immediately; and we passed the afternoon talking to and admiring the wit and loveliness of our fresh acquaintance, who was, we found, on a visit to Mrs. Leicester Stanhope for some ten days. Above the average height, with an exquisitely shaped head, Lady Lytton's eyes were the distinguishing feature of her face from their superb lustre and colour; but her mouth and nose were worthy neighbours of such eyes. Her hair and eyebrows were dark, while her complexion was brilliantly fair; and I was informed on speaking of her to dear old Mr. Edmund Byng, a very intimate friend of ours, that 'Rosina Wheeler was the most lovely girl ever seen in London' when she first came to town. He remembered her quite well.

"We did not see Lady Lytton again after this garden party, as she returned to Suffolk, where she was paying another visit, till early in the following year, when her maid arrived at my father's house one day with a note inviting my sister and myself to stay with Lady Lytton for a few days at East Ham, where she had taken part of a villa house. I was so completely fascinated at my first interview that I eagerly accepted the invitation; but the night of our arrival was passed by me in bitter tears for the heart-breaking sorrows which were the sad outpourings of the soul of my poor friend to one in whom she found she had inspired a passionate love for herself and a burning desire to serve her if possible. These sorrows would not have been confided to me on so short an acquaintance but for the fact that a letter had reached Lady Lytton *that very day* from a solicitor who had been instructed by the solicitor employed by her husband to offer her *certain terms* on which her debts would be paid, and a further allowance made to her. These terms were so shameful that her whole nature was shocked and repelled; and I

could but admire the courage (on hearing the particulars)
with which she had nerved herself to welcome and enter-
tain two comparative strangers, and put aside the tumult
of feeling which this letter had excited in her. Towards
evening, however, she broke down; and then I heard by
degrees of the treatment this lovely woman had experienced
for years, and the separation from her of her children, a
daughter, Emily, and a son, Robert (the present Earl of
Lytton), who were taken from her at an early age, and
whom she had never seen since. Ten years had nearly
elapsed since they were severed from her, and she had
vainly sought for her daughter. I made Lady Lytton a
promise there and then that I would do all I could to
obtain tidings of her daughter, and find her if possible ; and
the Almighty blessed my efforts, for in a *few months* from
that time I discovered Miss Lytton in a small lodging in
Brompton. I have given all the particulars of her death
in that lodging of typhoid fever in ' another place,' and the
cruel and inhuman treatment of her mother by the doctors
and *others*, so that it is not necessary to allude to it here
except to mention the fact that I was enabled to fulfil
my promise. After the tragedy of Miss Lytton's death
and burial, I persuaded Lady Lytton to leave East Ham
and reside with a clergyman and his wife, relations of my
own, to protect her from the perpetual annoyances she was
continually exposed to, and in that house I had more
opportunities of seeing and experience of the persecution
she so continually suffered from. Her nature was noble
and intensely loving, her temper hasty, but she was very
generous and forgiving if she saw the least possible sign of
repentance from any who insulted or injured her. She had
given me for her daughter, if I discovered her, a diamond
bracelet, a gift from the Duchess of Saxe Coburg Gotha
to Lady Lytton when at Geneva, where she lived for some
time before my acquaintance with her, and a packet containing the most loving address to her child, which on her
shocking death she made me read as I returned the

bracelet and packet to her. And I can testify to the fact
that her first thought and utterance of grief on my telling
her that her poor daughter was dead was praying for the
father of her child.

"I had another painful task of breaking to her the
death of her mother, Mrs. Wheeler, whom she described to
me as completely taken up with social questions and
lectures of the Miss Martineau type, and who had lived
with Sir John Doyle (Lady Lytton's great-uncle) in Guernsey, where the early days of Lady Lytton were passed.
Miss Wheeler came to London to school, I think, in Hans
Place, Sloane Street, Chelsea, amusingly described in her
'Autobiography of Miriam Sedley,' 1850; and she often told
me how grieved she was that she had not studied *music* more
than she had done.   She was passionately fond of animals,
especially dogs. 'There is no *deceit* or *treachery* in these
darlings,' she frequently said."

I append a letter from Lady Lytton to Miss
Planché.

LADY LYTTON TO MISS PLANCHÉ.

"*January 27th*, 1848.

"MY OWN DARLING KATE,—

"I have just received your kind little note of
yesterday, for which and all else God bless you. Do try
and thank the kind-hearted lawyer. Oh! what a dreadful
thing it is to be such a *fléau* as I am to every one! And
lion-hearted as you are, my own darling, I feel as if I were
dastardly enough to let you fight single-handed against
a fearful odds of fifty to one, or lead a forlorn hope against
a legion of devils, which Sir Liar, with his money, his infamy,
and his tools, unquestionably is. Eugène Sue, in one of
his letters to me, speaks of his admiration 'pour cette
femme fière et courageuse,' meaning your humble servant;
but what would he think of you, darling? I will be up (if
I am alive) on Saturday to receive you and your kind
friend. I cannot swallow anything without feeling nausea,

but it is no wonder, the prolonged and intense destitution
that fiend keeps me in is such a source of constant worry,
anxiety, and humiliation.   I could not help smiling, dearest,
when in one of your letters you talk to me of rigid economy,
and saving money out of my pittance to pay the interest of
the money I owe.   Alas! I should be too happy to have
the power of doing so; but when even that wretched driblet
is never paid me for weeks, sometimes months, after it is
due, how on earth am I to do so?   I have been at my old
extremity of selling things for almost nothing to get even
a few postage stamps, for *this is my sort of want*, not one
iota less imaginary than the *literal* fact of being *without
one sou* on earth, and Byrne crying and refusing to go and
sell the things, in the hope that to-morrow (that great
chronological swindler of the wretched) will bring my
money, whereas I know it will always bring me fresh
duns and fresh insults.   God keep you, my own darling,
from ever knowing the degradation of this sort of misery.
There is a dignity in great afflictions which suffices for
their own support, but these leprous gnat bites make one
almost loathe one's self.   Verily English men are charming
husbands ; and English laws are still more charming.
There was a man at Geneva who had taken all his children
away from his wife, even to the baby, and prevents her
seeing them, kindly assuring her (like Sir Liar) that her
consenting to a divorce is the only way to arrange matters
between them.   His poor heart-broken wife is now at
Brighton ; and, of course, upon her indignantly rejecting
this (as I did), he has threatened to get up some plot to
ruin her ; and being *rich, a husband*, and in *moral* England,
where all manly infamy is encouraged and protected, both
legally and socially, he will no doubt succeed.

" God bless you, my own noble-minded darling.

"Your

"ROSINA BULWER LYTTON."

CHAPTER XVII.

ILLNESS AND DEATH OF EMILY BULWER LYTTON.

I PASS on now to one of the most melancholy episodes of Lady Lytton's unhappy life : the illness and death of her beloved daughter, Emily Elizabeth Bulwer Lytton. The writer of the following is the same Mrs. Curteis Whelan to whom reference has been made above. Lady Lytton enlisted her services for obtaining any information about Miss Lytton, whose place of residence had always been carefully concealed from the mother. Inquiries among the friends of Sir Edward who were also her own had no satisfactory result, and she had despaired of success, when an accident procured all the information required ; but this had better be explained in her own words.

LETTER RESPECTING THE DEATH OF MISS LYTTON (1848) FROM MISS KATHERINE PLANCHÉ (AN EYE-WITNESS) TO THE BARONESS DE RITTER.

"THE LODGE, MICHAEL'S GROVE, BROMPTON,
"*May 28th*, 1848.

" MADAM,—

"Though a perfect stranger, I venture to address you on the part of Lady Bulwer Lytton, whose personal and most intimate friend I have the honour to be. Having heard her repeatedly express a deep anxiety to learn any particulars connected with her much-loved and unfortunate daughter, my wish to gratify so natural a desire has emboldened me to write to you, of whose kindness to Miss Lytton I have heard so much. I trust I am not the first person to acquaint you with the fatal termination of her illness, which ended in typhus fever on the 29th of April, two days after the arrival, at my instigation, of her mother. Her Ladyship hired the room which you had vacated, and remained during the whole night of the 27th on the staircase, listening to poor Emily's continued exclamations about ' my mother,' that mother having given her word of honour to the medical man, Mr. Rouse, that nothing should tempt her into her child's room, as he represented that any sudden emotion would endanger her life, at the same time assuring her mother that there was no danger to be apprehended at that moment, and that the poor young victim's illness was merely an attack of hysteria. The agony that Lady Lytton suffered during that night, hearing her child's voice for the first time for ten years, in supplication and pain, can easily be understood, madam, by you, who are a mother, and the unparalleled control she had over her feelings can only be believed by those who witnessed it.

" By some treachery the next morning Sir Edward was informed of Lady Lytton's arrival, and, remaining himself at Miss Greene's, ordered the medical men to desire Lady Lytton to leave the house, upon the plea that her presence in it had already endangered poor dear Emily's life, when she had not either seen or heard her mother, and had not the slightest suspicion of her being so near her. Dr. Marshall Hall and Mr. Rouse executed Sir Edward's orders in the most cruel and ungentlemanlike manner, as I am, unfortunately for them, a witness of; and dear Lady Lytton, at my entreaties (which were the more urgent from my suspicion that, if dear Emily died, Sir Edward would accuse Lady Lytton of being the cause of her death), left the house and went home with me in a state of mind which I cannot attempt to describe. Her poor child died the next evening, having been seen in her last moments by Dr. Tweedie (one of our most celebrated physicians) on the part of Lady Lytton, who pronounced her decease to be from typhus fever.

"On Sir Edward's first discovery of Lady Lytton's arrival, he suspected that she had been summoned by you to her daughter, which suspicion leads me to hope that you have sympathised with and pitied the dear girl's motherless position, and endeavoured to alleviate it as much as possible.

"I need scarcely say that any little circumstance connected with her beloved child will be vitally interesting to my dear friend; and she is, I know, most grateful to you and your daughter for the affection and kindness you manifested to poor Emily during her life. Poor child! by this most untimely end she is spared the cruel knowledge of all her mother has suffered through ten long years of separation from her children.

"I must entreat you to pardon my intrusion upon you, madam, and that you will kindly and charitably throw any light in your power upon the early portion of the poor girl's illness. I shall most anxiously look for an answer from you, and with the assurance of my respect,

"I have the honour to be, madam,
"Your obedient servant,
"KATHERINE FRANCES PLANCHÉ.
"To the Baroness de Ritter."

THE BARONESS DE RITTER'S ANSWER TO MISS PLANCHÉ'S LETTER.

"VIENNE, SPIEGELGASSE No. 1,098, le 7ième *Juin*, 1848.

"MADAME,—

"J'ai reçu hier votre lettre du 29 Mai, qui contient les premières nouvelles directes de la mort de la pauvre Emily Lytton, qui m'a fait une sensation inexprimable, car je puis bien vous assurer, que j'aimais cette douce et excellente enfant comme ma propre fille—qui est maintenant au désespoir, ayant perdu si imprévu, son unique amie, qu'elle adorait. Ma douleur en est extrême, et je regrette de tout mon cœur de ne pas être restée auprès d'Emily jusqu'à son dernier soupir; mais j'ai passée auprès d'elle tout l'été passée et une partie de l'hiver, et comme ma famille exigeait mon retour, je ne pouvais absolument rester plus longtemps en Angleterre.

"Je plains de tout mon cœur la pauvre mère de l'infortunée Emily, car je mesure ses sentiments d'après les miens, et je déplore les circonstances qui ne lui ont pas permis de s'approcher du lit de son pauvre enfant mourante, qui a très souvent prononcé le nom de sa mère pendant sa maladie. Je ne puis vous dire exactement la cause de sa maladie, car elle a été separée de moi plusieurs mois, ayant accepté une invitation amicale de la famille D'Eyncourt à Bayons, où elle a reçu un rhume très fort, de sorte qu'elle a continué de tousser d'une manière très inquietante à son retour chez moi à Londres ; j'ai eu tous les regards possibles pour elle, mais sans succès ; enfin elle a été forcée de se mettre au lit puisqu'un mal de tête affreux la tourmentait jour et nuit ; je n'ai pas quitté son lit pendant plusieurs semaines, et elle a reçu tous les soins possibles ; enfin on a pris une bonne pour la soigner encore mieux, et les medeçins m'ont priés de ne plus entrer dans sa chambre, craignant que la vue des personnes, qu'elle aimait ne l'excitait trop. On m'a assuré, qu'il n'y avait pas de danger pour sa vie ; et après avoir prié Sir Edward de m'amener ma douce Emily à Vienne après son rétablissement pour changer d'air, je partis dans l'espoir de trouver ici de bonnes nouvelles, qui m'auraient dédommagées de l'état déplorable dans lequel j'ai retrouvé ma patrie après une absence de dix mois, et je puis bien dire que j'ai passées les premières semaines en pleurs, et je me sens incapable de donner des consolations à Lady Lytton, que je n'ai l'honneur de connaître ; je puis seulement lui conseiller d'implorer le bon Dieu pour supporter cette perte douloureuse, et de se consoler avec l'idée assurante, que notre pauvre Emily a quitté une vie pleine de peines, pour recevoir près de Dieu les récompenses pour ses excellentes qualités, dont j'ai été témoin si longtemps.

"Agréez, quoique inconnue, l'assurance de respect de
"Votre sincère
"AMÉLIE DE RITTER."

The following is a more detailed account of the same event by Mrs. Whelan :—

"Singularly enough, one evening in the month of April, 1848, a friend of my father's came to see us, and said to me immediately on entering the room, ' Do you know that the young lady you are in search of is living close here ? ' He then explained that while sitting in the shop of a chemist in the Fulham Road, he was shown a prescription, and told that the daughter of Bulwer Lytton was lying dangerously ill at a small lodging-house in Pelham Terrace, Pelham Crescent, Brompton, and that Dr. Rouse, of Fulham, whom I knew, was attending her. Sad as such news was, I hastened next morning to Pelham Terrace, and seeing a shopboy knock at a door, I waited till he had been answered, and then hazarded the inquiry, ' How is Miss Lytton to-day ? ' when immediately came the reply, ' A little better, we think.' Overjoyed at my success, I flew home to the Lodge, Michael's Grove, to tell my father, and to send the information to Lady Bulwer Lytton ; but upon further consideration I determined to go myself to East Ham, thinking it better than writing, and never shall I forget the mixed pain and pleasure of my visit. It was soon arranged that Lady Lytton should come, with her old faithful servant Byrne (who had been Miss Lytton's nurse), to town, and see if she could possibly gain access to, and help to nurse her daughter, under conditions so unsuited to her position and age.

"I had soon observed from the style of house that it was let out in separate rooms and apartments, to people in a humble sphere of life, and was therefore most anxious that Lady Lytton should first come to us ; but she overruled my objections, and early next morning arrived at Pelham Terrace, where she engaged a room at the top of the same house for herself and Byrne, and then sent me a letter requesting me to come to her after dark. I did so, taking my own maid with me, and on ascending the wretched narrow staircase I passed the second-floor back room, which I then heard was Miss Lytton's, and was soon re-

ceived by Byrne and the dear and basely wronged wife
and mother. ' She is insensible, Kate,' cried Lady Lytton
on seeing me, ' and I am to see her in half an hour ; I have
bribed the nurse and landlady.' Then tears and sobs
broke forth from the overcharged heart, and Byrne and I
had enough to do to calm her preparatory to the interview.
When the time came I followed Lady Lytton downstairs
with Byrne to the door of the bedroom, which was open,
impressing on her the importance of keeping very quiet.
I had no need, however, to do so : the pitiful sight of this
young girl, without a relative near her, lying in a room
which was almost entirely taken up by the bedstead, which
stood nearly filling up the space between the door and the
window, was so startling that she remained for a time
speechless, as, almost transfixed, she gazed on the loved
form from which she had been so long separated ; lying
insensible, her features changed by fever, and hardly to be
recognised in the darkened room, where only the sheen
from her golden hair as it reflected the light of the single
candle guided the eye to the pillow and the sufferer. It
was thus, while Lady Lytton stood like a statue just inside
the room, that a knock was heard at the door; and lest she
should be discovered, Byrne and I hurried her upstairs.
The visitors were a Miss Greene (a nursery governess of
Lady Lytton's) and the present Earl of Lytton, a youth
about sixteen years of age, from Harrow. They came
to inquire about the patient, as they were not in the house.
My dear friend had thrown herself on her knees on reaching
the top room, and buried her face in the pillow of the
wretched bed in which she was to pass the night. No sobs
now, only convulsive throbbings of her whole frame, greatly
alarming us who were watching her ; but after a time she
became quiet, and I then took my leave, going home with
my servant, and promising to be there early in the morning.

" By ten o'clock I was there again, and found everything
had been discovered ! Dr. Rouse and Dr. Marshall Hall,
the other medical man (both of them are now dead—Dr.
Rouse soon after committed suicide), were commanded by
Sir Edward Lytton to get Lady Lytton out of the house

on the plea that her presence had aggravated the disorder (typhoid fever), which we afterwards discovered by our own medical attendant was advancing to its last stage. Miss Lytton had been delirious, and had spoken of her mother, who had sat on the stairs outside the door all night, sending to the room cooling beverages, and any things she had with her which might be of service for her daughter; for Miss Lytton's wardrobe was so scanty that she actually died in a nightdress lent her by the kind nurse, and which was afterwards in my possession.

"Dr. Rouse knowing me, sent for me on my arrival in Pelham Terrace; and he and Dr. Marshall Hall tried to intimidate me into making a promise to them that I would take Lady Lytton away.

"I told them I should do what Lady Lytton wished, that she had paid for her room for a week, and no one could turn her out but the landlady. They declared that Miss Lytton's life was endangered by the *knowledge* of her mother's presence! a most ridiculous assertion, as the poor girl knew no one, being delirious when not wholly unconscious.

" Our interview ended by my telling them I would hear what Lady Lytton herself said. Dr. Rouse followed me upstairs immediately, and then Lady Lytton threw herself on her knees to him, and implored him to let her stay to the end. I had in a life, then quite young, seen many stage representations of mental agony, but here was the *real anguish*, and every phase of it is burnt into my memory.

"Dr. Rouse himself would have given way, I saw, but he *dared* not; all he could do was to offer his carriage to take us away. He retired, and then I pointed out to the poor mother the risk she ran of misrepresentation that she had caused the death of her daughter through excitement, and further attempted to show that she would gain nothing by remaining; but in this I was wrong, and I have since deeply regretted it: she should have stayed, and I with her.

" However, I prevailed, on assuring her that I would go

to Dr. Rouse and obtain his promise to send to my father's house, or to come after every visit to his patient, that we might have the latest intelligence of her condition. I must now mention that the carriages of the two doctors were being driven up and down the little street while this conference was going on; and we had ascertained that Miss Greene lodged only two or three doors further, where the doctors were then in consultation while I was persuading Lady Lytton to return home with me. So I followed to the house, and was admitted by Miss Greene, who, with two men, completely blocked the small passage. 'Are the doctors here who attend Miss Lytton?' I said. They hurriedly answered, 'Yes,' and made way for me to pass.

" I entered the first room on the ground floor; and there sat Sir Edward Bulwer Lytton, Dr. Marshall Hall, and Dr. Rouse, the latter looking most wretched.

" I had had the questionable advantage of meeting Sir Edward Lytton in many distinguished houses, the owners of which were good enough to invite me, and of course I knew him; but I addressed myself to the medical men, and told them that 'Lady Lytton had consented to go with me to my father Mr. Planché's house, but that I came to hold Dr. Rouse to his promise.' Some remark, on my saying this, fell from this tender husband and father, the great novelist, dramatist, and poet; and I answered it. He kept his seat while I stood, but my reply intimated to him that I knew him, and it is almost amusing to recollect that he sent me an apology for not having risen : '*he was so distressed,*'—for I never saw any one less so; he was *very deaf*, and I regret to say, I think he did not hear what I said, for I had no feeling for him but of intense disgust, and he saw it. I returned trembling with anxiety for the task before me—the removal of this deeply injured innocent woman, wife, mother.

" But I need not have doubted her power over herself (of which I saw much more in after-days). God alone knows the agony of that mother's heart as she walked quietly past the closed door of the room where her poor dying girl was so soon to breathe her last.

"At ten o'clock I was obliged to accompany my father to a soirée at Mrs. Milner Gibson's (leaving dear Lady Lytton in my sister's care). I told them what had happened during the day. ' It was not possible,' people said; but it was not only possible, but *true*. Lady Lytton sent an eminent fever physician, Dr. Tweedie, to see Miss Lytton. His first words were, ' Too late, too late.' He asked for port wine; there was none in the house, and some was procured from a tavern at the end of the street.

" On the following evening, Saturday, the 29th of April, 1848, this poor young lady died; Dr. Rouse himself coming to announce to me the sad intelligence. The housekeeper from Knebworth was sent up to take possession of the body, which was conveyed to Knebworth and buried there.

" In the papers appeared the following :—

" 'At Knebworth ' (mark the veracity of our Colonial Secretary*), ' Emily Elizabeth, the only daughter of Edward Bulwer Lytton.'

" I had the satisfaction of putting in the *Morning Post*, and also the *Britannia*, a Sunday paper much read in those days, the correction of this mistake :—

" ' On Saturday, the 29th of April, at a lodging in Brompton, of typhoid fever, Emily Elizabeth, the only daughter of Sir Edward and Lady Bulwer Lytton, aged 20.'

" Sir Edward Bulwer Lytton sent my father a challenge. My father had many grand qualities, but a passage of arms was not at all to his taste (for he fainted at the sight of blood), so in reply he simply threatened to bind him over to keep the peace.

" I have letters and papers to corroborate this account, and passed the greater part of my time during three years, until my marriage in 1851, in Lady Lytton's company.

" Seldom has it been the fate of any one to be so maligned and crushed as this woman; it was even said of Lady Lytton that she did not love her children—this I

* Secretary of the Colonies 1858-9.

most emphatically deny. I have good reason to know how she loved her daughter, and, as to her son, she scarcely ever spoke of him to me without tears, in the early days of our acquaintance.

"KATHERINE CURTEIS WHELAN.

"*September*, 1883."

The following letters relate to the same tragic event :—

FROM MISS PLANCHÉ TO DR. ROUSE.

"ST. MICHAEL'S GROVE LODGE, *April 29th*, 1848.

"DEAR SIR,—

"Not only am I always so agitated when I speak to you upon this most grievous and unparalleled case of poor Lady Lytton's that I can scarcely hope to express myself as concisely and collectedly as so urgent and painful a subject requires, but as you also invariably cut me short, I adopt this plan of explaining to you that, natural and imperative as Lady Lytton's wishes were to call in medical advice on *her* side for her poor child, now lying in so critical a state, her friends would not consent to her doing so till she had consulted one of her legal advisers, Mr. Charles Hyde, upon the safety and feasibility of such a measure. Mr. Hyde having substantiated its perfect justice and propriety (especially under Miss Lytton's *extraordinary* position in a shabby, half-furnished lodging), Lady Lytton had resolved not to lose a moment in sending Mr. Hyde to a medical man. Lady Lytton saw perfectly the tendency of every move made since her expulsion from the lodging in Pelham Terrace yesterday. Sir Edward not being allowed to see his daughter affords the plausible ultimate assertion that Lady Lytton was not in fact more harshly dealt with as a mother than he was as a father, though in any case there is a wide difference between the feelings of a father and those of a mother. All this plausibility Lady Lytton is perfectly prepared for, as are her friends, for, as *she* says, 'Sir Edward Bulwer Lytton's *facts* are always made to order.' Though you must in truth and honour acknowledge, from the extraordinary and almost incredible command of herself that Lady Lytton had throughout that fearful night, that she listened to her poor child's ravings unseen, unheard, upon the stairs, her only design was to watch over her silently and unobserved, deserted as she was in a paltry lodging, with no other attendance but that of a hired nurse, who, however good and conscientious a person she may be, must certainly lack a mother's feelings.

"As Lady Lytton explained to you yesterday, had her daughter's malady been any other than so high a state of long-coming-on melancholy and nervous excitement, no *human* power should have prevented her establishing herself *openly* at her child's bedside.

"I must beg of you not to destroy this letter, which, of course, as a man of honour, you will not do when I tell you I have kept a copy of it.

　　　　"I have the honour to be, dear Sir,
　　　　　　"Your obedient servant,
　　　　　"KATHERINE FRANCES PLANCHÉ.
"To Dr. Rouse."

Miss Planché was acquainted with Dr. Rouse previously; he destroyed himself soon after.

The poor young lady died in the evening of the day this letter was written.

DR. TWEEDIE TO LADY LYTTON.

(Copied from his own note.)

"MONTAGUE PLACE, BEDFORD SQUARE, *May* 18*th*, 1848.

"Dr. Tweedie presents his compliments to Lady Bulwer Lytton. In acknowledging her kind note, Dr. Tweedie begs to express his deep sympathy with Lady Lytton on the cause of her recent affliction, and his sincere regret that at the time he saw her daughter medical aid could not possibly be of the slightest service in averting the fatal issue of the malady.

"There is one consolation—small indeed—that the last moments, or rather the last few hours, were passed without apparent suffering. As Lady Lytton has alluded to Dr. Tweedie not having received the usual fee for consultation with Dr. Hall and Mr. Rouse, he begs to name the most moderate sum for consultation—two guineas."

LADY LYTTON TO MISS PLANCHÉ.

"TOWER, THURSDAY EVENING, SEVEN O'CLOCK,
"*May 18th,* 1848.

"MY POOR LITTLE VICTIM OF A KATE,—

"Here am I boring you again to-day, but it is your own fault for having constituted yourself my rudder, chart, and anchor; and who else to turn to in all my difficulties I know not. Here is my present one. I *have just* received the enclosed from Dr. Tweedie, and all I possess in the world till July is £1 8*s.*, so what to do I know not, unless you can beg or borrow me a guinea till I see you, and then I will see what more I can sell, though really it seems to me that I have nothing left. In the hope that you will be able to do so, as you have achieved so many greater things in my troublesome behalf, I send you one guinea towards Dr. Tweedie's fee; and if you can get the other, will you have the kindness to write three lines to Dr. Tweedie, expressing my thanks to him, and saying (which God knows is true) that being too ill to write to him myself, I have begged you to do so, and enclose him the two guineas (with many regrets that it is not more), and take it or get some sure person to leave the note and its enclosure at his house. Forgive all this trouble, mine own darling Kate, as well as every other I have given you; and believe that had our positions been reversed (which God forbid !), I would with heart, soul, head, and hands do as much for you. I fear you will hardly be able to make this out, but the night is coming on ; for that matter, it is in my heart and eyes all day long. God bless you.

"Ever your grateful and affectionate
"ROSINA BULWER LYTTON."

The generosity of Sir Edward Lytton in leaving

his wife to pay Dr. Tweedie's fee needs no comment.

LADY LYTTON TO DR. MARSHALL HALL.

"*July 17th,* 1848.

"SIR,—

"Now that I am able to hold a pen, painful as it is to me to have any sort of communication with you, yet, as I understand that Sir Edward Bulwer Lytton (that incarnate lie of the nineteenth century) dares to give out that my poor angel child died of 'a natural decay,' you, as his accomplice in the last act of this at once awful and disgraceful tragedy, had better warn him to drop *this* cold-blooded falsehood, or I have friends and WITNESSES who are determined to make the TRUTH public, which is that the primary cause of my poor *murdered* child's illness was the life of hard labour she led to promote her father's ill-gotten and quacky literary reputation as a German scholar (*he not knowing one word of that language*), coupled with the terrific seclusion and privations of every sort that she endured. Witness her dying without the *commonest* necessaries of a sick-room about her, as *even* the wine poured down her throat (alas! too late) had to be sent for from a common public-house!

"The actual cause of her death was your gross ignorance, only to be equalled by the coarse and inhuman brutality of your manner. I shall ever look upon you and proclaim you as her murderer, for when this poor young victim of the parsimony and neglect of a profligate father, and the ignorance of a medical charlatan, was rapidly sinking under TYPHUS, did you not starve and bleed her as if for nervous fever, and so ensure and hasten her death?

"Remember, both you and your employer, that there are too many witnesses to all this for your or his falsehoods on the subject to avail. God forgive you both, but I never can.

"ROSINA BULWER LYTTON.

"I am aware that he tries to excuse the miserable hole

in which she died by giving out that she was on a visit to a German baroness. But was it right to let this poor young girl, without even a maid of her own, trapese about with German baronesses who lived in lodgings at thirty shillings a week, and where a commercial clerk was pacing up and down all night in the garret overhead ? "

"This inhuman creature pretended that my child's life was at stake if I did not leave the house. In vain I swore she should never know I was there, *nor did she*. He said *his* fame as a physician was at stake. 'Which,' said I, 'is of the most import, *your* fame as a physician or *my* feelings as a mother ?' 'Oh, my fame as a doctor, to be sure,' said he, with a horse-laugh."

EXTRACT FROM LETTER OF MRS. BRUCE, THE NURSE AT THE TIME OF LADY LYTTON'S POOR DAUGHTER'S DEATH.

"*December* 15*th*, 1849.

"MOST HONOURED LADY,—

"I cannot find words to express my grateful thanks for your Ladyship's benevolence. Bad and base a man as Sir Edward is, people are not aware of all his villainy to you. Many highly respectable families have heard much from me, amiable lady. Mr. Rouse made out that he was one of the best of men and fathers, and that he had a medical man in the house all the time your angel daughter was ill of a night ; but I soon contradicted that falsehood, and was believed before Mr. Rouse. I informed Sir Edward that she spoke of you in the most dutiful manner, saying, 'Oh, my mamma! I *reverence* my DEAR mamma.' He cannot deny it. I hope those words will be a comfort to your Ladyship, knowing that you have an angel to watch over you, who, I am convinced, really loved you, but dared not make it public.

"CHARLOTTE BRUCE."

The record of the next few years of Lady

Lytton's life, during which nothing of special importance occurred, is as follows :—

Soon after the events narrated above, she left the
Tower and lived until 1851 in apartments at 97,
Sloane Street. In 1852 she moved to a cottage in
the Fulham Road. In 1853 she went to Llangollen.
In 1855 she left for Taunton, where she resided
until her husband's death in 1873. But during this
last period many things happened which must be
detailed at some length.

I here insert a letter relating to her literary
labours.

FROM LADY LYTTON TO MR. SHOBERL,
THE PUBLISHER.

"97, SLOANE STREET, CADOGAN PLACE, CHELSEA,
"*January 20th*, 1851.

"DEAR SIR,—

"As there is nothing like a perfectly clear understanding in all matters of business, I trouble you with these
few lines, that I may ascertain from you whether I am
correct in considering that the arrangement between you
and me for my new novel of 'Miriam Sedley' is as
follows, viz., that *you* are to defray all the expenses of
printing, publishing, and advertising, and that *I* am to give
you £10 per cent. upon every £100 I receive from you of
the profits on the sale of the work, or £5 on every £50.
Never having before published a book on these terms, I am
doubly anxious to clearly understand them ; for, as I before
told you, nothing but the *terrible* want of money induces
me to write, and therefore I could not afford to *incur* £5
expense. This arrangement is to me a most woeful falling
off after receiving in days of yore £600, £500, and £400
for infinitely worse books than the one now in your hands.
The very least poor Mr. Bull ever gave me for the worst
book I ever wrote was £300 down on receipt of the MSS.
I am well aware that those palmy days are gone ; but I am

also perfectly aware that my books are a very good speculation to any publisher, as the *name* alone sells them, and
they have a certain sale in the provinces of the three
kingdoms, and a great one in America, which, being to
a certain degree reputation, ought in some measure at least
to be profit.

"Awaiting an early reply,

"I remain, dear Sir,

"Yours very truly,

"ROSINA BULWER LYTTON."

CHAPTER XVIII.

THE next few years of Lady Lytton's life contain nothing but a record of privations and persecutions, which culminated in the extraordinary madhouse conspiracy of 1858. Of the events which preceded that remarkable episode I propose to give but a very brief outline. In 1852 Lady Lytton was living in a small cottage in the Fulham Road. The repeated efforts of herself and her friends to obtain a more adequate allowance from Sir Edward had resulted in complete failure, and she was consequently even more embarrassed than she had ever been previously.*

"I had not a farthing," she writes, "till a publisher of the name of Shoberl's bills for between £400 and £500 became due, but at the end of that year Shoberl failed, and I did not get a penny! I really felt stunned, or rather crushed. I was for four months trying to let my cottage and as ineffectually trying to borrow money. At length a good Samaritan on the Stock Exchange, a stranger of course,

---

* The result of these efforts may be guessed from the following extract from the preface to "The School for Husbands," published by Lady Lytton in 1852 :—" For although about a year ago I received the munificent offer of an additional £100 a year if I would give up certain letters in my possession, and live out of England, much as I have suffered in this land, I preferred remaining in it and living down the whole clique to acceding to this additional outrage." —L. D.

said he had heard such a good character of my honesty from my creditors, that he most humanely and generously lent me £1,000 at five per cent. for ten years, I paying back £100 a year of the principal, and insuring both my tyrant's and my own life. With this drain on my already miserable pittance, I could not stay in London. My friends, to aid me in economising, asked me to go on visits to them, so I went first to Lady Hotham at Brighton and then to other friends there ; but I soon found out that there is nothing so expensive as visiting in great houses, so, after a short trip to Paris with Lady Hotham, I went to bury myself in the little Welsh village of Llangollen."

It was at Llangollen in 1854 that an extraordinary attempt was made, if not to poison Lady Lytton, at all events seriously to injure her health.

" A vulgar old woman, calling herself Mrs. P——, came down with her daughter to the village inn. She scraped an acquaintance with me, and obtruded herself upon me at all hours, at breakfast, dinner, and in my bedroom before I was up of a morning. One day before I came into the dining-room she had helped me to soup. I found her with her bonnet on, and before I had time to eat the soup she pretended she had had a sudden summons to London and was off. I had scarcely eaten the soup before I was seized with the most agonising pains and violent retchings ; my doctor gave me antidotes, and said that some attempt had been made to poison me, but the dose had not been sufficient. This seemed to be confirmed by my getting, about three weeks later, the following letter from Mrs. P—— :—

" 'HOTEL DE PROVENCE, *December 27th*, 1853.

" 'DEAR LADY L——,

" ' I am about to leave for Paris. I have lost my son, and my daughter her baby. Pity me. PRAY *be on your* GUARD, as a person will be sent down with a dog to attract you. Her name will begin with a G. Mind, I will come

to you to sooth my hevvy sorrows. *Pray be on your guard.*
Believe, I would not harm you in the least. Saying
good-bye,

<blockquote>

" ' Pity me, and believe,

　　" ' Ever your *friend,*

　　　　" ' T. P——.

" ' God bless you.'

</blockquote>

" About ten days after this Brellisford, the waitress, came
to me and said that an old woman, looking like a housekeeper, had just arrived from the station to take apartments for ' her young lady, a Miss Getting.' "

This person duly took up her quarters at the inn,
accompanied by the dog, but her efforts to make
Lady Lytton's acquaintance naturally failed, and she
was compelled to leave without effecting her object.
With reference to this Miss Getting, a gentleman
wrote from Brighton :

" I went to the party I spoke of last night ; and, sure
enough, the Miss G—— who I met there was the *sister* of
the Llangollen lady. They are both intimate friends of
Sir L. B——'s. Miss G—— spoke of Lady L—— as being
perfectly insane, and also very seriously ill in her bodily
health."

" She was scarcely gone," writes Lady Lytton, " when I
got letters from London, imploring me to be on my
guard, as these Gettings lived at Brighton, and the one sent
to Llangollen had a carriage always ready on the road in
order, if I could be found out walking, to kidnap me and
carry me off to a madhouse, as Sir Edward was giving out
all over London that I was quite mad. The summer after
this (1854) I left the hotel, and went into lodgings in a
small but nicely furnished house, of which I took the whole
except the parlours, which, as the woman only asked
twenty-five shillings a week for them, I told her on no
account to let to any one, but if she had an offer to do so, I
would pay her for them rather than have any other lodger in

the house after all I had suffered. But when I had been there about three weeks, to my great indignation she informed me that she had let her parlours to a lady and gentleman, who had given her two guineas a week for them. I have since heard upon indisputable authority that this Mr. and Mrs. B—— were always with Sir Edward at Knebworth and Ventnor and elsewhere.

"A few evenings after, the evening being sultry, I was obliged to leave my drawing-room door slightly ajar, when, to my horror, who should come tripping in, with a basket of strawberries, but Mrs. B——, dressed, or rather undressed, to a pitch that would have alarmed even an art-student! She made me a sort of theatrical speech, in which she introduced herself and her strawberries. I never eat strawberries; and in the absence of Wenham Lake ice, my reception of her must have been most refreshing or rather refrigerating! Nothing daunted, this woman spread her furbelows, and, uninvited, seated herself; and seeing her husband creeping up the stairs, she had the crowning impertinence to call him in and introduce him to me, I visibly petrifying the while, and darting into my bedroom, locked the door. The next day came a note from Mrs. B——, expressing her great sympathy with all I had suffered, and as the cuisine was not particularly good at those lodgings, would I do them the favour of dining with them at the hotel? I sent down a verbal message to say I never dined out. The next day the pair took their departure for London, but the people of the house became suddenly and unbearably insolent, and although I had taken the rooms for six months certain, said I must leave them immediately, as they had let them. This was pleasant, for lodgings are difficult to get at Llangollen; and, worse than that, it wanted six weeks to the time I should receive my parish allowance, and also to the time when the two months' rent of my cottage would become due. I had not a sou wherewith to meet this sudden and unfair demand in the teeth of a written agreement. But my kind old friend, Dr. Price, not only came to the rescue, rating these vile people soundly, and telling them they would repent their shameful conduct before they were much older (which they did), but he kindly got me another lodging, higher up, on the same road, in which I had not been installed a week, when Dr. Price wrote to me saying that horrid woman Mrs. B—— and a woman she called her maid were in my old lodgings. I put on my bonnet, and went out to pass the house, and what should I see but Mrs. B—— and her *soi-disant* maid sitting on the *sill* of the open drawing-room window, with a salver between them, with two decanters of wine on it, and glasses in their hands, over which they were laughing and singing ! and as soon as they saw me they set up a perfect shout. Two nights after this the *lady* and her maid were literally drummed out of the place for roaring and screaming about the streets with men at between one and two in the morning, and disturbing the quiet village. I, of course, could not stay in a place where I had been so outraged and persecuted ; and then it was that I wrote to a friend to engage me rooms in an hotel at Taunton, kept by Mrs. Clarke."

On this occasion Lady Lytton contrived for a time to elude the vigilance of her persecutors, as appears from the following letter written by her to Mr. A. E. Chalon :—

"DEAR MR. CHALON,—

"I don't know if I ever told you that when I made my escape from Llangollen and came here Sir Edward was perfectly rabid at his and his bloodhounds having lost my track. So well had I managed it, that all the wretches there thought I was gone to London, as I had had all my luggage forwarded to a friend in Hyde Park Terrace, and sent on here after, so that when my parish allowance became due, he and Loaden thought themselves *very* clever in saying they would not pay it till they had a clergyman's certificate of the place I was in, and of my existence ! My dear good old lion Hyde said he should have a better proof of my existence than *that*, as he, Hyde, would accompany me to Knebworth, and see me properly installed there, which, of course, brought the reptile instantly to his senses ; but as I was determined *not* to endure this infamy every time, and as poor Mr. Hodgson, though an excellent man, is a sort of legal Admiral Dundas, I determined to take the matter in hand myself, more especially as the spies were reappearing on the horizon.   About a week before my last parish allowance became due, a creature calling herself Miss Henna (why not Henbane at once ?) wrote to request an interview with me ; that is the way they generally begin ; but by her coming in the dusk of the evening, in a pouring rain, and refusing to say what her business was, and being so very urgent to see me, *only* to *see* me, Mrs. Clarke told her, without mincing the matter, that she firmly believed her to be one of Sir E——'s spies, and that therefore she might go back and tell him, after being hunted to death by his infamous emissaries, I saw *no one* not especially recommended to me, but that no doubt he would be delighted to hear that I had not been so well for years, and was going abroad in a day or two. 'Miss Henna' then, by way of establishing her respectability, said she was a governess.   'Oh ! very likely,' said Mrs. Clarke ; 'I understand most of that vile man's mistresses are, and they afterwards fill the equally honourable office of his spies.   Pray, where are you staying in Taunton ?'   She then got very red, stammered very much, and named some doctor living near Trinity Church (two miles from this).   'Oh! indeed !' said Mrs. Clarke, 'but it happens rather unfortunately that there is *no* doctor of law, physic, or divinity of *that* name in Taunton, so the sooner you return to your employer the better.'   Mrs. Clarke sent a policeman to watch her, and she decamped by the next London train, and Mr. Oakly, the governor of the gaol, made every inquiry, and no one of the name of ' Henna' nor answering her description was known at the post-office or in the town."

About this time Lady ˏLytton was persuaded into

sending a statement of her case to Lord Lyndhurst, but her papers were lost under mysterious and suspicious circumstances,* and her appeal resulted, as usual, in nothing. I pass on to the early part of 1857, when Lady Lytton was still at Mrs. Clarke's, the Giles Castle Hotel, Taunton. The following letters to Dr. Price explain her situation at that period. The book referred to was "Very Successful."

"MRS. CLARKE'S, AT GILES CASTLE HOTEL, TAUNTON,
"*Tuesday, January* 13*th*, 1857.

"MY DEAREST AND KINDEST DR. PRICE,—

"Thank you a thousand times for the *News of the World* just received, which pleases me, not for its praise, but for its *honesty*. Oh, dear Dr. Price, I care not, I assure you, one straw for all the bought abuse of that venal and infamous pressgang, further than that as it has crushed my poor book and effectually ruined poor me, for this dark, cold, bitter morning I know not, in God's name, which way to turn from the fearful ruin that has snared, and now compasses me as a net. Poor Miss Dickenson, who so kindly lent me that £400 for the Geneva infamy, being now by a swindling banker ruined herself, has for the last three months been pressing for the payment of the principal, the interest of which, with the interest of Mr. Wheeler's money, has, as you know, added to the additional infamy at Llangollen, exhausted my beggarly pittance, which, if I had it even *intact*, is not enough for bread and salt. Added to this, there is the £100 borrowed for this wretched book and Mrs. Clarke's bill, while Mr. Hodgson, with intended kindness, but real cruelty, has borrowed another £25 from dear Mr. Wheeler to get my things out of the Pantechnicon, and packed them down here, where I have

---

* General Thompson demanded an inquiry in the House of Commons into this affair, but nothing came of it.

not even standing room for them, and the carriage alone has cost me £4 16s. Now this poor book, without any great success, ought, had it been dealt with honestly, to have realised me by this time £700, and floated me out of all this, instead of which, owing to the unparalleled infamy with which I am so *effectually* compassed on *all* sides, it has only added another mountain of millstones to crush me ; and that is what it is done for. And I have no, nor indeed *any*, defence equal to the attack. You will see by the enclosed letter from Mudie that my last ghost of a hope has now failed me, for (under all the circumstances) returning to Skeet, as he recommends, would be the worst sort of financial suicide. The *only* thing that could be done for me, which I fear you nor no one else would do, would be to open a public subscription for me to sell my book with my *name*, and stating the full particulars of what had caused it. I have long deprived myself of the commonest comforts of life, and worked day and night, like fifty slaves, and all, all, no use. As fast as I fill my poor buckets, that fiend comes and kicks them down, and I have not a single hand to help me to refill them. If any one to-morrow was willing to lend me this £500, I could not borrow it, having now no means of paying it. It has been this cruel borrowing for sixteen years, with this fiend ever preventing my earning an honest independence, while others make fortunes out of the veriest trash, and *he* has become rich on his demoralising obscenity, which has at length ground me down into this utter ruin. I am now quite prostrate, body and mind, the blood gushing out like a fountain every cough I have. It is to be hoped it will please God to have mercy on me at last and take me, but I should be sorry to leave the world as a swindler ; and poor kind Miss Dickenson, and my friend's £100—oh! it is too, *too* much. DO, dear Dr. Price, throw *conventionality* to the winds, and try and get up this PUBLIC SUBSCRIPTION for me, or could your young printer recommend a publisher who would undertake the *London* agency of the book? For return to Skeet, you know I could not. I did not calculate on paying Miss

Dickenson the whole £400, only half, and the next book
the other half; but this infamy has effectually *ruined* me.
I hope you got my letter of yesterday with the bank post
bill.   God ever bless you, dear kind friend, will be the last
prayer of your grateful and affectionate

"R. B. LYTTON."

"GILES CASTLE HOTEL, TAUNTON,
" <i>Wednesday Night, January</i> 28<i>th</i>, 1857.</div>

"MY DEAREST DR. PRICE,—

" As every day I grow weaker and weaker, and every
day some fresh agony supervenes, I will try and scrawl
you these few lines to-night (though I cannot send them
till to-morrow), while they are making my bed.   The plot
thickens, and that fiend Sir Liar's game is evidently to
defame my book, so as to prevent my finding a publisher,
so that the following is the infamous advertisement he
is getting inserted in all the papers throughout the country :
' The eminent publishers Messrs. Whittaker, of Ave Maria
Lane, have repudiated all connection with Lady Bulwer
Lytton's " Very Successful," *that most disgraceful* work.'   Now,
of course, any *other* woman—that is, any woman with a
farthing in her pocket—could bring an action for defamation, and obtain swinging damages, and lawyers would
be only *too* glad of such a case; but as it is, *I* being a
pauper, and most Englishmen naturally toadies and
cowards respecting the powers that be when there is
no pecuniary advantage to be gained by courage and
honesty, I have, of course, no earthly chance, now that
I am so effectually trampled down in a corner, but that
of being quietly stabbed to death in cold blood by these
hired tools of that cowardly brute Sir Liar.   This
morning came a letter from Mudie saying he must
return the second hundred of my book, as the Whittakers
would not let him have the plates.   So, you see, the conspiracy is to effectually destroy the sale of the book, so as
to utterly ruin and disgrace me ; and I have no one of
sufficient energy and generosity to even make a *show*
(though it were but a sham) of making head against this

infamy, which might be done by putting an advertisement
in the *Times*, headed ' Notice '—and borrowing their *own
word*—' Notice.—From the very disgraceful means that
have been resorted to to suppress Lady Bulwer Lytton's
"Very Successful," the remaining copies of the edition
are selling at £3 a copy.' And I'm very certain such
a notice would fulfil its own statement, and worry that
wretch by foiling him at his own weapons (*i.e.*, a lie
and a puff) more than anything; and an advertisement
they can't refuse to put in. To-day, in my agony, I got
up and sent for Mr. E—— to go to London to see Mr. Hyde,
and one more person, who, if he can be found, *perhaps may*
stretch out a hand to save me by getting these infamous
facts properly before the public. But I have no hopes,
for if I were dying, as I trust and believe I am, all people
can ever manage to do for me is to bother me to help
myself, which, were I able to do, I should not trouble
them. Then Mr. E——, as he says himself, is worse than
ignorant in all publishing matters, and fears he may do
more harm than good (no doubt); and if even a publisher
could be found, still it would take at least a week to
negotiate so complex a matter properly, and find an honest
and spirited publisher that would make the enterprise his
own interest, and turn the whole of this conspiracy to the
advantage of the book as a spur to its sale, which
properly managed it would be; but who will so act for
a beggar against a rich influential villain? And Mr.
E—— can only stay one day in London; and even
catching at this, I fear, useless straw is for me as
ruinous in expense as it would be in life to open an
artery and let the last drop of my blood drain out. Each
day my miserable fate is hanging on some new thread,
which snaps the next and plunges me into a more fearful
abyss than before. The strength of a Hercules would fail
under such prolonged and ever *increasing* torture. But
one thing could help or save me, and enable me to baffle
my remorseless and unscrupulous enemy; and that I have
no more power of obtaining than I have of snatching one
of the stars out of the heavens. If Mr. E—— returns, as I

fully expect he will, with a shake of the head and a 'No use! he was not in town, and would not be till next week,' then all I pray is that they will let me die quietly, for more *talk* I cannot stand; and when it is known that I have *no* channel through which to sell my book, and consequently no earthly means of meeting my cruel and heavy liabilities, what can I do but die? Forgive me, dearest Dr. Price, for afflicting your kind heart all this time, but you kindly wish me to write nothing else. God bless you, and now good-night. I'll not close my letter till tomorrow (Thursday). If, dearest Dr. Price, Mr. E—— brings me any good news (?), you shall hear from me by Monday; but if not, as I fully expect, then indeed I cannot write, for my ruin will be too fully accomplished, and this will be the second murder Sir Edward Bulwer Lytton has achieved, for his poor young victim daughter could not weather it so long as her more inured mother. If it was merely the failure and dastardly lies and abuse of this poor book, it would not weigh with me a moment, nor even were it the heavy expenses I have incurred for it would *they* trouble me, as Clarke's claims against me could not trouble me, after the manner in which he and those Whittakers treated me; but there is my poor friend's £100, poor Miss Dickenson's money, and Mrs. Clarke's bill, and not one shilling to meet all this. As I before said, with honesty, intelligence, energy, zeal, and a proper indignation to expose such villainy, it might be all turned to account, and made the means of putting me effectually in a better and safer position than I have ever been in; but with only new and insignificant hirelings to fight the battle, and, as they *know*, not the means of adequately paying their hire, *what* earthly chance have *I*? God bless you, dearest Dr. Price. Give my best love to dear Mr. and Mrs. Wheeler; thank them for all their kindness to me. And if this should be the last letter you receive from me, pray believe that to the last moment of my miserable and cruelly tortured existence I shall never cease to be

" Your grateful and affectionate, and also theirs,

" ROSINA BULWER LYTTON."

Other extracts from this correspondence further illustrate the unfortunate lady's struggles and painful embarrassments.

"March 15th.

"What strange crotchet have you got into your dear kind head of my having sold the first thousand copies of my poor doomed book, when I wrote you word that the remaining six hundred copies so cruelly thrown back on my hands I had in vain tried to bring out as a second edition, Sir Edward having threatened every publisher with an injunction and so effectually prevented my getting one ? I have literally not one penny piece upon earth. In April I shall owe poor Mrs. Clarke, who has been most kind and Christian to wait so long, a nine months' hotel bill, and there is poor Miss Dickenson clamouring for her long-owing £400, which was to have been paid out of this poor strangled book in February. . . . I am in mourning, so far as a sheet of black-edged paper goes—other I cannot afford—for a poor aunt of mine, my mother's sister. Though an old maid, she was another victim to the grasping selfishness of man, her spendthrift brother having run through three large fortunes, got every shilling out of his poor sister, speculated and lost it, then died and left her in her old age, desolate and penniless, on the world. She had been very good and kind to me as a child, and I could not let her want necessaries in her declining days, so my miserable pittance has been still further curtailed this year ; hence my arrears to Mrs. Clarke. On the 18th of last month it pleased God to remove her to where there is neither sorrow, nor age, nor death. She wished, poor soul, to see me before she died; but had I not been myself stretched on a sick-bed, I had not a penny to go to London with, any more than I can pay her memory the respect of putting on mourning, for feelings are luxuries that beggars have no business to indulge in. I think you will own that my cup of misery has more than overflowed this year, but God's will be done."

"March 31st, 1857.

"At length I send you the only thing left for me to do: my appeal to public charity, which ought to have been ready three weeks ago. . . . This pamphlet is now making the tour of Europe, America, the colonies, and the Indies. I have sent it to the members of both Houses of Parliament, the mayors of every town, the magistrates of all the metropolitan police-offices, heads of colleges, all the clubs, and am trying to get copies of it sold at different libraries. Of course I have sent it to all my fashionable acquaintances of the *haute volée*, who may perhaps give a guinea and a half from their superfluous thousands out of curiosity. At all events, if they do not, I have nothing to do but beg my bread about the streets."*

"April 5th, 1857.

"Ten thousand thanks, my dearest and kindest Dr. Price, but no earthly power would induce me to borrow *now* another sixpence from any human being, as I have no certainty, or even chance, of being able to repay it; and, as I am not a swindler, ready to supply my own wants on any terms, why should I accept what I cannot repay, and more especially from *you?* But, with my whole heart, I thank you all the same for your great and constant kindness. . . . This is the third quarter I shall owe poor kind Mrs. Clarke, which will be £75, and my parish allowance is £47, even if I get it, which, now poor kind Mr. Hodgson is gone, I fully expect I shall not. But God's hand is so heavy upon me that I no longer kick against the pricks. . . . Oh, the bitter, bitter curse of being penniless! To do me any good I ought to be able to get ten thousand of these pamphlets circulated, and this I cannot afford."

"April 15th, 1857.

"I have received a great many orders for the pamphlet, for that gratifies curiosity, and only costs a shilling, but only three orders for the book, one from kind

---

* For Lady Lytton's "Appeal to the Justice and Charity of the English People," see Appendix I.

Lady Boynton at Brighton, upon whom I had certainly no claim; so I returned the post-office order, and sent her the book, but she again sent it back to me in so kind a manner that I could not refuse, without being ungracious, to keep it. Thank you, dear Dr. Price, for your kind advice about going out; but, like all other advice that I get (of which I get plenty and to spare), I have not the means of following it, as it is now nearly seven months since I have set my foot outside the door, and have, had I the strength, neither boots nor shoes to go out in, and every driblet I get for my book, or even for that pamphlet, I feel, in common honesty, bound to appropriate to paying what I owe, as far as it goes. However, I hope soon to have a nice long drive in my hearse, which, as Curran said, is the carriage after all!"

"April 28th.

"Lazarus being raised from the dead was scarcely more miraculous than the number of persons this pamphlet seems to have raised up who have heretofore appeared to have forgotten my existence, but not one from the Gold Coast yet."

"August 6th.

"Pray take every care of yourself, and do let me have one line as soon as you receive this to tell me, as I sincerely hope, that you have quite recovered from the effects of your last severe attack. As for my miserable affairs, while they are, like Mahomet's coffin, suspended between heaven and earth, you may guess the fearful wear and tear this suspense is to me. Good Mr. Ironside * is more sanguine every day, but twenty years of attested evidence against that monster is not to be collected in a day; meanwhile you may guess what I am suffering, without literally a penny piece in the world. My appeal to public charity brought me, besides the sale of the pamphlet, which went to pay its expenses and advertisements, £70 from seven good Samaritans, who each sent me

---

* Mr. Ironside was the publisher of Lady Lytton's "Appeal," and befriended her in many other ways.

a £10 note for one copy of my book, but all this has already gone in preliminary law expenses. You may imagine how all these ceaseless pecuniary drains and difficulties prey upon me body and soul, but I have no right to torment you with them, nor would I but that you so kindly ask me to tell you of my affairs, which is only another word for my miseries."

To Mrs. Jermyn.

"*September 11th*, 1857.

" How very kind you are to take such trouble to disseminate my 'Appeal.' I have written to Mr. Ironside to forward you another dozen. Alas ! they have been able to do nothing with that shuffling, lying monster, and I told them from the first they would do nothing by temporising gentlemanlike measures but achieve the work of cruel supererogation of prolonging my already insupportable trials and tortures. So now the plan is, as soon as this complicated Divorce Bill becomes law, to sue the wretch in the Ecclesiastical Court. . . . I deeply regret that I was not allowed to have my way seven months ago, when the wretch sealed my ruin by burking my last book, of organising a public penny subscription all over England, which would have effectually exposed him, and, I feel sure, would have rescued me out of this terrible Slough of Despond before this. . . . I cannot eat, and am nearly mad from total want of sleep, for if hope deferred maketh the heart sick, despair prolonged maketh it mad."

To Mrs. Jermyn.

"*September 28th*, 1857.

" Among the innumerable unthinking things poor Mr. Ironside has done to make me wince was his writing to *you* about forming a chimera committee ; did he ever trouble to consider or consult my feelings, he might have known that this spurring a willing horse to death would have pained and annoyed me, but, poor man, though full of the kindest and noblest impulses, he has no judgment, no knowledge of the world or of human nature, and consequently no tact. You may wonder how I could be so imprudent as to consign myself to a person of whom I knew nothing, but you know drowning wretches *will* catch at straws, and soon after he so kindly and warmly took up my 'Appeal' he wrote to me in an authoritative manner for a schedule of every shilling I owed, and upon receiving it wrote back, 'I shall only be able to allow you £150 a year.' Now, as I know positively nothing about money but the want of it, and have a vague idea that men of business have some occult way of managing monetary affairs, I gave a long sigh, and felt as if the incubus was already removed, and said I would live on £50 a year if he could contrive to make the other £350 pay the debts Sir E. L. B——'s infamous and cruel conspiracies had forced upon me. . . . But three months ago I found, after all Mr. Ironside's somewhat blasphemous 'By God, you shall be got out of this slough,' that he had no final or definite plan on earth. . . ."

To Dr. Price.

"*October 1st*, 1857.

"Your skill, which I know from experience to be as great as your kindness, cannot minister to a mind diseased, and that is my mortal malady, much augmented by now finding that this new Divorce Bill, which is, of course, a sham, like all their pretended law amendments, does not come into operation till January, 1858. What I am to do without a penny till then God alone knows. Added to all this, though scarcely able to hold up my head, and though writing is the most torturing and detrimental thing to my chest possible, I have to slave away at another book, doubtless to share the same fate as my last, and while I write I have to hold my handkerchief with my left hand to my mouth to prevent the blood gushing out."

CHAPTER XIX.

SPIES AT TAUNTON.—A BOGUS ACTION.

To Dr. Price.

" November 3rd, 1857.

"I will now tell you the last infamy. You have heard me speak of the wretch Laura Deacon, but calling herself Mrs. Beaumont, for whom I and my children were turned out of our home. Well, this wretch had established herself at Boulogne-sur-Mer, and by means of the story about Sir Edward's being the guardian of her bastards, had got into some sort of society there, when out came my pamphlet, and all the people were up in arms, and I was inundated with letters from Boulogne saying that the writers were sure this vulgar boasting impostor was one and the same person described therein. To one and all these inquiries I replied there could be no doubt she was the kept mistress, Beaumont, upon which she was summarily drummed out of Boulogne, which she left vowing vengeance upon me and the whole world. Now I come to her descent upon Taunton.

"Last Thursday, as I was propped up in bed, writing these eternal letters, I was brought a card with this engraved upon it :

"'Mrs. Sellers
"'(*Née* Hautenville),
"'14, *Woburn Place*,
"'*Russell Square*.'

And beside this was scrawled in pencil 'Late of London.' The message sent with this card was that 'the lady wished particularly to see me, as she was very intimate with some

of my most intimate friends abroad.' This alone made me
suspect that the Llangollen P—— affair was about to recommence, for a gentlewoman would have written a note
saying who these mutually intimate friends were. Unfortunately Mrs. Clarke was out at the time, and you never
can get a correct description of a person from a servant,
but Anne, the chambermaid, said she was old and haggard-
looking, light hair, blue eyes, very thin, etc. ; said she had
come that morning from London, but had not a stick of
luggage with her, only a little knitting box, not even a
nightcap. She ordered her luncheon, and said she would
sleep here. I felt sure she was a spy, told them to watch
her, and sent down word I was not well enough to see her.
' Oh, she would write to me,' which, of course, she never
did. It was then two o'clock ; she went out, and stayed till
eight o'clock, when she came in and went to bed, saying to
Anne, ' Oh, do put me next Lady Lytton's room.' Anne
said she could not, as the rooms were full, which they
were not.

"BEAUMONT: 'What is the number of Lady Lytton's
bedroom ?'

"ANNE: 'I forget.'

"BEAUMONT: 'Only tell me which side of the house
it is.'

"ANNE (quite angry): 'I never heard so many impertinent questions in my life, and I'm sure you can ask
them for no good.'

"BEAUMONT: 'Oh, I only wished to be put next to
Lady Lytton, as I'm afraid of being put next a gentleman.'

" The next morning I sent for Mrs. Clarke; and she said
that Beaumont came in asking for a good sitting-room, and
then added, ' I should like that one, with a bedroom adjoin-
ing, that a friend of mine had when she boarded here two
years ago.' Mrs. Clarke felt sure she was a spy, as these
were my rooms, and she had never boarded any one but me,
so she answered curtly, ' You can't have the rooms, as they
are engaged.' I then asked Mrs. Clarke for a minute description, and she gave me the exact one of the Boulogne

woman. I felt convinced that this wretch, the pretended Mrs. Sellers, was no other than Beaumont. She had come into the bar that morning, when the following colloquy ensued :—

"BEAUMONT: 'I want to hire one of your large ball-rooms, Mrs. Clarke, to give lectures in.'

"MRS. CLARKE: 'You had better hire the Assembly Rooms for that purpose.'

"BEAUMONT: 'I'm sorry Lady Lytton is ill, and I'm sure she would have seen *me* if she had not been.'

"MRS. CLARKE: 'I'm *sure* she would have done no such thing, for she sees no one that comes in the way you did.'

"BEAUMONT: 'Ah, but I'm so very intimate with some of her most intimate friends abroad.'

"MRS. CLARKE: 'What are their names?' Dead silence; pause.

"BEAUMONT: 'Ah, poor thing, I can feel for her, for *I* have a brute of a husband myself, from whom I am separated, and if the wretches would only let one alone, and not hunt and persecute one so! But now there is this new Divorce Bill, I would sue mine in the Ecclesiastical Court if I had money, but a poor woman can do nothing without money; how can they?' (This feeler I take to have been the pith and marrow of the spying expedition.)

"MRS. CLARKE: 'Ah, well, Sir Edward will find, to his sorrow, before he is many weeks older that Lady Lytton has found both money and friends.'

"BEAUMONT (evidently taken aback): 'Indeed! Do you know where Sir Edward is now?'

"MRS. CLARKE: 'No, nor do I want to know. Every one knows where such a villain *will* be.'

"BEAUMONT: 'Dear me! You seem very warm in Lady Lytton's cause.'

"MRS. CLARKE: 'Not more than any honest person who knows how much she has suffered and is suffering, and how uprightly she acts by every one, would be.'

"BEAUMONT (twirling round like a teetotum): 'I'm lucky in having only one child; and as that has been adopted, it is no bother to me. He! he! he   Oh, Mrs. Clarke, I'm very sorry I came away in a hurry without any money. *Could* you let me have that eighteen-pence back again that I paid you for my luncheon yesterday? and I'll send you the amount of my bill on Monday.'

"I then sent Mrs. Clarke to track the wretch through the town. She had been to Day's (a linen-draper's where *I* deal), and ordered five pounds' worth of things to be sent *here* for her without paying for them; to Bragg's, at the library, about the sham advertisement I enclose.* As soon as I got this advertisement I made two copies, and sent one to her infamous employer at Knebworth, the other to Park Lane, directed so as those that run may read: 'To Sir E. Bulwer Lytton, Bart., M.P. For the woman Beaumont, *alias* Laura Deacon, spy and mistress to that too contemptible Sir Liar Coward Bulwer Lytton.' I asked this monster if it were not enough to have turned me and my children out of our home, to have hunted me through the world, and beggared me by his dastardly conspiracies, without the crowning outrage of polluting the shelter I had found with this wretch, and if he did not like such truths publicly blazoned on the superscription of letters, to leave off sending his infamous prostitutes to spy upon me, for as sure as he did do so he should hear from me in this strain, and I did not care for all the conventional twaddle in England about my unladylike, coarse, and unfeminine language. I was past all *that*, so the only language to address him in *was* that of Billingsgate, and the *only* protection against such a low, cowardly ruffian was *public* exposure. Friday, the next morning, I sent Mrs. Clarke off to Weston to make inquiries about the sham Mrs. Sellers. They knew nothing of her there but that she had

---

* "Madame Sellers (*née* Hautenville de Hautenville), pupil of Signor Bordoni, principal maestro of La Scala, Milan, and of the Conservatoire at Paris and Royal Academy, London, and of the celebrated composer Alexander Lee, has some hours disengaged during the week, which she proposes to fill by giving lessons in singing and elocution at Taunton and its neighbourhood. Applications as to terms to be made, etc. Madame S—— is sister-in-law to the Rev. W. H. Sellers, late of Trull, and can furnish references in the metropolis from the College of Preceptors."

taken her lodgings at a school, 5, South Terrace, for two months; and from the mysterious manner in which she came there and the roundabout way of her proceedings, every one thought her a very improper person.—Tuesday night, eight o'clock : A lady has just arrived from Weston to tell me that the *soi-disant* Mrs. Sellers had been met in the street by a Major Simpson, 'who *had* been a very gay man,' and that he said he knew this woman formerly to be a most extensively improper person, and that he instantly returned to his hotel to leave word that if she presumed to call asking for patronage, she was upon no account to be shown up to his wife. This lady who brought me this news knows Mrs. Sellers the mother, who has but one son, the clergyman, now in Italy. She is going to write to his mother to-night, tell her the whole affair and the *charming* daughter-in-law she possesses (all in ignoring the fact). A thousand thanks for your kind advice, but even could I afford wine, which I cannot, my head is so bad, I should be afraid to take it. God bless you, my dearest and kindest Dr. Price.

"Believe me, ever your grateful and affectionate
"ROSINA BULWER LYTTON."

TO MRS. JERMYN.

"*October 23rd*, 1857.

"Scold you indeed, you dear, darling, golden-hearted woman! How could that be possible? But still, still you know not how you wring my heart with all these additions to my mountain. Here am I now £20 in your debt. Well, I'd rather have reason to be grateful to you than almost any one I know, so I shall keep your present of £5 to pay the laundress and the servants at Christmas, and bless you for saving me this additional humiliation."

TO MRS. JERMYN.

"*December 6th*, 1857.

"The worm that never dies within me is the thought and the fear that the poor people who have been so kind to me and would have trusted me to any amount should ultimately suffer. My poor excellent landlady, Mrs. Clarke, who has not seen the colour of my money for nine months (and you must know that all I pay her for *everything*—food, fires, wax lights, and my two excellent and well-furnished rooms—is two guineas a week, and I pay the servants £4 a quarter besides ; now I could not live for this in a beggarly lodging, and to be with such a good, honest woman is a great protection)—well, when I sent for her some time ago, as I only thought it right to do, and told her my horrible difficulties, and that I had not even a chance of paying her till January, the poor good creature said, with tears in her eyes, ' Oh, never mind me ; you only try and keep up, for to see how much you suffer and how hard you work, I'm sure no one out of hell could add to your annoyances. At least, I won't."

To Dr. Price.

"*November* 29*th*, 1857.

"Truly say you, dear Dr. Price, about my poor little darling Tiber, whose loss I feel more and more every day. I at least, with the exception of your dear kind self and three more, could better have spared all my worthless acquaintances than that true-hearted, intelligent, faithful darling dog. My last hope even seems to have died with him. For every evening I used to end my prayers over his innocent head with ' Never mind, my Tiber ; *this* day is over,' and ' Sure I am that the Lord will avenge the poor, and defend the cause of the helpless.' I have no kind darling eyes now to encourage me in this belief, so, having ceased to feel it, I have ceased to say it."

"*January* 14*th*, 1858.

"On Monday the siege commenced ; that is, Mr. Ironside wrote to Sir Edward enclosing him a circular from my friends appealing to public charity for funds to bring my case into court, and giving him one week to consider whether he will submit to this disgrace and exposure, or make me a suitable allowance. . . . Well may the proverb say there is a good side to every misfortune, for though being nearly bedridden weakens me to death, I have literally no clothes, that is no winter clothing, to put on, and all the shawls in the world don't keep one's limbs warm ; consequently every time I attempt to sit up I get a violent cold, for though during the two years and a half I have been here, by dint of hard labour, for which I have neither time nor health, I have contrived to keep my wardrobe mended till it will almost mend no longer, yet I cannot manufacture clothes, and I literally have not a dress or cloak fit to go out in were I able. But what grieves me most is the total destruction by moth, from having no one to look after them, of my beautiful ermine, sable, and grèbe, all of which the poor Princess Galitzin gave me, which £500 would not replace. But Sir Edward Bulwer Lytton is a great man, and it is very wrong of Mr. Hyde to call him a fiend in his letter of to-day, and say that his joining it has ruined the Conservative party. . . . I have now arrived nearly at the end of the third volume of another book. . . . God knows where I am even to find a publisher."

In the next letter she seems to have discovered that Mr. Ironside's well-meant assistance was worse than useless.

"*January 22nd*, 1858.

"Would to God I could see you, and you would soon understand that Mr. Ironside is not a clever man, but so self-sufficient and wanting in judgment that he would have undertaken to launch the leviathan with a push of his little finger, or to have quelled the Indian Mutiny with only a broken poker for arms, a snuff-box full of powder for ammunition, a solitary printer's devil for an army, and three-halfpence and a red herring for supplies. I do not recognise Mr. Ironside's right to act in his own way. I now know, as one knows everything too late, that Mr. Ironside is a man who undertakes more than he is able to perform.

"Like Cassandra, I am a fatally true prophetess. Months ago I said, 'Depend upon it, no good ever comes,

or can come, from a corrupt source; and all that juggle
of a Matrimonial Causes Bill, if it ever becomes law, will
do will be to enable common women to go to a police
magistrate and get a show of justice executed on their
tyrants, but all the poor wretched women in the upper
classes will have their whole fate left at the mercy of
a corrupt and venal judge.'   Read the case of Johnson
versus Sumner, that I send you, and Chief Baron Pollock's
disgraceful dictum that ' even if a husband had £10,000
a year, £200 a year is enough for the wife!'   Mr. Baron
Martin, indeed, thought that even if £200 a year was
enough for a wife, the decision ought to have been left to
a jury; but the Chief Baron thought not, so the rule was
granted accordingly.   Now tell me what chance have I,
or any other outraged woman in England, after this
iniquitous decision ?"

The following extract throws some light upon the
wonderful rapidity with which Lord Lytton wrote
the historical romance " Harold."   It was "completed in less than a month" (see "Life of Lord
Lytton," vol. ii., p. 163).

" February 3rd, 1858.

"I will send you an extract from Sir Charles Napier's
life, by which it appears that when he was at Caen, fired
with all the reminiscences of William the Conqueror so
rife there, he wrote an historical novel called ' Harold,' and
sent it to Colbourne, who wanted to publish it with the
author's name.   This Sir Charles would not agree to, but
could never get back his MS.   Years after, when he was in
India, out comes Sir Liar's ' Historical Romance of Harold '
—same plot, names, scenes, characters, everything, even to
a prophetess of the name of Vala, all except the battles
which the ' hero of a thousand fights ' had described so
vividly.   These were maudlin and tame, ' from,' says the
biographer, ' Sir Bulwer Lytton never having been in
battle.'   And this is the honourable way in which reputa-
tions are made in England !"

" February 21st, 1858.

" Last Thursday I was served with a writ to appear in the Queen's Bench next Thursday at the suit of Maria Sellers for defamation of character. Now I always understood that a married woman—and this creature pretends to have a husband—could not issue a writ without her husband's name being included in it. There is nothing of the kind in this one, only Sir Liar's name joined with mine. I instantly sent off to Mr. Hyde. . . . Mr. Kinglake, the Weston magistrate, says that, despite the writ, he cannot believe that Sellers woman, with her infamous character, will ever venture into a court of justice, which is all very fine to say."

" February 25th, 1858.

" With my usual good luck, Mr. Hyde was out of town, and my letter being forwarded to him caused another delay, so I did not get his letter till Tuesday morning. This is the substance of it : ' Your letter has quite upset me. To think that I should be laid up ill when you so much need my services ! for I plainly see you are about to be made the victim of a diabolical conspiracy. Sir E—— being made co-defendant, the game will be that he, virtuous creature, cannot countenance scandal, and so judgment will be let go by default, that you may be half beaten before you go into court, and he, being applied to for damages, will make that a pretext for stopping your beggarly pittance *in toto.* But I should think Mrs. Sellers' bad character would nonsuit her in any court. I have written to Ely Place to tell them to watch the case.' "

Lady Lytton instructed a Taunton solicitor to enter an appearance for her in this case. He interviewed Mr. Hyde at Langport, and received from him full information as to the extraordinary conspiracy, or rather series of conspiracies, of which she had been the victim.

" Both lawyers, who see the infamous sham of the whole thing, now think that when the fiend finds, to his astonishment, that I am both ready and able to defend this shameful suit when the time comes (and twenty-one days after the appearance is put in, according to the law, must elapse before the second step is taken), then there will be no Maria Sellers to prosecute, and so the wretches will, as usual, sneak out of it."

Such was the result of this precious action, for on the 26th of March Lady Lytton writes :

"I told Mr. Taunton I was not a fool, and would not submit to be treated like one; therefore, as my solicitor, I must insist upon his instantly writing a stringent letter to that Petgrave, this woman's attorney, saying that as we were perfectly aware of the whole conspiracy and determined to expose it, they had better lose no time in dropping this insulting farce, as nothing but the thorough conviction that there was no redress for wives in England prevented my bringing a counter-action. The result of this step, which I wanted taken a month ago, was that this morning I received a letter from Mr. Henry Hyde saying, to his great surprise (but not the least to mine) and delight, that the plaintiff had abandoned the suit, which, as I told them from the first, never was instituted but to get the last shilling out of poor hunted me."

In point of fact, this iniquitous action cost Lady Lytton between £60 and £70 in preliminary expenses, so her persecutors were at least partially successful in their amiable intentions.

The next move in this extraordinary game was made by Mr. Loaden, who came down to Taunton to try and discover from Mrs. Clarke particulars about the *soi-disant* Mrs. Sellers by professing to have become converted to the belief that Lady Lytton was a much-ill-used and persecuted woman. Mrs. Clarke, as usual, refused to give any informa-

tion whatever ; but this visit of Mr. Loaden's naturally caused poor Lady Lytton the greatest alarm and
annoyance.

"I could not have felt more deadly sick," she writes,
"with fright and disgust had I seen a venomous reptile
ready to spring at me. . . . Ever since that monster
has been here, I feel as if I had a vipers' nest under my
bed, and that if I dropped off to sleep, they would crawl
up and strangle me. All this, I know, is very wrong
and very silly, for even if there was one, God is here also.
But all else I can bear but the proximity of that creature."

"*May* 10*th*, 1858.

"I need not tell you that I am in my normal state,
full of troubles, worry, and misery, for Loaden, it
seems, went to Mr. Taunton to propose that I should
apologise to that infamous woman ! a thing which the
vile crocodile dared not hint at in this house, where
nothing was heard but his amiable anxiety to save me
expense. Taunton wrote to Mr. Hyde, who instantly
wrote to Loaden to say, ' No, I should not apologise to
that infamous woman, and so open their own trap-door for
them to escape.' We all know the sham. Mrs. Sellers
never can come into court, but still you may guess the wear
and tear it is upon my overworked nerves to have the
wretches carrying on this farce from assize to assize and
then withdrawing it."

"*May* 17*th*, 1858.

"I am certain they are hatching some fresh villainy,
for within the last week I have had the most flummerising
letters from the editor of the *Court Circular*, who is
also editor of the especial Derbyite organ called the
Constitutional Press, set up by them about eight weeks
ago. His first letter was wanting to enter into an engagement with me to write a novel to appear weekly in the
pages of the former, a copy of which he sent me, containing
an announcement of my writing the ' Life of Sonnini,' whose

life I really never attempted ; the others were assuring me of his sympathy for my wrongs, and saying that at all times I should have these two papers at my command."

Lady Lytton's forebodings were well founded, for it was about a month after this letter that she was entrapped into a madhouse.

CHAPTER XX.

IT was at this stage of her history that Lady Lytton resolved, in her despair, to go to Hertford, and expose her husband's conduct on the hustings. The following is her narrative of the episode as detailed in a letter to her friend Miss Augusta Boys.

"Friday, June 11th, 1858.

"MY DEAR AUGUSTA,—

"I could not thank you for your kind letter before, because it found me just setting off on Monday morning for the Hertford election, or rather nomination, for which purpose that paragon of landladies and pearl of women lent me the money, and accompanied me. The journey was terrific, for as I would not go by London, the direct way, for fear of meeting Sir Liar or some of his set bound for the same place, I went by Oxford, on which line all the trains were just twenty minutes behind their time (so much for Bradshaw), so that when we reached Bedford at eleven at night, the last train to Hertford had been gone a quarter of an hour, so we had to post the remaining thirty-five miles. I ascertained at Hitchin that it was the stinginess of the Grosvenors, as there would so soon be a general election, which had prevented their coming down adequately for the contest, at which the Corporation, who had made immense sacrifices to have one, were furious. It was five in the morning before we got to Hertford, and knocked the people up at the Dimsdale Arms; but by seven all my placards, which I had brought ready printed, inviting the electors and yeomen to meet *me* at noon, not indeed for their votes, but for their *interest*, were pasted all over the town, and produced the greatest excitement. Unfortunately the nomination was to take place at eleven, and just as we were setting off for the hustings, Mrs. Clarke discovered she had blue ribbons in her bonnet, vowed she would not wear his colours, and went to buy another; *this* lost hour was fatal to us, for when we arrived on the ground, Sir Liar had made his speech and been nominated. The electors after declared to a man, had I been in time, they would have spared him the trouble of his ignominious flight, and hurled him from the hustings; however, when I arrived, William Cowper was speaking. The moment I drove into the field the mob began to cheer; and even Sir Liar's two powdered flunkeys, and both his postilions, took off their hats and caps, and joined. I instantly alighted, and walked over calmly and deliberately to the hustings, just putting the crowd aside with my fan, and saying, ' My good people, make way for your member's wife.' They then began to cheer, and cry, ' Silence for Lady Lytton !' Sir Liar's head fell *literally* as if he had been shot; Mrs. Clarke said she *never* saw such a thing in her life; he staggered against the post, and seemed not to have strength to move. I then said, in a loud, calm, and stern voice, ' Sir Edward George Earle Bulwer Lytton, as I am not in the habit of stabbing in the back, it is to *you*, in the first instance, that I address myself. In the step your cruelty and your meanness have driven me into taking this day, I wish you to hear every word I have to say ; refute them if you can; deny them if you dare.' Then, turning to the crowd, I said, ' Men of Herts ! if you have the hearts of men, hear me !' ' We will. God bless you ! Speak out.' Here Sir Liar, with his hands before his face, made a rush from the hustings. The mob began to hiss, and cry, ' Ah, coward ! he's guilty; he dare not face her,' which *he* must have had the *pleasure* of hearing, for instead of attending the public breakfast in the Corn Exchange, he bolted from the town, and left them all in the lurch.

"I began by warning the people that one of two things would happen : either that not one syllable of the scene that had just taken place, or of what I was about to say, would be reported in the *Times*, or by the rest of the press, or else the most barefaced falsehoods would be propagated as to my having rushed on to the ground like a mad woman. Cries of 'Only let them dare to attempt it ; that's all!' 'Thank you, my friends, but I rather think it will be the silent and suppression system that will be adopted on this occasion.' 'Ay ; but he can't silence the county, and the next time he wants our votes, he may seek them in a horse-pond ;' and off went his colours, and they trampled them under foot. I then gave them a brief *resumé* of his infamies to me, assuring them it was a farce to look for political probity in England so long as private vice was made the high-road to public honours, and that road was macadam-ised with God's broken commandments.

"But though gentlemen in England have a perfect right to brutalise their wives as they please, our elastic conven-tionalities have not yet quite extended that autocratic power to the usage of their daughters ; and when I described the manner in which my poor child's young heart had been broken, how she had been slaved to death over her quack of a father's German translations (he not knowing one word of German !), her scanty wardrobe, the wretched house in which she died, which a clergyman in that county could certify, as *he* had sent to a public-house for some wine when it was too late, the poor boors gave me their tears, which I was more grateful to them for than for all their cheers. After a pause I rewhetted my razor, and, much in Dizzy's own unscrupulous style, began slicing the Derby Adminis-tration, and after a few remarks I said, 'So that, upon the whole, my friends, it is lucky for these honourable and right honourable *gentlemen* that the colonies are so *far*, but though the colonies are far, my Lord Derby's colonial secretary is near, terribly near, or I should not have the honour, and at the same time the deep affliction and humiliation, of addressing you this day ; but I am tired of having the most insulting calumnies publicly disseminated of me by Sir Edward Bulwer Lytton and his emissaries, the last of which, I understand, is that I am mad' (cries of 'Come, come, that won't do after to-day'), 'which calumnies are only denied on oath in the attorney Loaden's back office, where perjuries are plentiful and truth scarce. You know oaths cost nothing. So, in fact, my good friends, I am here to-day to do what the lawyers call "enter an appearance."' (Loud cheers.) 'I am, moreover, here to tell you that I *won't* be a peeress upon £180 a year, which, from his ceaseless and costly conspiracies, is what Sir E. B. Lytton's original swindle of £400 a year has dwindled down to ; and as you have so often disgraced yourselves by supporting *him*, you must now redeem yourselves by supporting me' ('That will we to a man') ; 'and as the right honourable baronet who has just been re-elected' (cries of 'No, no ; no election in the matter') 'cannot afford the legal encumbrance of a wife, why she will only, I suppose, have to continue to live, as she has been living for the last eighteen months, on charity.' (Cries of 'Shame! shame! Blackguard!') 'Nevertheless, my good people, *don't* suppose that I have lightly or without first trying everything made a show of myself here to-day. Friends and foes have for the last year warned Sir Edward Bulwer Lytton not to drive me to this public exposure, but he preferred parting with his character to his money, thereby at once evincing the Bulwer cleverness (which is somewhat crab-like) and his utilitarian theories, one of which is, "Always prefer the interest of the *greater* to the lesser number," and every one knows that he has plenty of money, and scarcely a shred of character ; so that it was all the more generous (a Lytton generous!) of him to part to-day unreservedly with so small a supply.' (Roars of laughter.) I said a great deal more, too long to repeat, and ended by thanking them cordially for the patient hearing and hearty sympathy they had accorded me, and apologising that 'unaccustomed as *I really was* to public speaking, I was unable to favour them with any of those oratorical gymnastics they were accustomed to be astounded by in the right honourable baronet

the new Colonial Secretary.' (Renewed roars of laughter.)
I then concluded with a short parody on Lord Lyttelton's
well-known lines —

> " 'If on *my* statements some few doubts *should* fall,
>   Look in *his* face, and you'll believe them *all.*'

" 'We do, we do, we do! God bless you, Lady Lytton;
you'll have your rights yet; and you'll see that the men of
Herts *have* the hearts of men.'

"The cheering then became uproarious as they followed
me to the Mayor's house. Mrs. Woodhouse, the Mayor's
wife, told me that as I drove up a poor old woman of
ninety, a tenant of Sir Liar's, who had been a tenant
of his father's and grandfather's, and who had brought
Mrs. Woodhouse some eggs and chickens in from Knebworth, when she heard it was I, fell upon her knees, and
said, ' Now I don't care how soon I die, for Heaven has
sent her here to-day to unmask that villain, who so cruelly
broke the heart of his poor young daughter, and has
behaved so inhumanly to her, poor lady.' I had brought
down all I had left of my ' Appeals ' (about thirty) to distribute, and when I got back to the hotel I found the landlady had sold them for ten times their value, and presented
me with a little *rouleau* of half-sovereigns; but I told her I
could not possibly take it, as I had not brought them to
sell, so she must give them to the poor, as far as they
would go. Then came in Rose, the bookseller, to know if
I had any more 'Appeals,' as he said, after my ' speech,' he
could have sold them at five guineas apiece. Unluckily
I had not. They wanted, right or wrong, not to let me pay
a *sou* at the hotel, till I told them I should be quite
offended (and oh ! such *delicious tea*, cream, and home-brewed
beer !). All the way to the station the crowd was dense,
every window full, and on the tops of the houses the people
waving their caps and handkerchiefs and crying, ' God
bless you ! God prosper you, brave noble woman ! You'll
defeat the wretch yet. He could never buy what you have
won to-day.'

"Again I thanked them all from my heart. While I

was sitting in the railway carriage at the station, I heard a portly, full-blown parson say to a lady, ' I hope you were in time to hear Lady Lytton's speech? How well she speaks, so much better than the Great Mogul! So much energy, yet quiet dignity ; such proper emphasis and discretion, yet not a shadow of boldness, notwithstanding the unfeminine proceeding. What Junius-like hits at the Ministry, and how they all told, and how she carried the people away ! Sir Edward's tough indeed if he gets over *this* day. Such a scene I never witnessed ; she *is* a brave woman.' Lady : ' Pooh ! he's as tough as what he looks like, a granite effigy of the d——l.' Clergyman : ' Ay, ay, but his pride, his vanity, his humbug, all to be demolished at one fell swoop by a wave of his wife's fan ! Certainly she did it *well*.'

"It seems this was to be a week of wonders, for when I got home here on Wednesday morning at four (another night), I found a copy of the *Constitutional Press*, the especial Derbyite organ, containing *the* most outrageous and unqualified praise of ' The World and his Wife,' cleverly selecting all the political scraps *I* meant for *them*, and applying them to Lord Palmerston, but they said that the book was far beyond their praise ; and not to garble any of the gems by short extracts, they should continue the review. I wrote to the editor to say that this was a capital bundle of thistles to throw to that docile donkey the British public, but that *I* was quite up to this cogged dice and *sauter la coupe* Dizzy dodge, while *they* were, *sub rosâ*, setting on their press to pour out their unscrupulous malignity, and quote things *not* in the book, that said sapient public may say, ' You see, so far from Sir Edward trying to decry or to injure the sale of her books, you must confess nothing can be so unqualified as the praise of his especial organ.' Oh, the slimy, tortuous serpents ! really a certain place *is* too good for them.

"To go to its antipodes. Wolff, the missionary (who married Lady Georgiana Walpole), and who has a living near this, has manifested a sudden and marvellous interest in me, and sends me a daily letter. I send you that of

to-day, in which he says Sir Charles Napier, the conqueror
of Scinde, used to speak so highly of me. This is *odd*,
as I never saw him. I wish you were here to help me
demolish such a magnificent pine dear kind Mrs. Jermyn
has just sent me. She must have sent to Brobdignag
for it.

"If you survive the reading of this gazette extraordinary,
will you kindly let me have it back by return of post, to
send to Miss Ryves and Dr. Price, as I am too dead tired
to rewrite it to them. If you have any fancy to keep it,
you shall have it back again. Let me also have back
Mr. Wolff's note. And with best love to your sister, kind
regards to Mr. G——, and all kinds of condolences to
poor Jerry,

"Believe me ever, my dearest Augusta,
"Your grateful and affectionate
"ROSINA BULWER LYTTON."

This episode took place on the 8th of June,
1858 ; and although the London press, almost without exception, ignored the whole proceedings, quite
enough sensation was created to make Sir Edward
Lytton's position exceedingly uncomfortable. He
lost no time in resorting to the desperate expedient
of incarcerating his wife in a lunatic asylum, and
to further this object he sent Mr. Hale Thomson
to Taunton to report upon the condition of Lady
Lytton's mind. Dr. Thomson's visit is fully
described in a second letter to Miss Boys, which
I append.

"TAUNTON, *Friday, June 18th*, 1858.

"MY DEAREST AUGUSTA,—

"I have been *so* ill all the week (which you will
not be surprised at when you hear the cause) that I could
only scrawl you that hasty line with the *Evening Star* of
Saturday, the 12th inst., containing that curtailed, garbled,

and *cooked* account of my advent at Hertford. That ruffian Sir Liar's villainy has now culminated; and even those who know him best, and consequently despise him most, are staggered at its fiendish unscrupulousness. It must be indeed outrageous when I tell you that it has actually roused the open-mouthed indignation of the Tauntonians; and the yeomanry have declared that should that vile wretch Loaden ever show his hideous face here again, they will publicly drive him out of the place. To show you how diabolical the conspiracy was, it appears that he, the viper, was down here the Thursday week before the Hertford election giving out everywhere that I was mad. Mrs. Clarke is convinced that some were bought over, for certain it is that without black treachery on the part of my pretended friends, or rather agents, no such infamy *could* have happened; but I'll bide my time, and they shall reap their reward. Poor dear good Mrs. Clarke is worth her weight in diamonds; but then she is a woman, and I've never yet known an Englishman who, if he were not against you, was not for you, which always plays an enemy's game *better* even than *active* rascality, for did not God Himself when on earth feel that the *neutral* was the hostile by asserting that 'those who are not for Me are against Me'?

"But now for the conspiracy itself. Last Saturday, the 12th inst., at two p.m., I was still in bed, not having recovered the dreadful fatigue of body of two consecutive nights' travelling, and the terrible prostration of mind from the overwrought excitement at Hertford, when Mrs. Clarke brought me up a card:

'MR. HALE THOMSON,
4, *Clarges Street, Piccadilly*,'

saying he wanted to see me on particular business. I sent word I was in bed, and could not see him, and either to write or tell his business to Mrs. Clarke. Still he persisted, saying he had papers in his pocket for my advantage to submit to me, that he was an old medical man of sixty, and that I need not mind seeing him in my room. I was very indignant at this unwarrantable and

vulgar perseverance in an utter stranger to obtrude himself upon me when I was ill in bed, and wrote upon a
piece of paper, 'Any communication for Lady Bulwer
Lytton's advantage or for her injury can be made to her
solicitor, Mr. Charles Hyde, 33, Ely Place, London.' At
this, said Mrs. Clarke, he flew into a great rage, and flung
out of the house, but soon returned with the ruffian
Loaden, that little Dr. Woodford, of Taunton, and a
great tall but very respectable-looking woman—a keeper
from Gillet's madhouse in this town. At this poor good
Mrs. Clarke was furious, rushed upstairs, locked both
my doors, and put the keys in her pocket, vowing they
should not enter my room but by first cutting her down.
Upon this the ruffian Loaden grinned in her face, said
he'd break open the door, and told her to make the most
of me, as they were going to carry me off to a madhouse,
and she should never see me more. Here, she says, Mr.
Thomson interposed, and said, 'No, I will not have any
violence or outrage offered to Lady Lytton. I have come
down to make a medical inquiry, and it shall be so strictly
and conscientiously ——.' Hearing this dreadful uproar
at my door, I called out to Mrs. Clarke to unlock it and
let Dr. Thomson in, but to come with him, as I would
not be left alone with any one capable of such an outrage as to force themselves into my bedroom. She did
so, and he entered, followed by the tall keeper. They
both looked at me, and then at each other in evident
surprise, for upon all these occasions of dastardly outrage
and moral earthquakes I have always sufficient command
over myself to be exteriorly deadly calm and cool.

"After opening the session with a deliberate lie that he
had *not* been sent by Sir Liar, which I nipped in the bud
with an 'Of course not; *he* never by any accident does his
own dirty work; but as the amiable, creditable, and manly
impeachment against me is lunacy, confine yourself to that
count, Dr. Thomson, and don't presume to presuppose me
an idiot by telling me such clumsy lies, for who *but* that
incarnate fiend my Lord Derby's new colonial secretary
could have authority to send any one to offer me this

crowning outrage?' he hung his head, and said, 'Lady Lytton, no one shall or can kidnap you; but did you write these letters?' producing some old letters of mine, four years ago directed to Sir Liar Coward Bulwer Lytton, and, with the same truths, to the ruffian Loaden.

"'*That* did I, and will do so again and again; but if those are the grounds upon which they found my insanity, pray why have they bottled them up all these years, and never acted upon them till now? Why also, when, eleven months ago, Mr. Ironside, of Sheffield, returned the ruffian Loaden one of his own letters, with the true bill of 'Liar, coward, and blackguard' written under the name of William Loaden, why, I say, did the reptile quietly pocket *that?* and why did he not either bring an action, or take out a statute of lunacy against Mr. Ironside, for those truths?'

"Not a word. Next Mr. Thomson produced a placard, printed on blue paper (as all Sir Liar's were at Hertford), which was dated 'Taunton, Sunday, June 6th, 1858,' and had been placarded all over the county (Hertford), sent to people, and among others to Sir Liar. It was purporting to be *his* address to his constituents, saying *his* beloved wife would accompany him on Tuesday, to receive their congratulations; he hoped theirs would also be with them, as he did not acknowledge any greatness but what emanated from the *domestic* hearth; and the pride he felt in their suffrages that day was from their heartfelt tribute to the purity of his private character. Then, in his own pompous, inflated, stilted style, which they had hit off to a *t, he* said, among public questions, he should labour in the cause of 'our great social evil.' In short, it was one of *the* best-done things I ever read, and I'll send it to you when I get it back. He asked me if I did not write it? Mrs. Clarke, who was standing by, before she even read it, said, '*No,* I can take my oath of that, for it was I who got all Lady Lytton's placards printed.' I then offered to give him my oath on the Bible that I had never seen it till then, adding, 'I should only be too happy to own it,' as I thought it, without exception, the very cleverest and best-done thing

I ever read, and it must have stung Sir Liar through
every nerve, like poisoned arrows, as it was evidently
written by some one who knew his chronic vice and
hypocrisy. Mr. Thomson refused to take my oath, saying
my simple negation was quite enough. He then got me
into a long argument, feeling my pulse, and looking into
my eyes and mouth the while as if I were a horse. After
this pretty little *scena*, he turned to the keeper, and said,
'Well, I must say I never found a clearer head, or a more
logical mind, or sounder flesh and blood, than Lady
Lytton's ; so far from being mad or dying, what do you
think ? '

" 'I think, sir,' said the woman, wiping the tears from
her eyes, 'that this is one of the cruellest outrages I ever
witnessed in my life to a person so pre-eminently in her
senses, as this lady appears ; and only half of what she has
told you would certainly have been enough to have driven
most ladies quite raving mad.'

" He then said it was my going to Hertford had made
Sir Liar think me mad. He does *not* think me mad, and
that is another lie, for Lady Glamis warned me months
ago that he was trying to hatch some such diabolical plot.
I always laughed the notion to scorn, as I said, and still
say, that cannot be managed on *one* tool's *ipse dixit ;* there
must be publicity and investigation, and then *I* have
nothing, and that cowardly brute everything, to fear. He
then took Mrs. Clarke into the drawing-room, and asked
if I was not occasionally very violent and very cruel to
her ? She laughed in his face, and said, 'she did not think
it was in my nature to be cruel to any living thing ; and
as to my violence, that was all concentrated upon my
wrongs and outrages, and l must indeed be a stick or a
stone if I were not violent on that score, seeing what they
were.' Afterwards the ruffian Loaden had all the servants up in another room, to ask them the same question,
when it appears that Anne and Frizzledom particularly
distinguished themselves, Anne by piously hoping they
might all drop down dead if they injured a hair of mine,
and Frizzledom modestly admitting that 'though he was

not much of a man to signify, he thought he should be quite
equal to putting them three fellers in a horsepond.' Next
the little provincial Dr. Woodford was had in to look at
the maniac! After he had heard the whole history of the
Llangollen conspiracy and old P——'s letter of warning to
me about the spy Getting, he said, in that little squeaky
grasshopper voice of his, 'And pray what right had you to
turn Miss Getting out of the house?'

" 'The same right that you would have to turn a burglar
out of *your* house if you had been forewarned that he was
in it.'

" Going away, the little man said, *a propos de bottes*,
which was no doubt included in his fee, 'Still, really, I
must say that I think, Lady Lytton, £400 a year is a very
adequate allowance for any lady.'

" 'Not for any lady, but decidedly most ample for a
Mrs. Woodford, a Mrs. Taunton, or any of that species of
provincial animalculæ, because, in every sense of the word,
more than they, their husbands, and their vulgarity all put
together are worth.'

" 'Oh! ah! hum!—yes!—perhaps; with Sir Edward's
fortune, certainly it ought to be more.'

" This cruel yet farcical outrage lasted from 2 p.m. till
nine at night. I heard Loaden was like a ramping madman when he heard the result of the medical inquiry.
When I thought the wretches were at length gone, Mr.
Thomson came sneaking back, and asked me, with some
hesitation, as a favour, if I would write down, in a note
addressed to him, what terms I would accept from Sir
Edward not again to publicly expose him? The very lenient
and moderate terms I required for such life-long villainy,
crowned by such a fiendish outrage, were that he should
be bound stringently, that is *legally* (his oath not being
worth the breath that went to form it), never again to
malign or molest me directly or indirectly; also that I
should be henceforth free to live where I liked, and go
where I pleased; that he must instantly pay into Coutts's
the sum of £4,500, the amount of legal and other expenses
his eighteen years of persecution had hampered me with,

and allow me the very small sum of £500 a year for *my* life, not *his*, like the present swindle of £400, and this intact, without deduction of income tax, made payable to my sole order, quarterly by £125 at Coutts's, for I never would again receive through Loaden, neither did I want to be put to the expense of employing an attorney to receive this pittance, or be insulted by a demand for clergymen's certificates to prove that I was alive. If he acceded to these mild and merciful terms, I would promise never to mention his wretched name, which I should be too happy to forget. I gave him till next Saturday (to-morrow) to consider this, which if he did not agree to, he might rely upon my being in London on Monday next and making Downing Street not only too hot for him, but for his whole set.

"Only think what his last lie has been, denying upon *oath* that I ever was at Hertford, that it was a mere electioneering flam, and ordering Chapman and Hall, the publishers in Piccadilly, to contradict it positively everywhere on his authority.

" Dr. Woodford was in the bar here the following Monday, Mrs. Clarke says, saying I was no more mad than he was. On the contrary, he had never seen so sane a person ; and he had no doubt I should gain my point, and get all I wanted, which indeed was but reasonable. I forgot to tell you that, after I had given Mr. Thomson the note he required, I said, ' But, pray, what guarantee have *I* that when they find your report is not amenable to their diabolical conspiracy, they will not employ *other* emissaries to repeat this disgraceful outrage ?' '*Mine*, Lady Lytton, for it would indeed be an outrage. I only hope that you will have no cause to regret my having forced my way into your room to-day, but that you will henceforth be happier than you have ever been.' Time will tell, but I confess I have little faith in the words of any man who could undertake such a mission for such a man as Sir Liar. Besides, the tariff of all men towards me seems to be the fairest possible profession and promises and the foulest possible deeds.

"The whole place is crying shame; and it must be bad indeed when Mrs. Clarke says she never saw a man so indignant as even Mr. E——. He says she ought to have sent for the police, and not have allowed them to force an entrance without producing their warrant. It is when one is bowed down by misery and oppression that one is so grateful for one touch of human feeling, of which there is so little in this great iron-bound, flint-paved country; and I never shall forget poor little Mrs. Blewett when she came the next morning after this infamy. She flung herself on my bed in such violent hysterics that I thought I should never get her out of them. Indeed, every one has been very kind, and begs me not to be afraid to go out, as every man, woman, and child in the place will protect me; but I am so ill and nervous with all this (the more so from having held up so superhumanly during the outrage), that God knows when I shall be able to go out again; and I was getting so miraculously well, thanks to that cerebisia I am taking. I must kindly beg of you to let me have this volume back to send on to my dear, kind friend Dr. Price, as I am so ill and so overwhelmed with business that I cannot rewrite it. You shall have it and the other safe back. With best love to F—— and kind regards to Mr. G——, believe me, my dearest Augusta (at least, as much as remains of me),

"Ever gratefully and affectionately yours,
"ROSINA BULWER LYTTON.

"I did not know till *to-day* that the wretches had actually brought two keepers, and *one* was posted outside my bedroom door the whole five hours the outrage lasted, and a carriage and four at Pattison's (the other hotel) *all* day ready to carry me off, as that vile wretch Loaden thought.

"Endorsed.—Upon going to London on Wednesday, the 22nd of June, 1858, after this, upon getting no answer to the demand Hale Thomson had made me write, I was kidnapped at his house, 4, Clarges Street, Piccadilly, and incarcerated, as all the world knows."

CHAPTER XXI.

MR. THOMSON had promised that Lady Lytton should receive a positive answer to her proposals within four days from their interview, which occurred on June 12th ; but when more than a week elapsed in silence, she lost patience, and determined to endeavour to bring matters to a crisis by going up to London.   She writes to Dr. Price on the 21st of June :—

"I am just starting for London by the mail train, determined that my very moderate demands shall not be kept shilly-shallying at the fiend's pleasure, but shall be decided at once, or he shall take the consequences."

So on Tuesday, June 21st, 1858, Lady Lytton and Mrs. Clarke set out for London.   They arrived there at eight o'clock the following morning, took rooms at the Hyde Park Hotel, opposite the Marble Arch, and went to Mr. Hale Thomson's house in Clarges Street at twelve o'clock.

"We were shown up into the drawing-room, and presently the fellow came to us, holding out both his hands, which, of course, I did not see, saying he was delighted to see me and hoped I had come to dine with him.   I said, 'Mr. Thomson, I have neither come to dine with you nor to be fooled by you.   You had better com-

municate with Sir Edward Lytton, and tell him I must
have a definite answer one way or the other, for which I
shall call at six o'clock this evening.' I then went to call
on Miss Ryves, and she asked to come with me to be
present when I returned to Thomson's, and fortunately I
gave her two important letters of Sir Edward's, in case I
should, in my agitation, drop or mislay them. At six she,
Mrs. Clarke, and I again drove to the corner of Clarges
Street, and there got out. As we did so I observed an
impudent-looking snub-nosed man, who was walking up
and down, and stared at me as if he had been watching
for us, as afterwards turned out to be the case. We were
again shown into the drawing-room at Thomson's, but this
time the folding-doors were closed between the two rooms,
and we heard the low murmuring of voices in the back
room. After being kept waiting more than half an hour,
he made his appearance, saying he had been detained
by patients ; and soon after him stalked into the room a
tall raw-boned Scotchman, with hay-coloured hair, who, I
subsequently learned, was an apothecary of the name of
Ross, keeping a druggist's shop in Fenchurch Street
(another friend of Loaden's), and the second with Thomson
who signed the certificate of my insanity, he never having
seen me or I him before, and I never having once spoken
to him. Finding I was to get no answer about the letter
from Thomson, I said to Miss Ryves and Mrs. Clarke,
'Come, don't let us waste any more time in being fooled
and insulted here; we'll go.' Easier said than done, for on
reaching the hall we found it literally filled with two mad
doctors, that fellow Hill, of Inverness Lodge, Brentford, his
assistant, the impudent snub-nosed man who had stared
so when I got out of the brougham, two women-keepers,
one a great thing of six feet high, the other a moderate-
sized and nice-looking woman, and a very idiotic-looking
footman of Thomson's, with his back against the hall door
to bar egress. Seeing this blockade, I exclaimed, "What
a set of blackguards !' to which Mr. Hill, wagging his head,
replied, ' I beg you will speak like a lady, Lady Lytton.' ' I
am treated so like one that I certainly ought,' I answered.

Hearing loud talking in the dining-room, into which Mrs. Clarke had been summoned by Thomson, I walked into it in time to hear her very energetically saying, ' I won't ! ' to some proposition they were making to her; and seeing a side door ajar that led into a back room, I looked in, and there saw those two precious scoundrels Sir Coward Bulwer Lytton and his attorney, Loaden. Boldly advancing towards him, ' You cowardly villain,' I said, ' this is the second time. I have confronted you this month. Why do you always do your dirty work by deputy ? ' At this he rushed as he had done from the Hertford hustings, but this time not into Mr. Austin's flower-garden, but down Mr. Hale Thomson's kitchen stairs and up his area steps into the street. I turned to Miss Ryves, who had followed me, and said, ' See, the contemptible wretch has again taken to his heels.' Whereupon, going into the hall, she pushed the idiotic footman aside, and said, ' Whatever villainy you may be paid to practise towards Lady Lytton, you have no right to detain *me*.' Thomson then ordered the hall door to be unchained and unlocked, and she rushed out into the street. Meanwhile I, who was sitting in Thomson's hall, said, ' Nothing shall get me out of this.' Whereupon the hall door was opened, and two policemen were brought in, at which I rose to my feet and said, ' Don't presume to touch me ! I'll go with these vile men, but the very stones of London will rise up against them and their infamous employer.' At the advent of the policemen I got into Hill's carriage, which was in waiting, he, the two keepers, Mrs. Clarke, and myself, inside, and the impudent-looking snub-nosed assistant on the box. The creatures took me all through the Park, and as there had been a breakfast at Chiswick that day, it was crowded. Many whom I knew kissed their hands in great surprise to see me. Arrived at Mr. Hill's stronghold (Inverness Lodge, Brentford), a very fine house, in fine grounds, which had formerly belonged to the Duke of Cumberland, and which since my incarceration Hill has been obliged to leave, and transfer himself to London, public indignation having made it too hot for him, I fortunately had the presence of mind

to ask the name and *locale* of my prison and write it down
on one of my cards for Mrs. Clarke, that she might bring
me my things from the Hyde Park Hotel. I was shown
upstairs, after she left me, into a large bedroom with the
two keepers, and the windows duly nailed down and only
opening about three inches from the top. After kneeling
down and praying to God in a perfect agony, I bathed my
face in cold water; and the little keeper was very kind and
feeling, and said to me, 'Oh, pray, my lady, try and keep
calm under this severe trial. It does seem to me to be
something very monstrous, and, depend upon it, God will
never let it go on.' 'I know He will not,' said I; and then,
looking through the window, I saw between thirty and
forty women walking in the grounds. 'Are all those un-
fortunates incarcerated here?' I asked of the little keeper.
'Those,' she said, rather evasively, 'are our ladies. They
are out gathering strawberries.' I then rang my bell, and
when it was answered, said, 'I want to see Mr. Hill.' He
came, and before I could speak, said, 'It is a lovely evening, Lady Lytton. You had better come out and take a
walk.'

"'Mr. Hill,' said I, 'I sent for you to *order* you to remove
those two keepers from my room, for I am *not* mad, *as you
very well know*, and I won't be driven mad by being treated
as a maniac, and as for walking out with or associating
with those poor creatures out there, if they really are
insane, I'll *not* do it, if I am kept in your madhouse ten
years.'

"'Madhouse! madhouse! nonsense, Lady Lytton! this
is no madhouse, and those are my children.'

"'Then you must be a perfect Danaus,' said I, 'for there
are about forty of them. But if you had a hundred, I
again *order* you to remove these women from my room, and
at your peril disobey me.'

"He then told them to leave the room, and went himself
soon after. In about half an hour I heard my door unlocked on the outside and a gentle knock at the door. I
said, 'Come in,' and a charming little girl of about fourteen,
with a pretty, gentle expression of face, soft chestnut hair,

and the prettiest and most dove-like dark hazel eyes I ever saw, came in with some tea and some strawberries. This was Hill's eldest daughter; and how he and his vulgar English wife came by such a child I can't imagine, unless the fairies stole theirs and left this one in exchange. This dear little girl, my only consolation while there, conceived the most violent affection for me, which I heartily returned, for she was a perfect star in the desert, and with a big fat, magnificent tortoiseshell cat, with the most fascinating manners, a perfect feline Chesterfield, and the poor cow, which Hill used to leave in an arid field, under a vertical sun, without water (the pump being deranged, like his patients), were my only comforts; and as I and poor little Mary Hill used to pump for hours at this crazy pump, till we filled the stone trough for the poor cow, which used to bound and caper like a dog when it saw us coming to the rescue, *this* was, no doubt, considered as a strong proof of my insanity, or at least of my having water on the brain. I never would go into the grounds with the keepers, only with my dear gentle, affectionate little companion Mary Hill; and, moreover, Mr. Hill sent *all* his 'children' to his other madhouse further on the road, so that I had the Palladian villa of Inverness Lodge, Brentford, all to myself, without even the three kings. The first evening poor Mrs. Clarke returned about ten o'clock with my scanty wardrobe. I *implored* her *not*, by way of consulting a lawyer, to go to Mr. Hyde, whom, after the Lyndhurst paper and Sellers affair, I believed to be trying to desert me, which affairs eventually proved to be true. But, unfortunately, at Miss Ryves's instigation, she *did*, for your friends always know your affairs better than you do yourself. It appeared that two days after I was incarcerated in Mr. Hill's stronghold, and Mrs. Clarke had returned to Taunton to rouse up the people, which she did to good purpose, Loaden went to Taunton to my hotel, with a solicitor of the town, saying he had come for my tin boxes and all my papers. 'Then,' said Mrs. Clarke, 'you won't have one of them.' Of course the provincial attorney thought the great man and that sacred Mumbo Jumbo a husband (no matter how bad his character) ought to be omnipotent, and that she should give them up. But she would not; and some commercial traveller in the hotel, hearing the altercation between them, very kindly called her out of the room, and said,

"'Ask him to show you his warrant or authority for making such a demand; and if the fellow won't or can't, then I'll know how to deal with him.'

"She did so, and the wretch said he had his order in his pocket. 'Well, then, produce it,' said the traveller, coming in; 'and if you won't, I'll send for a constable to turn you out of this.' At which the attorney, Mr. Edwards Beadon, said, in all humble sycophancy, to Loaden, 'My dear sir, you had better produce your authority.' But as the wretch, of course, could not produce what he had not got, the commercial traveller turned him out neck and crop. But as he went he turned to Mrs. Clarke, clenching his fist, and said, 'Take my word for it, you will never see Lady Lytton again, nor will any one else.' 'And take *my* word for it, Mr. Loaden, that *this* threat of yours will turn out as great a falsehood as everything else you have ever said,' was her answer."

With reference to this attempt to obtain possession of Lady Lytton's papers, the following letters may be interesting. Lady Lytton was incarcerated on the 22nd of June, and on the next day Mr. Loaden writes :—

To Mrs. Clarke.

"June 23rd, 1858.

"I forgot to ask you to-day if Lady Lytton gave you any papers or gave Miss Ryves any papers, and if she did, where the papers now are.

"Yours obediently,

"William Loaden.

"Thursday night. A verbal answer will do."

On hearing of this, Mr. Hyde at once wrote the following to Mrs. Clarke :—

"33, ELY PLACE, LONDON, E.C.,
" *June 24th*, 1858.

" MADAM,—

  "By a deed of separation between Sir Edward and Lady Lytton, dated April 19th, 1836, all property of every sort and description belongs to Lady Lytton that she shall at any time be possessed of ; and, as her solicitor, I request that you will not let any person interfere with what is at your house at Taunton ; and should any violence be attempted, you must apply to a magistrate, and show him this note, and he will afford you protection.   I shall take proper legal steps to have Lady Lytton released from the unlawful confinement she is now suffering under.

"I am, Madam,
"Yours very obediently,
"CHARLES HYDE.

"Mrs. Clarke, Giles' Castle Hotel, Taunton."

I now resume Lady Lytton's narrative.

"At Hill's the rule of the house was about two inches of candle to go to bed with, for fear of some mad incendiary, and then the door double-locked on you outside ; but as I was *not* either mad or an incendiary, and am in the habit of making my ablutions, and reading, and saying my prayers, before I go to bed, I could not do so within the two inches, and so effectually resisted the candle rule, but could do nothing against the locked door, and, therefore, was greatly frightened the next morning, for the first time one awakens in a strange place one cannot for a few seconds remember where one is, so I *was* frightened at seeing the great six-feet-high keeper standing over me, who said, ' I came to call you, but your Ladyship seemed in such a happy sleep, I did not like to wake you.'   I told Hill this must not happen again, but she must wait till I rang.   He then said, he meant to get me a *maid* next day,

which was a delicate way of putting it, considering that the
six-feet-high's successor was even *more* strapping, only
dark, and the image, or rather the facsimile, of 'the fair
Sophia' in Cruikshank's ballad of Lord Bateman, if she
had only worn a turban, instead of a cap, and had had a
gold warming-pan of a watch at her side.   Her name was
Sparrow, but she never was in the way when I wanted her,
her excuse being, as the house had a flat roof (Italian style),
she used to sit out there to work, the '*prospec*'' was so
'rural.'   'But, Sparrow,' said I, 'you were engaged to
attend upon me, and so should not, like the rest of your
species, sit alone upon the housetop.'   Everything was so
atrociously bad at this fine house, that I really could not
eat, and I believe Hill began to fear I should die upon his
hands, so, at the end of four days or five, he said to me,
'What can I get you? what do you have for breakfast at
Taunton?'   'What I am not likely to have here, Mr. Hill,
—an appetite.'   But what I really suffered most from in
that intensely hot summer,—being a water-drinker, and
the water at Taunton being the very finest I ever tasted in
any part of the world,—was the horribly tepid bad water
at Hill's ; and when I tried the soda-water, that was equally
bad.   I was also thoroughly wretched, without my clothes
and books or a single thing I was accustomed to.   Hill,
it was true, was *very* anxious to send for *all* my goods and
chattels to Taunton, which, you may be quite sure, I would
not let him do, as I told him it was not worth while for
the very short time, I was *sure*, public indignation would
allow me to remain incarcerated in his stronghold.   When
I had been there about ten days, the Commissioners made
their visit.   They were Dr. Hood, Dr. Conolly, and Mr.
Procter (Barry Cornwall), by far the best and most gentlemanlike of them, who listened to my statement with
marked attention, saying, with a shrug of his shoulders,
'Those letters, I confess, startled me.'   The letters he
alluded to were two I had written to Sir Edward touching some of his infamies, for there is *no* vice that he has left
unexhausted, and no virtue unassumed.   But, as I told Mr.
Proctor, the charges in those letters were no inventions of

mine ; and I gave him my authority, which was, that when I was at Geneva, my old friend, the Comtesse Marie de Warenzow, came to me one morning, and said she had got a letter from her niece, Lady Pembroke, and she must read me one paragraph. This was the paragraph : 'That wretch, Sir Edward Bulwer Lytton, has just been drummed out of Nice for his infamous conduct.' Before these commissioners I turned to Mr. Hill, who stood, like a footman, at a respectful distance in their presence, and I said, ' Now, Mr. Hill, I have been nearly a fortnight in your house, can you say from your conscience—if you have one —that I have said, done, or looked, any one thing that could in any way make you think I was not in the full and clear, ay and very analytic possession of my intellect ?' Hill wagged his head, twirled his thumbs, and rolled his poached egg orbs fearfully, as he mumbled in a low voice, ' I'd rather not give an opinion.' ' Of course not,' said I, ' having taken the ghost's word for a thousand pounds yearly. But pray if you believe me in *any*, even the slightest degree, insane, how can you reconcile it, to your conventionality towards these gentlemen, the Commissioners, to leave your very charming little daughter, unguarded, with me *all* day long, and worse still, allow her to drive out with me alone, when, from one minute to another, I might do her some grievous bodily harm, or make my escape with ease ?'

"At this, without wasting a reply on me, Mr. Hill began sonorously clearing some imaginary obstruction in his throat, and reminded the Commissioners that they would be late for the train.

" I may as well tell you here what, of course, I only heard after from Miss Ryves and others—namely, that Miss Ryves, after rushing out of Thomson's house, immediately drew up and sent to the papers a true and circumstantial account of my most iniquitous kidnapping and incarceration, which the time-serving *Times, of course*, did not insert. She also wrote to the Hertford papers to say she had been for years witness to and cognisant of Sir Edward Lytton's persecutions of me, and my maid was (and, thank God, *is*) still living, who had been witness to his personal brutalities in former times; and, in short, that there could not be on this earth a more iniquitous pair than my Lord Derby's colonial secretary and his attorney Loaden.

"The Sunday after the visit of the Commissioners, an oppressively hot day, the door was unlocked, and Mr. Hyde tottered into my room, for he was then suffering from softening of the brain, the complaint of which he afterwards died. His hands were full of papers; and he said, in his bluff bull-dog way, ' Well, I've seen Sir Edward in Downing Street. I saw him yesterday; and though it's almost too bad to show you, yet you must see it—I mean the statement he and Loaden drew up for the Commissioners respecting your insanity.' This precious documentary piece of rascality set forth that both my parents died mad. Now my father had had one of the most absurdly splendid public funerals for a commoner that ever was seen, being Grand Master of some Masonic lodge; and ostentatious burials are not generally bestowed on lunatics. And my poor mother having been dead only ten years, any one could have refuted *that* lie. But, like all Sir Edward's lies, they were only fabricated for the few and for the dark, and never allowed to appear in the honest, searching light of publicity. This tissue of lies went on to say that I had attempted to commit suicide, and that the family insanity in me had developed itself in delirium tremens from my intemperate habits. 'The dastardly fiend!' I exclaimed; 'so the sacrilegious monster would even desecrate my poor father and mother's graves! For what? To bury his life-long victim alive in a madhouse.'

"'Yes; 'pon my soul, it's too bad,' said the attorney; ' but I'm happy to tell you that I have now got you the £500 a year for *your* life.'

"I knew by this, though all papers but the conveniently reticent *Times* had been kept from me, that public indignation *must* be astir, and making things rather unpleasant for my Lord Derby's colonial secretary, in which I was right, for I afterwards heard that not only the people here

(Taunton) were holding committees and meetings every day on the outrage of which I had been the victim, and the Somersetshire Yeomanry were determined upon going mounted to London, and pulling his house about his ears, if I were not released, but his butler could *literally* scarcely stand under the loads of letters he had to bring in every morning of imprecations and threats by no means anonymous. And as poor Prince Albert was then living, my Lord Derby was sent for in hot haste by Her Majesty, and told either I must be *instantly* set at liberty, or his colonial secretary must resign ; for the outrage, or rather the *scandal*, was too great. Now my woman's intuition and common sense told me something of this sort must be going on, or I should never have heard a syllable about the £500 for my life. So, in reply to Mr. Hyde's communication, I said, ' What I are they trying to make me out an idiot, as well as a maniac, that they or you should suppose, after such an irreparable culminating outrage as he has inflicted upon me by this incarceration, I will let that meanest of creatures Sir Edward Bulwer Lytton off upon the beggarly pittance I would have accepted before it, and oblige him by vegetating upon it, in the exile of some living tomb, all the rest of the life he has so poisoned at every source ? No, thank you.'

" ' Well,' said Mr. Hyde, ' Sir Edward has shown me his rental, and how he is tied up ; and he really cannot——"

" ' Pray, Mr. Hyde,' said I, interrupting him, ' *are* you Sir Edward's solicitor or mine ? '

"Whereupon, not finding it convenient or agreeable to endure any probing, he scrambled up all his papers, and said, taking out his watch, ' Bless me ! I shall lose the train,' and darted out of the room.

" The next day Dr. Roberts, whom I had known a long time, called on me, and when I told him of Mr. Hyde's audacious proposition about the £500 a year, he urged me to be firm, and not take a doit less than a thousand a year, which, as he truly said, was little enough, after such an outrage, for which, said I, *no* money *could* compensate. ' Very true,' said he, and after assuring me of the universa indignation and sympathy my case had excited, he took his departure, promising soon to call again.

"The plot was now evidently thickening, for the next morning Sparrow, entering my room, said a groom had just ridden out in such haste that the horse was covered with foam to tell Mr. Hill he must go to London without a moment's delay; 'and I cannot but think and hope,' said she, 'that it means some good to your Ladyship.' About five o'clock Hill returned from town, more fat, head-wagging, and eye-rolling than ever, but desperately civil, and *aux petits soins*, and asked me if I would like a drive as far as Richmond ? I said yes, amazingly, provided Miss Hill went with us. 'Oh, yes, certainly,' said he ; 'for your Ladyship has quite bewitched my little Mary, and she cries every time a servant is sent up to you with anything instead of her.' Never was anything so beautiful as that always lovely view from Richmond Hill upon that glorious July evening, with the golden sun steeping it in light and turning the 'silver Thames' into a perfect Pactolus, while the fresh breeze from the river was a real luxury, after my nearly three weeks' incarceration in that large but low-ceilinged, stuffy room, with its nailed-down windows ; and as caged birds are always wild when they *do* get out, Mary Hill and I took to running races, not the least part of the pleasure of which was seeing fat old Hill, 'like panting Time, toiling after us in vain,' and puffing and blowing like a steam-engine, till he made almost as much noise as his ten children made under my windows of a morning when I was groaning in my cage. By the time we got back to Inverness Lodge the evening was fast closing in ; and though, as always, I had an invitation to sit below in a really magnificent lofty-roofed banqueting-room, some fifty feet long, I preferred my own society in my room."

As Lady Lytton writes above, the news of her confinement in Mr. Hill's asylum created such a scandal, in spite of the efforts of her husband and his friends to keep the affair quiet, that Sir Edward

Lytton found it absolutely necessary, for the sake of his own reputation, to take immediate steps for her release.   Negotiations were then set on foot, with the result that this persecuted lady at length agreed to go abroad with her son and Miss Ryves until the scandal had in some degree subsided, upon the distinct understanding that when she returned her debts should be paid, and she should receive an allowance of £1,000 a year.   How these promises were fulfilled will appear hereafter

CHAPTER XXII.

'HAVING been brought to Mr. Hill's stronghold on Wednesday, June 22nd, 1858, at 7 p.m., I left it on Saturday, July 17th, 1858, at 3 p.m. Poor little Mary Hill cried so violently that I was really grieved to leave her, and felt quite selfish in going, as I then thought, to be happy.

"Upon this memorable 17th of July, from 3 to 7 p.m., I had to drive all over London in quest of ready-made things, and then to go to Farrance's Hotel, to eat a hurried dinner, and after from Belgrave Square to London Bridge railway station, so that I was really quite worn out when at eleven at night I found myself in bed at the Lord Warden Hotel, Dover, from whence we did not cross to Calais till Monday, the 19th."

From Calais the party proceeded to Paris and thence to Bordeaux, where they stayed about a month. About the end of August they went on to Luchon. But I must now return to the events which were meanwhile happening in England. Sir Edward's object in sending his wife abroad in company with her son was of course to silence his detractors, who were becoming inconveniently clamorous; and with this end in view, he did his very utmost to stifle the voice of the press, and to persuade even Lady Lytton's own friends that he had at length determined upon an entire change of policy, and was willing to permit his unhappy wife to live in peace and comfort for the remainder of her life. In this design he was eminently successful, for, having sent his wife abroad with her son and Miss Ryves, he contrived to win over Mr. Hyde to a belief in the goodness of his intentions, as the following letter, written by that gentleman to Mrs. Clarke, will show :—

"33, ELY PLACE, *July 17th*, 1858.

"DEAR MADAM,—

"I am happy to say everything is in a fair way of settlement for Lady Lytton, and you will no doubt hear from her, with all particulars. She is to leave Brentford to-day. Mr. Edwin James, the Queen's counsel, and myself have fresh authority to settle her debts, and what I ask of you now is to be good enough to let me know what her Ladyship is indebted to you, and what other creditors at Taunton she has.

"I remain,
"Yours, etc.,
"CHAS. HYDE.

"Mrs. Clarke."

At this period Mr. Hyde was in failing health —he died of softening of the brain in September, 1859—and he was no doubt more easily dealt with than he might have been under different circumstances. As a matter of fact, these debts were not all paid off until April, 1860.

With reference to the part taken by the press in this matter, it is worthy of notice that the *Times* ignored the whole affair, the only allusion being this short note, published July 14th, 1858 :—

"LADY BULWER LYTTON.

"We are requested to state upon the best authority that all matters in reference to this lady, about whom certain statements have appeared in some of the public journals, are in process of being amicably settled by family arrangements to the satisfaction of all parties concerned."

Other papers, however, were not quite so amiably reticent. A long account of the whole case appeared in the *Somerset County Gazette* of July 13th, 1858, from which it will be sufficient to quote extracts.

From the " Somerset County Gazette and West of England Advertiser," July 13th, 1858.

"For some three years past a lady, rather above middle age, of somewhat portly figure and handsome countenance, has occupied apartments in the quiet, comfortable, and pleasant establishment at Taunton known as Clarke's Hotel. Her appearance, manners, and habits, so far as the latter were known, did not cause her to be particularly noticed as she walked in public; for she was much like ordinary ladies—plainly and becomingly dressed—conducted herself with propriety, remarked objects that were likely to attract attention, and passed without notice those that were not so. She sometimes did a little 'shopping,' as ladies generally are fond of doing, and when she asked for any particular article, she did so in ordinary terms, and answered questions in a rational manner, though at times with haughtiness. In her country walks she was occasionally accompanied by a female friend, though generally in these her only companion was a little dog, for which she always showed great fondness. Sometimes also she has been seen at public entertainments, though but seldom, and there her attire has been similarly becoming to that in her walks in town or country. In a place like Taunton, a person of any note does not long reside before he or she becomes known to many of the inhabitants; and soon after the arrival of the lady we have been describing, she was generally known to be Lady Bulwer Lytton, wife of the eminent novelist, who now holds the distinguished position of Colonial Secretary in her Majesty's Government.

"Persons who are in a state of madness give indications of their misfortunes at home and abroad. They

> ' Bend their eyes on vacancy,
> And with the incorporeal air do hold discourse ;
> Their words are loose
> As heaps of sand, and scattering wide from sense.'

But Lady Lytton, during the three years she was at Taunton, never did aught that we are aware of (and we have taken pains to ascertain the truth) to cause in any one with whom she had communication the slightest suspicion that in her case reason had been dethroned, or that her brain was in any degree affected with lunacy. Yet this lady has been taken from the quiet retreat she had chosen in this fair town of Somerset—perhaps we might say to which she was driven—and carried to one of those miserable abodes of the most hapless of human beings—a 'madhouse.'

"The circumstances under which Taunton has lost one of its inhabitants are so extraordinary and so shocking, that, as may be supposed, they have greatly excited the minds of the people generally. Upon those persons who were on terms of intimacy with Lady Lytton (they were only few, for she evinced little inclination to mix in society, and it was pretty well known that her pecuniary means were too limited to allow of her doing so), upon her personal friends the first mention of the fact fell like a clap of thunder when the skies give no sign of an approaching storm. They could not credit such strange information with truth ; but when convinced of its veracity their exclamation has been, 'Good heavens! Lady Lytton in a *madhouse !* For what ? Who can have sent her there ? She is no more mad than I am, or any one else.' And those who have merely seen her as she passed them in the streets or other public highways have been hardly less startled by the intelligence. There is on all hands a firm belief that this unfortunate lady—we say unfortunate in allusion only to her present lamentable position, and without reference to circumstances which have given both to herself and her husband an unenviable notoriety—there is, we say, a firm belief that Lady Lytton is the subject of a horrible and appalling injustice and wrong; that while perfectly sane she has been shut up in a lunatic asylum, merely in order that a woman who has, no doubt, been a constant source of annoyance to her husband may be prevented for ever from again giving him similar trouble, or again molesting him in any way. In ascribing to her the character we have given, we desire to avoid the indication of any opinion as to her conduct towards Sir Edward, or as to his general treatment of her. We only state a fact, that people among whom she has resided during a period of three years—to many of whom she is well and intimately known, and most of whom have had frequent opportunities of seeing her—believe that though sent to an asylum for lunatics, her intellect is perfectly sound, and therefore that she has been made, for some reason or other, the victim of an atrocity which a hundred years ago might have excited no great attention beyond the circle of the doomed one's own relatives, but which cannot be overlooked in the present age without danger to 'that liberty of the subject' which has been since achieved, and which is the highest boast and most glorious privilege of the people of this country.

"In giving to Lady Lytton the character we have ascribed, and in stating what is the general opinion of her in this town, we by no means wish to have it supposed that we regard her as one of the most pleasant or amiable of women. Her later literary works (for none of which can be claimed any considerable praise) seem to have been undertaken in a great measure for the purpose of publishing to the world her own sufferings, and of exposing what she conceived to be the foul treatment she received from one who vowed at the altar to ' love and cherish her ;' and in more than one instance her writings evince unkind and uncharitable feelings towards very estimable and excellent persons. We particularly allude to one of her

latest productions, entitled 'Very Successful,' in which
a lady of this town, who is only known to be respected
and esteemed, is held up to most undeserved ridicule for no
other reason than that she did not desire to cultivate her
Ladyship's acquaintance, having, probably from the nature
of her daily engagements, little time to give to the maintenance of friendships beyond the circle of associates she
had already gathered around her.* And we happen to
know that in several cases her Ladyship has manifested
much haughtiness to persons who have had occasion to
come in contact with her. But such things as these, however much to be deprecated in all persons, certainly cannot
be regarded as evidence of a deranged brain, for if unkind
and offensive personalities in print were so considered, few
writers would be safe from incarceration in a lunatic asylum ;
and if haughtiness were held to be a proof of lunacy, who
is there that should give the necessary 'certificates,' and
who become 'warders'? Displays of ill-temper and
malignity, of pride and arrogance, are never very reasonable ; they are in truth very ridiculous. Still there is much
yet to be learnt if they are to be held as indications of
madness. We make these remarks to show that, while
under an impression—we will say a conviction—that in
Lady Lytton's transfer to a lunatic asylum she has been
made the victim of a shocking outrage and crime, we
are not unacquainted with, or insensible to, her weaknesses
and defects. And we may here state that our object in
alluding to her case at all is to enforce by its publicity
that strict investigation into its circumstances to which
she is in common justice entitled, and which society
demands for its own satisfaction and as its own safeguard.

"Four hundred a year being unequal to the require-

* I have not thought it advisable to omit this passage, though it
is based upon a misconception. One of the characters in "Very
Successful" bears the same name as a lady who lived in Taunton
at this period, but when the novel was written Lady Lytton was not
even aware of her existence. It is of course true that Lady Lytton,
owing to her unfortunate position, avoided mixing much in Taunton
society, and thereby offended certain worthy people in all innocence.
—L. D.

ments of a lady who had moved in the higher classes of
society—leaving luxuries out of the question—Lady Lytton
became involved in debt, which of late has claimed about
one-half of her income, and of course every year saw her
sink deeper and deeper into the mire. One of her chief
complaints against her husband was the smallness of the
means he allowed her for her support ; and certainly if, as
is stated, his own income is £10,000, it is a very reasonable
one, for the allowance of £8 a year to his wife by a man
whose income is £200 would be just in the same propor-
tion ; and there are few who would not decry and condemn
the injustice which such a payment by a person having £200
a year would exhibit. By the deed of separation Lady
Lytton was to possess in her own right any property she
then had or might acquire thereafter, which has been chiefly
from her publications—in some cases remunerative, but in
others miserable failures. She has been severely censured
for the bitterness displayed in some of her writings, but
perhaps not altogether with justice. Let those who would
condemn the use of harsh language just learn under what
circumstances it has been used ; and if they find the
author's life has been one of excessive trial and suffering—
that she has either been compelled to quit, or has felt it
imperatively necessary to flee from, the house of her
husband—that from a position of pecuniary ease she has
been cast down to a condition of humiliating poverty—that
instead of her society being courted by numerous 'friends,'
whose acts of kindness caused her days to pass lightly and
happily, she is shunned by most of them as no longer
worthy of their regard—that while her husband still moves
among the gayest and noblest of society, she remains the
occupant of two small rooms in a country hotel—if they
make in her case the allowance which such an accumulation of woes and miseries ought to ensure, they will not
fail to be very sparing of censure ; they will hardly
express surprise, perhaps, at the display of ill-feeling,
however bitter or general it may be. When a person
is treated as an Ishmael, it is not to be wondered at if
he regards himself as such ; and the best of tempers will

at last be soured and ruined by constant irritation and suffering."

Then follows a narrative of Lady Lytton's visit to Hertford election, of Dr. Thomson's appearance at Taunton, and of Lady Lytton's deportation to Brentford, events which I have already chronicled. The article continues :—

"We have said Lady Lytton's capture, and the circumstances connected with it, have caused a great degree of excitement among the inhabitants of this town ; and if any proof of this were called for, or any evidence of the opinion generally entertained required, we could hardly give more indubitable testimony than is contained in the following resolutions, which were adopted at a meeting of inhabitants called by a gentleman who, though a perfect stranger to Lady Lytton, felt that a monstrous injustice had been inflicted upon her, and determined to use the very considerable influence he possessed to obtain her freedom if really not insane, or at least to force on such an inquiry into her mental condition as to satisfy the public that she is not in a fit state to be at liberty. The gentleman in question arrived in this town only a day or two before the case came to his knowledge ; and immediately upon becoming acquainted with it he proceeded into the street, called together such of the more influential inhabitants as he met, and within an hour the meeting took place. After a discussion of the subject, the resolutions were thrown into the following form :—

"'At a meeting of certain inhabitants of Taunton and the neighbourhood, held at Clarke's Hotel on the 6th of July, 1858, Mr. Hitchcock in the chair, it was resolved :—

"'On the motion of Captain Jones, seconded by R. Easton, Esq.—

"'1. That the removal of Lady Bulwer Lytton to a lunatic asylum, or other place of confinement, and the circumstances under which she was incarcerated therein, call for a public expression of alarm for the rights and liberties of the subject, and particularly of distrust of the treatment to which her Ladyship is said to have been subjected.

"'2. That a committee be now appointed to watch the result of the extraordinary measures reported to have been adopted in Lady Lytton's case, to the end that the public mind may be satisfied, through their report, that in her Ladyship's case justice may be done.—W. R. HITCHCOCK.

"'The meeting was then adjourned for a week.'

"Here we will leave this miserable tale; but we are anxious, before closing our remarks, to avow that in taking it upon ourselves to set it before the public, we are actuated only by a sense of duty and justice. For the truth of the narrative, we can refer to the lady who accompanied Lady Lytton to London; the details are given as they were furnished to us—without exaggeration or distortion. If her Ladyship's mind is in such a state that she is a fit subject for a lunatic asylum, and an asylum is the only suitable place for her, no harm can come from the publicity we give to her case; if not, then much good must inevitably arise from its publicity, to her chiefly, and in an immeasurable degree, but also to society in no unimportant measure. The whole question is, of course, Is Lady Lytton actually insane? We have said, from what we have seen and heard of her, she is not; and this view is entertained by all we have heard express any opinion on the subject. It is a question of deep importance whether it is not utterly wrong, and most dangerous to the liberties of individuals, that upon the word of two medical men persons may be taken to a madhouse, when, if not already insane, they are undoubtedly placed in circumstances in every way calculated, by their horrible and frightful character, to destroy reason and produce insanity. We say nothing of their continued confinement, but of their being consigned to such a place even for a moment. On every account a power of such awful magnitude should be destroyed, and confinement in a lunatic asylum be possible only after a public inquiry, similar to that which must precede the committal of a person accused of felony to the common gaol. Society in general demands this; helpless women require it ; and if there are any individuals for the sake of whose character and reputation before the world the change should be made, they are those who occupy such a position as Sir Edward Lytton now holds in her Majesty's Government. As a Secretary of State, he, as is well known, exercises great authority in such cases ; and men so highly stationed can always find ready tools for any work, however nefarious. It is right, then, that suspicion against them should be rendered impossible, that no reasonable person should have ground for the supposition that they have committed or connived at an atrocity at which the body shudders and the mind is appalled. It is true that investigation into cases like that of Lady Lytton is compelled when demanded by the friends of the incarcerated person; but the system is altogether contrary to the general equity of British laws and customs. To send to a madhouse a person suspected of lunacy, and afterwards institute an inquiry whether he is mad or not, is a mode of procedure very unworthy of a civilised nation, and one which the people of this country ought no longer to endure. Lady Lytton's case will no doubt have the effect of drawing general attention to this great anomaly, and probably it will tend in a great measure to the accomplishment of the desired change. Heaven grant it may be so!"

The *Daily Telegraph* also took up the injured lady's cause with justifiable warmth, as will be seen from the appended article of July 15th, 1858.

" Daily Telegraph," July 15th, 1858.

" Sir Edward Bulwer Lytton has succeeded in hushing up the scandal of his wife's arrest and conveyance to a madhouse at Brentford. The matters in dispute, so say the persons interested, will be arranged to the satisfaction of all concerned. For the sake of the lady herself, the public will rejoice that such a compromise has been extorted

from the Secretary of State; if the victim be content, no
one has a right to complain, but it must be remembered
that Sir Bulwer Lytton alone has gained by the suppression of inquiry. We are now told that he will seal a
treaty of perpetual truce with the woman who was, apparently under his instruction, dragged by policemen into
a carriage, hurried to a lunatic asylum, and there compelled
to sign a compact of forbearance towards the individual
by whom, according to her statement, she had been grossly
and flagitiously wronged. It is with pleasure we record
that this ignominious family war has been terminated,
and the accusation of insanity has been abandoned; that
Lady Lytton is confessedly qualified to treat with her
husband upon terms of equality. Justice may boast of a
triumph, for though it would have been more satisfactory
to have forced the entire transaction before an authentic
tribunal, it may suffice to know that popular opinion has
driven Lord Derby's choice and brilliant colleague into a
virtual surrender. It matters little whether Sir Bulwer
Lytton, under Cabinet influence, has found it necessary
to save the reputation of the Government as well as his
own, but it is not to be forgotten that he employed
attorneys, nurses, and policemen to capture his wife; that
she was forcibly consigned to a lunatic asylum; that
medical certificates were obtained to prove her insanity;
and that now, an explosion of national feeling having taken
place, she is to be released, and allowed to live in personal
independence.

"All that now remains for investigation is who and
what the professional gentlemen were who handed over
this lady to the keepers of a madhouse, whether she was
sane at the time of her capture, and whether she was not
kidnapped by the myrmidons of her flattered and successful husband. Individually she may benefit by the
compromise, though it may be that a salutary exposure
has been stifled. On one point the public are agreed : the
power at present exercised under the lunacy law of England is dangerous to social liberty. Any one, by obtaining
the certificate of two medical men, may imprison wife,

child, or other relative for years, perhaps for life, in a mad-house. The Lunacy Commissioners, we are reminded, may interfere with its machinery of visitors' inspections and reports, but what is the result? Men might be named who open establishments of this character, accumulate fortunes, and live in affluence, and are pointed at by their neighbours as the creatures of conspiracy. Their resi-dences are nobly furnished, their grounds rival those of the nobility, and when official visitors, after sumptuous luncheons, pass their patients in review, and an exasperated captive pours forth his vehement denunciations, 'they write him down mad,' and the wretch is left for another year, to be goaded by a sense of wrong, wrought upon by the contagious presence of insanity, and at length made all that his officious friends desire him to be. Without casting a general slur upon a body of men many of whom are highly respectable, we may state it as the conviction of those who stand above all prejudice in their profession, that the lunatic asylums of this country are frequently applied to the same uses as the Bastille, where the Man in the Iron Mask was immured for life and buried in secrecy because his pretensions were considered dangerous by claimants to estates and titles, or perpetrators of un-searched crimes.

"But a social question of far more universal importance is connected with the deplorable disclosure in the case of Sir Bulwer Lytton. The baronet's wife may be released from the terrible captivity to which, by the practical con-fession of her persecutors, she never ought to have been for a moment consigned, and from which we have made no unsuccessful effort to deliver her; but what of humbler persons? What of the domestic victims in whose name no publicity is invoked? We hear of jealous and bitter-tongued women, of outcast wives, who go down to bury their humiliation in the shade of equivocal watering-places, of ladies whose 'fashionable' manners shock the propriety of German spas; but when these scandals are the popular table-talk, in the name of justice let the woman be con-sidered. The lord and the lady, the baronet and his wife, the parents of children, do they stand in the eyes of the world upon a level? We hear of a man who has been compelled to part with the mother of his children, and we know that while she goes into retirement, with her happiness blasted in her declining years, his car of triumph rolls on, he is still the ornament and delight of society. But when the forsaken woman glides into the shadow of suspicion, who cares to remind us that a cluster of children call her mother; that twenty years of married life should have made her sacred; that even her failings should have been holy to her husband; that bitterness itself is pardonable when it rises from the fountains of love; that what by the triumphing 'lord of the creation' is termed 'incompatibility' may be nothing more than the satiety of a selfish affection? If manliness, if chivalry, if the noble principles of honour dominated more supremely than they do in the circles of our English life, would these published separations so continually feed the mass of scandal to the detriment of names once invoked in confidence and affection at the altar? Let cynicism utter what it will, let irony do its worst, let men affect to despise the heart-born passions, the chief happiness of every human being is at home; neither Church, nor State, nor military glory, nor political conflict can destroy the supremacy of that instinct which makes joy itself a virtue—the pride of an honest man in his family. How implacable then must be the antipathy be that breaks these consecrated bonds; how utterly exhausted and callous must be the affection that permits this last repudiation of a moral tie, linking children with children, and teaching those children to reverence their parents."

In answer to these damaging statements, Mr. Robert Lytton wrote to the *Daily Telegraph* on July 17th.

To the Editor of the "Daily Telegraph."

" SIR,—

"As the son of Lady Bulwer Lytton, with the

best right to speak on her behalf, and so obviously with the best means of information as to warrant the hope that my simple assertion will be at once believed in the matter to which I am compelled to refer, I beg to say that the statements which have appeared in some of the public journals are exaggerated and distorted, and that they are calculated to convey to the public mind impressions the most erroneous and unjust. As was natural, I put myself into constant communication with my mother, and with the gentleman in whose family, in his private house, she was placed (for I beg distinctly to state she was never for a moment taken to a lunatic asylum); and I carried out the injunctions of my father, who confided to me implicitly every arrangement which my affection could suggest, and enjoined me to avail myself of the advice of Lord Shaftesbury in whatever was judged best and kindest for Lady Lytton.

"My mother is now with me, free from all restraint, and about, at her own wish, to travel for a short time, in company with myself and a female friend and relation, of her own selection.

"From the moment my father felt compelled to authorise those steps which have been made the subject of so much misrepresentation, the anxiety was to obtain the most experienced and able physician, in order that my mother should not be subject to restraint for one moment longer than was strictly justifiable. Such was his charge to me.

"The certificates given by Dr. Forbes Winslow and Dr. Connolly are subjoined, and I ought to add that Dr. Connolly was the physician whom my father had requested to see Lady Lytton, that Dr. Forbes Winslow was consulted by my mother's legal advisers, and I felt anxious to obtain the additional authority of the opinion of the latter gentleman, and requested my friend, Mr. Edwin James, to place himself in communication with him. I trust that such journals as have given publicity to partial and inaccurate statements will do me the justice to publish this communication, to which I need add no more than to

say that this painful matter has been arranged, as it ought
to be, by the members of the family whom it exclusively
regards.

" I have the honour to be, sir,

"Your most obedient servant,

"ROBERT B. LYTTON.

" 1, Park Lane, July 17th, 1858."

[Copy No. 1.]

"To Edwin James, Esq., Q.C.

" Having at your request examined Lady B. Lytton
this day as to her state of mind, I beg to report to you
that in my opinion it is such as to justify her liberation
from restraint.

" I think it but an act of justice to Sir Edward B. Lytton
to state that upon the facts which I have ascertained were
submitted to him, and upon the certificates of the medical
men* whom he was advised to consult, the course which
he has pursued throughout these painful proceedings cannot
be considered harsh or unjustifiable.

" I remain, sir,

"Your obedient servant,

"FORBES WINSLOW, M.D., D.C.L.

" 23, Cavendish Square, July 16th, 1858."

[Copy No. 2.]

"LONDON, *July 17th*, 1858.

" SIR,—

"Notwithstanding the decided opinion which I
felt it my duty to express with reference to Lady Lytton,
after my visit to her at the private residence of Mr. and
Mrs. Hill, and which, I need not repeat, justified the course
you adopted, I have much satisfaction in hearing of the
arrangements which have been made for her Ladyship

---

* The " medical men " here referred to are Mr. Ross, an apothecary, of Farringdon Street, City, and Mr. Hale Thomson, of
Clarges Street, formerly connected with the Westminster Hospital.

leaving their family in the society of her son and her female friend.

> "I have the honour to be, sir,
> > "Very faithfully,
> > > "Your obedient servant,
> > > > "G. CONNOLLY, M.D."

It is necessary to bear in mind that Lady Lytton never saw this letter of her son's, nor ever heard of it until long after her departure from England.*

Neither was she aware that Mr. Hyde had written the remarkable letter to the editor of the *Hertford Mercury* which ran as follows :—

> "33, ELY PLACE, *July* 19*th*, 1858.
>
> "SIR,—
>
> "As the legal adviser of Lady Bulwer Lytton, I am fully authorised to state that the family arrangements which are about to terminate the differences between Sir Edward Bulwer Lytton and my client are in every respect satisfactory ; and I feel it due to Sir Edward B. Lytton to add that explanations have been given which have entirely removed any impression that his conduct was dictated by any feeling of harshness or severity towards Lady Lytton. I believe it to be most consonant with the feelings and most compatible with the future welfare of Lady Lytton that these private misunderstandings should cease to be the subject of public discussion.
> > "I am, sir,
> > > "Yours, etc.,
> > > > "CHARLES HYDE."

But the explanations of Mr. Lytton and Mr. Hyde do not seem to have been universally accepted as

---

* On her return to England, Lady Lytton writes to Mrs. Curteis Whelan, November 3rd, 1858, "Had I but seen that tissue of lies (which they took care I should not see), neither force nor fraud should have got me out of England."

conclusive. The following letter appeared in a subsequent issue of the *Daily Telegraph :—*

"*To the Editor of the 'Daily Telegraph.'*

"SIR,—

"Thanks to you for your noble and eloquent defence of Lady Lytton, and the outrage on public justice perpetrated by her husband. Your watchfulness may have been rendered unnecessary by the family 'arrangement' which has been announced; but Heaven help Lady Lytton, travelling abroad under the guardianship of such 'affection,' with the stigma of insanity upon her, available for any purpose.

"The letter of Mr. Robert Lytton explains nothing, answers nothing. It does not even show where his mother is. He writes—'My mother is now with me, free from all restraint.' This letter is dated 1, Park Lane, the town residence of Sir Bulwer Lytton, who is now in London. Does Mr. Lytton mean to say that his mother is or was on Saturday last under the roof of her husband? There is more than meets the eye in this. Is Lady Lytton free from all restraint? Whatever the 'arrangement' is, it was made when she was in durance, and not a free agent; and if that arrangement has taken her from the custody of Mr. Hill, of Brentford, to that of her own son and husband, it is only that her prison-house has been changed. 'From the moment my father felt compelled to authorise those steps which have been made the subject of so much misrepresentation, etc., in order that my mother should not be subject to restraint for one moment longer than was strictly justifiable, such was his charge to me.' If Sir Edward was so solicitous to procure the opinions of the most able physicians, we may ask how it happened, instead of consulting Dr. Forbes Winslow and Dr. Connolly in the first instance, that he employed a Mr. Thomson to kidnap the lady at his own residence. Mr. Lytton says the statements are 'exaggerated' and 'distorted,' but he does not explain how. He says he has the best right to speak on behalf of his mother, and has the 'best means of information,' and that his assertion will be at once believed. It is hard to refuse this to a son, and in ordinary cases one would not feel inclined to do so; but he seems to have acted entirely under the influence of the father, and to have been from first to last so directly opposed to his mother, that before we give him the credence he asks there are several questions he ought to answer. Is it true he has neither sought after nor corresponded with his mother, nor even seen her, for nearly seventeen years, until he met her at the hustings at Hertford, during the recent election there? Is it true that on that occasion he made the preliminary attempt which culminated at the house of Mr. Thomson, in Clarges Street, to put his mother in a mad-house by sending a physician to the house of the Mayor of Hertford, where she was on a visit? Is it true that when his mother was kidnapped in Clarges Street, and Miss Ryves ran out into the street, and seeing Mr. Lytton waiting outside, entreated him to interfere and procure assistance to prevent his mother being carried off to Brent-ford, he refused to have anything to do with the matter? Other questions suggest themselves, not directly affecting Mr. Lytton, but important to an understanding of this painful case. He says, 'I put myself in constant com-munication with my mother. . . . I carried out the in-junctions of my father, who confided in me implicitly, . . . enjoined me to avail myself of the advice of Lord Shaftes-bury in whatever was judged best and kindest for Lady Lytton.' Is this a solemn farce, a piece of well-acted hypo-crisy, or a truth in letter and spirit? Is it conceivable that Sir Edward Lytton, not having set eyes on his wife for seventeen years, and leaving her to live and suffer and complain during all that time on £400 a year, suddenly became so tenderly solicitous on her behalf, as to require 'all that was best and kindest' should be done for her? Why is Lord Shaftesbury introduced? Is it to give the shelter of his sanctity to a cruel outrage? Mephistopheles might envy the genius which suggested the mention of Lord Shaftesbury as the adviser and referee of Sir Bulwer Lytton.

"The certificates appended to Mr. Lytton's letter are not properly 'certificates;' they are intended as apologies for the conduct of Sir Bulwer Lytton. But though put forward with this view, they substantiate that the state of Lady Lytton's mind 'is such as to justify her liberation from restraint,' and prove nothing to his honour. It is easy to see that the 'certificate' of Dr. Forbes Winslow is but an answer to certain questions put by Mr. Edwin James, who was strangely employed by Mr. Lytton, and whose object was to extract from the doctor everything that he could on behalf of Sir Edward. On this part of the question we are all competent to form an opinion, and if it should appear that the facts submitted to Sir Edward were facts suggested by himself, and the medical men, on whose certificates he acted, were employed by him, which is the fact, Dr. Forbes Winslow's opinion upon this part of the question goes for nothing.

"The more inquiries we make into the matter the more convinced we are that a great wrong was attempted, and has now been glossed over. That wrong was not done to Lady Lytton alone, but to all society. Her wrath may have been appeased, her personal wounds may have received a plaster, and her friends may have been flattered and cajoled into silence, but is the public satisfied, or has the wrong to society been atoned for, while the case of Lady Lytton remains uninvestigated, and the conduct of her husband escapes official and public censure? Is any one of us safe so long as the law permits the 'next of kin' to do what has been done to her?

"AN ENGLISHMAN."

And on the 21st of July, the *Daily Telegraph* returned to the charge.

"Daily Telegraph," July 21st, 1858.

"We return unwillingly, and, we trust, for the last time, to the melancholy scandal in which Sir Bulwer Lytton has involved himself. It had been our intention not to carry further this painful controversy, yet additional ex planations are extorted from us by the peculiar tactics, not only of particular individuals, but of some among our contemporaries. There have been allusions to 'misrepresentations' contained in 'paragraphs,' and 'exaggerated and distorted statements,' circulated with reference to the lady who a few days since was spirited away by stratagem to Brentford. Now in respect of the persons principally concerned, nothing more need be said; if the Right Hon. Secretary for the Colonies has effected a settlement agreeable to his conscience and his wife, none has a right to interfere; if the electors of Hertford are satisfied, the general public has perhaps little reason to complain; and if legality and justice are not to be permanently outraged, we rejoice that family negotiations have been successful. Yet there are points connected with our own position which should be clearly set forth. The vague and solemn rebukes that have been set forth were addressed almost exclusively to ourselves, not of paragraphs, but of articles based upon a well-prepared narrative published in a provincial journal, no one assertion of which to the present moment has been invalidated. But if there has been 'exaggeration,' if there has been 'falsity,' who was the person and what was the time to correct them? The proper individual was the son of Sir Bulwer Lytton himself; and the proper time was upon one of the occasions when, since the exposure in our columns, he called at the *Daily Telegraph* office, sometimes not alone. Did we hear then anything about 'distortion' or 'misrepresentation'? Most certainly not a word. Mr. Robert Lytton acted then as the champion of his mother, and not he only, but her personal friends also, appeared delighted that upon public grounds an appeal had been made bearing so directly upon their private interests. Then, we think, was the moment for substituting accurate for erroneous impressions; but since this retort is forced upon us, what if we suggest that the original case was not one to be explained away? Lady Lytton was by no means the person interested in a concealment of the facts or in hushing up the affair before it was dragged before a Commission of Lunacy. W are now told, indeed, that the baronet was satisfied in the course he adopted, which we have never pretended to deny, for we have insisted only on inquiry. We asked whether the allegations against him were true, and we pointed out the impossibility of allowing a public man to remain under an imputation so scathing, and we expressed our hope that the sinister rumours afloat would be set at rest by an ample vindication of the Privy Councillor's conduct. Is it our fault, then, that no such vindication has been attempted, that Sir Bulwer Lytton has preferred a private arrangement, that he has defied the written opinion of two professional men, and allowed his so-called insane wife to be once more at large upon terms to which he had previously refused his consent? Nothing would have been more satisfactory to ourselves and the public than that Lord Derby's colonial secretary, after a strict judicial investigation, should have demonstrated himself a man of honour, incapable of kidnapping an obnoxious wife.

"But upon whose authority was Lady Lytton captured and sent to Brentford? Not originally, as has been stated, upon that of Dr. Connolly. The certificates were signed by a Mr. Hale Thomson, once known at Westminster Hospital, and by a Mr. Ross, an apothecary of Farringdon Street, whose medical reputation seems to have travelled providentially from east of Temple Bar to an official residence in Downing Street. The sanction of these 'eminent' gentlemen enabled the policemen and nurses to place Lady Lytton by force in a carriage, but through a humane after-thought, Dr. Connolly was ultimately called in and despatched to the residence of Mr. Robert Gardiner Hill, at Brentford. There he certified that Lady Lytton was a demented patient. There, however, Dr. Forbes Winslow, within a day or two, certified, in singularly cautious and ambiguous terms, that she was *not* a demented patient, she was, in fact, fit and unfit to live without restraint, and the result is that, with her son and a female relation, she is to enjoy a Continental tour. At all events, it is gratifying to know that whatever has been the effect on the lady's

nerves, she has been benefited by the public discussion
of her case.   Instead of the Brentford process, she will
sojourn at the spas, and Florentine gaiety may compensate
her for three weeks of Middlesex gloom under the lunacy
law.

"Concerning the Brentford question, Mr. Robert Gardiner
Hill is pleased to think himself aggrieved.   We may remark
that Mr. Hill claims to have penetrated the secrets of
physiological science.   That he is not the proprietor of a
'notorious madhouse' we will admit, if he will allow that
he is the principal of a 'celebrated lunatic asylum.'

"What consolation would it be to any of our readers, if
falsely accused of insanity, that a 'lunatic asylum,' and
not a 'madhouse,' shuts its doors upon them?   Would a
paltry verbal quibble reconcile them to captivity among
maniacs and the mentally afflicted?   He is among the
proprietors, he confesses, of Wyke House, which, if he will
not permit us to describe it as 'notorious,' is at least well
known as a madhouse, or, if the term be offensive, of a
lunatic asylum.

"Though not standing alone in this controversy, we
have been solitary among the organs of the press in claiming
a public inquiry on behalf of Lady Lytton.   In our main
object we have succeeded.   The 'patient' is no longer in
legal or in medical clutches.   Her position has totally
changed since the protest of public indignation rose against
the treatment to which she had been subject.   The Taunton
people are satisfied that a great wrong is not to be perpetrated, and Lady Lytton's friends, who rejoiced in the
original exposure, are now at liberty to be as ungrateful
as they please.   They will not induce us, at all events, to
state whence our information was derived, or how far the
right honourable baronet is indebted to themselves for the
publication of a monstrous scandal.   But it was due to
ourselves, to our readers, and to the innumerable corre-
spondents whose letters we have felt it necessary to suppress, to remind Mr. Robert Lytton and his colleagues in
the negotiation just concluded, that they have to thank
the press for the publicity which spared them the painful

alternative of a judicial investigation. It fell to us, fortunately, to produce a movement of public opinion in favour of Lady Lytton ; and it is not for her personal advocates to blame the persistency with which we have followed it to its final issue. Least of all, whatever gracelessness may be exhibited in Park Lane, do we regret a course of proceedings without which, in all probability, the wife of Sir Bulwer Lytton might have been still, and possibly for the rest of her life, subject to the galling tendernesses of our asylums for lunatics."

CHAPTER XXIII.

I WILL now resume my account of Lady Lytton's journey from her letters to Dr. Price.

"HOTEL DE FRANCE, BORDEAUX, *Aug. 6th*, 1858.

"Daily and hourly I wish for you in this delicious climate and paradise of fruits and flowers. We only stayed a week in Paris, and have some thoughts of going on to Madrid."

"*Aug.* 21*st*, 1858.

"I scrawl these few lines in great haste, as we leave this to-day, but all our plans of going to St. Sebastian and Madrid were suddenly changed yesterday, for I grieve to tell you that poor dear Robert has been so ill from the terrible excitement before we left England and the equally trying pleasurable reaction, that yesterday his doctor peremptorily forbade his encountering the discomforts of Spanish travelling, and ordered him to the baths of Luchon, in the south of France. . . . You may guess, therefore, how anxious I am to get to Luchon."

"BAGNÈRES DE LUCHON, AUX PYRENÉES,
"HOTEL BONNE MAISON, *Aug.* 31*st*, 1858.

"We arrived here safely last Monday week, and Robert, I am happy to say, is, thank God, much better already, as he gets up at six, takes his bath at half-past, drinks the waters (an exaggeration upon those of Harrogate, so you may guess how nice they are!), returns to bed, breakfasts at ten. About two I beat him up a couple of new-laid eggs, with some sherry and hot water; he then walks, rides, or drives out with us, and most lovely the rides and drives

are, more especially the former. We dine at seven, and to
bed at ten, a regimen that agrees with him admirably.
This is one of the most charming and original nooks you
can imagine, at the foot of the vine-clad and purple Pyrenees; at least, I never saw anything like it. You come
upon it from a gorge of the mountains, and do not see it
till you are in it. Luchon itself consists of a long avenue,
about a mile and a half long, of gigantic and umbrageous
limetrees, with rows of gay-looking booths of toys, clothes,
fruit, confectionery, jewellery, etc., decorated with bright
flags and garlands of flowers, which give it the air of a
perpetual fair. The houses are picturesque in the extreme,
being built like Swiss châlets and snow-white, with gold-
coloured broad wooden balconies and verandahs. Gardens
the most luxuriant are spread out all over the place, literally like a carpet, while the Pyrenees encircle and rise
above them like a screen. At the end of this lime avenue,
near this hotel, is an amphitheatre of white Doric columns;
this is the Baths. The picturesquely dressed Spanish
pedlars, displaying their Barcelona silks and Aragon hats,
the bells of the muleteers, the constant and really musical
cracking of the whips of the mountain guides, the bands of
music, the gaily attired ladies promenading about from
morning till night, dress the place with an eternal holiday
look. The fruit—figs, peaches, melons, mountain or wood
strawberries, and grapes—are in profusion, the latter, large
black ones, only three sous a pound; but with all this, the
cuisine is so bad that I often long to be back at Taunton,
dining *tête-à-tête* with my dear Dr. Price, which, if you
knew how thoroughly happy I am, you would say was very
good of me; for my dear boy is never tired of repeating to
me that I am now his sole object in life, and, God knows,
his every act proves it."

This is, unfortunately, the last letter which the
poor lady wrote in so happy a frame of mind. Very
shortly afterwards disagreements arose between
mother and son. She discovered that she had
been deceived, and that her letter requesting Lord

Shaftesbury to become one of her trustees had never been sent to him, though before she left the asylum her son informed her that Lord Shaftesbury had consented. Mr. Lytton suddenly left his mother at Luchon. She saw him once more in Paris on her journey home, and there mother and son parted, never to meet again. She returned to Taunton on October 23rd, 1858, going back, of course, to her staunch friend Mrs. Clarke, at the Giles Castle Hotel.

" The good people of Taunton," she writes, " when they heard I was to return safe and sound, wanted to give me a triumphal entry from the station. I wrote, however, to Mrs. Clarke to say how grateful I felt, and always should feel, to them for their great kindness and zeal on my behalf, but that they would greatly add to their kindness if they would allow me to return to them as quietly as possible—I was so far from well."

It was not until her return to Taunton that she found out that Mr. Hyde had been throughout the recent negotiations much more anxious to shield Sir Edward's reputation than to extract from him good terms for herself, that her debts were not even yet paid, owing to the shuffling delays of Mr. Edwin James, who acted no doubt by the express directions of his patron, and that a final settlement of her affairs upon a satisfactory basis was almost as far off as ever. She saw, moreover, for the first time the letters of her son and of Mr. Hyde to the newspapers, which were calculated to give an entirely false impression of the circumstances attending her trip abroad.

The result of Lady Lytton's discoveries was embodied in a letter to Lord Shaftesbury, from which I append extracts.

"TAUNTON, *Oct. 25th*, 1858.

"MY LORD,—

"Having returned to England on Saturday, I have this moment seen, for the first time, a letter in the *Times*, bearing date the 17th of last July, signed by my son, and, therefore, purporting to be written by him and advised by your Lordship. I sincerely hope, in justice to you both, that these statements are. utterly without foundation, as this letter contains the most deliberate and utter lies. The truth of the iniquitous transaction is this. From a sick-bed, to which I was brought by the crowning outrage of an incarceration in the house of a mad doctor, at the end of twenty years of fabulous villainy and persecution, I was half bullied, half cajoled, to leave the country, or rather smuggled out of it, to patch up Sir E. B. Lytton's somewhat damaged reputation, and shield him from the storm of public indignation his unparalleled cruelty to me had so justly excited. I was assailed at the point where the mother has no stronghold, the interest and the urgent appeals of my child. Here I gave way. . . . I now understand · why I was smuggled abroad in such electric telegraph haste. It was that I might not see that cruel and cold-blooded letter. I was also informed that your Lordship had consented to being one of my trustees, but I learnt for the first time at Bordeaux that you had never consented to anything of the kind."

On the same subject, to Mrs. Curteis Whelan :—

"TAUNTON, *Nov. 3rd*, 1858.

"Never believe that my poor calumniated boy wrote that infamous letter which appeared in the papers on the 17th of July.* It was the creditable joint production of the ruffian Loaden ánd the Colonial Secretary's legal Mephistopheles, Mr. Edwin James, to which they dared to affix

* Mr. Lytton soon afterwards acknowledged to his mother that he wrote this letter.—L. D.

poor Robert's name. Had I but seen that tissue of lies, neither force nor fraud should have got me out of England, and one of the greatest lies in it is that of Miss Ryves being a relation of mine—a relationship which I never heard of even from her till then! As for my selecting her to travel with me, I should far rather have been alone with my son."

To Dr. Price.

"TAUNTON, *Nov. 4th*, 1858.

"I am sick—sick at heart. The day I arrived Mrs. Clarke had to show them my letter of urgent entreaty that there might be no public demonstration, and it was only by main force that she prevented their ringing the bells and drawing me from the station. But last Friday, the first day I went out, they instantly set all the bells ringing; and the crowd gathered and cried, 'God bless your Ladyship!'

    *   *   *   *   *

"Poor Mr. Hyde's health totally incapacitates him from business, added to which he has evidently been intoxicated by the air of Downing Street and the blandishments of the Colonial Secretary. Dr. Roberts was the only one who had the sense to stand out that after so gross and irreparable an outrage I ought at least to have double the paltry £500 I asked two years ago. Mr. Hyde was quite satisfied when the veracious Colonial Secretary told him that he could not afford it, and never had the sense to say, or rather to insist, that if he could pay Mr. Hill £1,000 for incarcerating me for life in a madhouse, he certainly could equally well afford to pay it to me for the rest of my miserable existence.

"I left England under the solemn assurance that *all* my debts, more especially Miss Dickenson's and the other debts of honour, should be immediately paid, and the beggarly £500 a year settled upon me for my life. Well, I return to England and find that, as usual, faith has been broken with me. Mr. Hyde was sent down to Taunton in hot haste to pay the tradespeople and try to stop their

mouths, which it didn't, for they say that since the civil
wars, when the amiable Colonel Kirke broke faith with
his victims and shot them all down wholesale from the
windows of the White Hart, no affair, private or public,
has made such an indelible impression.   Poor Miss Dickenson was paid the day after I arrived in England, and not
one of the other debts of honour has been paid yet, and
Dr. Roberts wrote me word yesterday that when Mr. Hyde
had drawn up the deed settling the £500 a year upon me
for my life, Sir Edward, by the advice of his lawyer—for
you know he always has some convenient scapegoat—
objected to the deed *in toto*."

I here append a copy of the deed of October,
1858, of which mention has frequently been made
above.

"DEED OF OCTOBER 1ST, 1858.

"This indenture made 1st of October, one thousand
eight hundred and fifty-eight.   Between the Right Hon.
Sir Edward George Earle Lytton Bulwer Lytton, of
Knebworth Park, in the county of Hertfordshire, Baronet,
on the one part, and the Right Hon. Charles Tennyson
d'Eyncourt, of Bayons Manor, in the county of Lincoln,
and Edwin James, of the Inner Temple, London, Esq.,
one of her Majesty's counsel, and John Roberts, of 75,
Grosvenor Street, in the parish of St. George, in the
county of Middlesex, doctor of medicine, of the other
part.

" *Whereas* the within-named Eliza Barbara Bulwer, Sir
Francis Hastings Doyle, and Sir Thomas Geary Cullum
have all respectively departed this life, and the within-
named Edward G. E. L. B. Lytton hath since been created
a baronet and hath taken the surname of Lytton.   And
whereas the said Sir Edward G. E. L. B. Lytton and Dame
Rosina Anne, his wife, still continue to live separate, as
heretofore, and the said Dame Rosina Anne Lytton applied
to the said Sir Edward G. E. L. B. Lytton that the allowance for her maintenance should be increased from four

hundred pounds to five hundred pounds per annum, and made payable during her life, and that debts she had contracted during such separation, amounting to about three thousand pounds, should be paid by the said Sir Edward G. E. L. B. Lytton, which, for the comfort and better maintenance of his said wife, he had agreed to do on the understanding that he is in no way legally liable to pay such debts, and in or towards liquidation of such debts hath deposited with the said Edwin James the sum of two thousand seven hundred and seventy-four pounds seventeen shillings and fourpence, being the net proceeds of the sale of an estate* in the county of Limerick belonging to the said Rosina Anne Lytton, and which was many years since sold with their joint consent. And whereas, for securing the payment of the said annuity and for the considerations aforesaid, the said Edward G. E. L. B. Lytton hath agreed to enter into the covenants with the said Charles Tennyson d'Eyncourt, Edwin James, and John Roberts as hereinafter contained. Now this indenture witnesseth that in pursuance and performance of the said agreement on the part of the said Sir Edward G. E. L. B. Lytton, he, the said Sir Edward G. E. L. B. Lytton, doth for himself, his heirs, executors, and administrators, covenant, promise, and agree with and to the said Charles Tennyson d'Eyncourt, Edwin James, and John Roberts, and the survivor of them, and the executors and administrators of such survivor, by these presents in manner following, that is to say, that he, the said Sir Edward G. E. L. B. Lytton, will well and truly pay, or cause to be paid, unto the said Charles Tennyson d'Eyncourt, Edwin James, and John Roberts, and the survivor of them, and the executors, administrators, or assigns of such survivor, during the life of the said Dame Rosina Anne Bulwer Lytton, or during the said separation, the clear yearly sum of five hundred pounds of lawful money of Great Britain, by even and equal quarterly payments on the tenth day of October, the tenth day of January, the tenth

---

* Not an estate, for that my cousin, Mr. Bolton Massy, had bought years before, but of a few acres appended to it, which he wanted to enclose.—R. L.

day of April, and the tenth day of July in every year, and
shall and will make the first payment on the tenth of October now next ensuing the day of the date of these presents,
without deduction or abatement for income tax or any
other account whatsoever, upon the trusts within expressed
with regard to the four hundred pounds and in lieu and sub-
stitution thereof; and further that he, the said Sir Edward
G. E. L. B. Lytton, his heirs, executors, and administrators,
shall and will well and truly perform and keep all and
singular other the covenants, conditions, and agreements in
the within-written indenture on his and their parts to be
performed and observed, it being the intention of all parties
to this deed that the within indenture is not to be altered
or abrogated in any other respect than appears by this
deed.   In witness whereof the said parties to these presents
have thereunto set their hands and seals the day and year
first above written.

> "EDWARD GEORGE EARLE LYTTON
>   BULWER LYTTON.
> "CHARLES TENNYSON D'EYNCOURT.
> "EDWIN JAMES.
> "JOHN ROBERTS.

"Signed, sealed, and delivered by the above-named
John Roberts, in the presence of Chas. Hyde, 33, Ely Place.

"Signed, sealed, and delivered by the above-named
Edwin James, in the presence of Chas. O. Hyde, clerk to
Messrs. Hyde, solicitors, 33, Ely Place.

"Signed, sealed, and delivered by the above-named
Sir Edward George Earle Lytton Bulwer Lytton, in
the presence of Wm. Hughes Brabant, Savile Place.

"Signed, sealed, and delivered by the above-named
Charles Tennyson d'Eyncourt, in the presence of Thos. S
Morrell, land agent, Tealby, Lincolnshire."

CHAPTER XXIV.

THIS deed, which merely provided for the payment of Lady Lytton's debts out of the small fortune she brought to her husband, and gave her the inadequate income of £500 a year, by no means put an end to her troubles, as will appear from the following extracts from her correspondence.

TO DR. PRICE.

"TAUNTON, *January 6th*, 1859.

"I have at length got back my letters. They were returned yesterday only, and the night before I had had the expense of sending Captain Jones to London, he having been the head of my July committee, a noble-hearted chivalrous sailor, not to be tampered with. . . . I shall have all this expense for nothing, except that I shall be glad of his having an opportunity of giving them a bit of his mind."

These letters were two highly important and compromising epistles written by the late Lord Lytton to his wife. They were handed to Miss Ryves by Lady Lytton on the occasion of her visit to Dr.

Thomson in Clarges Street, and she experienced the greatest possible difficulty in recovering them.*

"February 4th, 1859.

"DEAR DR. ROBERTS,—

"A letter from Mrs. Hyde informs me that efforts are being made by Sir Edward Lytton and his infamous myrmidon Mr. Edwin James to obtain the deed securing me the beggarly £500 a year for life, and then vaunting Mr. Hyde's and your staunchness in refusing to give it up. Truly Mr. Hyde might be struck off the rolls for such a dastardly act, so of course he will not dare to give it up. And, of course, you would never so ruin yourself in your profession and in public opinion, as to be accessory to having me swindled out of it while acting as my trustee."

TO DR. PRICE.

"February 15th, 1859.

"All faith has been broken with me, and the chief part of my debts of honour, Mr. Wheeler's included, has not been paid yet, which is done to injure and embroil me with Mr. Wheeler and others."

TO THE SAME.

"February 27th, 1859.

"You are quite right. It is all a farce to fob me off with about the creditors bringing an action against Mr. Edwin James. No one but Sir Liar could do that, and therein this contemptible quibble of these two ineffable *vauriens* lies. As I have told that unscrupulous Mr. Edwin James, he and his client are merely enacting the fable of the two thieves in the cook's shop : the one who stole the piece of meat, having passed it to his accomplice, when taxed with the theft says, 'I have not got it,' while the other exclaims, with characteristic truth, 'I did not take it,' but the cook, not being a trustee, very soundly beat them both."

* Her legal right to them, however, was never disputed,—a fact which has an important bearing upon Lord Lytton's action against me for their recovery, which was commenced in November 1884, and is still pending.—L. D.

" March 2nd, 1859.

" I don't believe that Sir Liar ever gave Mr. James the money. He would have been the very first to fly at him and go to law with him for breach of trust if he had. I am very sure it is only an infamous quibble between them to worry, annoy, and degrade me, and as for *my* breaking faith, as I also told Dr. Roberts, *that* is all fudge, for he must remember the faith-breaker is the one who first violates a treaty, which Sir Liar did by, the moment he smuggled me out of England, disseminating every imaginable lie about me, which he still continues to do, and, above all, by the non-payment of my beggarly debts. I do hope, however, that Mr. Wheeler, Mr. Errington, and Mr. Sandby will lose no time in serving Mr. James with a writ, as Sir Liar says he gave him the money."

TO MR. EDWIN JAMES.

" March 8th, 1859.

" The remaining debts are, with Laurence the Quaker's little bill of £4 10s., I think five in number instead of two, *i.e.,* those of Mr. Errington, Mr. Wheeler, Mr. Sandby, and Mrs. Hardinge Tyler, the latter £45.. As for the too contemptible quibble of the debts amounting to more than the rough guess ' Lady Lytton made ' without pen and ink in the presto-begone style in which I was *esclandré* last July from the madhouse, that stupendous fact was duly announced to me as far back as August, 1858. . . . What on earth have your false and most ill-judged allegations against me of not keeping the gag in my mouth to do with your oft-repeated and as oft-broken promises to pay the remainder of my beggarly debts immediately, lastly fixing on the 11th of January for so doing ? And, above all, what had they to do with the new act of this black and truly infamous conspiracy, of which, Mr. Hyde being ill, his wife warned me on the 1st of February in these words, ' He thinks you ought to be apprised of the strenuous efforts which are being made to get from him the deed securing you that £500 a year ' ? I assure you, sir, I regret as deeply or rather more deeply than any one the subversion of my whole nature in being compelled to adopt such a tone and such language to any one in the rank of a gentleman, more especially to a man of your splendid and indisputable talents, and holding what should be such an honourable position in your profession, but desperate cases require desperate remedies."

To Dr. Price.

" *March 16th*, 1859.

" The moment Dizzy's swindle of a Reform Bill gave its first squeak I was amused to hear of the accelerated court a certain set paid to Lord Palmerston, for it reminded me forcibly of a story Smollett tells of an Englishman going into the Campidòglio at Rome, and before the Pope and a whole conclave of cardinals marching up to a bust of Jupiter, and after making it a profound bow, saying very solemnly, ' I hope, sir, if you ever get your head above water again, you will remember that I paid my respects to you in your adversity ! ' "

To the Same.

" *March 29th*, 1859.

" I have this moment got back my letters. Dr. Roberts preserves a hermetical silence to all my anxiously pressing letters about the rest of the debts, so Heaven only knows what they are or are not doing."

To the Same.

" *April 8th*, 1859.

" The remainder of my debts are not yet paid, and I doubt if they ever will be. I told Mr. Hyde at the mad doctor's house at a rough guess without pen and ink that my debts would amount to from £2,500 to £3,000, no such very monstrous sum * at the end of twenty years' ceaseless and costly persecution on an irregularly paid stipend of £400 a year minus the income-tax ! Ever since last

---

* As a matter of fact, the sum in question was considerably less than the fortune Lady Lytton brought to her husband at her marriage, so the vaunted generosity of Sir Edward simply meant that he paid her back her own money.—L. D.

August Mr. Hyde has been blowing loud clarions about his present patron's vast generosity, saying that though ruy debts amounted to considerably more than the sum named, Sir Edward had paid them without a murmur, the truth being that these mighty debts are not paid *yet*, and the sum total of their amount is £2,760 10*s.*, just £260 more than the smaller sum I named and £240 less than the larger one."

To the Same.

"*May 8th*, 1859.

"Dr. Roberts writes me word that Sir E——'s illness is not *all* an electioneering sham, for it is neither more nor less than that his brain and mind are seriously affected. What a fearful retribution it would be if he ended his days in the place where he incarcerated me! Dr. Verity said twenty years ago that he was as mad as Bedlam, when we were at Naples."

To the Same.

"*May 29th*, 1859.

"I am going to London to-morrow for a month, having much business, but the mad woman is determined to show herself everywhere well dressed for the first time this many a year. I take a very old friend of mine with me to town, for as long as Sir E—— lives I shall be afraid even to stir two yards alone. My address for the present will be 38, Norfolk Square, Hyde Park."

To the Same.

"*June 5th*, 1859.

"I'm sure I ought to be flattered; all my friends make so much of me, and are so glad to see me, but after the oysterish life I have so long led, never quitting my shell, driving about all the morning on business, and dinners, balls, plays, and concerts every evening, are almost too much for me."

To the Same.

"*June 18th*, 1859.

"My friends are so kind that I ought to be cut up in mincemeat to suffice for all the parties they make for me.

Tuesday I go to the opera with Mrs. Wheeler, and on Wednesday with them to a whitebait dinner at Greenwich. The Hardinge Tylers are pressing me to meet Dhuleep Singh on the 28th at dinner, which is a great temptation, but I am really worn out with all this dissipation, and must get back. Mr. James, who may well be ashamed to meet me, refused to see me, but I insisted, so now he writes to say he will receive me at six o'clock next Monday evening. I am going out to dine in the country with Judge and Mrs. Haliburton."

To the Same.

"*June 25th*, 1859.

"I had an hour and a quarter's broadside with that slippery *vaurien* Mr. Edwin James on Monday. I have not time to give you particulars of all his lies, save that, like all liars, he is a great coward. Said *anything* I wished should be done, the remaining debts paid immediately."

Mr. Edwin James's promises were, however, again broken, as the following letter shows.

To Mr. Edwin James.

"*June 27th*, 1859.

"Dear Sir,—

"I was much annoyed and disgusted to find last night that Mrs. Hardinge Tyler had not yet been paid her £45, though I cannot say that I was surprised. . . . Allowing for the drains upon your client's exchequer for hush-money and other back-stair outlays, it is really most impolitic that his parsimony should be the only portion of his money allotted to me, and that while you committed the Bœotian blunder of boasting to me of having paid one of his tools, the sham Mrs. Sellers, £50 for her dirty work against me, you go on worrying and torturing me by the non-payment of my paltry but just debts. I am aware that you have been much occupied with that Ruck case,

but now that infamous old Dr. Connolly * has been exposed,
and the amiable Mr. Ruck, though owning to an almost
permanent state of delirium tremens and strange delusions,
has got his £500 damages for false imprisonment, I beg
you will have the goodness, without further delay, to
discharge my few remaining debts."

Lady Lytton returned to Taunton on June 30th.

To Dr. Price.

"July 10th, 1859.

" Mr. Edwin James has not yet paid the remainder of
my debts. I have put the matter into the hands of my
solicitor, Mr. Hawke, a shrewd, clever, yet honest man. I
feel safe in Mr. Hawke's hands, because I was placed there
by my friend Mr. Henry Cole, the barrister."

The result of the wholly unjustifiable delay in
paying off Lady Lytton's debts accordingly was
that she was compelled to throw away more money
by employing lawyers and agents to bring her husband to reason. I can hardly suppose that Sir
Edward and Mr. James were ignorant of the effect
their procrastination would produce, or that they
acted without premeditation, their object being to
cause the unfortunate lady as much annoyance and
embarrassment as possible. Lawyers' bills and frequent journeys to London on business thus kept up
a perpetual drain on Lady Lytton's slender means,
but the real strength of Sir Edward's position will
be gathered from the following letter from Miss
Augusta Boys.

To Lady Lytton.

"July 29th, 1859.

" Dearest Lady Lytton,—
" You have unfortunately allowed your adversary

---

* Dr. Connolly certified that Lady Lytton was insane when at
Mr. Hill's.

to see your game by telling both Mr. James and Mr. Lytton that, for the sake of the latter, you will not act or do anything that will show Sir Edward up. All this has been told Sir Edward, and they laugh at your threats, for as Sir Edward does not possess one grain of honour or any other redeeming quality, you must know that did he possess but one tittle of facts against you out of the thousand you have against him, neither his affection for his son nor anything else would prevent his exposing you to the utmost. . . . As to the debts not being paid, I told Mr. Hawke in my letter of yesterday the Q.C. did not dovetail his story well, for, admitting only those on the list were to be paid, how came it Mr. Errington was only paid half, and did he think it likely you would omit your own personal friend Mrs. Tyler? Let the Q.C. produce your list and your stipulation. Again, if they have agreed to pay some even of your debts, why have obliged Mr. Wheeler to sue for his?"

To Dr. Price.

" *August 1st,* 1859.

"After that slippery Mephistopheles Mr. Edwin James' solemn promises to Dr. Roberts and myself when I was in town last June that the remainder of my beggarly debts should be paid immediately, what do you think his fresh lie to Mr. Hawke is? Why, that Sir E—— did not promise to pay all my debts, but only a certain number, which have been paid! If so, how came Mr. Wheeler, the *first* claimant on my list, to have been obliged to serve Mr. Edwin James with a writ before he could get his money? and how came Mr. Errington, the second on the list, instead of being paid his full claim of £400, to have been only paid £300 and asked to wait for the other £100? Mr. Hawke wanted to know if I had any written proof of Sir E——'s having promised to pay *all* my debts, so I sent him pretty plain proof in two letters of Mr. Hyde's to me at Bordeaux, one of the 29th July, 1858, wherein he says, ' Sir Edward has authorised Mr. Edwin James and myself to satisfy *all* demands made upon us for you,' and another of August 28th, 1858, where this occurs : 'Sir Edward has lodged in Mr. Edwin James's hands for the payment of your debts £2,700, which, I'm sure you will be glad to know, is your own money, but he says he will give as much more as is required.'"

Months passed, and the debts were not paid. Fresh expenses were of course incurred by Lady Lytton in trying to obtain a settlement, but her new solicitor, Mr. Hawke, seemed to be no more capable of bringing about a satisfactory result than her previous advisers had been, and meanwhile fresh embarrassments increased the poor lady's distress.

To Dr. Price.

"October 28th, 1859.

"Little did I think when I wrote to you last that I should be driven into availing myself of your always generous kindness so soon, though not to the extent you offered. To my great consternation, a large linen-draper here, of the name of Day, went to smash a month ago, and, to my great inconvenience, my half-yearly bill with him that was to have been paid at Christmas, and which amounted to £22, I had to pay yesterday to his assignees, which has left me just 5s. 9d. to go on with till January, so if you could kindly lend me £5, you would be doing me, as you have so often done before, a great service. Mrs. Clarke would of course lend it me in a moment, but till I pay her the last instalment of the £100 she lent me in June I should not like to ask her. There is a certain £15 long owing to me from a friend; I have written to ask for £10 of it."

To the Same.

"October 20th, 1859.

"You ask me to tell you what Mr. Hawke is doing. Alas! I can only answer you, as Lord Albemarle did his lady-love, 'Don't wish for that star, dearest, because I cannot give it thee'! Don't ask me what Mr. Hawke is doing, because I cannot tell you, not being able to extract a line from him."

TO THE SAME.

"*November 6th*, 1859.

"I have been waiting from day to day in the hope of an answer to my application for my £15, that I might return you the £10 you so very kindly lent me. The answer has arrived at last, and is another put-off."

TO THE SAME.

"*November 17th*, 1859.

"I am harassed and worried to death at Mr. Hawke's unwarrantable silence, but will still wait for the 11th of December, and then will tell him that after having fooled and tortured me all these months, if he does not choose to do my business I must find some one who will."

TO THE SAME.

"*November 19th*, 1859.

"My eyes are streaming with influenza, so that I can hardly see to scrawl these few lines, but I send you a Spanish ballad. I think I should die if I did not some-times vent my cruel outrages in this way."

SPANISH BALLAD.

DON POMPOSO FANFAROSO
  Who never moved except on stilts,
Had such eyes and such a nose O
  They shook the rapiers to their hilts.

HE proclaimed he *was* a wonder!
  And who *should* know if he did not?
He who had been weaned on thunder
  And quaffed the lightning seething hot!

The Guzman blue blood, of old Spain,
  For his quick pulse, was all too slow;
No,—*his*, the blood of Tubal Cain,
  Black fused in regions down below.

DON POMPOSO FANFAROSO
  With fury shut his castle gates
'Gainst his spouse and children, those a—
  —Cursèd fetters on great men's fates!

Don Pomposo full ofttimes bid
   His page the golden Xeres pour,
But *certes* not to pledge the Cid,
   Nor the bones of Campéadore !

But to chase those pushing spectres
   Which *will* haunt e'en great men's brains,
Bullying them, like vulgar Hectors,
   With buried sins and living pains.

Phantoms of betrayed senoras,
   With deep-drugged cups and loaded dice,
Witches, with their weird angoras,
   Transforming stalwart men to mice.

False promises and broken vows,—
   By judgment heaped, as preachers tell,
Beneath the shade of pleasure's boughs,
   To make the downward road to hell.

It was whispered, that Pomposo
   Once late, upon a fearful night,
Lost a jewel of Formosa,
   And lo ! brought back a strange pale light,

Flitting, flitting—round about him,
   Now in his eyes, now in his hair ;
Not so much it seemed to flout him,
   As all the world beside to scare.

Certain it was, that from that time,
   Whate'er he said, whate'er he did,
Though called by common mortals " crime,"
   Was puffed from Cadiz to Madrid.

Then his wisdom was so solid,
   It turned to lead ; the lightest joke
Won him votes at Valladolid
   To be Lord Rector of Pig-poke !

Among the Cortes, made him first,
   In legislative foodledom,
To gag the masses, who had cursed
   Hereditary noodledom.

From the Escurial's treasured tomes,
   He excavated dead men's brains,
As the free bee all Flowerland roams,
   And hives *their* sweetness for its pains.

So, too, Pomposo culled a thought,
   And then a quip, now here, now there ;
And thus his wondrous works were wrought
   From out a harvest sown elsewhere.

Soon he hived—'tis true, *not* honey,
   But what's more sweet, though join'd with moon !
Which was heaps of golden money,
   That bought the sun of Fortune's noon.

The world all cried, " Oh ! how clever !
   Surely *he'll* live when Spain's no more ? "
Echo woke, and yawned out, " Never !
   Pray give poor Spain a loud *encore !* "

The great man turned upon his heel,
   To give his genius wider scope ;
He made a progress through Castile ;
   Boors asked how HE ! " was off for soap " ?

DON POMPOSO FANFAROSO
   Could not brook such low-bred Spanish !
So where Guadalquiver flows O !—
   Presto ! he thought fit to vanish !

'Tis true, strange noises in the air
   Make crones think he still inhabits
One of his many castles there,
   And perhaps is shooting rabbits !

Empécinados, with their mules,
   In those awful mountain passes
(Being themselves such arrant fools),
   Treat the poor things just like asses ;

And fright them forward with his name
   As the shades of evening close in,
So deathless is the tide of fame !
   Such strange channels still it flows in !

And mothers, with unruly brats,
   That *will* talk, and shun repose O !
Cry out, " Hobgoblins ! owls ! and bats !
   Here's POMPOSO ! FANFAROSO !

To " point a moral " without fail
   Requires the reader to be warned ;
And he who now " adorns *this* tale "
   Perchance may be by *tail* adorned !

TO THE SAME.

" November 29th, 1859.

" For the last four days I have been in terrible affliction,
crying my eyes out, which always makes me seriously ill in
other ways. I must have told you of that dear, kind, good
Samaritan Mrs. Jermyn, whom I had never seen, but who,
when I published my 'Appeal,' upon an average twice a week
kept sending me £10 notes, pretending, dear angel of a
woman, that she had sold single numbers of it for that,
and who, when I was incarcerated in the madhouse, sent

Miss Ryves £50 for lawyers, and told her to ask for whatever more was wanted, and who, in fact, has been heaping kindnesses of every description on me ever since. Well, after a second fit of apoplexy, she died, a ready-made angel if ever there was one, last Friday at Leamington. I could not have believed it possible to have grieved as I have done for a person one had never seen and only known as one knows God, from the help and blessings one receives from them."

TO THE SAME.

"*December* 24*th*, 1859.

"Quite ill with suspense ; not a word from Mr. Hawke, good, bad, or indifferent."

TO THE SAME.

"*January* 28*th*, 1860.

"I received this morning a kind note from Mr. Cole. He had called twice on Mr. Hawke without being able to see him. He says he will persevere till he catches Mr. Hawke, and will 'pitch into him,' and not fail to let me know the result. As for Mr. Hawke, he is a legal riddle that the Sphinx itself could not solve. I wrote to him four days ago, insisting upon no longer being kept in the dark as to what so vitally concerned me, or else on having all my papers back, that I might employ some one else; still no answer! If hope deferred maketh the heart sick, what must despair prolonged do ?"

TO THE SAME.

"*February* 18*th*, 1860.

"I am so ill from this inhumanly prolonged suspense that I have neither heart nor strength to write. It is very easy to talk of exposing such conduct, but without money, and without a man of any kind belonging to me, how is it to be done ? I do think it is a burning shame of Mr. Cole not to have written again before this; and as for the vulture that preyed on the vitals of Prometheus, it was a tame sparrow compared to the Hawke that is preying upon mine."

Lady Lytton again travelled to London in the middle of March, in the hope of getting her affairs finally settled. She had a very unsatisfactory interview with Mr. Hawke, who seemed to have done practically nothing during the past nine months, and returned to Taunton on the 17th in a more hopeless frame of mind than ever. And so the dreary business went on.

To Dr. Price.

"*April 9th*, 1860.

"I told Mr. Hawke I *must* have my bill and my papers back, and we must proceed with our action against Clarke,* and I wrote a month ago requesting Dr. Roberts to follow up Mr. Hawke and see this was. done, but from neither of them have I had any sign since, and unless I break into Mr. Hawke's office and steal my papers, I don't really see how I am to get them. . . . I had such a present last Thursday, a most beautiful and thorough-bred Blenheim. The gentleman who sent him to me from Woodstock says that when the Duchess of Marlborough saw what a perfect beauty he was she did not like his leaving Blenheim. I have christened my doggie Daisy, feeling I shall soon have a daisy quilt over me."

To the Same.

"*April 12th*, 1860.

"I am worried to death, and have been drained dry by the active infamy of my enemies and the passive folly of my friends ; and I am both grieved and heartily ashamed at being only able to send you £5 this quarter out of the £10 you so kindly lent me to go to town last month. You talk, dear Dr. Price, of employing some respectable solicitor. *Imprimis*, where find such a thing, more especially nailed down here as I am? Every journey is ruinous to me in point of expense, as I am not like a

---

* For having published a second edition of Lady Lytton's novel "Very Successful" without her authority.

man, who can go alone, and always have two or three people to pay for. I am, morever, in a cruelly false position, hampered with a beggarly title, and in a sphere of life from which I reap only imposition and disadvantages of every sort, so that I can compare my whole life to nothing but ascending, or rather in vain trying to ascend, a slippery mountain of ice, so heavily laden that even walking on smooth ground would be difficult."

CHAPTER XXV.

CONTINUED STRUGGLES.

At the end of May I again find Lady Lytton in London, endeavouring to obtain a settlement of her dispute with Mr. Clarke, the publisher, and also to wind up her business with Mr. Hawke, from whom she was still unable to obtain any satisfaction. She writes to Dr. Price :—

"I thought I had explained to you long ago that last year I took counsel's opinion, which was all in my favour, and made my copyright over to what in law is called a 'next friend,' to sue Clarke, so that my married woman fetters are thereby knocked off, which makes Mr. Hawke's conduct the worse. But I will not leave his office without my papers this time."

To the Same.

"Great Western Hotel, London,
" *May 29th,* 1860.

"In the morning by ten I was at that attorney's office. He was out of town. I then went to Dr. Roberts. He said the last time he had seen Mr. Hawke he said, 'he did not really see what he could do in Clarke's affair,' though he had told Mr. Cole five months ago that 'it was all right, and he should go into Court with that;' and in February, when I was there, after first telling me the lie that he did not think I cared about it, which was what I alone employed him for a year ago, the rest being his own volunteering, his last words were: 'Oh, well, I'll go on with it !' . . . . Yesterday I dined with the Tylers, and at nine this morning I was at Dr. Roberts' door, and at Clarke's in Paternoster Row at half-past nine. They pretended he was out. Dr. Roberts wrote him a note, saying he must produce the written authority he pretended he had from me for republishing 'Very Successful,' or the law must take its course. By three o'clock Dr. R. receives a letter, saying he had bought the copyright of 'Cheveley' from Mr. Bull, as I and everyone else knows he had, and then it turned out Dr. Roberts, in his muddle, had written 'Cheveley' instead of 'Very Successful;' and this is a pretty good type of the clear and zealous way in which all my business is done, and so the matter rests for the present. . . . . I appointed a quarter-past four for Dr. R. to go with me again to Mr. Hawke's. . . . . The attorney could not look me in the face. I said, 'I have come for my papers, and I mean to have them.' 'I have told Dr. Roberts you shall have them to-morrow.' 'I am tired of your to-morrows, and must and will have them *now* if I stay here all night.' 'Then you may stay here all night,' said the fellow; 'for you sha'n't have them.' 'Mr. Cole,' I said, 'ought to be ashamed of himself to place me in such hands and then leave me. What a set I have had to deal with!' 'Oh yes! Everyone ill-uses you,' he answered with a grin. 'That,' said I, 'is the only truth I have ever heard you utter;' whereupon he put on his hat, walked out of the office, and left me and Dr. Roberts there, and so the matter rests. Dr. Roberts is now furious with Sir Liar, and that blackguard Mr. Edwin James, and owns he has been regularly sold, but when I warned him of that long ago I was not listened to."

TO THE SAME.

"*June 1st,* 1860.

"I returned here at three yesterday morning in a deluge of rain, so stiff from my increased cold that I could scarcely turn in bed. Of course, the first step is to get Mr. Hawke's bill and have it taxed, which is what I have in vain been trying to do for the last five months. The great thing is to bell the cat, but who is to do it? As a proof of Dr. Roberts' practical lucidity, he said to me the other day, after telling me that Sir E. still gave out that I was quite deranged, and that my appearance was something too disgusting, 'I'd give my right hand if you were in London going out everywhere. That would be the true and effectual way to crush him.' 'And,' replied I, 'I would give both my hands if you would in any way point out to me the means of doing this, which I have been aware all along is precisely what I ought to do; but Sir E., being equally aware of this, takes good care that I should not have those means, and you all quietly let him do so.' "

To THE SAME.

"*June 8th*, 1860.

"As for a maid I would, you may be sure, have had one long ago, could I in any way have afforded to do so. It is not the wages, which would have been saved over and over again in needlework, but Mrs. Clarke charges 15s. a week for their board. Moreover, you must know when I was in the Pyrenees two years ago Mr. Lytton sentimentalised greatly over a poor lame girl of fifteen, whom he proposed taking to Paris with us; but I, delighted to recognise and encourage such humane feelings in him, put this poor young girl into a convent at Luchon, not to be a nun, but to be boarded, educated, and clothed. This, I need not tell you, as things have turned out, is a great drain upon me, but, of course, I cannot vent my trials upon this poor girl, but must continue, as long as I live, to provide for her.* So you see, dear Dr. Price, there can be no maid nor even a drive during the summer months for me."

To THE SAME.

"*June 13th*, 1860.

"I wrote on Monday to Mr. Cole, telling him how cruel and ungentlemanly I thought his conduct in placing me

* This is only a single instance of Lady Lytton's unselfish generosity. She was for ever stinting herself to relieve distress in others, and thereby incurred the charge of reckless extravagance from her enemies.—L. D.

in such hands as Mr. Hawke's, then coolly leaving me, and not even having the common courtesy to answer my urgent letters. Yesterday I received a long letter from him, expressing his regret that he should have recommended Mr. Hawke, of whom he knew nothing but in a business way, but that, if he might presume to advise, it would be for my trustee instantly to bring an action against Hawke for detaining my papers, of which action he would have to pay the costs. I forwarded this letter to Dr. Roberts."

To the Same.

"*June 18th*, 1860.

"I have had a letter of apology from Mr. Cole, owning how very wrong he has been ; therefore, I have forgiven him, as I do every one who *owns* they are wrong."

To the Same.

"*June 22nd*, 1860.

"I have written three times to Dr. Roberts, requesting one line to know whether he has commenced proceedings against Mr. Hawke, but not a single answer have I had."

To the Same.

"*June 27th*, 1860.

"I this morning at length received a much-ado-about-nothing letter from Dr. Roberts. He begins by saying he has not had time to attend to anything but his professional duties, but that he *had* commenced proceedings against Mr. Hawke, who had not sent in his bill, but said he wanted between £30 and £40, and would then give up my papers. . . . I told Dr. Roberts, that had he eighteen months ago, as I begged of him, written to Mr. Ironside, sending him my own written and positive denial to Captain Jones of ever having given Clarke leave to re-issue 'Very Successful,' with Clarke's counter-statement, or had he, as every one says it was his bounden duty to do, written not a courteous and palavering letter to Sir Edward, but a stringent and determined one, I should never have been driven into Mr. Hawke's clutches at all ; and even had he, Dr. Roberts, four months ago, as I prayed of him, pro-

ceeded against this fellow, or made an effort to obtain my
papers from him, I should have been spared the, to me,
ruinous expense of a second journey to London. . . .
I think Mr. Cole will be a little surprised at Mr. Hawke's
proceedings."

To the Same.

"*July 2nd*, 1860.

" Dr. Roberts is now trying to get out of even attempting to get my papers from Mr. Hawke. . . . . He writes
that he is so ' stung ' at my accusing him of double dealing
—which I never did accuse him of, but merely of verbal
sugar and water—that ' he must decline any farther
interference in my affairs beyond what concerns the trust.'
I have written to Mr. Cole, saying that, as it is very certain
Dr. Roberts will persevere in his cruel course of doing
nothing, I must beg of him, Mr. Cole, to really act for me
in this affair, for which I will send him an adequate fee in
October."

Extract from Letter of Mr. Cole to Lady Lytton.

" I return you the doctor's letter. Mr. Hawke's demand is
simply absurd ; he will find great difficulty in making it out
even on paper, and will never obtain it on taxation. What
your trustee ought to do is instantly to take out a summons
at Judges' Chambers, citing Mr. Hawke to show cause why
he does not send in his bill that it may be taxed, and
instantly deliver up your documents. This would bring
him to his bearings at once. It is really abominable that
you should be so harassed, and I feel truly sorry I should
have been in any way the means of bringing you in contact
with this man."

It will easily be seen from the foregoing extracts
how persistent was the ill-fortune which attended
Lady Lytton in the choice of her so-called friends
and legal advisers, and how financially ruinous was
the result of all her struggles to obtain justice

Endless lawyers' bills, repeated journeys to London, the machinations of her enemies and the apathy of her friends—all constituted a perpetual drain upon her scanty resources, which made her life a long struggle against embarrassment and poverty. After her dealings with Mr. Hawke, she employed Mr. Cole to conduct her affairs, not as a friend, but as a barrister. She writes to Dr. Price : " I cannot consent to be under any obligation to him, so I have told him that the fact of his not acting for me professionally is an additional reason why I have no right to encroach upon his time, and as I am to have my parish allowance to-morrow, I borrowed £10 from Mrs. Clarke and enclosed it to him, telling him it was useless to return it to me as it would only give me the additional trouble of continuing to send it." Mr. Cole employed a new solicitor, Mr. Comyn.

To Dr. Price.

" *July 18th*, 1860.

" Indeed, dear Dr. Price, it is not either kindness or generosity that makes me send Mr. Cole such a fee for doing nothing but having put me into the hands of Mr. Hawke and coolly left me there much longer than, according to my notions of right and wrong, he ought to have done. No, it is pride, which will not allow me to accept even half an hour of a man's time, unless I can approve of his conduct. There is not another man in England besides your dear noble-minded self from whom I would condescend to accept the most humiliating of all services, *i.e.*, pecuniary ones."

To the Same.

" *August 2nd*, 1860.

" I am told I want total change of air and scene : very likely, but there is much use in telling a poor wretch this

who has been literally so skinned that she cannot even
afford as much change of air as a drive into the country
would give her. Not a word from Mr. Cole! The other
day Foden Lawrence, a Quaker upholsterer here, and one of
my firmest allies and fighters in the incarceration of 1858,
wrote to Sir E. himself for his little bill of £5, which Mr.
Hyde omitted to pay. Sir E. wrote him a contemptible
quibble back, that he should apply to my trustees to pay it
out of my allowance, as he was not responsible for any of
my debts, as if it had been a new one! This production
Lawrence enclosed to Dr. Roberts in a very stringent but
respectful letter, telling him it was his bounden duty, as my
trustee, to enforce the payment of these paltry debts, and
that, if he would not do his duty, he, Lawrence, would by
suing Sir E. in the county court."

To the Same.

"*August 5th*, 1860.

"In reply to Lawrence the Quaker's letter, Dr. Roberts
has written to say that his (Lawrence's) bill not having
been on the original list, he fears they won't pay it. Meanwhile Lawrence has a letter from that scamp Edwin James,
saying that Hyde should pay his bill, and I wish you could
have seen the letter he wrote to the Q.C. yesterday, saying,
'If I could be surprised at anything thee did, I should be
surprised at thy foolish and Sir E. Lytton's contemptible
quibble: he affecting to think this a fresh bill incurred by
his wife, and referring me to her trustees to get it paid.
Were it so there would be no necessity for such roundabout
proceedings, as she always pays her bills punctually, and,
moreover, scrupulously fulfils her promises. Thee cannot
surely suppose that the men of Taunton forget the disgraceful
and illegal kidnapping and incarceration in June 1858, as our
indignant zeal it was that stirred up the general public to
insist upon her release; neither do they ignore that one of
the chief motives for this much-injured lady consenting to
hush up that disgraceful business was the solemn promise
that all her debts should be instantly paid, and though she

may be fettered into not publicly exposing that iniquity, for which she might have recovered such heavy damages, from the fear of irrevocably injuring her son, thee must remember that others are not impeded by any such obstacles, and a creditable figure thee and thy client, Sir E. Lytton, would cut in the county court.'"

To the Same.

"August 15th, 1860.

"I am well aware that God can at all times and in all places, and under all circumstances, at His own good pleasure, work wonders; but I know that my besetting sin has been kicking against the pricks, that is, not sufficiently remembering while writhing under the blows that, after all, the secondary causes which so persecute and maltreat us are but God's instruments, and could have no power over us, were it not His will, to which we *must* submit, and ought to bow. But one is but human, and in the heat of a cruel, and, humanly speaking, unjust and unequal contest, it is hard at all times to act up to this conviction! However, I do hope that, through God's mercy, what began in despair is now fructifying into resignation with me, and, instead of unavailing lamentations over all my withered gourds, I can kneel down among them and pray, 'Thy will be done.' No tidings of the barrister or attorney."

To the Same.

"August 21st, 1860.

" Last Friday I had another severe blow on hearing of the death of that aunt of the Queen's, that dear, kind Grand Duchess Anne. Nothing could exceed her great and constant kindness to me during the five years I was in Switzerland; indeed, the few valuable ornaments I still possess which have not been melted down to pay swindling attorneys and supply my daily bread were her gifts. I think her liking for me began in heartfelt sympathy, as a greater and meaner brute, with one exception, than that Grand Duke Constantine, her husband, could not be. Unlike her

THE GRAND DUCHESS ANNE.

sister, the Duchess of Kent, she had, besides her great beauty, that greatest of all charms,—the sweetest of sweet voices; a truer heart, brighter soul, or nobler mind never went to heaven. She can but gain by the change; but oh! how additionally dark and cold the world looks and feels when these pure unworldly spirits quit it to return home! Poor soul, she was but a few days ill, and her death was as gentle and lovely as her life had been. Peace be with her!

*   *   *   *   *

Dr. Roberts will be rather surprised to hear, as he will to-day, that Foden Lawrence, the Quaker, by going properly to work has got his money. The way in which Lawrence won the battle was this. In reply to his letter, the copy of which I sent you, the Q.C. wrote an inane bluster, saying he always treated intimidation with contempt, but would consult his co-trustee about paying the bill. Of this the Quaker took no notice; but three days later served Sir E. with a writ! Yesterday, so that the letter must have been written on Tuesday, which shows the fright they were in, comes another letter from Mr. Edwin James, enclosing a cheque for the money, but with a last dying flourish, saying he paid it, though 'morally and legally Sir E. was not obliged to pay it.' To which asinine lie Lawrence, in enclosing his receipt, returns the following reply, ' Law and equity, as we all know, are two very different things; but I always thought that when a person made a solemn promise, they were morally bound to abide by it; and had not thy client, Sir E. Lytton, solemnly promised in 1858 to pay all his wife's debts, I should not have sent in my claim. Such being the case, I am sorry to have been kept two years applying for my bill, and ultimately been compelled to serve thy client with a writ, which has at last ensured the payment of my claim; but if he is not legally obliged to pay. it, thee must be no lawyer to have allowed him to pay it, and that in all haste when compelled to do so.' My belief is that, were the invasion really to take place to-morrow, the Quakers would be the only people who would show fight, John Bright and the rest of the Peace Society at the head of them!'"

To the Same.

"*September* 21*st*, 1860.

" Of course, I was obliged to employ another solicitor here to write to Mr. Ironside touching Clarke's allegation of his having made him, Clarke, a present of all my copyrights. At first he did not answer, and at last wrote to Mr. Easton to say that he had given a full explanation to Dr. Roberts, and referred him to the latter. Upon Mr. Easton writing to Dr. Roberts, and desiring that Mr. Ironside's letters on the subject might be sent to me, an answer comes from a clerk or someone, saying Dr. R. had gone abroad. Oh, how I wish I had some enterprising person who would get up a penny subscription throughout England for me, and then I might hope to weather at least this pecuniary fleecing, and effectually expose the shufflers! . . . I only wish I had been at Naples at the Marylebone mountebank's * advent, and I'd have got my friends, the Lazzaroni, to whom I used to give a dinner, *i.e.*, a ton of macaroni once a fortnight, to give him the reception he deserves."

To the Same.

"*September* 26*th*, 1860.

" I wrote to Mr. Cole again to-day to know when this cruel farce was to end. . . . If you can read novels *do* read ' The Woman in White ' by Wilkie Collins. It will remind you slightly of my history. Sir Percival Glyde and Count Fosco are very pretty rascals as far as they go, but mere sucking doves compared to the fiends I have to deal with."

To the Same.

"*September* 30*th*, 1860.

" You need not tell me to avoid stimulants,† as I never drink anything but water, for two excellent reasons, one of which would suffice. Imprimis, I cannot afford anything else, and, secondly, nothing else agrees with me half so well."

* Mr. Edwin James.

† One of the most cruel and unfounded charges brought against Lady Lytton by her enemies was that she occasionally gave way to habits of intoxication. Upon this point see Appendix II.—L. D.

To the Same.

"*October 5th*, 1860.

" I send you Mr. Cole's last letter. I shudder at the prospect of the additional expense and infamy that awaits me. I wonder what was the affidavit I was to make. However, Mr. Comyn was right in saving me the expense of another journey to London, seeing how I have been beggared in this way already. I had a great shock yesterday morning in receiving a letter in an unknown hand, with an enormously broad black edge. It was to announce the death on that morning, the 3rd inst., of poor Mr. Alfred Chalon, the painter."

To the Same.

"*October 13th*, 1860.

" I have had another blow in the sudden death of that poor Admiral Gordon, that kind friend of my childhood, that I told you of a fortnight ago, that Lord Blayney brought me the message from. I was planning to go and see him and his wife in the spring. To show you the strength and universal ramification of the deeply organised and chronic conspiracy against me, I must tell you that, finding all the cruel expenses into which Sir L. was as usual plunging me, I last October got ready a one volume book to be out by Christmas, for £100, which it ought to have brought, would have been salvation to me. It was not a novel, and had nothing that could be construed into personality, but was a series of essays. This I wrote under the name of Robert Denham, and sent it to Judge Haliburton, to get published for me. He and Mrs. Haliburton thought very highly of it, and he sent it to Bentley, who kept it six weeks, professed himself delighted with it, but insisted upon knowing the author's real name. The moment he heard it was mine he shuffled out of publishing it, saying his engagements would not allow him to do so! Nothing daunted, six months ago I returned to the charge, and got the MS. copied, so that my writing, which is well known to the trade, might not betray me, for which I paid three pounds. I then begged of a lady of whom I knew little and who is quite out of my beat of acquaintances, and, therefore, not likely to be suspected of being my agent, to try and have the goodness to dispose of the MS. for me. I gave her the whole history of Judge H.'s failure with Bentley, that she might avoid this Charybdis. Well, would you believe it, this woman wrote me word about six weeks ago, saying, 'I hope I have not done wrong, but I have sent your MS. to Bentley!'"

To the Same.

"*October 15th*, 1860.

"No parish allowance yet. The contemptible cowards! I despise them too cordially to fear them, and this is at once my battle-axe and my shield, and as for my 'violent language,' so shocking to ears polite, it is my only safety-valve, my only relief. For, gorged as I am with ever-increasing and never-redressed outrages and insults, I should have burst long ago but for it. Well can I sympathise with, and enter into the explosive feelings of, that old gentleman of whom Montaigne tells us, who, being a martyr to gout, was ordered as he valued his life to abstain from provocations of it, such as hams, tongues, Bologna sausages, and all salt meats. 'Abstain from them!' he roared, 'Never, sir, never! I should die if I had not those damned hams and tongues to swear at as the cause of all my sufferings.'"

To the Same.

"*October 17th*, 1860.

"Parish allowance come. I am really ashamed always to encroach upon your generous kindness by still continuing five pounds in your debt, and being only able to send you ten pounds, the half of which is enclosed. I am *only* seventy-eight pounds behindhand with poor good Mrs. Clarke, which is a serious grief to me, and then Mr. Hawke's bill hanging over me—what is to become of me God only knows. You will say that there is no end to my luck when I tell you that I had a letter from a lady who tells me Mr. Chalon had made a will, and she believes had left me two or three thousand pounds; but, owing to his having made it himself, and it not having been witnessed, it is invalid, and all his beautiful pictures, instead of going as he left them, will be sent to the hammer. But what I think far worse, his poor, old, faithful Swiss servant, who had worn out his life with him, will be left unprovided for."

To the Same.

"*October 26th*, 1860.

" I tried to write to you yesterday, but was prostrated by one of my splitting headaches, which was by no means relieved by a rigmarole from Mr. Cole, and Mr. Hawke's bill. I do not see how, unless he had quadrupled the 6s. 8d.'s, he could have inflated it more. . . . As to Mr. Hawke's making a fancy demand of £30 or £40 to Dr. Roberts, and then another of £60 to Mr. Comyn, that only proves what sort of a man he is. . . . I sent Mr. Cole a list of the papers sent to Mr. Hawke, and said that when they were returned I would pay the extortionate bill. I also begged to know how much I was in Mr. Comyn's debt, which, of course, will be another £10, and, as I shall have at least that sum to pay the little attorney here, Mr. Easton, you may guess the more than terrible state I should be in but for your generous kindness. . . . That £10 that Mr. Cole mentions as Mr. Comyn having to my credit, is the £10 I sent Mr. Cole, which he would not take, but which saved me nothing, as I ordered him a very handsome silver tankard which cost me £12, for I certainly could not remain under an obligation to a man who has acted as he has done."

To the Same.

"*November 1st*, 1860.

" I, alas! have it not in my power to do good to anyone beyond the very poor, properly so-called, and when one sees the joy that a single sovereign, or even half a one, with a few old clothes can create in a destitute family, one cannot help wondering that those who have the means, and spend thousands upon pictures and old masters, have no

fancy to lay out a few pounds upon originals and God's
servants. . . . Mr. Cole now expresses a fear that Mr.
Hawke will still persist in not giving up my papers. I
wrote, 'What, then, in the name of horsehair and humbug
is the use of the judge farce, if the said judge cannot
compel the fellow to disgorge his prey ? As for Mr. Comyn,
I know no more of him than he does of my business. He
may, for aught I know, be an angel in parchment ; but all I
contend for is, that, were it six, four, three, two, or even one
month since Mr. Comyn had been employed, after Mr.
Hawke's eighteen months' lies and game at hide-and-seek,
he, Mr. Comyn, should not have wasted his own time and
my patience in calling, waiting, and asking this fellow for
my papers, but should at once have done what he has done
now, whatever that was, as it instantly produced that fancy
article, his bill.' . . . In my former letter I said to Mr.
Cole that I did him the justice to believe he was quite
incapable of actively and knowingly aiding and abetting
this iniquitous conspiracy, but he must remember that
'evil is wrought by want of thought as well as by want
of heart.'"

To the Same.

"November 15th, 1860.

"I now send you Dr. Roberts' last letter. You must
bear in mind that two years ago, on my return from abroad,
in the teeth of Mr. Ironside's solemn denial of ever having
given Clarke permission to republish my works, Dr. R.
told me he could not force or induce Clarke to produce
his written authority. Yet six months ago he went through
the farce of writing to Clarke, and the authority was said
to have been produced, though I never saw it. Dr. R.
then wrote me word he had written to Mr. Ironside, who
owned having given Clarke the permission. Whereupon,
in the teeth of his former denial, I naturally asked to see
this letter, but of this request, though thrice repeated, the
doctor took no notice. Now, observe, he says to Mr.
Easton he has lost the letter, and Mr. Ironside says it was
so long ago (two years !) that he really cannot remember

whether he had given Clarke leave to republish the books or not. Couple this with Hawke's pretending, first, that he had sent Captain Jones' letter containing Ironside's denial back to me, or to Miss Boys, then, that he had never had it, and, lastly, that he had lost it, and you will own that a more precious set of traitors never lived!"

TO THE SAME.

"December 17th, 1860.

"The enclosed little epigram was written by the Chief Baron, Sir F. Pollock, who gave it to Judge H., but he, not daring to corrupt my morals openly, gave it to his wife to send to me. I forward it to you in the hope that you, like me, will be bad enough to laugh heartily at it.

"'On the Court of Queen's Bench, in Dublin, committing Miss Aylward to the Richmond Bridewell, for contempt of court in refusing to produce a child under a writ of Habeus Corpus. That prison is appropriated to men only.

> "'"In most earthly tribunals some harshness prevails,
> But the Irish Queen's Bench is both prudent and mild;
> Miss Aylward they sent to a prison for males,
> As the likeliest way of producing a child." ' "

The bulk of Lady Lytton's debts had now been paid off, but she was left saddled with the burden of lawyers' and other bills which she had been compelled to incur in order to enforce her rights, and from this state of embarrassment she never contrived, in spite of the most rigid economy, to extricate herself. On February 13th, 1861, she writes :—

"Mrs. Tyler writes me word that she has *not* been paid."

Again, March 13th :—

"Alas! you are quite right. I am **eaten up with interest** and eternal payment of arrears."

To Dr. Price.

"*May 17th*, 1861.

" Much to my surprise, I receive a letter from Mr. Watkins, the Queen's photographer, saying, that having attended the sale of poor Mr. Chalon's pictures at Christie's, he had bought Mr. Chalon's last picture of me, and as he thought I ought to have it, he would sell it to me for less than to any one else, viz., £15. I wrote back, saying, I would buy it, but could not do so until the middle of next October, if he would keep it till then. This morning I got the enclosed very civil letter from him, and a dozen small photos done from Chalon's head, which is life-size. . . . The man in the paragraph does not allude to the right man in the right place, but to Colonel or Mr. Stewart. Dizzy having mustered the lame, the halt, the mad, and blind for the great sham fight on the Budget, this Mr. Stewart, the member for Cambridge, was there with his keeper, and Lord Adolphus Vane Tempest with his, both returning back to their respective asylums as soon as they had voted. But why not madmen as well as fools ? "

To the Same.

" *May 26th*, 1861.

" If you have not burnt my letters, as I told you once or twice before, please put them all in any common deal box and send them to me, for, as I am writing my miserable life that the truth may at least be known after I am gone, there may be incidents in them that would save me the trouble of rewriting."

The above is the last letter to Dr. Price which I can find. I presume the rest were burnt.

CHAPTER XXVI.

FAILURE OF VARIOUS SCHEMES FOR RELIEF.—DR KENEALY.

DURING the next few years of Lady Lytton's life nothing occurred of any special interest or importance. She continued to live on at Taunton down to 1873, the date of Lord Lytton's death, as, in spite of the lonely and humdrum nature of her existence there, she felt at all events comparatively safe from fresh plots and conspiracies. The greater part of her debts was indeed discharged, but some remained unpaid, more especially the interest of a sum of £400 lent to her by Lady Blackburne, which she could not in honour leave unpaid. In consequence of this obligation, she was again compelled to borrow money at ruinous interest, and afterwards, in 1874, being then seventy-two years of age, she finally arranged for a loan through an insurance office of sufficient amount to defray all remaining claims; but this reduced her annuity of £500 a year by £256 a year, so that she had left only £244 a year for her own use. In the summer of 1864 Lady Lytton left the Giles Castle Hotel, and took up her residence at a small house, " Brenton Villa," where she remained during the rest of her stay at Taunton.

I will pass on to the year 1867, when a new

scheme for the amelioration of Lady Lytton's condition was first mooted. She had drawn up a full
and unreserved statement of her wrongs in 1866,
when a literary gentleman made a request in the
press that all experiences of unjust or illegal incarceration in asylums should be sent to him. In an evil
hour, Lady Lytton forwarded a statement of her case
to this gentleman, who, however, made no use of it.
It was now proposed that this MS., which was never
intended for publication in its original form, should
be revised and amended, and thus utilised in some
way or another for the unfortunate lady's benefit.
In 1884 a gentleman wrote to me :—

"Mrs. ——, who was much interested in the case of
Lady Lytton, invited me to assist in a scheme for its
amelioration. In 1867 Lady Lytton sent me a long statement of her wrongs, which she desired to publish.* Granting
that the details were true, it was still evident that they
contained matter on which to ground unbounded actions
for libel against every one concerned in the publication. I
referred it to Dr. Kenealy, who confirmed my opinion.
We therefore suggested very great modifications, and that
the statement should take the form of a letter to the Queen.
Lady Lytton gave us *carte blanche* as to the alterations.
Dr. Kenealy was then too much engaged in professional
work to lend his aid gratis, and I was going abroad, and
unwilling to undertake so delicate a task alone: So the
matter dropped."

Unhappily, however, the matter did not drop, for

* This is inaccurate. Lady Lytton never meant the MS. to be
published as it stood. It was merely a statement of facts, many of
a sufficiently scandalous nature, which, although true, were only
intended for private cars. In fact, on the inside of the cover of the
MS. was written, "Disseminate these facts everywhere, short of
publication."—L. D.

this very MS. was published, without Lady Lytton's authority or consent, in 1880, under the title of " A Blighted Life."

I will return to this outrage hereafter. Meanwhile I append a few extracts from various letters which contain references to the subject.

" September 26th, 1867.

" I think the statement should begin as from her to a kind and generous public, and be signed with her name. It must be stated that every appeal has been made to him before her being forced to take this painful step. It must also be shown that her grinding poverty prevents her ever going into the Divorce Court, but before we launch this I will ascertain what chance of success she would have in court, or whether she is barred from availing herself of it. I think she wants to get her life written, and a full statement of all she endured would be parading that in a form she does not contemplate. If you are so kind as to revise the ' Madhouse MS.,' as she would call it, I will send it to you."

" October 3rd, 1867.

" The added rank* must make a difference since the deed of separation was drawn up. He has been applied to for help, and been told that a public subscription would be raised, and has only written in reply an insolent letter to Dr. Roberts, the trustee, telling him he will not pay a farthing, and that he (Dr. Roberts) does not do his duty as trustee, as he ought to prevent her getting into debt, and save him (Lord L.) from being worried.

" There is one thing in your friend's letter which is quite wrong. She says, ' She must be coarse-minded.' You may take my word for it she is not. I think thirty years of brooding over her miseries and wrongs has brought her to hate and despise the shams of society so much that she has brought herself into the contrary habit, and so calls a liar a liar, and a villain a villain, and so on. . . . I can but

* Sir Edward was created Lord Lytton in 1866.

do my best, and cannot leave her to starve, and I can't see
how she can get on. She says that by her next quarter she
will have to receive only about £20. Now she would rather
starve herself than let those dependent on her want, for
instance, this poor dying maid, who stood by her through
all her troubles till she was forced to part with her.* Lady
Lytton is not a woman at the best who can rough it, as it
is called, and now, the greater part of her time in bed and
suffering, she is quite helpless. I am looking for a letter
to send you which gives an idea of the true feeling such a
person as she has, banished to a spot void of anything like
intellectual society. All there is on the lowest scale of
country-townism. She says it is terrible to contrast this
life with what her early years were, when she lived amongst
and mixed in all that was high and courtly, not only in
social position, but in intellectual life. At Louis Philippe's
court she was ever most welcome ; the Queen Amélie took
her especially to her *heart*, I was going to say, but received
and protected her. Paris was the only place in which her
husband could not succeed in crushing her. Lord Aylmer
stood her friend, and the King and Queen. You must
remember that this unfortunate woman had a little property
of her own, which was probably the reason of his marrying
her, as it gave him his qualification for Parliament, which
his mother was too avaricious to give him. To bar dower
he settled £1,000 on her, and then, wanting money on some
occasion, he asked her to give up this settlement, and his
brother, William Bulwer, being the only remaining trustee,
gave it up. Thus she was at his mercy, as he often reminded her. She was not a penniless girl when she married,
for her property was £300 odd a year. All this should go
into the statement."

Under the date of October 10th, 1867, I find a
long letter from Dr. Kenealy to a friend, advising
Lady Lytton to proceed for a divorce, and assuring

---

* Lady Lytton allowed this maid, who died of a long and painful
illness, £20 a year.

her that no funds were necessary, as the husband would have to pay all expenses. He also expresses a desire to know whether there was any truth in the report which Lord Lytton sedulously propagated that his wife had herself committed adultery, and was thereby debarred from taking any action against him, and advises that before publishing the proposed account of his behaviour her friends should try to ascertain if Lord Lytton had any chance of proving his allegations.

As a matter of fact, the real reason why Lady Lytton shrank from divorce proceedings was a promise she had made to her son while she was incarcerated in the madhouse. The libels which Lord Lytton promulgated about his wife were utterly destitute of foundation, and as cruel as they were baseless.

Dr. Kenealy subsequently wrote on October 13th :—

"I am very much pleased with your packet of notes received this morning, the postscript to one of which leaves no doubt on my mind that I have been misinformed, and redoubles my indignation against a wretch capable of so vile and odious a falsehood, disseminated, I have no doubt, widely, and emanating directly from himself at his own table."

In the following a lady plainly informs Lady Lytton of the slanders which were current against her :—

"*October 29th*, 1867.

"MY DEAR LADY LYTTON,—

"I think it is best and fairest always to tell the exact truth. One of the gentlemen whom I have interested in your affairs has just come down from town to see me and speak about you. It appears that things are paralysed owing to some reports having been brought to them regarding certain tales which they have been told were public and notorious at Florence regarding your conduct while residing there. They say naturally it would be utter madness, indeed they positively decline having any hand in publishing anything or making any public appeal, unless there can be some absolute denial given to this, and unless they can be put in communication with persons who can absolutely and authoritatively refute the report of misconduct on your part. What am I to say? The mere fact of my simply stating my unbelief is useless. Do pray show me how your innocence of all cause for scandal can be established past contradiction."

FROM A FRIEND.

" *October* 31*st*, 1867.

" I enclose Lady L.'s letter. I am surprised how quietly she has taken this, and also the letter I sent her before of Dr. Kenealy's. I fear you will think that I did too much, as she spoke of the baseness of the accusation in telling her this scandal connected her name with a Mr. ——. I have written in confidence to ask some of Mr. ——'s friends likely to know what was passing at Florence twenty-five years ago."

FROM A FRIEND.

" *November* 4*th*, 1867.

" I send you this letter of Lady Lytton's, as it is all literary, in reply to my asking why she did not do something in the book way for her necessities. You will see how the ground has been cut from under her, as she says, and as you understand these things, you will appreciate the situation. I had asked if any of the tradesmen had entered an action against Lord L.; she at first said she believed not, but she wrote to ——, the money-lender, who has her in his power, and she sends me his letter to-day, saying that they or some of them had entered an action, thinking it would bring Lord L. to. However, that it had not done, and he supposed the action still lies with, he presumes, Lord L.'s appearance against it. He sent her yesterday exactly the moneys she had borrowed. She thought she was borrowing two sums of £750 at ten per cent., whereas she found out afterwards that she had agreed to pay £40 in thirty quarterly instalments, so that in the end she will have paid £1,200 for the £750. She is now so entangled that I do not see how she can be disentangled."

FROM A FRIEND.

"*November*, 1867.

"In reply to your letter relative to the two headings of 'Letter' and 'Narrative,' Lady Lytton says, 'To tell the truth, I don't care how it is done so long as it *is* done.' She wrote from her bed, poor woman, in a handwriting very unlike her usual one. She seems to be very ill. I think she is anxious not only to pay her debts, but to put her name before the world with truth and let it know how ill-used she has been before earth closes over her, and none are left to vindicate her character."

On the 6th of November, 1867, Dr. Kenealy writes to say that he is so overpowered with business as to be quite unable to devote much time to Lady Lytton's proposed letter, but that if she will send her MS., he will correct and revise it. And the MS. was accordingly sent, and subsequently returned to Lady Lytton. No practical result, however, followed these negotiations, and Lady Lytton's hopes were once more doomed to disappointment.

A scheme for a public subscription was eventually abandoned, and neither Dr. Kenealy nor any of the other gentlemen who professed themselves so anxious to serve her cause ever succeeded in finding time or opportunity for advancing it. Meanwhile the unfortunate lady's embarrassments increased instead of diminishing, and the following extracts from her letters to friends may serve to show the despair into which these repeated disappointments had plunged her :—

"BRENTON VILLA, TAUNTON,
"*November 23rd*, 1867.

"Having this morning received, for the first time, a paper of 'headings' or a prospectus of what *ought* to have been done in the matter of my appealing to the public *viâ* a letter to the Queen, like all English plans for the redress of public or private grievances, it is so redolent of *l'esprit du lendemain* that in self-defence I must trouble you with a *resumé* of this more than painful subject. When Mrs. ——, with the kindest intentions, more than two months ago told me she had applied to you to do what neither my too burning and bitter sense of chronic outrage enables me morally to do, nor my present miserable health leaves me power to undertake, I thought it exceedingly kind of her to enlist you in the cause and equally kind of you to be so enlisted. Well, poor Mrs. ——, in her great kindness of heart, *gave* you that MS. narrating my Lord Lytton's mad-house conspiracy, which was written as one would write a private letter, writhing under a sense of cruel wrong, and never, beyond the mere facts, intended for publication.* The first douche of iced water I got in this too cruel phantom of false hope and factitious help was your pious horror, sir, of my 'violent language,' while the unparalleled infamy which had caused it did not seem to elicit the slightest surprise. The 'certainty' was a poor foundation to build any chance of success upon; nevertheless, when Mrs. —— informed me of this, and said the language must be altered, I gave her *carte blanche* to do this, or, as I wrote, gratefully accepted the offer 'to have my claws cut, and my teeth drawn.'

"Then ensued more talk, more ruinous delays, and up

---

*This statement is highly important, bearing in mind the fact that this MS., under the name of "A Blighted Life," was afterwards published without Lady Lytton's knowledge or authority.—L. D.

sprang a crop of frivolous and vexatious chimerical obstacles, so that I soon perceived that the only efforts being made were those of how *not* to do anything in the matter; next came the *coup de théâtre* of all the Knebworth lies, which were duly conveyed to me, and when I had been effectually tortured and insulted in every way I considered the matter was at an end. Mrs. ——, it is true, wrote me word after this, saying, 'And now I have all my work to do over again.' What this meant I could not tell, but lo! soon after arrives Mr. Kenealy's note about my writing a letter to the Queen, which he would correct, and then came one of Mrs. ——'s telegrams, in which she said, 'If you have not got the headings' (headings of what ?), 'Mr. —— will write them over again.' Now, as this was the very first I had heard of any headings, though they were mentioned as if I was perfectly *au fait* with them, and in the note in which Mrs. —— enclosed Dr. K——'s letter to you there was no reference made to any 'headings,' I felt not only mystified, but insulted, as if all this was done to make my last chance impossible; that this method was resorted to in order to goad me into taking the initiative of ending it, which I did in such a summary way that I have no doubt Dr. Kenealy might do my Lord Lytton further service by endorsing his assertion of my being a mad woman. Mrs. —— also told me in a former letter, 'Mr. —— has arranged all the narrative,' and yet afterwards in another letter telling me she had got the MS. back, she adds, 'It has not been touched.' Now how does that tally with your having arranged it all? and what was I to make out of such a cruel and unfathomable muddle of cross purposes, what but to add another proof of the truth of the old saying, 'Mieux vaut au sage ennemi qu'un maladroit ami'?

"The paper of headings and the prospectus would have been invaluable to me had I received them six weeks ago, whereas, now that the evil and the failure are accomplished, it is only a bitter, cruel, and most superfluous mockery to send them. But it is the old—world-old—story, for history and fate are always repeating themselves. 'Ah, cruel friend, had you *only* written me this letter while I was at Athens,

I should not now be eating figs at Syracuse.' My position is truly frightful, and so imminently perilous that anywhere but in England the very stones might be moved to compassion. I beg, sir, you will accept my apologies for all the trouble you have had in this truly unfortunate affair."

FROM A FRIEND.

"*December 6th*, 1867.

" I spoke to Mr. —— of the bitter disappointment I had had and was forced to inflict upon you. Now I am going to take upon myself to authorise him to lay the deed of settlement before counsel. As we know Lord Lytton cannot lay any charge of adultery against you, *I* have always thought that your best chance was to claim an increase of allowance. At all events, no harm can be done by taking counsel's opinion on the deed.

" I have returned from Chancery Lane ; how can I write what I have to say ? I really am distressed, and more than distressed, to tell you that the whole thing has failed. I had a long interview with the lawyer, but the more he conned over the terms of your settlement the less he could, in common honesty to his clients, recommend them to grant this insurance from the clause empowering Lord Lytton to stop the £500 a year in the event of your doing anything which he might consider annoyance and molestation, thus rendering your settlement liable to contingencies which might arise, and which prevents your settlement from being the slightest security. I am really quite upset by this failure, for I very stupidly did not look on that clause in the light in which I now see it. I am so distressed for you and your disappointment, I can find no words adequately to express my feelings. The lawyer said he had heard from a friend now dead of instances of Lord Lytton's conduct to you which, if his friend had not vouched for the truth of them, he could not have believed. Once he was present on an occasion when Lord Lytton threw a glass of wine in your face."

It was not until 1874, after her husband's death,

that Lady Lyttton was enabled to effect with an insurance office the loan to which the above letter refers.

Dr. Roberts writes :—

"*December 14th*, 1867.

"I am sorry to hear that you have failed in your endeavour to obtain a loan from the insurance office. I cannot devise any means for obtaining the sum Lady Lytton requires. We must, therefore, as a forlorn hope, apply again to Lord Lytton. I have written to his Lordship on the subject."

It is scarcely necessary to add that Dr. Roberts' appeal was again unsuccessful.

CHAPTER XXVII.

"A BLIGHTED LIFE."—CONCLUSION.

LADY LYTTON continued to live at Taunton in the same miserably embarrassed condition until the death of her husband, which took place in January, 1873. In October of the same year, her son offered her an additional allowance of £200 a year, which she at first refused to accept, but was afterwards persuaded by Dr. Roberts and other friends to avail herself of. In the following year (October, 1874), Lady Lytton removed to Upper Norwood, but the house taken for her by her trustee being unsuitable to her requirements, she quitted it early in 1875 for "Glenômera," a small house at Upper Sydenham, where she spent the remaining years of her life. The circumstances under which that allowance was withdrawn in 1880 need a few words of explanation. I have already given some account of the scheme by which it was proposed to lay Lady Lytton's wrongs before the public in the form of a letter to the Queen, and of the part played in it by Dr. Kenealy and other gentlemen. Lady Lytton's MS., which these gentlemen had undertaken to edit and revise, was, as a matter of fact, returned to her absolutely untouched, the plan fell through, and all idea of publishing it was abandoned. But in 1880, to

Lady Lytton's unbounded horror and amazement, this identical MS. appeared in print with her own name attached to it, in its original form, and containing every word of the undoubtedly strong language in which she had detailed her sufferings for the information of her own friends, and not for that of the public. But the facts of the case had better be set forth as she described them, in a pamphlet issued by way of refuting this audacious forgery of her name. The following extracts sufficiently explain the circumstances :—

"That the Dowager Lady Lytton's life has been 'A Blighted Life' is a sad and undoubted truth ; but that she has had any knowledge of, or part in, the publication of a recent work bearing that title, she and those who know all the facts distinctly and most solemnly deny. She was equally amazed and indignant when, many weeks after the appearance of this catch-penny, it came to her knowledge ; and that its editor, not content with the violation of all honour and probity, in pirating and publishing a private correspondence of hers, that had unfortunately been entrusted to Dr. Kenealy in 1866, had actually forged her name on the title-page, as if it had just issued fresh from this poor outraged lady's hands, when in reality the shock of this totally unexpected blow caused her a severe fit of illness. But in order to make the facts of this most iniquitous proceeding intelligible to the reader, these facts must be stated categorically, which shall be done as concisely as lucidity will allow.

"First, premising that the moment the Dowager Lady Lytton heard of this most shameful outrage, she resolved to bring an action against its perpetrator ; but upon consulting her solicitor, she had of course to run the blockade of all the obstacles usually thrown in the way of poor and therefore defenceless women. She was strongly dissuaded from any such course, as it would be sure to give this catch-penny additional sale and circulation, and raise a hornet's nest about her ears.

"She then thought that she would at least have the poor alternative of publishing a disclaimer as to all knowledge of, much less complicity in, this cruel outrage against herself, *viâ* an advertisement in a number of the leading newspapers. But here again she reckoned without her host. The *Times* would not insert it unless some gentleman of standing and position guaranteed the proprietors against an action, not a very easy thing to obtain, as no one cared to be mixed up in such a case. *Bref,* no journal would insert her denial, with one honourable exception, *Truth,* which, true to its name, *did* publish her refutation.

"And now to explain how the Dowager Lady Lytton's letters came to be made so shameful and dishonourable a means of outraging and injuring her.

"So far back as 1866, a literary gentleman made a public appeal, *viâ* the press, to all persons who could furnish him with authentic experiences of unjust and illegal incarceration in madhouses.

"Now as, some eight years before this, the Dowager Lady Lytton, as the public were well aware, had been a very signal instance of this peculiar species of injustice, as public indignation it was which, in three weeks, liberated her from durance, and as she was writhing under all the falsehoods and false promises that had been resorted to to gag her when thus forced *out* of the madhouse, every faith having been broken with her when once the safety of her oppressor had been secured, she, in an evil hour, sent a statement of her case, written in desperate haste, *in every sense* of the term, to this literary 'gentleman,' who was also in such haste to expose the terrible abuses of the lunacy laws, and have them altered, and who kept her statement five months, and then returned it to her, not having stirred a finger to redress her wrongs, or reform the laws in question.

"A friend wishing to know the history of Lady Lytton's incarceration, the latter sent this same statement to her, with a permission to let the truth be known *as widely as possible short of publication.* 'But, oh, the horribly strong and violent language, so unladylike, so unwomanly!' say the readers of that statement. Alas! yes, and deeply do her friends deplore that she should have been goaded into using such, and no one more sincerely deplores it than herself, to whom it has done more harm than any- body else. But if persons would sometimes

> 'Look into their own hearts
> For the key to others' lives,'

it would explain, if not atone, for a great many mysteries now masquerading about the world.

" Just let any impartial and equitable human being for one moment put him or herself in the place of this cruelly outraged and utterly defenceless woman, betrayed on all sides, fresh calumnies continually being disseminated against her, with every channel both of refutation and redress closed to her; what wonder? for indeed the wonder would have been if she had not done so. We repeat it, what wonder, so long and so uniquely tried, if she *had* been goaded past endurance into following Quintilian's rule for forcible writing, *i.e.*, 'always to adapt your language to the subject upon which you are speaking or writing'?

" But to return to this ill-fated MS. The lady to whom Lady Lytton had sent it, with reiterated injunctions that it was not for publication, only as a sort of *mémoire pour servir* for any calm dispassionate statement that might be drawn up on her behalf, in an evil hour, but with the best intentions, sent it to a then rising barrister, and so far no possible blame could be attached to this lady, as the reputation of the barrister in question was at that time unimpeached ; his unenviable notoriety at a later period of his career she could not have foreseen.

" All possible pressure was put on her to let the case go into court, but she had repeatedly assured her friend that no amount of provocation would ever make her consent to that, as eight years before she had promised her son, at the sacrifice of her own interests, that she would never

expose his father in open court. Then the venue was
changed, and the barrister in question was to write a sort
of pamphlet containing a calm judicial statement of the
Dowager Lady Lytton's persecution so far as the phase
of the madhouse conspiracy went, which was already so
notoriously known to the public. 'For,' wrote her friend,
' he says your MS. is so full of libels that it could not be
published.' To which Lady Lytton somewhat indignantly
replied, 'Of course not; for, as I have stringently tried to
impress upon you from the first, it was especially prohibited to be published.'

"Well, at the end of five weeks the rising barrister was
overwhelmed with sorrow! But he found he had such
a press of business that he could not fulfil his promise
about the pamphlet.

"Lady Lytton's friend after this second failure then,
through another gentleman, a mutual friend of hers and
of the barrister's, wanted Lady Lytton to undertake the
pamphlet affair herself, but she, being heartily sick of the
whole thing, explicitly refused to do so. And now comes
the most mysterious and inexplicable part of this iniquitous affair.

"In 1866 her MS. was duly returned to her, and has
been carefully locked up in a despatch box in her
possession ever since; so how any one could come by it
to commit the gross outrage upon her by publishing it,
and springing this mine under her in this present year
1880, passes her and all her friends' comprehension, and
the only conclusion that either she or they can arrive at
is that it must most unwarrantably and dishonourably have
been copied by some person fourteen years ago, when
in the rising barrister's possession."

The pamphlet goes on to mention the additional
allowance of £200 a year granted to his mother
by the present Lord Lytton shortly after his father's
death in 1873, which at first she refused to accept.

"For a year and a half she firmly adhered to this

resolution, despite innumerable schemes and stratagems on the part of her trustee, Dr. Roberts, to beguile her into taking it.* In 1874 this trustee took a house for her at Upper Norwood, and he very kindly, as she thought, insisted on lending her £300 at three per cent., to pay a premium on this house. But ever on her guard about that £200, and aware that the year and a half he had been trying to induce her to take would just make £300, she looked him full in the face and said, ' Now, Dr. Roberts, can you and will you give me your solemn word of honour that this is not Lord Lytton's bitter pill of £200 a year that you are wrapping up in the currant jelly of pretended kindness to get me to swallow ? '

" ' I give you my word of honour,' he replied, ' that it has nothing to do with Lord Lytton's money. Should I take three per cent. from you if it had ? '

" ' Oh ! *cela est un détail*, as the French say, and there is no going to a masquerade without a mask,' said Lady Lytton, still far from satisfied, and before taking this money, she sent a lady to catechise him the next day. To this lady he went through the same *manège*, and assured her that the £300 he had offered Lady Lytton had nothing on earth to do with Lord Lytton's money.

" Lady Lytton at length accepted it, but no sooner had she paid it away to her landlord than her trustee laughed in her face, and owned that this £300 was Lord Lytton's year and a half—£200 a year—adding, ' I knew I should never get you to take it unless I deceived you into it ! ' at which she, poor victim, was naturally most bitterly indignant. ' But,' said her trustee, ' how upon earth can you possibly exist without it ? It is quite bad and difficult enough to pinch on as it is, for since that mortgage of £1,500, you have to pay £64 5s. a quarter, which leaves

---

* In June, 1874, Dr. Roberts saying that he had seen a benevolent old lady who insisted upon Lady Lytton's acceptance of £250, as a small relief from her wants, Lady Lytton endorses the letter, " Poor Dr. Roberts' last attempt to smuggle Lord L——'s £250 into my pocket under the myth of a benevolent old lady's gift ! No, no, that won't do ! ' Marchand d'oignons s'y connaît en ciboules.' "—L. D.

you just £444 a year, including this £200 a year, to struggle hard upon, and you *must* live.'

" Now the effect of the publication of that most iniquitous catch-penny ' A Blighted Life ' was that very shortly after (*i.e.*, last October, when her quarterly pittance was due) her present bankers, Messrs. Coutts, informed her that only £125, viz., her own £500 a year, had been paid in to her account, whereupon the same friend who had thrown herself into the breach about her former banking difficulties went to Coutts's and found such was the fact, so she went from thence to Cavendish Square to Sir S. Scott (Lord Lytton's banker) to inquire the cause of this. They did not know, but informed her Lord Lytton had given orders to reduce the £700 a year paid to the Dowager Lady Lytton to £500.*

* * * * *

" We have only to add that in allowing her friends to make the foregoing statement, the Dowager Lady Lytton has but one motive, one aim, purely and simply in view : certainly not to expose her enemies, but to exonerate herself from the odious calumny of having published that cruel outrage upon herself and violation of all honour and honesty entitled ' A Blighted Life.' "

The pamphlet is endorsed by Lady Lytton as follows : —

" I certify that every circumstance narrated in the foregoing statement is strictly true.

" ROSINA LYTTON, DOWAGER, *December* 15*th*, 1880."

There are but a few more facts to narrate before I close this melancholy history. For the last seven years of her life Lady Lytton resided at a small

---

* This allowance was afterwards renewed by Lord Lytton, presumably because he discovered that his mother had nothing to do with the publication of "A Blighted Life," and paid down to the day of her death.—L. D.

house, "Glenômera," at Upper Sydenham, latterly with only one servant. She rarely left her room, and the house once only during the last five years. Naturally of a too generous disposition,* wholly unselfish, and frequently left to the care of a servant who was equally unable to comprehend or to supply her requirements, she could hardly have lived so long had it not been for friends who commiserated her neglected and desolate condition, and tried to alleviate her sorrows and to supply what were really necessities by assisting her to the utmost extent of their ability. Although in her eightieth year, she possessed to the last the remains of a beauty that had been so noted in her youth Neither her general tone nor manners had deteriorated through adversity, but remained to the last as distinguished as they were polished and winning. She was full of anecdote and wit, and though not reticent on the subject of her wrongs, she never failed to impress upon her hearers a feeling of sadness and regret that so much capacity for all that was loving and affectionate had been so ruthlessly destroyed by neglect, wrong, and persecution. No one can defend some of her published extravagances, but our blame should more justly be laid upon those who abused her highly sensitive nature, and induced those feelings of exasperation under the infliction of wrong which she had no other opportunity to express.

* Numerous letters of gratitude bear witness to her charitable deeds, which were strictly guided by the injunction, "Let not thy right hand know what thy left hand doeth." Even when in very straitened circumstances, and up to the day of her death, she assisted a relative of her husband, who is still living.—L. D.

Worn out by sorrow, afflicted with much bodily suffering, and tormented with constant mental distress, this poor lady died rather suddenly on the 12th of March, 1882, in her eightieth year.

Her funeral was paid for by the present Earl; the only followers were Mr. Shakespeare, the solicitor representing the Earl of Lytton, the Rev. Freeman Wills, a distant relative of Lady Lytton, Mr. Ancona, a friend, and the Misses Devey, her coexecutrices. Her remains are buried in the pretty churchyard of St. John the Evangelist at Shirley, in Surrey. There is no monument over the grave, but facing the foot one has been erected to her memory by those who loved her, which marks it sufficiently for identification. Her furniture and effects were sold by auction, and realised a sum which enabled the solicitors to the executrices to distribute among her few remaining creditors a dividend of about ten shillings in the pound.

In her will * she expressed a wish to have inscribed on the tombstone (which does not exist) the following words (Isa. xiv. 3), with which I may fittingly conclude this work :—

"The Lord shall give thee rest from thy sorrow, and from thy fear, and from the hard bondage wherein thou wast made to serve."

* See Appendix IV.

APPENDIX.

APPENDIX I.

"LADY BULWER LYTTON'S APPEAL TO THE JUSTICE AND CHARITY OF THE ENGLISH PUBLIC."

THIS pamphlet was printed and published in 1857 by Mr. Isaac Ironside at the Free Press Office, Fargate, Sheffield, and enjoyed at one period a considerable circulation. It contained an account of Lady Lytton's wrongs, or rather of some of the most flagrant of them, and as most of the matters alluded to have already been detailed in the foregoing narrative, I do not propose to reproduce it *in extenso*, but merely to append a few extracts.

"PRELIMINARY ANNOUNCEMENT.

"The following appeal to public justice and public charity was intended as a preface to a second edition of 'Very Successful,' but Lady Bulwer Lytton's lawyer has just returned from London, having found it impossible to obtain a publisher, from a threat having been ubiquitously circulated through 'the trade' that an injunction * would be obtained against the work if republished. Now, this is a mere threat, and nothing more, as even 'the trade' are well aware, that the FACT-exposing ordeal of a court of justice is the very last that any of the *dramatis personæ* of 'Very Successful' would subject themselves to ; but as the bare threat effectually answers their leader's noble (!) and gentlemanlike (!) purpose of starving the authoress out of the market, and involving her in the most utter pecuniary ruin, she can only more urgently reiterate her appeal to public charity, by stating that subscriptions of £1 11s. 6d. sent to

* And yet what lost labour, as no injunction can be threatened, much less got, against the recording angel's eternal archives !

Lady Bulwer Lytton, care of Mr. W. Bragg, librarian, Parade, Taunton, Somerset, will be most gratefully acknowledged, and a copy of the book forwarded to any address. As, amid modern progressions, there are yet no workhouses for the destitute wives of rich men, Lady Bulwer Lytton, as her last hope, trusts this appeal to public charity will not be made in vain.

* * * * * * *

"She wishes it to be clearly understood that this is a painful and crying appeal to public CHARITY and not to public sympathy; for she is well aware that in a state of society where every vice is not only chartered, but adulated, in men, there is no sympathy for a woman who, passing the conventional Rubicon, presumes to complain, let her outrages be what they may, more especially if she has not made to herself friends of the mammon of unrighteousness among men. Accustomed as she now so long has been year after year, and day after day, to curtail some comfort or some absolute necessary, a little more or a little less to her individually could certainly never drive her into appealing to PUBLIC CHARITY! but the claims that others have on her have; and therefore it behoves her to leave no stone unturned or unbroken, however painful and humiliating the task may be, to prevent herself being made a compulsory swindler.

* * * * * * *

"'The ruinous climax of this conspiracy to suppress my only means of subsistence' (her novels) 'necessitates my making ONE more appeal to the candour and conscience of the public, in anticipation of the one-sided anathema that awaits a woman, under *any* outrages, under the hot pressure of any provocation, daring to expose the conventionally held sacred vices of a husband. But it is to YOU, GOOD men and true, who have no such sins to answer for, that I appeal, and of YOU I ask out of the bitter agony of my own heart.

"'Oh! women of England, in your happy homes—wives, mothers, and daughters—how would *you* feel, how would *you* act under similar outrages, if such should befall you?

which God forbid! How would *you* like to have had your first child turned out of the house the moment it was born, with the summary announcement from your lord and master *that " he would not have your time and attention taken up with any d——d child" ?* And though in after-years a whole page in a stilted novel. (*vide* " Zanoni ") might be devoted to blowing prismatic bubbles about the "depth and purity of a father's love for his first-born "—as a few natural feelings on *paper* entail neither trouble nor expense, but are, on the contrary, extremely lucrative—I doubt whether this public tribute would not in your hearts, as well as in mine, instead of atoning for (on account of that greatest of all irritants—hypocrisy!), have still further lacerated the wound caused by this brutal private fact. The mode in which I was expelled from my home I have already told you, for Sir Edward Bulwer Lytton is a "great man " (?), and the world is a poor little miserable narrow world, and there is only room for him in it, so his wife being in the way, he kicked her out of it ; his children were in his way, so he suppressed them ; God's commandments were in his way, so he broke them. It is his own confession that I had been to him an incom-parable wife. I will not take any credit to myself for an endurance I cannot call heroic, since it had too much abject physical fear in it to deserve that name ; but I *did* return good for evil ; I did for nine miserable years, under every outrage, injury, and provocation that a wife could be subjected to, conceal and forgive what I never ought to have forgiven. In moral England, where there is *no* redress for moral injuries, had I rushed to a magistrate with my hanging, bleeding cheek, for this ONE bit of quivering flesh I could have got an equally fragmentary piece of vulgar redress ; but there is none for a whole being and an im-mortal soul far worse tortured.

" 'So far, however, from exposing the perpetration of this outrage, and many others, as I *ought* to have done, I hushed it up, and actually compassionated into an object of deferential forbearance the poor creature who had so degraded himself, in return for which, some months after,

he turned me and my children out of our home, that
he might pursue his career of unbridled profligacy without even the *nominal* restraint of our presence; and when
I reminded him that when *I* had it in my power to
crush and fully expose him I had shielded and forgiven him, his answer was neither polished as to style
nor profound in anything save cold-blooded brutality,
for it was "More fool you! for I'll not give you another
opportunity." Oh, shade of Goethe! pardon that I should,
with all *your* cold calculated profligacy, have compared
you to this man! for *you*, who really had a drunken
termagant of a wife, knowing your own delinquencies,
yet treated her with the greatest kindness, endurance,
and forbearance. But all this was only to *me*, when
the tragedy progressed, and the heroine became my own
child—she who had been turned out of the house the
moment she was born. *My* endurance was exhausted,
which no doubt was very wrong, as of course, looking
back, I should have remembered that the cries of an infant,
like the tears of a mother, come under the head of "IN-
COMPATIBILITY OF TEMPER!" and justified marital
supremacy in any cruelties it might like to exercise. The
next thing I heard of this poor young victim, on my return
to England, was that she was dying *alone* in a miserable
lodging at Brompton, and this I heard through one of
those strange "chances" which, when we find in works of
fiction, are called improbably romantic, but which in real
life so often contradict experience and distance probability.
I could not, had I space, dwell on this last fearful act of
Sir Edward Bulwer Lytton's *only* original drama; may it
remain unique as well as original! Enough to state that
I saw while she slept the poor young ruin. Unseen by, unknown to her, I supplied the wants where everything was
wanting. I *heard* the poor young martyr's praises of the
beverages the nurse brought her, saying, "Oh, Mrs. Bruce,
how good everything is to-day! Do you know, they remind me of poor dear mamma. *He* says she does not care
for us, *but I know everything now.*" And again through
that fearful night, as I lay like a dog across the threshold

of her open door, I heard her tell the nurse, as a sort of explanation of her illness, how she had been slaved to death
over her father's German translations, and I bit my lips
through till the blood came, to prevent a shriek of agony
escaping me. But even *this* Sir Edward Bulwer Lytton
thought too great a luxury for me, and so, my arrival
having been betrayed by an apothecary of the name of
Rouse, he had me forcibly dragged from the house the
next day. But in stirring up these ashes of the past, I
am desecrating my own heart; and it is the present
maelstrom of misery—vulgar pecuniary ruin—which this
last conspiracy has entailed upon me which makes me
reiterate my urgent appeal to your charity; for indeed a
strong-minded *man*, forgetting that, whoever and whatever
His instruments may be, it is God who ordains the blows,
would load a pistol, and enter an impious caveat against
His decrees; but "I will trust Him though He slay me,"
and hope in *you* to whom I appeal. I am no hypocrite.
Sir Edward Bulwer Lytton has circled my life with a
snare, and crowned it with a curse; my miserable, lonely,
laborious, and disinherited existence *he* has made ONE
GREAT AGONY, composed of innumerable exquisite, infinitesimal tortures, for each and all of which, as there is
BUT ONE SOURCE, I have but ONE NAME; surely to the
most forbearing and least logical mind the inference is
obvious. "But forgiveness?" I hear the word; I acknowledge the strong claim the Redeemer of the world has
given it upon *every* erring heart. BUT DOES GOD HIM-
SELF FORGIVE TILL HIS FORGIVENESS IS ASKED? OR
CAN EVEN HE BE APPEASED WITHOUT REPENTANCE AND
CESSATION FROM SIN?

"' ROSINA BULWER LYTTON.

"' *March*, 1857.'"

APPENDIX II.

"AND LADY LYTTON, WAS SHE SO VERY BEAUTIFUL?"

This question was put to me quite recently, by one who wished to hear some particulars of my dearly loved friend Rosina, wife of the first Baron ——, and his victim—victim of a man whose whole nature was so intensely selfish, that it had not an inch of space for anything that did not satisfy the greedy adulation of *himself*, in which he had been born and bred. Until his deluded wife discovered (which she did very early after her marriage) what was the idol he really worshipped, she had been induced to believe that she was the object of his adoration.* And she had yielded her whole most noble nature to the insinuating and snake-like fascination of being idolised by a young man of at that period trifling literary merit, good lineage, and in a *presumptively* good monetary position, for his income was very small, and depended in a great measure on the caprice of his mother and his own pen, while Rosina Wheeler, I have always understood, had at least £300 a year when she married. She was at the time of her introduction into London society "one of the most, if not *the* most beautiful girl that was ever seen," as the Hon. Mr. Edmund Byng, who was a most intimate friend of my own, told me, and a fact of which many others, amongst them those of her own sex and rank (not usually given to speak rapturously of one another), have repeatedly

* *Vide* the dedication of "Owen," one of Bulwer's first poems, to her.

assured me when I was mixing in society, and I was known to be very intimate with her in 1847 and for some years afterwards, when my own great admiration of, and love for her was, as a literary lady said to me, "quite a proverb."

The form of Lady Lytton's head was one of her many beauties. Her hair was of a beautiful dark brown, her eyes indescribable as to colour and expression, ever varying with each emotion, so lustrous, so sweet, so tender and starlike, but when roused by her wrongs and cruel treatment, they shone with the greatest indignation and contempt. Her mouth was a true Cupid's bow, her straight, delicately-shaped nose of the most refined type, with arched nostrils, and her eyebrows, so delicately pencilled, and forehead were perfect.

When I first saw her at a garden party at the Countess of Harrington's (then Mrs. Leicester Stanhope) she was just past her prime, but gloriously beautiful still, and she retained her beauty to old age, for I spent some time with her in 1869 at Brenton Villa, Taunton, a few years after she had been released from the madhouse in which her wretched husband incarcerated her, and from which he had orders from high quarters to release her, and that quickly, on pain of forfeiting his seat in the Cabinet of the late Lord Derby. I am told by those who witnessed her suffering life near its end (unhappily I was out of England at the time) that she was even then a most hand-some woman.

Many an hour have I wept with her over the cruel and bitter wrongs to which she was perpetually subjected by the man who had vowed before God to " forsake all other " and " cherish her in sickness and in health "—vows which he so very soon broke. Oh ! if the readers of his works could have witnessed the scenes in some of which I took sorrow-ing part, and could hear of the dastardly treatment of my darling friend by this man and his agents, they would, I think, eschew their admiration of the writer !

I was at one of dear Mr. Rogers' breakfasts with my father, and some ladies and gentlemen of high rank, on one

special occasion when Bulwer was spoken of, and I confess
to the thrill of satisfied justice I experienced (knowing the
man's character so well) when the accomplished and vene-
rable poet picked the said Bulwer to pieces, metaphorically
speaking, like a rotten chestnut! No description of mine
can give any idea of the contempt of Mr. Rogers' manner,
and I sat facing him and longing to thank him before the
whole company for the outspoken opinion he had given
of the merit of such a man as I knew Sir Edward Bulwer
to be.

"WAS LADY LYTTON GIVEN TO HABITS OF INTEM-
PERANCE?"*

Certainly not, if you mean taking more stimulants than
was good for her. I was with her almost daily for nearly
three years, and never during that time did she take more
wine than was ordered for her by the medical man who
attended us for years, and who attended her. She drank
wine and water only, and the wine was mostly port wine.
She was extremely fastidious in the matter of water, and
particular that it should be "pure spring water." In spite
of all the trouble of mind she continually endured, she was
most careful in her housekeeping, and the surroundings in
which she lived (almost alone at times) were those of a
perfect gentlewoman. I hired several of her servants, and
she treated them with the greatest kindness and consideration, but it was not easy to please her, owing to her great
nicety and keen knowledge of how every trifling service
should be performed not for herself only, but for every one.
Later on in my own life I had to bless her for the

---

* I particularly requested Mrs. Whelan to allude to this, for I
was told a few years ago that Lady Lytton was in a state of
intoxication when she appeared on the hustings at Hertford in 1858.
This lie I refuted at the time, and since Lady Lytton's death, I have
written to Dr. Woodhouse (who was mayor of Hertford at the time,
and who is still living) begging him to state the true facts of the
case. I have his letter testifying to the falseness of the accusation,
and entirely exonerating Lady Lytton from this most cruel slander.
—L. D.

unflinching severity of her rules, as my own mother died while I was quite a girl, and dear Lady Lytton supplied her place to me at an age when young women mostly require one—on their entrance into society. Her knowledge of human nature has been a pilot to me through many a boisterous voyage, and I often think what her own dear daughter must have lost, wanting such a mother as she proved herself to me. I took a greater pleasure and deeper interest in my own household after my marriage than I should have done had she not taught me many things that were eminently useful to me and my dear husband, as I had treble the amount of housekeeping, in all its manifold branches, to undertake when I left London for a large country house in place of my father's modest establishment. Lady Lytton's extravagant generosity was her extravagance for others, not table luxuries nor luxuries of toilet or any luxury for self. It was other people's needs that drove her wild to help them, and I have known her to sacrifice her own jewellery and even her comforts to assist people who were pressed for money or in any trouble. Her heart was golden, and her generosity lavish. She had suffered too much to enjoy life, but we passed many happy and alas! many unhappy hours together, her wit and inborn gaiety alternating with her tears and pathetic sayings, and keeping me her prisoner of love. She had been a guest at the French court of Louis Philippe, and intimate with all the French royal family, and also much in the company of the Grand Duchess of Saxe Coburg Gotha, the Duchess of Kent's sister, and she would tell me in the most graphic manner many of the sayings and doings of the distinguished people, who fully appreciated her, as I knew by their letters to her, several of which she retained, and some of which she permitted me to reply to for her, a privilege I found most valuable in after-years.

I said once to her, "Why do you not go down to Knebworth and take your lawful place there? You are only *separated*, not *divorced*. I will go with you. We will post down and see what will be done. *I* am not afraid of Sir Edward Bulwer Lytton."

Her answer came slowly and assuredly—" He would employ some one to *kill* me, or he would *shut me up in a madhouse.*"

" Nonsense !" I answered ; "such things are not done in the nineteenth century."

Many years after that I had to write to Lady Palmerston and others to beg them to deliver her out of a madhouse into which she had been snared, and her life had been attempted by poison in Wales, as Dr. Price, her medical man, was ready to swear in any court of justice. I cannot give personal evidence of this attempt, as I was far away, nursing a sick child of my own, at the time, but I have seen Dr. Price's letters, and know all the particulars of the visit to my dear friend of a certain woman and what took place. So her astounding reply to my suggestion was thoroughly verified in both particulars. A diabolical plot was frustrated once, while she lived in Paris, by her maid, who betrayed the man (the chief mover in it) who was caught opening her desk by the police, they having been placed on the watch for him after the maid had mentioned the plot to her mistress. The great *avocat* Berryer was her counsel, as she brought an action on that occasion against the plotters, and her appearance in court was described to me by a countess who was well acquainted with her "as enough to turn the heads of all the young and old counsel present, she was so beautiful."

She would have won the trial but for the ridiculous fact that an English woman married could not bring an action in those days, let her cause be ever so just, the act ever so unjust, which forced her into court.

Her own life was purity itself, but her words were bitter, sarcastic, pungent, and powerful, on seeing and hearing, as she was often compelled to do, women, and men too, whom she well knew to be steeped in iniquity, walking in the midst of the first society in England, fêted, petted, in easy happy circumstances, while she, whose only fault was that she spoke the bare and unvarnished truth in plain straight-out English, was despised and vilified, deserted, and in a false position as to means. Her title only entailed on her extra payment for everything, and expensive lodging also. I have often gone alone into shops when walking with her, and purchased things to be sent home in my own name, to save her the immediate addition of £ s. d. which "Milady" involves. I have heard that on being congratulated on Sir Edward Bulwer's "making a Lady of her," she said "she wished she could return the compliment and make a gentleman of him." I can well believe she said it, her sense of humour would be roused by the vulgarity of the congratulation, and she could not resist the repartee. Her adjectives were decidedly a strong feature in her correspondence and conversation, and she lived in days when "manners" were certainly more part of one's education they they are now, so I was often addressed with this phrase when speaking of her (which was stereotyped with some people) : "Oh, yes, it's all true, but it's so shocking for a woman to speak against her husband!" the truth being entirely set aside, though acknowledged, for the conventionality of pharisaical England!

Well! "nous avons changé tout cela," as the French say, and this is the era of calling a spade a spade.

On one occasion it is quite just to state that I declined to post a letter for her to Dr. Marshall Hall, after the heart-rending death of her daughter in a wretched lodging of typhus fever, when the mother was denied access to her by the father, and I took Lady Lytton away to my home. She had written this letter, in the bitterness of her grief, to Dr. Marshall Hall, who had been the agent of this enchanting novelist, poet, and dramatic author. And she had *fully* expressed herself in the letter. She read it to me previously to sealing it, and asked me to post it as I returned home from the Tower of London, where she was then living with my uncle, the vice-chaplain, and my aunt and cousin, their daughter. I absolutely declined to do so. Not that the letter was not every word of it substantially true, and no language could be considered too strong for such unmitigated cruelty as she was subjected to, but I would not let her, if I could help it, furnish her bitter enemies with a cause of offence against her, and in spite of her anger at me and the terrible pitifulness of the case, I steadily refused to post the letter. She was most bitter in her language, most trying in her manner, on my refusal, and I left the room for an hour. On returning she quite broke my heart with her repentant words, begging me to pardon her for her, as she called it, ' impatience towards me," and adding more and more to my admiration of her character. It is needless to say I forgave her, and loved her if possible more than ever. Any one who has taken the trouble to read the Earl of Lytton's two volumes of his father's life will find letters of the Earl's mother which show how she humbled herself to his grand-mother, whose persecution of her was well known, and who had again and again nearly parted the lovers, as they were. Would that she had succeeded ! To quote, or rather to paraphrase, the remark of the husband, dearest Lady Lytton would have "gone farther" (and not very far, either) ' and fared well. Her exquisite beauty, her talents, and noble nature, would have made the happiness of many a man in the highest position. And her own happiness always was that of others. I could fill volumes with anecdotes of her delicate kindness and thoughtfulness for any and every one she came in contact with, and the amazing ingratitude with which she was repaid. The last part of her sorrowful life was cheered by the entire devotion of friends, who can bear equal testimony with myself as to her worth and excellence ; and having suffered severe bodily pain from rheumatism, etc., she passed away without a sigh, having asked for iced water. Before it could touch her lips she was gone from this cruel world, and to that "where the wicked cease from troubling, and the weary are at rest." Her faith was firm in the merits of our Redeemer, and her days of tribulation " overcome."

Her son declined to take the chair at a dramatic dinner on account "of the death of his mother," but he also declined to follow her remains to the still nameless grave in Shirley Churchyard, Croydon, where she was interred. The church is a beautiful structure, noted as "one of Mr. Ruskin's churches ; " and his father's tomb is not far from Lady Lytton's grave. In the church a communion table has been placed which bears her name and ours, the few faithful ones who loved her to the end, and which is the only tribute to her dear memory.*

KATHERINE CURTEIS WHELAN.

* Since the above was written a monument to the memory of Rosina Dowager Lady Lytton has been erected by her executrices, facing the foot of her nameless grave.—L. D.

APPENDIX III.

following extracts from letters written by the valier de Bérard relate to Lady Lytton's literary work eriodicals. The Chevalier was connected with Mr. , editor of the *London Journal*. Lady Lytton contri-d for some years to this publication.

"January 29th, 1854.

Mr. Stiff asked me yesterday to inform Lady Lytton shall feel very thankful if she would write me a short for the *Journal* of about three pages; should it spin to a tenth column, no matter.' I said he must not e your work at 25s. per page. He said he would think of doing such a thing, but would be liberal, would give more than any one else, and would feel ured if you would condescend to become a regular ributor to the *Journal*. He also published the *Weekly es*, which has a sale of ninety thousand. Mr. Stiff kind man. When I was ill he advanced me a few nds, or we must have gone to the workhouse. I do e, if you have leisure, you will compose a short tale for ; it may lead to something better; and, let me add, happy it would make me if I could be the means of ing you—you, who are so good, so generous, and so lfish! I have felt more for your undeserved mis-nes—wrongs, I should say—than any other; and ough age has crept on me, it has not blunted my ngs."

"Brighton, February 2nd, 1854.

I am here on a visit to Lady Hotham. Yours received erday. All I can say at present is, Can such things be ? When I have made the requisite inquiries you shall hear from me more at large. As you so peremptorily requested me to give the thing every publicity possible, I showed it to Lady Hotham."

"*February 24th*, 1854.

"Vous peignez si bien les personnages, que la ressemblance s'apperçoit au premier coup-d'œil. En vérité, madame, vous rivalisez Alexandre Dumas dans vos portraits graphiques. Votre stile est grandiose, et vous nous montrez bien que vous savez apprécier l'étendue de vos forces et de cette intelligence que les lords de la création s'attribuent exclusivement, et auxquels vous joignez la douceur et le raffinement de votre sexe, et en déployant les vastes inépuisables facultés de votre esprit."

"*March 5th*, 1854.

" Mr. Stiff tells me that he wants short tales of about four pages of the *Journal*, amusing and interesting, so as to suit the palate of all. He will pay liberally ; name your own price. Nor does he object to your writing for any other periodical at the same time ; I thought it proper to ascertain this point at once, to prevent all future cavil on this point, so that you can have one or two more strings to your bow. The sale of the *London Journal* now exceeds 400,000 a week ! *Voilà la pierre philosophale !*

" Sir Liar is very *shaky*, they say, and, unless excited, his faculties are dormant and failing him ; and it is reported he is troubled with the *argenté* paucity. Consolez-vous donc et riez. ' Rira bien qui rira le *dernier !* ' Chacun à son tour. Sir Henry n'a de quoi se consoler si il ne réussit pas ; du moins, vous avez la bonté de le mettre ' *à la porte*.'

" Bravo, madame ! le petit mot pour rire ne vous manque jamais. Continuez, je vous prie, dans cette belle humeur qui vous sied si bien."

"*April 2nd*, 1854.

" Stiff says, ' Tell Lady Lytton I care not what I pay to further the interest of the *Journal*, which now surpasses by some thousands the 400,000 per week, and I look forward to one million by Christmas.'

" Mr. Stiff is endeavouring to secure as much talent as

can, and I hope you will eclipse them all. Next week
will give ' Behind the Scenes' a good *review*, such as it
serves, in the *Weekly Times*. He has repeatedly thanked
e for having introduced him to you.

"The people at the *Home Circle* will insert your three
says next week or the week after; they say 'The Supper
Sallust's' is too *good* for their paper, and decline taking
You know one cannot 'make a silk purse,' etc.

Madame de Bérard has read your book with much plea-
re. She says that roses spring up under your pen, for your
oughts have all the beauty and fragrance of those flowers,
d your wit prevents one being cloyed by too much sweet-
ss; you have such endless variety, and come before the
blic with a mind as fresh and buoyant as if you had not
pended such a multiplicity of thoughts upon paper; and
it you possess an inexhaustible mine of brilliant talents,
ll in embryo. Burke himself could not write better, and
ry often not half so well."

"Saturday, April 15th, 1854.

" One of your articles has appeared in the *Home Circle*,
d will be continued next Monday and the following,
lich will complete the whole; they could not spare room
insert the three in one number."

The Chevalier tries to find out Mrs. Braine, the governess
the two children.

"May 15th, 1854.

' The person's name is Mrs. Braine, at Auckland Cottage,
orth End, Fulham Road. She was tall, and appears to
: Irish. I introduced my business by inquiring what her
ws had been in writing to you; she replied, ' I know
dy Lytton by name, and have felt much interest for her
d her misfortunes, on account of the strong affection I
re to her poor dear child, and which I cultivated as long
she lived, as these her letters will prove, for she wrote to
: as often as she could contrive to do so unknown to her
her. In the year 1839 I became the governess of the
ldren at Cheltenham, and continued so under Miss
eene, when I married and left.' She says she and the
ldren were almost starved. She wants you to use your

influence in placing her eldest son in a public school. I closely questioned her if she knew anything of Sir Liar; she had not seen him for years, but once lodged in a house where Mrs. Beaumont had lodged, with two boys and a girl; the boys, she says, were the very picture of Sir Edward. The landlady told her Lady Lytton was very ill, and that as soon as she died Mrs. Beaumont was to take her place. Mrs. Braine says Mrs. Beaumont is at present residing with the Hon. Mrs. Yelverton, Whitland Abbey, in Pembrokeshire. Mrs. Braine's maiden name was Phillips. She will send me a letter for you to-morrow, with your dear girl's hair and her letters.

" In the course of conversation I endeavoured to find out if she knew anything of P—— or Getting, but she does not. I should think the woman is straightforward; if not, she is the best actor I ever met with, for she appears very sincere in what she says."

This letter confirms Mrs. Braine's account of the children.

"*May 26th*, 1854.

" I have received yours of yesterday, with its enclosure. Unless you know the writer *well*, I would have you be on your guard. It appears to me as if intended as an attack upon your purse. One of the plans of the gang will be to cripple your means, among their other villainies, and every penny they may extract from your very slender means is so much gained by them. Therefore pray be on your guard; you may defend yourself from your *enemies*, but beware of your *friends !* As to what your correspondent says about a madhouse, it was certainly the case some twenty years back, but now these houses are visited by the Commissioners, and every patient brought before the Board and examined separately and alone; therefore the thing is impossible. My authority is Mr. Briant; for when, some time back, I spoke to him about it, he said that it ought not to make *you* uneasy, for, in his opinion, you most assuredly had not the *faintest* taint of madness. This took place at Brighton, and Dr. Turner was present, who concurred in the opinion. 'If Lady Lytton is mad,' said he, 'it is one of the most rational madnesses I ever saw or heard of.' Soyez donc tranquille, ma belle dame. Sir Liar is in a state, if not mad, of *monomania*. I have not been able to hear anything of him."

WALTER SAVAGE LANDOR, 1839.

Lady Lytton met Landor at Bath about 1839, and writes of him :—

"He used to say, in his peculiar way of pronouncing the word 'wonderful,' which he always called 'woonderful,' 'It is the most woonderfully beautiful city in the world ; Bath and Florence are the only two places where I can live.' No one ever appreciated so fully either his jests or his *bons mots* as he did himself; at all events, it would have been impossible for them to do so as loudly ; but then all Landor did was *fortissimo*, incisive, and trenchant.

"When he gave—and, though by no means rich, he gave often—it was always fully, freely, and thoroughly; for, despite his old gabardine of a brown surtout, shining at the seams, etc., yet was the lining—that is, the man—thoroughly *grand seigneur* of the days when that now nearly extinct race existed as the rule, and not as the exception. Yet no butterfly, emerged from its chrysalis state into its purple, gold, and winged glories, could be more different than the matutinal Walter Savage Landor in the aforesaid old brown surtout and the thoroughbred, noble-headed, distinguished-looking man who bore that name when dressed for dinner. If his laughter was muscular and stentorian, the thews and sinews of his vituperation or his indignation, even with regard to his historical or archæological feuds, were equally athletic. It happened there was a young artist at Bath whom Landor patronised—no, not patronised, for that was not his way, but whom he tried to serve. He had sat to him for his portrait, *en buste*, which he gave me—a perfect *replica* of the magnificent head, and admirable as to tone and *pose*, with just the faintest *soupçon* of the immortal old brown coat. Mr. Landor insisted that I should sit for my picture to his *protégé;* I consented, upon the express proviso that he should always be there, so that

I might not die of *ennui* during the penance. Some time before he had promised to send me his 'Pericles and Aspasia,' but so long was he in doing so, that I thought he had forgotten all about it; but not so. One morning a kind of champagne case arrived, containing not only 'Pericles and Aspasia,' but 'Imaginary Conversations' and all his other works, splendidly bound in russia, quarto editions, lined with blue *moire*, as if they had been for a royal presentation. During one of the sittings the artist happened to speak enthusiastically about some lines of Ben Jonson, whereupon Mr. Landor, who was seated at the time, bounded from his chair, and began pacing the room and shaking his tightly clenched hands as he thundered out, Ben Jonson! Not another word about him! It makes my blood boil! I haven't patience to hear the fellow's name. A pigmy! an upstart! a presumptuous varlet who dared to be thought more of than Shakespeare was in his day!' 'But surely,' ventured the artist, 'that was not poor Ben Jonson's fault, but the fault of the undiscriminating generation in which they both lived.' 'Not at all!' roared Landor, his eyeballs becoming bloodshot and his nostrils dilating, 'not at all! The fellow should have walled himself up in his own brick and mortar before he had connived at and allowed such sacrilege!' 'But,' said I—for the painter could not speak for laughter—'even if Ben Jonson had been able to achieve such a *tour de force*, I am very certain, Mr. Landor, that, "*taking every man in his humour*," Shakespeare would have been the very first to pull down his friend's handiwork and restore him to the world.' 'No such thing!' rejoined Mr. Landor, turning fiercely upon me; 'Shakespeare never wasted his time; and, with his woonderful imagination, he'd have known he could have created fifty better.'"

ANECDOTES OF DISRAELI AND MRS. WYNDHAM LEWIS.

Mrs. Bulwer was sitting by the side of Rogers in the drawing-room after a dinner-party, when Disraeli, who had been lounging in a cane-seated chair, crossed the room, with his coat-tails, as usual, over each arm, leaving his dark green velvet adorables, with the marks of the chair on them, fully visible. Rogers asked, "Who is that ?" "Oh! young Disraeli, the Jew," answered Mrs. Bulwer. "Rather the wandering Jew, with the brand of *Cane* on him," said Rogers. Disraeli heard the laugh these words evoked, and turning round, glanced scornfully at them. When Lady Lytton repeated this to me, I remarked, "Now I am certain it must have been *you*, and not Rogers, who uttered this *bon mot*." "No, indeed. I assure you it was Rogers, and not I, who said it."

When Mrs. Bulwer asked Disraeli to take Mrs. Wyndham Lewis down to dinner, "Oh! anything rather than that insufferable woman," he would answer; "but Allah is great." And putting his thumbs into the arm-holes of his waistcoat, he would walk up to her and then offer his arm.

As a pendant to the above. It was during a dinner at the Bulwers' that Swift had been a topic of conversation, and when the ladies retired, "Who is this Dr. Swift, Rosina?" said Mrs. W. Lewis, "that they have been talking about? Can I ask him to my parties?" "Hardly so." "Why not?" "Because he did a thing some years since which effectually prevented his ever appearing again in society." "What was that?" "Why, he only died about a hundred years ago."

Lady Lytton told me she honoured Disraeli for one thing : he always behaved well to his wife.

EXTRACT FROM LADY LYTTON'S NOVEL OF "VERY SUCCESSFUL," 1856.

"At a Dinner-party," Sketch of Disraeli.

"Will you tell me," said Mr. Phippen, "who are those two men opposite, the one with black ringlets and the other with a head of light hair and moustachios like a distaff gone mad?" "Oh! those," laughed Mr. Bouverie, "are Mr. Jericho Jabber and Sir Janus Allpuff, my Lord

Oaks' two leading acrobats." "Good heavens! How can
Lord Oaks think of balancing his political ladder on the
chins of two such mountebanks? 'Pon my life! Their hair
alone is worth paying a shilling to see, and reminds me of
the intrigues that used to be carried on when Bonaparte was
First Consul by means of locks of hair. But you'll be tired
of my stories." "Indeed, no. Pray let me hear what you
were going to say." "Well, you must know that during the
Consulate great excitement all of a sudden reigned in Paris
at the First Consul having frequently appeared in powder;
for, 'gad! sir, it turned out that his barber was no other than
the famous Ex-Chouan in disguise, who had undertaken to
give signals to the partisans of *Louis Dix-huite* by his
manner of powdering and frizzing the Chief Consul. It
was observed that two expresses were sent off to Warsaw
the day he first appeared in powder, and this circumstance
having been communicated to Fouché, that sleepless dragon
Commissary of Police, he arrested the *Barbier Comte*, who
had been long a marked *suspecte* in Fouche's private book,
and when arrested upon him were found a very curious
cipher in curls, chignons, straight, long, and short hair,
together with several hieroglyphics in curling-irons. It
seems that powder and curls, or *canons,* as they were called,
were very significant, intimating *war,* and plain and straight
hair denoted *peace ;* and all this handiwork of the Tuileries
Figaro it was that had made the *Tiers Consolidés* fall to
54, as the right side of the Consul's head described
the French republic, while the rest was geographically
sectioned out for the rest of Europe, so that a prominent
curl in any particular division, powdered more or less,
denoted hostility. It was actually sworn on the *procès
verbal* that the Swiss cantons, which stood very high and
close to the centre of the Chief Consul's *toupée,* were
powdered thick, that Spain was particularly frosted, and
upon the right side of the head there was combed a prospectus of a new constitution. The Consul's head, on being
compared with this cipher, left no doubt of the conspiracy,
besides which several false curls, in the shape of ships,
artillery, and bastions, had been found on the culprit, who

was handed over to the prefects of the palace, to be tried by a jury, half crops and half *gens de poudre*.   Ha! ha! ha! Such were the *jeux d'esprit* in *those* days, and I was just thinking, as our friend the *Jew*-d'esprit opposite has oiled the ringlets on one side of his head more than the other, whether the oleaginous side might not be intended as a cipher as well."   There was a hush for a moment as some exquisite music floated from one of the hidden bands. And then Mr. Jericho Jabber displayed some wonderful *tours de force* he had got up on his return from the Pyramids upon ancient Greek, Assyrian, and Ethiopian music, which naturally whirled him off into a twin ecstacy upon dancing, which he designated as the photograph of motion, explaining that there was no person or thing that might not be imitated by gesture, and then almost pantomimically showing, by means of a gold spoon and a terrible hurling of his ringlets to the back of his chair, how the Lacædemonians and Thebans used to attack their enemies dancing; and on bounded Mr. Jericho Jabber, till he got back again to Thebes, and for change of air from thence to Athens; and winding up with one of those fine presto! begone! perorations and hocus-pocus arguments with which he was wont to beguile listening senates upon much more vital matters, he burst forth with, "Why, as a proof that there *must be*, that there *is*, something Divine in the origin of dancing, look at the religious rites into which it has been introduced, not only among the sacrifices of the mysteries of Delii and round the fountain of Hippocrene, from whence Pindar calls Apollo DANCER, but" (and here, as a culminating and irrefragable argument, he drew the handkerchief he was flourishing in his right hand hastily across his left), "more than all this, as an appeal to *our*" (?) "Christianity, did not David dance before the ark?"   And here Mr. Jericho Jabber leant back exhausted (as well he might be), whereupon Mr. Abner Haystack, taking advantage of the halcyon silence that reigned for a moment, when a good thing would be sure to tell, bent forward and said, "After all, Jabber, you must allow that there's nothing like the good old English country dance, as it is the only one where one is constantly *changing sides*, and one has to give hands across and set to the *opposite party ;* and, indeed, the original directions, printed on 'Sir Roger de Coverley' and another contemporary country dance called 'CAVEN-DISH COURT ; OR, LOOK SHARP!' after the *changing sides*, are, 'First couple *cast up*, and *cast off*, and hands round.'" The but ill-suppressed laugh being now decidedly against Mr. Jericho Jabber, he had nothing for it but to resort to his favourite attitude of sticking his thumbs in the arm-holes of his waistcoat and uttering his usual Caucasian truism of "God is great," after which he suddenly took to admiring the mouldings of the ceiling.

POEMS BY LADY LYTTON.

NOT the green graves where loved ones sleep,
    And friends strew grief with flowers,
Where circling years their vigils keep,
    'Mid snows and summer hours,

Nor yet those unrecorded tombs
    Palled within the treacherous deep,
Are among the saddest dooms
    The Fates on mortals heap.

For with healing on its wings,
    Through which gleam angels' eyes,
Time o'er all these a halo flings ;
    That softens as he flies.

No,— 'tis those dark undaisied graves,
    Dug deep within the heart,
Where memory like a maniac raves
    O'er wrongs that *can't* depart :

Whole trust by treachery repaid ;
    Truth springed, and crush'd with lies ;
Love only sought to be betray'd,
    As cobweb human ties ;

All that was holiest, brightest, best,
    From nature's dower within,
Made a sacrilegious guest
    To gild a bad man's sin.

On *these* lone graves, no blossom opes;
   No human tears are shed;
They're only strew'd with wither'd hopes
   Dead—burying their dead!

Poor ghosts! it was no honest foe,
   In fair and open fight,
Who dealt ye all the mortal blow
   That swiftly quench'd your light.

'Twas on a moral Marathon,
   Where a filial Theseus cast
The shadow of a loyal son,
   That murdered as it past!

Well! all his mammon spoils he's gain'd,
   And all the tinsel shams,
Of low ambition, conscience stain'd
   As mire a river dams.

God's priceless Koh-i-noor his soul
   All dimmed with worldly guiles,
Barter'd for glass of Satan's dole
   From *his* Philippine Isles.

While by *his* worshipped Babylon
   I've sat down and wept,
Pitying angels looked upon
   The grief that never slept.

And they brought, as they always do
   To such poor ruined shrines,
Blest gifts, of sacred rue
   Which God with His chastening twines.

For those bitter herbs of sorrow,
   By resignation crush'd,
Incense rise on mercy's morrow,
   To where all storms are hush'd.

Then, since God to me has sent
   That peace the world *can't* give,
Share it with me; and be content,
   Though late, to learn to live.

Now that young souls are given you,
  To ruin or to save,
As you shall make them false or true,
  God's servant or sin's slave.

Your mildew'd childhood knew no care,
  Poor hapless son of clay!
Deceit's foul mask aye forced to wear;
  It scared all truth away.

Tear off the vile, accursèd thing!
  That's tainted your whole life;
Be what you'd seem, and bring
  To God the struggle of each strife.

Forgiveness is the only boon
  You've left me to bestow;
Take it, and may you now full soon
  Its utmost value know.

Yet think not there's *no* happy state
  For broken hearts in store;
God's given us all that glorious *fête*
  The blessed *Jour des Morts.**

WE WERE THREE.

WE were three! three, so fond and true;
  No cloud between us ever came;
For, let what changes would ensue,
  Our firm of three was still the same.

We made and peopled our own world;
  No human vices entered there;
No treachery at trust was hurled;
  All *was* what it seemed, full and fair.

* Lady Lytton's birthday was the 2nd November, 1802, the *Jour des Morts.*

We were three ! with one common heart
　　My dogs and I all things did share ;
Being best, they'd the better part
　　Of all that they or I deemed rare.

'Mid the family portraits hung,
　　By time and change undimmed,
Their great Aunt Fairy, lovely, young,
　　By Edwin Landseer limned.

Than his true art, there's none grander,
　　For in every touch, all well is ;
Each dog feels, like Alexander,
　　That he's got his *own* Apelles.

But how describe those matchless two, ·
　　My Daisy and his darling wife ?
Their beauty, though it daily grew,
　　Paled by the beauty of their life.

My Tiny, with her wondrous eyes !
　　So soft ! like stars on velvet spread ;
Each look so gentle, and so wise !
　　They seem like garnered tears unshed.

Daisy, dog of the velvet ears,
　　And pretty truant, trying ways !
The mischief children pay in fears
　　Was always sure to gain him praise.

True to the instincts of his sex,
　　Which *must* the despot play,
The cats he'd chase, the sheep he'd vex,
　　And bark the birds and bees away.

But *this* was but his public life,
　　That bubble sham of dogs and men ;
All social good in him was rife,
　　And *tact* to know how, where, and when

The finest canine gentleman
　　That ever yet in dog-skin stepped,
Whether he swift through meadows ran,
　　Or gracefully on hearthrug slept,

Or, with true pet dog chivalry,
  Gave up to Tiny the best place ;
Not even chicken-bones would he
  Take without ref'rence to *her* face.

While she, as on my lap she sat,
  With ears like meteors streaming,
"Si grande dame ! jusq'au bout des pattes,"
  Just half waking and half dreaming,

Like Waller's Saccharissa, would
  " Suffer herself to be admired,"
Which Daisy dog quite understood
  Meant, " Keep your distance ; for I'm tired."

Then the hay, the sweet new hay,
  We've raked and tossed together !
E'en on the very dullest day,
  Our fun made sunny weather.

For we would make the welkin ring
  With the Blenheim nation air ;
It's not, of course, " God save the King,"
  But just " Marlbrook s'en va-t-en guerre."

E'en I, who shudder at the storm
  Of slang in this *too* vulgar age,
Must own my darlings *were* " good form " !
  That's perfect as to beauty's gauge.

True, " happiness *was* born a twin,"
  But a twin whose days were numbered,
As its first cradle death crept in,
  And stole its life while it slumbered.

For fate's dark funeral pyre he
  Always builds up with heart treasure,
And bequeaths ten " DIEI IRÆ"
  For each ONE *we've* known of pleasure.

So on a cruel bright May morn*
  A silence and a shadow fell
Upon our hearts, and left a thorn
  In place of him we loved so well.

---

* Daisy *obit* Wednesday, May 18th, 1870, 5 p.m

At first we *could* not think it true
   That we were now no longer three !
We watched the door,—as if *it* knew !
   But time has taught us, woe is me !

Where Daisy played, now daisies grow,
   But closed, as if in twilight hours ;
There's something sacred in the woe
   Of these, his little kinsfolk flowers.

There seems less verdure on the trees,
   Less splendour in the sun,
Since we were doomed to tell the bees*
   Our Daisy's course was run.

All nature then was out of tune,
   And jarred upon our hearts ;
We thought it midnight when 'twas noon ;
   And all the hours seemed poisoned darts,

Still piercing every vacant spot,
   Thus to cruelly remind us
Of him who *was*, and now is not ;
   For grief, like sin, is sure to find us.

We try to learn this lore of worth
   As our fancies upward rise ;
That daisies are the stars of earth,
   And stars the daisies of the skies.

An only dog's a fearful thing,
   Which sets our heart upon a cast,
Warning us that fate doth fling
   Us none but joys that cannot last.

Ah ! not e'en love's glamour shows 'em
   In all their value till they are
E'en *iter tenebricosum*,
   Lost stars, " so near and' yet so far."

---

* In Devonshire it is the custom, whenever a death occurs in a house, for one of the members to go instantly and tell the bees of it, the superstition being that the bees would be offended if they had not a *faire part*, and would revenge the neglect by bringing fresh losses and misfortunes upon the bereaved family.

As it's twined, so doth the tree grow;
    And heliotropes turn to the sun;
Tiny's now my *alter ego;*   •
    In fact, we twain are only ONE.

Her human sense and deep, deep love
    Share every thought, soothe every grief;
And daily bring, like Noah's dove,
    To my lone life its ONE green leaf.

We're all in all to each other,
    Joy, hope, fear, trust, kith, and kin,
Without tyrant spouse or brother
    To make a breach and let strife in.

Save us from biped friends (?); they're all
    " Cousin Amy's shallow-hearted; "
They give but *words* of honeyed gall,
    And probe the wounds that most have smarted.

Their bills on time are all *still* due;
    They'd not stir to see one righted,—
For *self's* ever friendship's mildew,
    And to worldliness is plighted.

Then, Tiny mine, since we are bound
    Together by one fast heart link,
Oh! may we *both* by Death be found
    Upon the great dark river's brink,

One prey for him, as we have been
    For all else this many a year;
And on our grave be ever green
    Those daisy gems we held so dear.

                  ROSINA LYTTON.

Monday, August 12th, 1872.

LIST OF NOVELS BY THE LATE DOWAGER LADY LYTTON.

1839. "Cheveley; or, The Man of Honour" . . . . *Published by Bull.*
1840. "Budget of the Bubble Family" . ,, *Bull.*
1842. "Bianca Capello" . . . ,, *Bull.*
1843. "Memoirs of a Muscovite" . . ,, *Newby.*
1849. "The Peer's Daughters" . . ,, *Newby.*
1850. "Miriam Sedley" . . . ,, *Shoberl.*
1851. "Molière's Life and Times; or, The School for Husbands" . ,, *Skeet.*
1854. "Behind the Scenes" . . . ,, *Skeet.*
1856. "Very Successful" . . . ,, *Whittaker.*
1858. "The World and his Wife" . ,, *Skeet.*
1871. "Where there's a Will there's a Way" . . . . . *Published anonymously in August by Bacon.*
1871. "Clumber Chase" and "Mauleverer's Divorce" were also *published anonymously,* I believe in the name of the Hon. George Scott.

"The Household Fairy." *By Virtue and Sons.* A most charming Manual for Young Housekeepers.
Essays : "Shells from the Sands of Time." *Bickers.* 1876.

APPENDIX IV.

LADY LYTTON'S WILLS.—HER EPITAPH.

WILL OF ROSINA ANNE DOYLE WHEELER.

" Dated 3rd January, 1827.

"This is the last will and testament of me, Rosina Anne Doyle Wheeler, now residing in Somerset Street, in the parish of Saint Marylebone, in the county of Middlesex, spinster. I do hereby charge and make liable all my real and personal estate and effects with and to the payment of my just debts, funeral and testamentary expenses. I do will and direct that my remains be interred in a plain elm coffin, without any furniture thereto or put or placed thereon, or about the same, and that the letters and papers contained in a small mahogany box, on which are my initials in ivory, be placed in my coffin and interred with me without being opened by my executors or any other persons whomsoever. And I do by this my will strictly enjoin my executors to comply with this my will and request. I further will and direct my funeral to be conducted in a plain manner, and without ostentation or parade of any kind whatsoever. I do will and bequeath all and every real estate and estates, as also my copyhold and customary estate or estates, of whatsoever nature, kind, or quality, that I have the power of giving, bequeathing, or disposing, limiting or appointing, unto my executors hereinafter named, their heirs, executors, administrators, and assigns. And I do direct and will and appoint all persons who have to convey and assign such estate and estates, as I shall by will direct or appoint to convey and assign the same estate and estates, to my said executors. And I do

will and bequeath, direct and appoint, that my said
executors, their heirs, executors, or administrators, and
assigns, shall stand possessed of all and every such estate
and estates, and the rents, issues, and proceeds thereof.
Upon the trusts hereinafter mentioned, I do give and
bequeath all my personal estate and effects, be the same
of whatsoever nature, kind, or quality, unto my executors
upon trust to convert the same into money, and when so
converted into money to stand possessed thereof upon
trust to invest the same in the Government funds or on
real security, and to stand possessed thereof and of the
interest, dividends, and proceeds thereof upon the trusts
hereinafter mentioned. And I do hereby will and declare
that my said trustees shall stand possessed of the rents,
issues, and proceeds of my said real estate and estates, and
the interest, dividends, and proceeds of my personal estate,
upon trust to pay the same from time to time, as they
shall become due and payable, or otherwise permit and
suffer my mother to receive and take the same for and
during her natural life as and for her own proper
moneys and effects. And subject thereto I will and direct
my said executors to stand possessed of the whole of the
said trust estate and estates and the interest, dividends,
rents, issues, and proceeds thereof upon trust for
Mary Letitia Greene, of Swords, near Dublin, spinster,
her heirs, executors, administrators, and assigns, absolutely.
Provided and in case of the decease of the said Mary
Letitia Greene in my lifetime or in the lifetime of my
mother, I then will and direct my said executors to stand
possessed of the whole of the said trust estate and estates
and the interest, dividends, rents, issues, and proceeds
thereof upon trust for the niece of the said Mary Letitia
Greene, namely Mary Anne Greene, the eldest daughter
of Philip Greene, of Dundalk, Esquire, her heirs, executors,
administrators, and assigns, absolutely, and during her
minority to apply the interest and proceeds in and about
her education. I will and direct that the bequests made
to or in favour of my said mother and the said Mary
Letitia Greene and Mary Anne Greene by this my will are

to and for their respective sole use and benefit, and shall not be liable to the debts, controul, or engagements of any husband or husbands they may at any time have or do intermarry, and their respective receipt and receipts, deed and deeds, alone shall be sufficient discharges and discharge to my executors without their requiring the concurrence of any husband or husbands of the said respective parties. I do appoint my uncle, General Sir John Doyle, of Somerset Street aforesaid, and Colonel Francis Doyle, of Montague Square, in the parish of Saint Marylebone aforesaid, executors of this my will, and in the event of both or either of them dying or declining or becoming incapable of acting in the trusts of this my will, it shall be lawful for my said mother during her life to appoint others in the room or stead of such of them as shall die, decline, or become incapable of acting, and such executor and executors so appointed shall have the same powers and authorities as though they were appointed by this my will. I revoke all wills by me heretofore made, and do declare this to be my last will and testament. As witness my hand and seal this third day of January, One thousand eight hundred and twenty-seven.

"Signed, sealed, published, and declared by the said Rosina Anne Wheeler, as and for her last will, in the presence of us, who in her presence, at her request, and in the presence of each other, have subscribed our names as witnesses.

ROSINA ANNE WHEELER.

JAS. GOREN, *Solicitor*,
ORCHARD STREET, PORTMAN SQUARE.

GEORGE HOLDING.
FRANCES DAWSON.

"I further desire that my heart be taken out and embalmed and sent as a letter I shall leave in my red morocco jewel box shall direct.

"ROSINA A. WHEELER."

This will is at striking variance with Lord Lytton's

assertion in the Life of his father (vol. ii., p. 155) that his mother's fortune "consisted of a little property in Limerick, encumbered by a jointure to her mother, which reduced the income derived from it to about £80 a year." It will be observed that there is no mention of any jointure in this will; and had there been a jointure, it would have been impossible for Mr. Bulwer to sell all his wife's property soon after their marriage, as he actually did, subsequently remarking to her that "he had got every shilling of her property, and she was completely in his power."

EXTRACTS FROM THE WILL OF THE DOWAGER LADY LYTTON.

"Being of sound mind and body this Monday, the eighth day of October, in the year of our Lord one thousand eight hundred and seventy-seven (1877), I hereby revoke all former wills and bequests, more especially the will made in favour of Mrs. Charlotte Cholmondeley Dering, *née* Yea, daughter of Sir J. Yea, Bart., of Pyrland Hall, Somersetshire, at this time residing at No. 12, St. George's Road, Eccleston Square, London, S.W., in the possession of her solicitor, Mr. Giles Symonds, of Dorchester, and do hereby will and bequeath absolutely to my good and more than valued friends Miss Louisa and Miss Rose Devey, of Cairnbrock Lodge, Tudor Road, Upper Norwood, in the county of Surrey, all I may die possessed of, which, I deeply regret, is only personalty—viz., oil paintings, portraits, engravings framed and in books, furniture, rare wood carvings, books, bronzes, ornamental china, *bric-à-brac*, glass, plate, household linen, wearing apparel, china dinner, tea, and dessert services, also all my tin boxes containing letters and other documents, and likewise my, up to this time unfinished, MSS. of my autobiography. That as I appoint the aforesaid Louisa and Rose Devey my sole executrices, they will upon no account, pretext, representation, pressure, or inducement whatever, however plausible and apparently truthful or reasonable, allow any of the aforesaid MS. autobiography to fall into the hands of any member of either the Bulwer, Lytton, Doyle, or Wheeler family, for as no one, including the late Lord Lytton's son, the present Viceroy of India, has the slightest legal right or authority to interfere with my testamentary dispositions as a freed woman or widow, so nothing could excuse a violation of this sacred trust reposed in all confidence in the aforesaid Louisa and Rose Devey.

"I can but state in addition to this clause yet another, which is that in the event of my living to finish my autobiography, or being able to find a literary executor whom I could trust to do so, I shall be of course at full liberty to repossess myself of the aforesaid MSS. and the tin boxes containing the aforesaid letters and documents and transfer them to the said literary executor. I must again express my deep regret that I have no large and real property to leave my two good Samaritan friends Louisa and Rose Devey, for had I the *carte blanche* of the Rothschilds to bequeath them, I should still feel that I had not and could not repay even a tithe of all their truly noble generosity to me.

"All that I may possess at my death of any and every kind of property I leave to the aforesaid Louisa and Rose Devey, to be equally divided between them as they themselves may select and determine, with one exception, which is my fine large jewelled Sèvres *écuelle*, cover and saucer, with a portrait of Louis Quinze on one side and that of the Duchesse de Chateauroux, one of the four Demoiselles de Nèsles, on the other, which *écuelle* was given by Louis Quinze to poor Marie Antoinette when she was Dauphine, who after she became queen gave it to the Comte d'Artois, Charles Dix; he gave it to his cousin Philippe d'Auvergne, Duc de Bouillon, who in 1813 gave it to my mother. Now they must on no account sell or give away this *écuelle*, unless indeed they leave it to the British Museum, as I do not wish a shred belonging to me to fall into the hands of the present Lord Lytton.

"Upon my tombstone I wish the following verses from Isaiah to be engraved :—

"' The Lord will give thee rest from thy sorrow, and from thy fear, and from the hard bondage wherein thou wast made to serve.'

"ROSINA BULWER LYTTON."

"MY EPITAPH."

BY LADY LYTTON.

LONG has been the way, and very dreary,
  With heavy clouds of blackest wrongs o'ercast;
But the pilgrim, spent and weary,
  Gladly sees the goal at last.

When Death o'erthrows the glass of time,
  He scatters all its sands of sorrow;
And the freed soul doth upward climb
  To welcome God's eternal morrow.

INDEX.

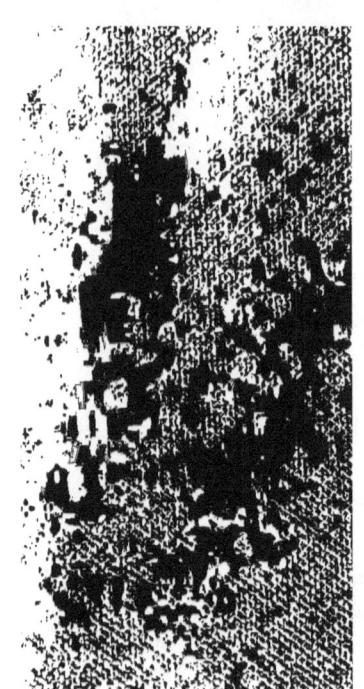

www.ingramcontent.com/pod-product-compliance
Lightning Source LLC
Chambersburg PA
CBHW031058110726
47900CB00003B/975